Night Marcher

Other Ben McMillen Hawaiian mysteries by Mark Brown:

Game Face
Yellowfin
The Puna Kahuna

Night Marcher

Mark Brown

For Sally and Morgan,
Thanks for being such great friends.
Hope you enjoy Ben McMillen's newest adventure.
With much aloha,
Mark B
10/15/03

iUniverse, Inc.
New York Lincoln Shanghai

Night Marcher

iUniverse, Inc.

For information address:
iUniverse, Inc.
2021 Pine Lake Road, Suite 100
Lincoln, NE 68512
www.iuniverse.com

ISBN: 0-595-27417-X

Printed in the United States of America

For Israel Kamakawiwo'ole whose music inspires much of my writing… may you rest in peace with your ancestors…*facing future*.

One After the Other

We walk across the land to the sea…
      one foot in front of the other.

We build sailing ships and cross the ocean…
      one crest after the other.

We come to land again
      and build homes
      and towns
      and cities…
      one after the other.

We cut through the thick forests,
      pushing back the people
      who were there before us…
      one village after the other.

We see the giant mountains
      and strip the earth
      and clog the rivers and streams,
      and the fish gasp for breath
      and die on the muddy banks…
      one after the other.

And on the other side of the mountains,
      we come once more to the sea,
      and we build faster and bigger vessels,
      and let the trade winds carry us to the
      Islands…
      one ship after the other.

We find more natives there
and trade them religion for land,
and slaughter the sacred whales,
and spread disease,
killing human and animal…
one after the other.

And as the sun sinks into the Pacific,
and the summer moon rises,
we climb up above civilization
and come to rest for a moment
on an ancient lava rock,
and we look up and wonder about the
stars…
one after the other.

You call someplace paradise…kiss it good-bye.

—*The Last Resort*

Acknowledgements

My thanks to Carol Lovell and the Kaua'i Museum; John Daley and Na Pali Explorer; the Kaua'i Police Force and Eros; the Honolulu Public Library and its wonderful staff; Ha Ola; and my wife, Zelda, whose patience with my projects is only exceeded by my love for her.

Prologue

An old Hawaiian couple stood motionless in the sand, hidden from the moonlight by the trunk of an ancient ironwood tree.

They watched flames and bobbing orange heads coming up from the beach. The freakish light made it impossible to count heads. While the procession passed them, the wide-eyed couple did something they hadn't done in a long time...they held hands. Even the rich scent of the humid night-time forest and air heavy with salt couldn't mask their fear. Only when the marchers disappeared into the ironwoods, did the couple look at one another. Without a word, hands still joined, they backtracked, then swung around and hurried across the sand and broken lava, headed for home. Each thinking about tales of old...about night marchers.

Praying that the ghosts hunted for someone else.

They completely forgot about their mullet nets and left them behind.

Through the dense forest, along an ancient trail, the procession of flickering torches continued. Seemingly suspended in air, the floating stream of yellow light illuminated the tree trunks and the *'ama'u* ferns that encircled them. The early morning mist swirled away from the path as the marchers passed, gray plumes reaching high into the trees, then spreading outward along the bottom of the forest canopy, mimicking the slow lava flows of years before.

Ahead, a plantation house, built too close to the trail. Inside, an old man who lived alone with his dog.

The man inside the great house was asleep, atop a magnificent four-corner *koa* bed, neatly tucked under a lightweight blanket, breathing peacefully, dreaming of the landscape, much of which he owned. Suspended above his bed was an old quilt. It hung above Queen Lili'uokalani's bed in 'Iolani Palace on O'ahu until January 16, 1893. The next day it disappeared.

Unlike his master, the dog was awake, head raised, eyes darting back and forth, tail straight to a point. The dog got up, then lumbered out of the bedroom. Down the hallway, down the wide curved stairway, into the parlor, up onto the big sofa with just enough bounce to propel him through the open window, which led to the screened *lānai* on the right side of the house. The dog pressed his nose against the screen and peered at the tree-lined path. The reflection of torch light flickered in his apprehensive eyes, but it was his nose that detected the danger.

The marchers neared the plantation house and began to chant. Their *mele* was a mourning song, a song that told of two chiefs, *ali'i*, who long ago waged war for control of the Island. The beagle joined the chant, wailing plaintively, high-pitched and sorrowful, a humanlike sense of doom in his howling.

Meanwhile, the man in the bedroom slowly raised himself to his elbows and stared at the light and long shadows marching across the panes of his bedroom window.

This had happened before.

For a long time a single marcher stood silently in front of the large home, breathing slowly through his nose, his face and neck perspiring underneath the *mākini*, a helmet carved from a gourd, which covered his head and rested on his shoulders. He wished for a breath of wind and waited.

In his right hand…a lava rock with rough edges that sparkled with torch light. He wore nothing but a *malo* around his waist and the canoeman's helmet on his head. The loincloth was light brown and streaked with a deep orange dye from the red earth, a symbol of the clan of his ancestors. The orange gourd had a large, sideways, figure-eight opening for his eyes. Strips of tapa cloth, decorated with brownish circles, hung from the bottom of the gourd and rested on the marcher's shoulders, chest, and back. Peering inside the eye holes, you could see nothing…the invisible face of a ghost.

Abruptly, the marcher brought the torch to the ground, extinguished it in the sandy soil, and let it drop. He walked forward, opened the gate, and followed a crushed lava path to the front steps. The howling stopped. The night marcher heard the retreating clicks of the beagle's feet. Then a bump…then nothing.

The man in the bed, seeing the last light disappear, and hearing the wail of the dog cease, slowly sunk back into his bed and drew up the damp blanket to his neck. He thought, like before, that the marchers were gone. He was confident that they wouldn't return until the next full moon. Exhaling a sharp, deep breath, he moved to his side, tucked his hands underneath his pillow, and closed his eyes.

Stepping onto the verandah, the man wearing the gourd found the front door unlocked. He entered. He walked straight to the stairs, then he climbed. At the landing he turned left and headed for the master bedroom where the old man slept. He found the door open a quarter of the way. With his free hand, he pushed it ajar. The door made no sound except one small groan just as the marcher's hand let go. The man wearing the helmet heard a blanket being thrown aside. Moments later he could see the old man's eyes, which seemed to glow in the dark like those of a night creature. Then he heard a gasp. The sight of an ancient Hawaiian warrior wearing a canoeman's helmet was pretty scary. The night marcher took much satisfaction in that. He smiled to himself and raised his right hand, revealing the magic lava rock. The rock began to glow, then it burst into flame, and the night marcher hurled it at the man in the bed. The old man tried to duck, but too late. The fireball, *pōpōahi,* hit him on the side of his neck and knocked him to the floor, motionless. The rock came to rest in the middle of the bed. Quickly, the night marcher came forward, ignoring the body, barely noticing the glowing orange circle that slowly burned the bed sheet. Stepping up onto the bed, straddling the sacred rock, he reached for the old Hawaiian quilt, lifting it from the wall with both hands. Then he jumped off the bed, steadied himself, and with a flick of his wrists made the quilt billow and settle over the burning circle, extinguishing the small flames. His attention now turned to his victim. He scooped up the body and placed it on top of the quilt, then wrapped his victim until all that remained uncovered were the old man's feet. The intruder reached underneath the strips of tapa that hung from his mask and unclasped his necklace. He held it in front of his face for a few seconds, fastened it, and hung it around one of the bedposts.

From his knees the night marcher lifted the limp body of Walter Churchwell and hoisted the corpse onto his left shoulder. He bent, picked up the cooling lava rock and left.

Soon he was outside feeling the first breath of pre-dawn trade winds. The cool sandy path felt good—it helped relieve some of his tension. Gave him the energy for what lay ahead. After adjusting the load on his shoulder for better balance, he marched back along the path, lava rock tucked into the band of his *malo*, torch once again lighted and held aloft. Headed to where he'd come from, to the water, carrying his victim, thinking—*For the Queen*.

Chapter 1

Standing on the *lānai* that extended across the back of his house, Ben McMillen leaned against the wooden railing and stared at the ocean, a disillusioned look etched deeply into his face.

Twenty yards from him the shoreline waves gently tumbled over the loose stones at the base of the small lava rock wall. Beyond, in the bay, before the reef, the water looked calm, a few ripples on the surface, the only real disturbance a family of green sea turtles, *honu*, headed out toward the reef's edge. Farther out past the coral and sea plants, were streaks of white foam where hundreds of noisy petrel, *'ua 'u*, knifed through the surface spearing baby squid and small fish.

Closer to the house there was a faint smell of the plumeria, petals unfolding to greet the first rays of sunlight angling over the mountain tops. High above, the fronds of the palms hung dead, exhausted from the night's constant wind.

It was Saturday. It promised to be a beautiful, high-sky day. But Ben couldn't remember a time when he felt worse.

A staggering caseload. Nothing even close to being solved and most cases many weeks old. He was sick of tracking down stolen items taken from unlocked tourist rentals. Tired of tracing missing young people who he knew, after interviewing family members, had left for the mainland in search of better wages or respite from overbearing parents. Boredom had set in with his job, only one case held his interest—the bank robbery. But he had made little progress on that. There were too many distractions balancing the caseload, dividing his time trying to make headway on each jacket stacked on his desk. Maybe if he just concentrated on the robbery. Maybe that would help his mood.

Ben sat on a wooden deck chair, slipped on his ankle length socks, then his New Balance running shoes, laced them, not too tightly, and stood to stretch. First, he leaned forward, left leg leading, right foot flat on the *lānai*, right hamstring muscle elongated. Slowly, no jerking movements, holding the position for a count of ten. Then the left. He repeated the exercise three times. Next he grabbed the top of his right foot and brought his leg back until his heel touched his buttocks. Twenty seconds. Then the left. Ben repeated the quad stretch three times, too.

He donned his racing cap, bent back the brim, exposing more of his forehead, and headed back into the house, through the kitchen, and out the front door. Jumping down from the front steps, he reset his watch and was off on the first of twelve miles.

Although he'd never admit it to anyone, what he wanted was a homicide. That's when the job intrigued him, heightened his senses, and when he felt like his work meant something.

A police detective hoping for a homicide. How sick is that?

He ran along the one-lane dirt path that connected his house with a roughly paved road then wound up the hillside to Highway 11 at a spot mid-way between the towns of Kealakekua and Captain Cook. Turning onto the uneven asphalt road, Ben already achieved a rhythm. His breathing was steady, inhaling on strides one and two, exhaling on three and four. This uphill part, which took him from sea-level to fourteen-hundred feet in just over two miles, was pure torture after the first half mile. He attacked this route only on Saturday. Ben felt it was what gave him the strength to finish the Ironman, knowing that the last six miles of the marathon, the section where most triathletes dropped out, cramped up, or began to walk, was nowhere near as demanding as his weekly ascent to Highway 11.

His confidence peaked too soon, or maybe it was his state of depression. Ben felt his legs fatiguing. His pace slowed. He knew it would come to almost walking at the top, but that first step onto the highway would be heaven, flat—even some downhill—and the worst part of the run would be over. His mind drifted from his running to the heavy, dull pain filling his stomach. Distaste for his job wasn't the only thing bothering him. It was something he'd been fighting with for a long time, much longer than the recent case assignments. His relationship with Lisa.

They had been together for almost three years. After the first few month's infatuation waned, Ben decided to transform Lisa from mainland *haole* to someone more in tune with Hawaiian culture. Encourage her to care about the things that mattered to him. His customs, his ancestors, the folklore and mythology, the plight of current-day Hawaiians. After awhile he got his wish, only now he felt that she was gaining ground, or that he was losing it, like it had become a contest who could be more Hawaiian. *He* was the Hawaiian.

She talked about changing jobs, getting out of sales for the hotel and into their community relations program, working with native Hawaiians to preserve the culture and blend it into the workings of the hotel property. Ben resented the idea, thinking it was just a marketing ploy. And here he was apprehending people, in a melting pot of cultures, now more Caucasian than anything else, where the lawbreakers were mainly Hawaiians forced into low income jobs and high property taxes, people trying to survive who took to drinking, dealing, or petty theft—people just sick of the white man's rain. He smirked to himself at his pun, but inside his stomach churned, spreading the dull pain up into his throat. He wondered what life was like before the outsiders came ashore. He'd heard stories, but there were no pictures, at least none he considered authentic. Drawings and other renditions only came after the early sailors and missionaries introduced the written language. Until then, everything was verbal, except for the petroglyphs carved into the frozen lava flows, the mysterious symbols of the past.

The land transferred from Hawaiian to *haole*, from native to Asian. Ben feared his race would soon vanish, as well. But was he unfairly taking his frustration out on Lisa, letting his resentment build? Probably. These innermost feelings he kept to himself. Lisa had no clue. And that just made it worse. She thought things were getting better, that they were getting closer.

Legs burning, right hand shading his eyes from the sun's glare reflecting off the jagged mountain peak dead ahead, Ben shortened his stride, dropped his hand, and reached for the water bottle tucked into his shorts against his back. After a quick drink, he poured a little water on the back of his neck and shook the sweat from his drenched hair. At the same time he tried to shake off thoughts of Lisa and concentrate on the bank job. Right now it seemed his only salvation.

The week before, someone robbed the Kona branch of the First Hawaiian Bank. Two in the afternoon, the slowest time of day the manager told him. There were no customers inside the bank, only two tellers and the assistant manager. The manager and another teller were at lunch. The robber, dressed in tan work pants and a light brown T-shirt, wore a blue nylon cap and silver-coated wraparound sunglasses. He was about five-seven and heavy, more than two-hundred pounds, and dark-skinned, probably Hawaiian. The teller he'd chosen, Maria Gomez, couldn't describe much more than that. She was too busy staring at the man's gun, which he'd hidden under a newspaper. The only thing she added when Ben spoke with her a second time was that the man wore a black plastic digital watch with 'lots of buttons.' She said she noticed it when he lifted the newspaper to show her that he really had a gun.

Maria was unable to trip the alarm because the first thing the man said to her was to keep both hands in sight, on the counter, or in the drawer, but not below the drawer. Ben wondered how the robber knew exactly where the silent alarm button was installed. But on a second inspection, he realized the alarm button was fairly easy to spot from either of the chairs in front of the assistant manager's desk.

The robbery took place so quickly that the other teller, who was servicing someone at the drive-up, didn't notice a thing until Maria screamed after the robber fled.

Physical evidence? The thief left nothing behind.

Suspect? A five-seven, two-hundred pound local. With a runner's or sailor's black watch. Maria struggled with the police artist and turned up her nose at the composite he came up with, like it was his fault.

Ben breathed hard now as he neared the top of the hill. In the distance he heard cars on Highway 11 and the first direct rays of sunlight struck his face. His thighs burned—he was barely running. Still there was a quarter mile more. He lowered the flexible brim of his runner's cap and thought of his sunglasses at home on the kitchen counter. Then he spotted Fernando Gonsalves, sweeping the walk in front of his bakery.

Between breaths. "Morning…Fernando."

"Hey, Ben. Howzit?"

Ben was down to a crawl now.

"Say, when you gonna win your age group?" Fernando chided.

"When I'm sixty."

Fernando grinned and waved, then raised his broom to break up a spider's web that blossomed during the night between the overhang and one of the supporting posts.

Top of the hill. Finally.

▼▲▼

With his tank top wrapped around his waist and just three miles of Highway 11 remaining in front of him, Ben, on the *mauka*, inland, shady side of the road, facing traffic, fully recovered from the treacherous climb, quickened his pace to six-minute miles. There were few cars to worry about, only those on the blind curves where a motorist might jockey the white line. So around the curves, Ben purposely hugged the inside, even though the tips of small branches protruding from the hillside left one leg and arm covered with small red scratches. His thoughts returned to the bank robbery.

A check of prior bank robberies came up with only two suspects, neither lived on the Big Island, both men were from O'ahu. One was paroled, the other still serving time, but neither came anywhere close to matching the description of the First Hawaiian Bank robbery suspect.

A further search of men with recent priors for armed robbery yielded a much larger list. There were more than eighty. Matching descriptions—six came close. Four on O'ahu, which Honolulu checked, one on Maui, who was a tall *haole*, and one on the Big Island. The Big Island man, who'd been released from Kūlani Honor Camp in the Hilo District within the last year, had an alibi. He'd been with his parole officer, Hilo-side, when the bank robbery took place.

One of the better alibis.

Ben glanced at his watch. His pace slipped a bit. He found that happened often when he became immersed in figuring out his cases. Except when it was a homicide, when his pace always quickened. Ben knew it was the sense of urgency associated with a murder. If he was stuck with petty thefts much longer, he supposed he'd become some guy out for a stroll instead of a man working to complete the Ironman in less than ten hours.

Crossing the roadway in the center of the town of Hōnaunau, he greeted several early risers, then headed downhill amidst orchards of papaya and coffee trees. The sun felt much warmer and his shoulders and torso glistened with perspiration. His running shorts soaked through. Ben wished he'd put balm on his lips—they were salty and dry and he could feel the sting of several small splits. All these years of running, he thought he could at least remember the coconut lip balm.

After a mile he reached a narrow road that ran parallel to Highway 11 and led to St. Benedict's Church, more commonly known as Painted Church for its mixture of religious and tropical murals that covered the interior. Ben passed Painted Church, then dowsed himself with more water, laughed when he realized he did that every time at the same spot, as if he felt required to baptize himself. But this time something was different. He felt a chill all over his body. Quickly, the sensation disappeared. Looking back over his shoulder, he suddenly had a feeling that something bad had happened there. He almost stopped, but fought off the urge to go back and have a look around. Shaking his head, dismayed how strange he felt, he continued on and pulled himself back to the bank robbery to think about how to flush out a suspect.

He could assume that the bank teller's description was wrong, that the man didn't weigh as much—sometimes short people just appeared to be heavier—and most times criminals looked bigger to victims than they really were. With a hat and sunglasses—a hat without a logo—the teller wasn't able to give the police artist anything about the man's eyes. And the eyes were what gave a person a face.

Would he strike again? Always a two-edged sword for a police officer. More clues, a pattern developed, a chance for the perpetrator to make a mistake, maybe even a chance to catch him in the act, but it also meant there would be another victim. And statistics showed a progression to violence directly proportional to the number of crimes an individual committed. Was it a two-edged sword for him? Did the prospect of working a homicide seem to have less appeal now? The first thoughts of quitting slipped into his mind.

Jesus!

He ran faster.

▼▲▼

Seventeen hundred dollars wasn't much. This was random and pulled off by an amateur. Ben concluded a first-timer, someone who needed money, any money.

He had another idea. Something that was part of everyone's description that few policemen asked about, but something that most witnesses, when prodded a little, remembered. What did the perp smell like? In Hawai'i where so much of the population labored outside among exotic fruits and flowers, an odor might lead you to where the suspect worked or lived. Ben felt a little nauseated just then, thinking back to another case, one where he interviewed a coffee farmer. Nothing smelled more revolting than a twenty-foot high mountain of coffee berry skins piled in the sun to rot. It gave the phrase *mountain-grown* an entire new meaning.

With something new to check out, Ben stopped thinking about the case and decided to push his personal problems to the back of his mind and enjoy the run along the ocean that would take him past several old battlegrounds, *heiau*—Hawaiian temples—and bring him to Kealakekua Bay. Here, it was believed that gods slid down the cliffs to quickly cross to the other side of the bay. Kealakekua—'pathway of the gods.'

Maybe the gods had a solution for him.

Just before the bay, Ben passed a place known as Moku'ōhai, site of the battle for the land districts of Kona, Kohala, and Hāmākua, where Kamehameha defeated rival chiefs Kīwala'ō and Keōua, thus gaining control of the Island of Hawai'i. These landmarks made Ben ponder the past again, when Kamehameha tried to conquer and unify the Islands, and when the first outsiders had arrived only a few years before, introducing a much different way of life, a way of life that changed the land and the people forever. His grandmother once told him that the 'people of old' knew in their hearts that the end of their culture and customs approached, yet they were frightened to speak of their fears, since so many of the *ali'i,* chiefs, were enamored with the great sailing ships—vessels of the gods, they believed. The chiefs marveled at the inventions of the white man, especially firearms and iron nails. Although Ben wished Captain Cook never made it to Kealakekua Bay, he realized someone else would have eventually. Someone to spread the word to the friendly heathens. Missionaries have amazing stamina for travel and speech.

He'd run eleven miles by now and scampered across the rocky beach that rimmed the bay. The temptation to jump into the cool water was great, but he'd save swimming for the end, after he'd reached his house, which sat on Nāwāwā Bay, just two miles north, or two miles *Kona*, as the locals say.

Sweat dripped from his nose, his eyes began to sting, and Ben's legs began to ache again. He was careful of where he placed his feet. The surface turned to *pāhoehoe* lava, ribbonlike, frozen magma, which was reasonably smooth. But bad placement into one of the ridges usually meant a twisted ankle and a hard fall. His friends and other triathletes thought him crazy to risk an injury training on the lava flows, but Ben thought it was how the old Hawaiians would have done it if they created the Ironman, so he ran dangerously.

The bank robber wore a black watch. The teller, Maria, thought the buttons were yellow or orange. Not much help there because Ben knew just about all the racing watches had bright orange or yellow buttons. Maria knew nothing of guns. Even when Ben showed her pictures of .38s, .357s, and 9mms, she drew a blank, shrugged her shoulders.

Spotting the end of the smooth lava just ahead, Ben increased his pace, as he always did, making believe the Ironman finish line was in sight, and most important, that the yellow band was unbroken, waiting for the victor.

With his chest out, as if he were holding the imaginary ribbon up across his shoulders, Ben crossed the 'finish line' first, then, cooling down, walked the last half-mile home.

▼▲▼

Across the ocean almost two hundred miles away on the eastern shore of Kaua'i, the sun began to warm the cane fields and the moisture-laden vegetation inhaled the sunlight. In the distance a dog barked. A man, weary from just two hours sleep, an arduous ocean voyage, and a trek into a remote valley, stood on his *lānai* and gazed eastward. He seemed mesmerized by the wide expanse of the sparkling Pacific. He thought about his next move, his head nodding ever so slightly. Now to escalate the action. Make the people aware of the injustice, the absurdity of a hundred years of deception.

He researched this thoroughly, who to kill and in what order, but one person he wanted was miles away…out there. The man's eyes widened. *That detective on the Big Island. The one who thinks he knows everything. Solved a series of killings. How tough was that? It was his partner!*

Has this 'insight' how Hawaiian folklore and mythology plays a part in everything. The great Hawaiian detective…hell, he's fifty percent Hawaiian. A half-breed…

Yes, it's time to plant the seed. Get the Chief to bring him here. Find the connection. Solve these horrible crimes. Put an end to this madness.

Well, we'll see about that.

Half-breed.

▼▲▼

After a quick swim in Nāwāwā Bay, Ben gathered his tank top, running shoes, socks, and water bottle. Donning his cap, he walked up the rocky incline, through the patch of *pili* grass, and up the steps of the *lānai.* He checked his watch. Seven-thirty. Then he saw Lisa in the kitchen, standing in front of the refrigerator, door open, scratching her head as if she was having trouble making a choice. Ben knew there were no choices to be made. He promised to stop at the market on the way home the night before, but forgot. All he picked up was a pizza, which he ate alone when Lisa called and said she'd be late.

"I thought the late nights were over," he said.

Lisa turned and smiled, then closed the refrigerator door. She came to him, stood back a second, realizing he was wet. She held his shoulders, bodies separated, and gave him a quick kiss on the lips. Then, hands on her hips, she said, "You haven't asked me where I was last night."

"When did you get home?"

"After eleven."

"Okay, where were you?" Ben sidestepped Lisa and opened the refrigerator door. He knew there was a bottle of orange Gatorade. He chugged from the bottle.

"I quit my job. I was working out the details on my new job."

Ben jerked his head. "You quit?"

"I said I have a new job."

"Where?" he asked. He replaced the bottle and closed the door.

Lisa leaned against the counter. "I'm the new community relations director at the Ritz."

"Community relations?" They had a community relations officer at the police station, Vinny Perez. His job was to work with the Citizens Against Crime group, give tours to the school children, explain to the kids about drugs, show them impounded cars from drunk driving accidents, explain what they should do if approached by a stranger, things like that. "What do you do?"

"I make sure we let the community know what we're planning, make sure we protect the environment," she waited, seemingly for effect, "...make sure we observe Hawaiian customs and the culture...and do it authentically."

"Yeah?" Ben cocked his head. "No offense, but you..."

"You're my experience. You're my background."

Ben nodded, but inside he felt he was being used.

"I'm trying to be less *haole*...I thought you'd like that."

"I do, but..."

"But what?"

"Nothing."

"C'mon...what gives?"

"Nothing...I've just got my caseload on my mind. Congratulations." He gave her a peck on the cheek. "I'm going to take a shower. We'll talk about it over breakfast."

"You forgot the groceries last night."

"All gone...had a party," he joked.

Lisa slapped him on the butt, told him to take his shower, then they'd go out for breakfast and groceries.

Ben headed for the bedroom. "The Ritz?"

"I like it. It's smaller. It's more like a family…the bigger hotels are full of strangers and I don't mean the guests."

The Ritz didn't sound like family to him.

▼▲▼

The Manago Hotel, third generation, family-owned, is located in Captain Cook *makai*, ocean side, of Highway 11. The old section of the hotel, which fronts the highway, is three stories with inexpensive rooms and a restaurant popular with the locals. Service at lunch and dinner is family style. A black plastic board with white press-in letters describes the menu, which changes daily. Seating capacity is around forty and The Manago has made the tourist guides, so there's usually a wait for tables at lunch and dinner. The smell of teriyaki and sesame oil seeps from the wood walls.

The Manago's new section has slightly more expensive rooms—the view from the hilltop is better—but the real treasure is the beautiful Japanese garden between the two buildings featuring a *koi* pond that meanders among the guava, mango, hibiscus, and a variety of ferns.

Ben and Lisa were squeezed into a small corner of the restaurant, but next to a window, enjoying the cool air. After they worked their way through Swiss-cheese and bean sprout omelets, rice, Portuguese sausage, bagels with cream cheese and strawberry-guava jam, and mango juice, they settled back in their chairs. Refills of Kona coffee in front of them, the early morning breeze pushing trails of rich-smelling coffee steam across the table.

They talked about Lisa's new job. And as they did, Ben thought back to when they first met and how each of them changed since then.

Lisa Scott was a transplanted mainlander who worked for the Hyatt Hotel chain since receiving her masters in hotel management. Her step-father was well-to-do, and, although she never flaunted her wealth, she always dressed nicely, ate at good restaurants, and generally thought that life would basically take care of itself.

She worked in the sales department in one of their smaller Hyatt properties. Seven years later, after four different hotels, each larger than the previous, she was offered a transfer to the Hyatt in Ka'anapali on Maui, which she accepted, viewing it as just one more gorgeous layover on her trip through life.

An unlikely surf shop owner, Ben never had been on a surf board. He came to Maui after resigning from the Kona Police Force, after his mentor, then Lieutenant of Detectives, Tobi Otaki, was passed over for a well-deserved promotion to Captain. What got to Ben then, was that Tobi quit the Force, something totally out of character for him, not turning the other cheek. There was a part of Tobi, a Hawaiian of Japanese ancestry, that always accepted one's fate as a matter of a higher deity. But when Tobi left, angry and disillusioned, Ben, in turn, reacted quickly, handed in his badge and gun, and literally ran three miles to his apartment in Kailua. He packed his clothes and a few personal items, and was on a plane to Maui within a few hours, to stay with a friend and decide what to do next.

He ran away.

His partner came to Maui to convince him to reconsider. Instead, Ben took all his money, which wasn't much, and invested it in a small, broken-down surf shop at the north end of Front Street in Lahaina, away from the tourists, a shop that mainly serviced locals.

Life then consisted of a few hours at work, a few more training for the Ironman Triathlon, and too many nights in the bars along Front Street, followed by too many hung-over mornings. When he thought about it now, training for the Ironman and downing beers most nights, was like a chain-smoking vegetarian.

And as for the women he met, he never knew their last names and usually couldn't remember their first.

But one evening, early, while sipping a Beck's at Longhi's Bar, he spotted Lisa walking by. His eyes followed her across the street and through the entrance to Kimo's, another popular eating spot on Lahaina's main drag. He paid his tab, charged down the crowded street, crossed between moving cars, and marched into Kimo's. Ben took a table on the verandah, and watched intently as Lisa sat at the bar, obviously waiting for someone, someone Ben hoped wouldn't show.

Finally, after ten minutes, he approached. 'I followed you from the mainland.'

'You must be patient because I've been here more than two years.'

He countered with an outstretched hand and, 'Ben McMillen, patient man.'

Now it seemed, he'd gotten his wish. Or had he? Lisa compromising more than he. He felt uncomfortable, as if he was being cheated out of his birthright like so many other Hawaiians. The breeze seemed hot, the room stuffy, and Ben's mouth felt dry. He exhaled…slowly.

Breakfast began to settle like sludge in his stomach.

Lisa nudged him. "What are you thinking about?"

"Oh…nothing."

"Here we go again."

Ben took a sip of coffee, cleared his throat. "When I first met you, I liked being with a *haole*. I liked doing *haole* things, like eating in nice places, staying overnight in the Hyatt, relaxing at brunch…But when I rejoined the Force and really got involved with the people…it's funny, but I needed to be like them…needed to become aware of what it really meant to be Hawaiian. Becoming more interested in what my grandmother tried to teach me about my ancestors, about the land…Then you, becoming interested in Hawai'i, in my culture, and now, with your new job…" He was babbling, stalling, and he knew it.

Lisa reached out and placed her hand over his and gently rubbed his wrist. "I guess one day we'll be so damned compatible, we'll have no choice but to get married."

She wasn't getting it and Ben wasn't ready to be totally honest with her, so he decided to joke about it. "Married?…you still don't know how to fold a tube of toothpaste. But you'd be good at strangling chickens."

"And I suppose the toilet seat cover is too heavy to lift? Maybe if we added a button on the remote?"

Lisa grinned. Ben's smile was forced. He couldn't believe he felt this way about their relationship, but it was there.

Pushing her chair away from the table and stretching, Lisa inquired, "Did you figure out the bank robbery while you were running?"

He was thankful for the change in subject. "Nope."

"No suspects?"

"No one with robbery priors who fits the description."

"Bad description?"

"Maybe."

"First-timer?"

"Hope not, but probably." Another sip of coffee.

"Any clues in what he was wearing?"

Ben explained that the suspect's shirt and cap were non-descript, no logos, no printing, and that he wore dark, wraparound sunglasses, the kind you can buy for $4.99 in any ABC. He told her about the newspaper and the gun. "He did have a black plastic watch with lots of buttons."

"Like your Ironman watch?" she asked.

"Don't know. The teller only said it was black plastic and had bright yellow or orange buttons. She couldn't even remember exactly what color they were."

"What kind of gun?"

"She can't identify it."

Lisa checked the time, then eyed Ben's coffee cup. "Done?"

He nodded.
"Let's get the groceries."

When they finished shopping, Lisa stopped a few feet short of the checkout. "Oh…we need toothpaste."
Ben snorted. "How could you possibly tell?"
She slapped him on the arm. "Watch it, chicken neck."

Chapter 2

At dawn Monday morning on the upslope of Kohala Mountain Range, just a half mile off Kawaihae Road, within walking distance of the base of Kemole Falls, Tobi Otaki sat on a bamboo mat, facing east. His palms rested on his thighs, his head bowed, eyes closed. Tobi's thoughts were of another world where the ocean waves uncurled onto virgin beaches, where tiny palm shoots took hold from a bulging coconut feeding small water-seeking roots into the speckled sand. Inland, there was a giant mountain, still for the time-being but for a steady plume of dark smoke rising from a crack in a frozen lava pond, hidden just below the crater rim. The wind came and sent the smoke westward out to sea. And between the mountain and the sea were bubbling rivulets of reddish-orange lava, burning shrubs, and protected places, *kīpuka,* where a lowland forest began to take hold amidst the network of molten streams.

Above there were small birds that went where the wind took them. Their feathers mostly brown and black and gray. Only later, when the rain forests were lush, would the honeycreeper's feathers begin to turn red and yellow and lime green.

The sun had risen but only faint trails of muted orange light reflected off the back side of the mountains—although that was enough to interrupt Tobi's meditation. Concentration this morning was not easy. He felt the heavy humid air pressing down on his shoulders. He raised his head and opened his eyes and gazed at the orange mist that hung beneath the deep purple storm clouds, covering the Kohala Mountains. He stood, rising effortlessly, needing no support from his hands, the Captain of Detectives considered Major Serrao's request. Send Ben to Kaua'i.

Tobi rarely sighed. He allowed himself a long, deep one now. He didn't feel good about this. Not because of the friction it would cause between Ben and the detectives there. That was to be expected. And although he felt Ben might be more at risk dealing with multiple homicides and maybe a maniac killer...that really wasn't the main cause of his anxiety. What bothered him was that when he called his old friend Bill Johnson, Chief of Kaua'i's detectives, and asked him who suggested the temporary assignment for Ben, all he got was 'someone here thought it might be a good idea.'

Good friends don't act that way unless something is very wrong. Friends say 'I shouldn't be telling you this, but...'

Walking back to his house through the garden, rolled bamboo mat under his arm, he paused to pinch off the yellow leaves of a rose apple, *'ōhi'a loke*. Tobi continued to the decking that surrounded a small garden of bonsai and native flowers, stepped up, and crossed the wood planks, leaving the ridged footprints made by his dew-laden straw zories. He wondered what Ben would say, wondered if he'd be hesitant. Was he putting his best detective in real danger? A confrontation with a serial killer with some strange link to the ghosts of the past.

Somebody thought it would be a good idea.

▼▲▼

Nearly an hour later as the faint glimmer of a new day ebbed toward Kaua'i, a man who'd been up all night, this time because he just couldn't sleep, trudged up the beach at Hā'ena Point. When he reached the seaside grove of pandanus, he twisted his tired body around to face the water and dropped to the sand.

He visualized racing across the moonlighted sea in a motorized rubber raft, cold sea spray everywhere. Returning later to his canoe, then paddling the small craft through the swells, securing it deep inside the ocean cave, swimming back out...shivering.

He pushed his sunglasses to his forehead and let out a tired sigh. Still transfixed by the sea, he subconsciously reached for his nylon belt, which held among other things, a plastic water bottle. The man slipped the bottle from its pouch, pulled up the stopper, and drank. He drank until he noticed his hands shaking. He dropped the bottle and buried his head in his hands. Only when he smelled the coppery scent of blood did he lower his hands and stare at them. There was nothing there. How could there be? It was three days ago. He'd washed them dozens of times. But as he examined his palms, he realized it took a long time before the smell of blood disappeared. Wash it from your skin. Yes. From your mind was another matter.

And now he had to do it again. He thought about the next victim on his list.

▼▲▼

On the beach at the entrance to Honokōhau Harbor, Ben increased his pace, sprinting now, running shoes kicking up the hard sand in his wake. Ahead, the channel through the dunes was visible. A charter boat slipped quietly through the man-made waterway, open sea just in sight. Ben squinted at the charter, wondering if it was Danny Mitchell. The boat looked like his, but it wasn't. The spotting tower was taller and there was a double red stripe running along the hull, not a single purple one.

Several heron watching the incoming tide, waiting for the tide pools to fill with baby mullet, cranked their necks as Ben approached, then dashed left along the water's edge before finally taking flight. They soared above the sunken lava beds, then flapped furiously as they turned into the wind and headed farther up the beach.

His lungs burning, perspiration dripping down his face, running shorts and top plastered to his body, Ben's heavy legs crossed the imaginary finish line. He bent over and rested his hands on his thighs. A minute later he walked up the road, past dozens of docked charters, waving at the crews hosing decks, polishing hardware, and loading supplies. He reached Highway 19, waited for the traffic to ease, then darted across, and climbed the hill to Kona Headquarters. The end of the brisk early Monday morning workout. The start of another week.

When Ben entered Tobi's office, he found the Captain of Detectives standing behind his desk, facing the window, hands clasped behind his back, his shoulders rising and sagging as he breathed. Obviously, in deep thought. Concentrating.

"Morning, Tobi."

Tobi turned and faced his protégé. "Good morning, Ben. How was your run?"

"Good." Coffee cup in hand, Ben carefully sank into one of Tobi's armchairs. "Joyce said you wanted to see me."

Tobi nodded, then pulled back his desk chair, stepped around, and sat.

Ben thought Tobi looked tired, weary, and the expression on his face unusual for him, reserved for when something bothered him that he didn't like dealing with.

"What's up?"

Tobi brought his fingers together, tip-to-tip, flexing, like synchronized spiders doing push-ups. Then he placed his hands on his desk, spiders intact but still. "Major Serrao was asked a favor by the Chief in Līhu'e. Also, the Chief there and I are good friends."

Tobi paused and Ben thought he detected a bit of a frown.

"They have two disappearances…two *similar* disappearances. They fear homicides. The evidence points to a single perpetrator…they think they might have a serial killer."

Ben put down his coffee on the glass table next to the chair. His thoughts immediately went back to Kona's serial killer. It was several years now, but the memories and the pain were fresh, always would be, he thought. Maybe he no longer thought about it everyday, but it crept back often enough, there were plenty of reminders—the places they found the victims, even Honokōhau Harbor, where he ran each weekday before work, was the site of the third killing. Sometimes he'd see people who had nothing to do with it, but somehow they reminded him of that case, that Lisa could have been a victim, that his partner…

"Serial killer? Maybe a kidnapper," he offered.

Tobi responded, taking his time. "The victims…both men…"

Ben's eyes narrowed. He'd mainly thought of serial killing victims as women. He watched as Tobi pursed his lips.

"…have not been found…their bed covers burned, although not completely…more like the center of their bed sheets burned through. And hanging around the bedpost of one and by the foot of the bed of the other…were carved fish hooks. Ancient Hawaiian fish hooks. They have been tested. They are authentic…very old. No fingerprints."

"Why does Līhu'e think the men are dead? Was there blood?"

"No blood…no burned flesh…"

Ben's skin crawled. Fire. Another tie to *his* serial killer…the burning boat. His partner burning. Ben opened his mouth, tried to form a question, but couldn't.

Tobi's hands were now folded across his chest. "Given the circumstances, Līhu'e is treating them as homicides."

"The favor the major asked?…for me to help out, right?"

Tobi looked at Ben for a few seconds, then nodded.

Ben tried to sound less than enthusiastic, although inside he felt the rush of adrenaline. "For a few days?"

"A little more than that. They want you to take the case…until it is solved."

He felt his skin tingle. He took a few deep breaths. Then Ben thought about Lisa, wondered how she'd take the news. Thought about the Ironman, only five weeks away. But mainly considered how strange it was that his wish to exchange his current caseload for a homicide actually had happened…and so quickly.

Tobi got up and went to his window. "Looks like rain."

"I'm to leave right away?"

"You can refuse."

"Hardly. But what a distinction…serial killer expert." Actually, it didn't sound so bad…

"Ben? What do you know about fireballs?"

"*Kāhuna*?" Ben moved forward to the edge of the chair.

"Yes, *kāhuna*…sorcerers."

"Not much about the evil ones. That's something my grandmother never told me about."

"They are called *kāhuna 'ana'ana.* They practice black magic. It is said that they can wish a person to death by praying or chanting. And certain *kāhuna* can conjure up fireballs and hurl them at someone who they wish to kill." Tobi leaned against the window sill—his fingers, now just below his chin, assumed spider push-up position again. "Do you believe it?"

"I believe there's an explanation for it."

"And that is?"

Ben had no explanation and shrugged his shoulders. "And you?…you used the present tense to describe them."

"I did."

Ben's face held a small grin and his eyes gleamed. "You think these," searching for the right word, in his own mind he hadn't yet classified the vanished victims as homicides, "…disappearances are connected to someone practicing sorcery?"

"You will have to check the reports and see the evidence for yourself, but the way it was described to me was that nothing burned except for a two-foot wide circle…and there were no signs of an attempt to douse the flames…no water anyway."

"Sounds mystical, but a blanket could smother the flames."

Tobi didn't comment, but sat and offered Ben a slip of paper. "A friend of mine on Kaua'i who might be able to help if there is a sorcerer about."

Ben read the woman's name, wrinkled his brow, then slid the note paper into his wallet.

"I'll look her up."

They discussed the case for only a short time more, agreeing they were speculating and that the sooner Ben was there, the sooner they'd have some first-hand information to go on. Tobi told Ben Līhu'e arranged for him to stay at a bed and breakfast near Wailua and that an expense advance waited for him in clerical. He also gave Ben his contact in Līhu'e, Detective Mike Gamos, and asked Ben to give the bank robbery case to Detective Cooper or Ha'aino and the rest of his crime jackets to him for reassignment.

The mention of the bank robbery triggered something in Ben's mind. It was something about the suspect's watch.

"Wrap this up quickly and come home."

"Miss me already?" Ben said with a grin.

"Do not want any more victims. You be careful…I can not pinpoint why, but I do not feel good about this. Keep your eyes open…and remember," Tobi pointed to his own eyes, "to watch the eyes of others."

Ben's smile disappeared. Tobi's tone scared him.

▼▲▼

Jack Cooper was at his desk, entering information into his computer, a bran muffin and plastic container of juice near his mouse pad. He waved his hand briefly as Ben walked into CIS, Criminal Investigation Section, his eyes gestured to the computer screen like he'd be done in a minute.

Ben went to the coffee pot, glanced over his shoulder at the bran muffin and juice and thought about the transformation in Jack since he started dating Helen Hata. Jack, a Kona Force veteran of thirteen years, worked his way up from uniform patrol to detective. He'd lived on the Big Island his entire life, grew up Hilo-side, graduated from UH—Hilo with a degree in criminal justice. He wanted to work on the Hilo Force, but the only Island opening at the time was in Kona.

Jack had many friends, but no best friend. Until Helen came along, Jack was overweight—the doctor who administered the annual police physical didn't even bother to weigh him, just lectured him sternly before writing down the maximum allowed, knowing Jack would be much worse off if he couldn't be a detective. Until recently, Jack resigned himself to being the hard-working, good-natured, food-loving officer, who everyone invited out for a beer, but hardly anyone brought home.

Ben tried to be a good friend, tried to involve Jack in his life. But when much of his spare time was spent training for the Ironman, a two-hundred-thirty pound sidekick soon falls by the wayside.

Helen changed that. Coffee and sugar donuts gone, Jack was down to one ninety-five.

"How's it going, partner?"

"Okay. You hear I'm off to Kaua'i on a case?"

Jack hadn't and Ben explained.

"Just disappeared, huh?"

"No bodies yet. What about the Dillon case?"

Jack struck a couple of keys, Ben saw the PRINT light blink on the printer, then Jack spun around in his chair.

"Nobody liked this Dillon guy…I can tell you that. He extorted money, pushed people around, got in more bar fights than we have bars…a high-school bully who never grew up. Probably still uses Brillcreme."

"And now he's gone. Any chance he just headed for the mainland?"

"Not unless he left everything behind. Unfortunately, I think he pushed someone too far. Now, an otherwise innocent citizen is probably a murderer."

After a sip of coffee, Ben pointed to the phone book on Jack's desk. "There you go. Based on what you said about this guy, there's an alphabetical list of suspects."

Detective Cooper snorted and rocked in his chair. "Thanks. So, when you leaving?"

Ben took a glance at his desk, figuring how much time it would take to clean up his paperwork. "I'll go home and pack around noon. Be there by two or three."

"What about your bank robber?" asked Jack.

"I got one thing I want to check out before I leave. You want it after that? Tobi said to give it to you or Ha'aino."

"Ha'aino can have it. The phone book might be a bit of a stretch…but Dillon's whole neighborhood isn't."

"Maybe it was."

"Was what?"

"His whole neighborhood…wouldn't be the first time."

Chapter 3

Driving his Wrangler, beyond Keauhou heading toward Kealakekua, Ben focused in on his robbery suspect. He wondered beside Kona Hospital how many outpatient clinics there were in the Kona District. He knew of one in Kailua off Kuakini. He guessed there were several others. Then adding the number of doctors' offices, checking out his hunch might take the rest of the day. After Tobi's 'do not want any more victims,' Ben knew he should get to Kaua'i as soon as possible. But on the other hand, an armed bank robber, unlike a purse snatcher, was the type of criminal who could commit a violent crime. He decided to check with the hospital in person, then get a list of the clinics and doctors and phone them if the hospital didn't pan out. He'd split the list with Ha'aino. As badly as he desired to get to Kaua'i, he wanted one last shot at the bank case.

Fifteen minutes later, Ben turned left when he reached the center of Kealakekua, followed the winding uphill road through the heavy shadows of the eucalyptus trees that lined the street, past the circular drive in front of the main entrance to the hospital, and continued on to the old lot. He parked on an incline, under a large moneypod tree, the shade savior from the Kona sun.

Ben hopped out of his Jeep and walked briskly across the parking lot. When he reached the main entrance door, Ken Asumura, the Kona Hospital pathologist and de facto medical examiner, bumped into him.

"Whoa...where you headed in such a hurry?"

Ben answered, "To Kaua'i, actually."

Ken thumbed over his shoulder. "Airport that way, bruddah."

Ken and Ben had been friends for years. They went fishing every other Sunday afternoon with another friend, Danny Mitchell, who owned a thirty-four-foot charter. Sometimes, if Ben was going to run a short distance, like four miles, then swim, then run another four, Ken would join him, sit out the swim, and then run back with him.

But the foundation of their friendship was based on something more important. Ben's grandmother, who died more than ten years before, had been a *kahuna lapa 'au*, and Ken's mother, who lived in the Puna District, in the coastal town of Opihikao, was a healer as well. Wise in the old ways of treating sickness. They made remedies from the roots and leaves of the plants and herbs that grew in the Hawaiian forests. They knew how to encourage a patient into the right frame of mind. This bond to heritage presented separate problems for each. For Ben, a feeling of guilt and helplessness whenever he had to defend the property of the wealthy against a native trespasser claiming his birthright. Whatever the situation, it seemed, most times, *haole* won over Hawaiian. For Ken, an entirely different problem. The conflict of being a professional physician in the modern world, yet believing in the cures of his ancestors.

When he was an intern, Ken once wrapped the vines of a parasitic plant that grows on the sea morning glory around the neck of a throat cancer patient. He'd pounded some of the leaves and made a tea from the juice, water, and sea salt, and given it to the patient to drink. He repeated it for five days. When the *haole* floor nurse learned of Ken's late evening treatments, she made quite a fuss, and Ken almost lost his internship. But a few days later, when the patient's tumor shrunk, it was the nurse who received another assignment and the *haole* doctors who came around to 'talk story' with the young intern.

Ben explained the disappearances on Kaua'i. Ken shook his head sadly when he described the fireballs and the premise of a serial killer.

"What are you doing here?" the pathologist asked.

"I have a theory on the First Hawaiian Bank robbery…want to check it out before I leave. Our man just might have been a recent patient here."

Glancing at his watch, Ken said, "Love to hear about it, but I'm late for an appointment. So, no fishing Sunday?"

"Hey…we'll have Kaua'i wrapped up by then."

"Seeya, brah."

"Later."

Inside, Ben marched straight to the Records Office, anxious to test his theory.

The woman behind the counter looked new. She was Hawaiian, of medium height, with short, straight dark hair, and had large teeth that were as white as sun-baked coral. Her gold hoop earrings were huge, touching her shoulders even when she raised her head straight up as he approached. Ben introduced himself, then handed her his card.

"Ben McMillen. I'm a Kona detective."

Smiling as she read the card, she said, "I'm Cheryl Malakua. How can I help you?"

"I'd like to know if anyone came in for treatment for a hand, wrist, or arm injury within the last week."

"We keep them by name, not date."

There was a frown, but she seemed intrigued.

"A suspect?" she asked.

Ben nodded. "No computer?"

"Not yet for E.R. patients...only hospital admissions. You said treatment, right."

"Right."

"What a minute...I just started using new file folders last week for E.R. They're light gray. The others are manila and yellow."

"Great. Need some help?"

"No, I can go through them pretty quickly." The woman brushed back her thick bangs. "I'll be right back."

Ben watched as Cheryl moved toward the first of six aisles each containing hanging file folders from the floor to a height of five feet on both sides of the aisle. Starting on her left, she scanned the tops of the folders, and quickly, just like she said, extracted only the gray folders, stacking them in the crook of her arm. She did an about face and came back down the aisle toward him. Ben counted six files from the first pass, so he assumed there'd be about seventy folders to go through. He eyed the wall clock, checked it against his watch, and figured if he got something here that it would be late afternoon before he'd be on his way to Kaua'i. He thought about the other hospitals, Waimea and Hilo. But he doubted his theory pertained to those. He believed the bank robber lived Kona-side. Probably even banked at a First Hawaiian branch, or at least lived nearby.

"Got 'em all. I'll show you where to look. We can split them up. Left or right arm?"

The teller said the gun was in his left hand. "Right...and we can ignore this weekend and today."

"Okay. Here's what you do..."

Five minutes later, not believing his good fortune, Ben exclaimed, "Here he is."

Ray Ahuna. Five-six. One ninety-five. Came to E.R. on the morning of the ninth. *Jeeez...just before he hit the bank.* Right wrist injury. Said he slammed his truck door on it as he was getting out his duffel bag. The strap caught on the stick shift. X-ray showed a bad bone bruise, nothing broken. The attending physician gave some pain killer and wrapped the wrist in an Ace bandage. Ice it the first day, then heat thereafter.

Ben took out his notepad and copied down the man's address.

"Want to check the remaining folders?" Cheryl asked.

"No need...I think this guy fits perfectly. I'll check it out with E.R. Mahalo, Cheryl."

"Anytime, Ben." She brushed back her bangs again. This time she caught her thumb in her earring.

The nurse behind the desk in the Emergency Room remembered Ray Ahuna She even described what he wore. Tan pants and a light brown T-shirt, a blue nylon cap and silver, wrap-around sunglasses hanging from his neck. Said he was in a hurry. Acted agitated. The nurse said she thought his behavior was normal. After all, the bruise to his wrist was bad. Hold a gun? She told Ben Ahuna probably couldn't even shake hands.

▼▲▼

Ray Ahuna lived in Kealakekua, just past Kona Waena High School, about a mile up a dirt road in the hills. The house looked in bad repair, sagging roof, a single redwood catchment barrel with a worn split down one of its seams, a variety of plants and seedlings growing from the chimney where it met the roof shingles. An old rusted back hoe sat next to the carport, four cement foundation blocks wedged underneath the left rear axle in place of the wheel. Fresh tire marks cut through the series of puddles in the pair of strips of bare earth that formed a circular driveway in front of the house, but there was no '93 black Chevy Bronco that Ben found out belonged to his suspect.

Ray Ahuna...about to be caught simply because his watch was on the same wrist as the hand that held the gun. Because he couldn't hold the gun in his bruised right hand.

Wiping the perspiration from his neck and pulling his shirt away from his back, Ben skirted the mud puddles in front of the house. He knocked on the screen door. Right away, he heard someone shuffle toward him. He expected an adult, but the small shadow that finally reached the doorway gave way to an empty face of a little boy, no more than ten years old. He had dark hair, not combed, and wore only a faded pair of swimming trunks far too big for him. The ragged bottoms went well below his knees and the drawstring, tied in a huge bow, pinched the waist so tightly that Ben wondered if more string showed than was around the boy's waist. The boy's anxious look was as if he was caught skipping school.

Ben bent over and placed his hands on his knees. "What's your name?"

"Loki."

"Is your father home, Loki?"

"He went to work."

"Where does he work?"

The boy pointed toward Captain Cook.

"On a farm?" asked Ben.

The boy smiled slightly and nodded.

"Loki, is your mother home?"

The boy's grin faded. He pressed his lips together and blinked his eyes several times, eyes that appeared to have run out of tears some time ago.

"What about sisters and brothers?"

He shook his head. "Grandma stays with us sometimes, but she's not here."

Ben knelt. "Loki, I'm a police officer. I'd like to talk with your dad. Do you know which farm he works at?"

A worried look filled the boy's face. "Is he in trouble?"

Ben shook his head, though slightly, as if that would minimize his hiding the truth.

Loki thought for a while but shook his head again.

"Does he come home for lunch?"

The boy beamed. "Everyday."

"Mind if I wait for him?"

The boy pushed at the screen door.

Ben gently placed his hand against the frame. "That's okay…I think I'll wait in my Jeep. What time does he come home?"

"Soon."

"Okay…I'll just pull up in the shade and wait there."

"Okay." Loki turned and disappeared into the darkness of the house.

Ben walked back to his Jeep, detached the blue strobe light from his roll bar, placed it on the floor behind his seat, and climbed inside. He radioed HQ, told Tobi what he had, said he didn't need backup, but wanted someone from Juvenile to get there right away to take the boy.

Tobi talked him into a backup. "We know he used a gun *and*...we also know you never take your gun out of your glove compartment."

Laughing a little, Ben asked, "Have you?"

"I can defend myself without it."

While Ben waited, he thought about the small boy inside the house. What would become of him with his only parent in jail? Armed robbery would get Ray Ahuna up to fifteen years even though his prior record was clean. Was the grandmother fit to take care of the boy? Then Ben realized that he'd assumed from the boy's expression that his mother had died. But maybe she hadn't. Maybe she lived somewhere else. Maybe the boy's parents were divorced. But then, how fit of a mother could she be if a man who could rob a bank had won custody?

Looking around at the house and grounds, Ben guessed that Ray Ahuna was desperate. He needed money. Most likely he was dealing with a man with bad judgment and bad credit. But in any case, Loki probably was headed to a foster home.

At eleven fifteen Julie Washburn from the Juvenile Section came. Ben convinced Loki that it was okay to go with her. Loki put on a shirt and a baseball cap and a battered pair of flip-flops, which required curled toes to keep on. When Julie and the boy walked by him, Loki's eyes told Ben that Loki knew his father was in trouble.

Ben patted him on the head as he passed.

Five minutes later, George Borges, Uniform Patrol arrived. Ben briefed him and asked him to pull around the back of the house and wait. It was a good spot for backup. More important, Ben thought two vehicles in front of the house might scare Ahuna and result in a chase. He wanted this to be easy. For the boy's sake and he guessed for Ray Ahuna's as well.

By eleven forty-five, Ray Ahuna hadn't shown and Ben began to worry that they'd been spotted. He decided to check out the rear of the house. Maybe there was another entrance, a path through the woods that hooked up with one of the other dirt roads, which made up the maze of back country access in the hills of

South Kona. Ben drove around to the back and pulled up along side of Borges. Just then his radio crackled and the dispatcher's voice came on.

"I'm here, Sarg."

"Your suspect just turned himself in."

"Really? Are you sure?"

"Raymond Thomas Ahuna, five-six, about two-hundred. Blue cap. Hawaiian. Right hand's bandaged. He's in HOLDING and Tobi's with him."

"I'll be there in a half hour." Ben felt better. Ahuna couldn't have known they were on to him, yet he turned himself in. If only he hadn't used a gun.

▼▲▼

Ben examined the gun. It was, just like Ray Ahuna said, not in working order. The trigger was jammed and the clip was missing, although Ahuna could have dumped the clip after the robbery. Ray Ahuna said he'd bought it at a pawn shop in Hilo a few months before.

"I was gonna lose the house. The man from the bank said 'no more.' I'm six months behind. I only work part-time picking coffee berries. Can't find no other work 'cept the night-shift stuff. But Loki'd be alone..."

Ben wondered what he could do to make things easier. "Ray, this is a serious crime. Bank robbery is not something that'll get you a suspended sentence."

Ahuna hung his head.

"And your boy."

Ahuna's head jerked. "What will happen to him?"

"Is there someone who can take care of him...his grandmother? Where's your wife?"

"She left me a few years ago. I was drinking then...she met some guy. They moved to Oahu...then the mainland. Don't know where."

"Your mother?"

"She's too old. She comes over a few times a week. Loki helps her more than she helps him...what will happen to Loki? He's a good boy."

"Doesn't he go to school?"

Ahuna sighed heavily. "The other boys make fun of him. He has no clothes...not good clothes...no money for even shave ice. He hates to go to school, but he likes to learn. I spend time with him and teach him things. He's as smart as the other *keiki*."

Ben got up from the stool he'd been sitting on and began to pace. He looked at Ray Ahuna who now stared expectantly at him, the shadows of the cell bars falling across the poor man's face. Ben stopped and stood in front of Ahuna's cell. "Turning yourself in was good. The gun not working…no bullets…that's good. This is your first offense. That's good, too." Then he asked Ahuna where the money was and found out that he paid off his late mortgage payments and kept nothing for himself. Robbed one bank to pay another. "Ray, robbing a bank is a felony…you're going to have to serve *some* time." Ben paused when he saw Ray Ahuna's big black eyes fighting back tears. "You'll get a reduced sentence. Maybe only a year or eighteen months. Loki will be placed in a foster home. He'll be fed and clothed and go to school. I'll see to it myself. Promise."

"You will?" He stood and shook Ben's hand with both of his. "…but will I get him back when I get out?"

"That I don't know…we'll do what we can. Wherever they send you…you be perfect, do what they tell you, stay away from the other prisoners, be respectful, but keep clear of them. That'll help."

Ahuna nodded. Kept nodding.

Ben nodded back, then walked away, almost wishing this was one case he hadn't figured out.

It made no sense to go to Kaua'i now—by the time he went home, packed, and drove back to the airport, it'd be after five. So Ben decided to catch the first flight in the morning.

He caught Lisa just before she was about to leave work. He explained that he was leaving in the morning. They agreed on dinner at home, sunset on the *lānai*, then early to bed. After he hung up, Ben found Julie Washburn, filled her in on the details of Ray Ahuna's circumstances and requested that she make sure that Loki got to see his father that night. And most important, that the boy not become lost in the system.

And then, after filing his report and picking up his plane ticket and cash advance, a sobering thought hit him. Unrelated to Ahuna, but directly connected to his destination. The last time he'd worked a case that took him to Kaua'i was the first and only time he'd been shot at.

▼▲▼

You're coming! You're coming! Have I got surprises for you.

We'll see how good you are, McMillen. If you're not so good, maybe we'll let you live. But if you are this great apprehender of serial killers, this expert in the ways of old…well then…we can't let you live, can we?

It's me or you. I think I like me better.

Chapter 4

Looking at the landscape reminded Ben how quickly nature repaired herself—at least from natural, not man-made, disasters. Green taro fields stretched from the lowlands west of Līhu'e northward along the base of the Makaleha Mountains, finally melting into the gray rain clouds that shrouded the northeastern tip of the Island. New palms and banana trees sprouted by the bases of their predecessors. Ferns and ti plants covered the forest floor. Only on the upper mountain slopes, near the edges of the great ragged valleys, remained the gray ghosts of the giant trees that were stripped clean, bark removed and smoothed in hours, reminders of that terrible September day when Hurricane Iniki's monstrous winds and driving rain swept across Kaua'i.

The Hawaiian Air 737 descended on final approach. Ben peered through the portal and thought about coming to Kaua'i a year after Iniki. He'd seen the workmen and scaffolding on the damaged Westin, which now was a sparkling Marriott property. Back then there were large brown palm fronds strewn across the hotel's roof. Now there were gleaming air conditioning compressors. He remembered gawking at the resort's golf course fairways, which were streaked with gray, like the paths of lightning bolts gone underground. Hundreds of them. And there were many other things he saw as he traveled about the Island back then—abandoned homes along the coastline, a huge temporary dump north of Līhu'e, filled with scraps of wood, roof shingles, refrigerators, washing machines, shredded tree limbs and shrubs, broken telephone poles, mangled street lights—anything the storm left not salvageable.

The Hawaiian gods repainted the foliage, workers from everywhere repaired the buildings, and the people of Kaua'i recovered and started over, some for the second time.

Ben tried to imagine what it was like that day. Winds so strong that people couldn't stand, waves so high and relentless that the beaches at Po'ipū were dramatically reshaped, sand pushed hundreds of feet inland collapsing homes, filling the lobbies of hotels. He pictured the brownish-gray web that covered so much of the vegetation, when finally the sun returned and burned the ocean salt that covered the leaves of the plants and trees.

The small jolt of the plane's wheels hitting the runway separated Ben from thoughts of the hurricane.

When he stepped out of the jetway into the terminal, a man came forward and offered his hand. He was Ben's height, jet-black hair combed back and tied in a small pony-tail, a narrow mustache, and deep gray eyes. He looked like a coffee grower Ben knew back home.

"Detective Gamos."

Ben shook his hand. "Ben McMillen. Glad to meet you. Got a first name?"

"Yeah. Miguel...Mike. Got more baggage?"

"Just these two," Ben said, gesturing to the hanging bag and his sports duffel.

Gamos took the sports bag. "That's what I like...optimism."

Ben narrowed his eyes. Gamos's tone was a little too sarcastic. Then he smiled to himself, remembering Tobi's warning to keep his eyes open. He was the outsider here, the one who had to prove himself.

Ben knew Gamos must be frustrated. Two unsolved cases, both possible homicides. The prospect that there would be more. And probably put off that his superiors thought he needed help from another Island.

Gamos jerked his head. "This way..."

Winding around slow-moving tourists in the terminal, Ben asked about the cases. Gamos gave him short answers, almost like a need-to-know briefing, so Ben had to continue probing to keep the Līhu'e detective talking. He learned that both victims were well-to-do, retired for the most part, each with philanthropic interests—Gamos coughed when he said that and Ben wondered if it was intentional—lived alone, both disappeared from their summer homes.

Ben didn't ask about their winter homes, but wasted no time inquiring about the fireballs and the ancient fish hooks.

Gamos stopped, looked at Ben with one open eye, then continued walking. "You believe in that crap?"

Well, we're off to a good start. "The fish hooks were there, right."

"Yeah, those are evidence. I meant the fireballs."

"I don't expect people who are not Hawaiian to believe in *kahuna* magic. On the other hand, there are many stories about some pretty amazing things…some I've been told first-hand. I guess I tend not to discount anything, especially the possibility of someone *imitating* folklore." Ben looked outside, saw the dark clouds above the mountains, spotted a muted rainbow. "Never saw more rainbows than on Kaua'i."

"I guess," Gamos said. He pointed to the right to a restricted parking area next to the terminal. "Over here."

"Where to first?"

"To see the Chief. Think he's worried about the local paper picking up on your being here. You know, serial killer expert from the Big Island to assist on a couple of Missing Person investigations."

"Whose idea was this anyhow?"

"To bring you in? No clue."

Bet you thought it was a bad idea.

In the car Ben ignored the other detective, stared out of the window, and gave the fireballs some thought. He couldn't remember anything specific his grandmother told him, rather he remembered something Ken Asumura discussed with him. That a fireball meant the *kahuna* wanted revenge in the worst way. That the victim had done something terrible to someone. Like a fireball was the ultimate retaliation. He tried to remember what Ken said the fireballs were made from but he couldn't.

If someone were re-enacting beliefs of the past, what would he use? A torch to throw?…to light something with?…maybe a dried coconut husk?

Gamos made a sharp left, which brought Ben forward in his seat. The Līhu'e detective then pulled into the front lot on Umi Street and angle parked the mud-caked Ford Explorer. He quickly opened the door and said, "Let's get a move on it…lots to do today."

Gamos hurried up to the front entrance, seeming not to care if Ben followed.

Hurrying to catch up, Ben glanced to his right and saw three large steel containers sitting on the grass just beyond the right wing of the building. The doors were supported by heavy reinforced hinges and were secured by huge padlocks the size of an out-stretched hand. Gamos told him that they were evidence storage containers. Strange looking as they were, the containers certainly appeared burglar proof.

Gamos led him down a glowing hallway that suffered from fluorescent overload. There were offices on both sides of the corridor, most of the doors were closed. The Līhu'e Detective nodded at a woman officer, who seemed more interested in Ben than the handcuffed man she was leading down the hallway.

The detectives turned the corner and headed down another hallway where the overhead lighting was turned off. A door ahead was slightly open, a crack of sunlight cut through the shadows. Gold painted lettering on the door read CHIEF OF POLICE.

Detective Gamos knocked, pushed the door fully open, and said to the slender man seated behind a huge steel desk, "We're here."

The Chief stood, pushing his chair back with a quick movement of the backs of his legs, came around the desk, walked straight toward Ben, and extended his hand. "Chief Johnson, Ben. Tobi's an old friend...glad to have you aboard."

"Thanks, Chief. Hope I can help."

"I'm sure you can. Coffee?"

Ben shook his head.

Chief Johnson gestured to the chairs in front of his desk and went back to his seat.

Chief Johnson was nothing like Kona's Major Serrao who was burly, loud, intimidating at first. The Līhu'e Chief was short, maybe five-seven, and very thin, no more than one-forty. His hair was light, close-cut on top, slightly longer on the sides, glistening with gel and brushed back. He looked like a miniature Marine drill sergeant, except that the pitch of his voice was too high.

Behind his desk, hanging on the wall, were a pair of orange boxing gloves. Ben eyed them, then looked at the Chief, and figured him for a street-wise policeman whom many probably underestimated. He wondered where the Chief and Tobi met.

"What's Mike told you?"

Ben shifted in his chair. "Just the background stuff...the ride's too short. I do have a few questions before I see the reports."

"Shoot."

"Tobi said the fish hooks are authentic. How old?"

"Forensic says they were made from whale bone...made a long time ago...before 1800." The Chief brought his arms up and locked them behind his head. His eyes blinked a few times. "Your next question about the fireballs?"

"Okay."

"Forensic says the fire seemed to be confined to a two-foot circle. There were traces of lava rock…what was described to me as *recently burned* lava rock."

Ben formed a tent with his hands, like he was about to pray. Slowing he raised his hands to his mouth, resting his chin on his thumbs. "Do you have the bed sheets?"

"One's in the evidence lockers, sealed in plastic. The second's still at the crime scene."

"Anything taken from the houses?"

Chief Johnson shifted his eyes toward Detective Gamos.

Gamos cleared his throat. "The first victim, the one in Kalihiwai…"

"Where exactly is that?" asked Ben.

Gamos gave him a bored look. "Small town…just Hanalei-side of Kīlauea. You follow the road along 'Anini Beach to the end. "The first victim, Walter Churchwell, lived with his son. His son was on O'ahu that night…strange guy, his son. Basically a thirty-six year-old beach bum living off the old man. He was a suspect, could have had it arranged…until the second one happened. Son had a bruise on his cheek when we first questioned him. Said he got it in a fight. We checked it out. That night Honolulu arrested him and another guy in a bar near Aloha Tower. Kept him overnight. Still was a suspect in my mind…maybe the brawl in Honolulu was staged. But Frobert's vanishing under the same circumstances made us turn down the heat on him. Anyhow, to answer your question, he said the only thing missing was an old Hawaiian quilt that hung above his father's bed.

"Like I said before, it's the old man's *summer* home. The main house is on the eastern shore, north of Anahola, near where the family cane operation is. Old Churchwell doesn't have much to do with it anymore. We talked with the workers there. Didn't get anything. Most never met him."

He talks up a storm when the Chief's around to impress.

"Tell me more about the second victim?"

"Samuel Frobert lived alone on the North Shore, just past Wainiha…that's past Hanalei, maybe nine or ten miles from the Churchwell place. Frobert was seventy-three. Found a stack of *Playboys* in his closet." Gamos snickered.

The Chief cleared his throat and Gamos gave him a resigned look.

Ben got up and walked to the small window that fronted the other side of police headquarters, facing the three storage containers. He turned and looked at Gamos. "Who kept house for him?"

"Apparently he did. We talked with a few people who live out that way…no one really knew him…his property is at least a quarter mile from the closest neighbor, and most of the places are rentals. There's private property signs all over his place. Found his checkbook. Didn't find any record of him paying anyone to clean or tend to the grounds. The house was spotless...the yard needed some work, though."

"Relatives?" asked Ben.

"Some on O'ahu...they don't have much to do with him." Gamos wet his lips. "We're still checking."

"Then who reported him missing...?"

Gamos turned and looked to the Chief.

The chief's fingers massaged his temples. "That's something we haven't made public, yet. It's why, after the second one, we were sure we had a serial killer...errr...a serial something on the loose. We got an anonymous tip."

"Phone call?" asked Ben.

"Uh huh. Said, 'Anybody know where Samuel Frobert's gone?'"

"That's it?"

"That's it."

"Man or a woman?"

"Man."

"On tape?"

Gamos answered, "Not 9-1-1...just a regular line."

"So you don't know if anything's missing from the house."

"No idea," answered the detective.

Ben came away from the window and leaned against the door frame. "No other clues?"

"We took our dog out to both places. He had no trouble following the scent to the water. And he didn't get sidetracked...the perp and the victim were together, close together...like the perpetrator carried the victim to the ocean. To a boat, we theorize, then disappeared into the night."

"The night?"

"Figure of speech." Mike Gamos grinned. "Night be kinda risky in the ocean, but if one guy planned both of these, he probably knows the territory pretty well, including the water."

Ben asked, "Footprints?"

"Rain." Gamos snorted, "North Shore...hell, it rains when it's not raining."

"This dog...?"

"A tracking dog."

"We have a drug dog back home...actually Hilo does."

"We have two dogs…the other's a drug sniffer. Eros tracks people. Wanna meet him?" Gamos gave Ben a big inviting smile.

"Sure…and I'd like to see the bed sheet and the other evidence."

"Listen, Ben." The Chief stood, pushing his chair back with his legs once more. "The reason you're here, in case you're really wondering, is only partially because you have some experience with a serial killer. It's also because a local reporter's gotten wind of this. He's picked up on the fish hooks and the burnt sheets and has written it up as some kind of mystical mystery…something connected to old Hawai'i. He's gotten some people scared. Especially some rich ones who live alone in remote areas. I don't hold back punches…"

Ben's peripheral vision quickly took in the boxing gloves on the wall behind the desk.

"…Tobi and I go back a long way…I'm as far from being Hawaiian or Japanese as you can be, but I'm a believer in…I guess you'd call it the spiritual part of Hawai'i. Not that I believe in all of it, but I know there are some serious people out there, people who believe in the *Menehune* and believe in *Kahuna* magic…and that some things happen that you can't logically explain. I just thought it wise to have someone on the case who might be able to interpret what's happening a little better than we're prepared to do here. I don't have a Hawaiian detective who's tuned into any of the old ways. I asked Tobi for help. He said you'd be perfect on both counts." He folded his arms across his chest. "I don't mind you talking with the newspaper if they find you." Chief Johnson paused, then nodded to himself. "Probably it's a good idea. Otherwise they'll think we're hiding something and dig deeper. But keep it brief, leave out the folklore stuff best you can and talk about disappearances, not a serial killer."

"So it was your idea to bring me here?"

The Chief pursed his lips. "Well, not exactly."

"Okay, who?"

Red-faced, he answered, "It was a suggestion from…from an anonymous caller."

"Say again."

Big exhale from the Chief. "You heard me…some concerned citizen called me and suggested it and quite frankly, it made sense."

"Some concerned citizen here knows about me?" Ben's face filled with doubt.

Ben moved his eyes to Gamos, and when Gamos saw he was looking at him, the Līhu'e detective lowered his head and stared at the floor.

Ben knew who called. The same citizen who 'wondered' where Samuel Frobert was. Serial killers are compulsive about reading about other serial killers. It's like

'I can top that...I'm the clever one.' Who's the guy who caught you?...he won't catch me.

Eyes open, bruddah.

▼▲▼

Gamos said, "This is patrolman Ernie Dumas. He's Eros's trainer."

"Ben McMillen, Ernie, glad to meet you."

"Same here, Ben."

"Let's go meet Eros."

Ben asked what kind of dog Eros was. He was told a Belgian Shepherd. Three years old. Trained in California to track fugitives and missing people. Extremely loyal to and protective of his trainer. Any doubts Ben had about that were put to rest when they stepped outside and walked toward the kennel.

The enclosure was about twenty feet square, heavy chain link fencing about ten feet high. Inside, tail straight and still, ears up, eyes unblinking, facial expression barely hiding his teeth, front paws dug in as if he were ready to burst through the fencing, stood Eros. Ben, Gamos, and Patrolman Dumas approached the kennel. Eros's eyes never left Ben.

Ernie called out, "Eros!"

The dog, ever so slightly, shifted its eyes to its trainer. Ben could see a twitching hind leg muscle.

Ernie stopped, put his left arm around Ben's shoulder, then tapped Ben's chest with his right hand. "*'Ohana!*"

The transformation was amazing. Eros relaxed, tail wagged, tongue licked around his mouth. Then the Belgian Shepherd sat. The stranger was *family*.

Ernie walked toward the kennel, opened the gate, but Eros remained seated inside. Ernie tapped his right thigh. Quickly, Eros was by his side, standing, waiting for his next instruction. "Come over, Ben...meet my brah, here, Eros."

Ben came, then asked, "Can I pet him?"

"Sure. He knows you're part of the family. But it'll take a few more meetings before he *really* trusts you."

Ben stroked the dog's coat a few times. "What's that around his neck?"

"It a receiver. It's how we communicate when we're not within eyesight and the situation is such that it wouldn't be a good idea for me to shout."

"Smart dog."

"He's unbelievable. Sometimes I think he's smarter than dolphin."

"Funny you should say that. Spinner dolphin are my *'aumakua*, my family's guardian spirit."

"Eros is all the guardian I'll ever need."

Mike Gamos interjected, "Eros is with Ernie day and night. End of the shift, they go home together."

Ben snorted. "Must make dating tough."

Gamos made a clicking noise with his cheek. "Ernie's married. His wife doesn't mind sleeping outside."

Ernie said to the dog, "Eros, how'd you like Detective Mike for lunch?"

Eros licked his lips.

Ben smiled but got down to business. "Ernie, tell me about tracking the two disappearances on the North Shore."

"Eros, *hale*!"

The Shepherd walked back into the kennel, hung his right paw in one of the diamond-shaped gate links, pulled hard, and stepped back. The heavy kennel gate slammed shut. Eros sat.

"Siesta!"

Eros laid down.

Ernie said, "He understands Spanish, too."

Ben shook his head.

Ernie walked over to a white pickup parked in the shade of the overhang, which ran along most of the back of Police HQ. The detectives followed.

"Same thing both times. First we let Eros sniff some clothes we found in the bedroom closet. He circled the room for a few seconds, then left the bedroom, went straight out the front door, and headed for the water. There are paths to the beach from both houses and streams that follow the paths and connect with the ocean. He never left the path. The scent took him straight to the water...at Churchwell's place to the ocean. At Frobert's to the mouth of the stream. The stream at Frobert's is too narrow for a boat and very shallow. Someone could have walked down the stream to the ocean. At both crime scenes he sniffed a few yards up and down, but came right back to the spot where he first stopped. So that's where the victims were taken...to the water. We searched the water, streams and oceans—a mile each way along the shoreline, no bodies, no other clues.

"Then we went back to the bedroom and let Eros sniff the fish hook. I held it by the rope, couldn't touch it...hadn't been dusted, and we can't dust it until Eros has a chance to sniff it. The fish hook necklace, assuming the perp wore it around his neck, would have absorbed some body oils, sweat from the perp. Eros tracked the fish hook smell the same way as the victims' clothes. Except at the Wainiha scene, Frobert's house. He went into the library first, then back to the bedroom. Both places, out the door. Right down the same path as before. My guess is the murderer carried the victims away. And at Frobert's he went into the library before leaving...maybe to take something, like the quilt he took from Churchwell's."

Ben was thinking about the coarsely braided coconut husk his people used to make rope a long time ago. He looked at Detective Gamos. "Was the rope authentic?"

"No. We're trying to trace it, but it's just about impossible."

Ben pinched the bridge of his nose and squeezed. "Ernie, you, Mike, and the Chief, all say murderer. Why? Why do you feel the victims were murdered and not kidnapped?"

"Just a hunch, I guess." He shrugged as he looked at Gamos.

The Līhu'e detective said, "One crime and no body, maybe a kidnapping. Two and bodies or not...homicide."

Ben faced Ernie. "Okay if we take Eros out there again?"

"Sure, but it's rained a lot the last few days. Makes finding anything new harder."

Ben patted the patrolman on the back. Out of the corner of his eye, he saw Eros get up and press his nose against the kennel gate.

"Not a good idea, huh?"

"No problem...he'd chew you up a little...but he wouldn't swallow."

They passed a badly destroyed car on the way to the evidence containers. Ben gestured at the twisted wreckage. Gamos explained that there was a head-on a week before near Hanapēpē. Two drunk drivers, killed instantly. He said they decided to keep this car, shards of glass, blood stains, empty beer cans and all, to show to the school kids when they came for a tour of Police Headquarters. Let them see first-hand what drinking and driving were all about.

What Ben saw in the evidence container mystified him. A bed sheet with a two-foot hole, brown strands of fabric surrounding the area that was burned. He expected the edges of the burned part to be more uneven. This hole was very much a near perfect circle.

"The other one the same?"

"Yeah."

"What are the dates, again?"

"First one, Churchwell, almost two weeks ago, Thursday early morning, September first. Frobert, just last Friday late or Saturday…early morning."

When he asked Gamos about traces of chemicals that might have been used to fuel the fire, the Līhu'e detective shook his head. After a few seconds, he answered, "What you find in burning lava…*natural* burning lava forensic said."

"Still don't believe in fireballs?" Ben grinned.

Gamos just walked away.

CHAPTER 5

The house where the first victim lived reminded Ben of a mansion situated on a flat plateau high above Captain Cook on the western slopes of the Big Island. The only difference was that this home was built near the sea.

The *koa* siding was stained gray by years' of rain, large ragged circles marked the knots in the wood, smaller gray spots peppered the side—rows of nail heads that looked like the path of a methodical woodpecker as he searched for insects. The wood shingle roof on the main structure had a slight pitch. Double chimneys protruded about a third of the distance in from the sides. From where Ben stood, on the dirt circular driveway, he saw that the left side of the property was bounded by a lava cliff, which disappeared into dense foliage. On the other side was a fairly wide stream that emptied into the sea several hundred yards farther on. He pictured Churchwell, wrapped in a quilt, being carried to the stream. He squinted as if that would change the shadowy image of the man carrying Churchwell into a person with a face.

Mike Gamos closed the car door with a push from his right hip. "Let's go."

Ben looked back at him and gestured for the other detective to lead the way.

They climbed the verandah steps and Gamos rapped on the screen door frame. Ben heard a door close from within, then footsteps coming down stairs. A man of medium height appeared, opened the front door and gestured them inside. He simply said, "Been expecting you." Without a handshake or even a push to open the door, he headed down a long hallway, never checking to see if his visitors followed.

The detectives were close behind.

When the man reached a sliding screen door, he warned without turning, "Watch your step."

There was no step, just a drop of more than a foot and a half, which Ben misjudged, causing him to stumble onto the small patio. He heard Gamos clear his throat, and Ben turned around.

Gamos descended neatly, gesturing with his hands, 'Look, no hands.'

Ben, already tired from Gamos's act, decided to confront him about it after they finished with Churchwell's son.

The son took a seat on one of the wrought iron chairs.

The detectives stood.

Ben studied the victim's son. To Ben, the way he greeted them made him a suspect. He was aloof, looked bothered but not worried, certainly not remorseful or anxious. He was dressed in below-the-knee, baggy navy shorts, no belt, and wore a plain, faded, oversized yellow tank-top. His feet were bare. The gold Rolex on his left wrist and heavy gold link chain around his neck glittered in the bright sunlight. He wore no rings. Except for the wrinkles in his face, Ben would have gauged him to be in his late twenties. He seemed out-of-place for this house. Young Churchwell looked like someone who belonged in an old beach shack, where everything would be a mess except, of course, for the surfboard, which would have a polish that reflected like a mirror.

Gamos said, "This is Detective McMillen…"

John Churchwell didn't say anything—just ^ and folded his arms across his chest and stared off into the distance.

"I know you've been over this before," Ben said, "but let's hear it one more time. Tell us what you found when you came home…you spent the night of your father's disappearance in jail on O'ahu, right?"

Gamos gave Ben a quick sideways glance.

Ben stared back. His expression saying 'let me do this my way.'

"Yeah…O'ahu," the son turned his head and for the first time looked Ben in the eye.

And Ben realized why. Churchwell's cheek was bruised, purple and yellow, and the flesh around the eye was noticeably swollen. *He really must have been nailed to still have that much discoloration after nearly two weeks.* "When did you get home?"

"Next day, man."

"What time?"

"Around noon, maybe one."

"How'd you find the house?"

"Been here before."

Gamos leaned forward and gave Churchwell a penetrating look. "Listen wise guy, play it straight. What'd this place look like when you returned?"

"Hey…let's remember one thing. I'm the victim…my father's missing, probably dead. Got it?"

Gamos bit his lip and continued staring at the son. Then he let out his breath. "What about the house, Churchwell?"

Churchwell's expression finally lightened up. "Nothing except the burned bed sheet…then I noticed the quilt was gone."

"When you first walked inside, could you smell anything burning?" Ben asked.

"No…just went looking for my father, thought he was taking a nap."

"Then what'd you do?" asked Ben.

"Searched around, then called the police."

"Wouldn't you call some of his friends, first? See if he was there?"

"Not with a burned bed sheet. And the quilt…I mean why would it be gone? It's hung there forever."

"What else you find?" asked Ben.

"Nothing. The police found that fish hook necklace on the bedpost……that's it."

"Tell me about this bar fight."

"Just some slammer who got mean."

"Slammer?"

"Some asshole slamming them down…a drunk looking for a fight."

"The report says he says the same thing about you."

Churchwell, sounding bored, "Fuck him."

"You know this slammer?" Ben watched Churchwell's eyes.

"Whaddaya mean, know him?"

"Met him before?"

"No way, man. Just some slammer."

"Well, we're going to check that out. Be a problem for you if we find out you know him."

Churchwell's eyes narrowed and he frowned.

Ben couldn't tell if Churchwell was worried or just thought he was dealing with two idiots, but he knew Churchwell understood what he meant—that the fight was staged to give Churchwell an alibi.

Rubbing the back of his neck, Churchwell said, "I thought another guy disappeared."

Gamos took a step forward. "Figured that would let you off the hook? Not a bad plan."

Churchwell looked at Gamos. "There is no plan, man. You guys leaving?"

"Mind if we take a look upstairs?" Ben asked.

Churchwell hesitated, but said, "Go ahead."

"You want to come along?"

"Why…you guys gonna steal something?"

But he got up and led the way.

The bedroom was large, Ben guessed at least twenty by thirty. The four-poster bed was against the far wall between two windows. The bed was stripped. Ben knelt on the mattress. There were no signs of fire. He pressed his nose against the material and sniffed. No odor. He got up and asked Churchwell on which post the necklace was found. The son of the missing man pointed to the left one at the foot of the bed.

"And you didn't see it."

"Wasn't looking there, man…just popped my head in to check on my father. Then the sheet got my full attention."

Ben gazed out of the window for a few seconds where the view of Kaua'i's north coast line was broken by tall palms and ironwood trees, except to the east, where the Kīlauea Lighthouse was visible.

Now facing the son, "Did your father keep valuables in the house…like jewelry or money?"

Churchwell ran his hand through his long hair. Then he twisted his neck like he was trying to get a kink out. "There's a safe in the library. Like I said, only the quilt was taken."

"So you checked in there…you know the combination."

"Course, man. Why shouldn't I?"

Ben could think of a thousand reasons.

After a quick inspection of the library, Ben said they'd take a look around outside before leaving. He asked Churchwell to double-check for missing items. Churchwell gave him a pained look, then shrugged his shoulders.

When they were fifty feet from the house, Ben said, "What do you make of him?"

Gamos didn't answer.

Ben grabbed his arm and brought him to a stop. Held his arm tightly. When he felt Gamos stop struggling, he let Gamos wrestle his arm free.

"What the fuck is that about?"

"About your attitude. I came to help. I didn't come for headlines. Now...we're either partners, or I go to the Chief and ask for someone else."

"We can handle this here with our own people."

"Fine, then drive me to the airport." Ben turned and headed back toward the Explorer.

Finally, Gamos shouted, "All right...all right."

Ben turned but held his ground. Wiped some sweat out of the corner of his eyes.

Gamos walked toward him. When they were face-to-face, he said, "Put yourself in my place."

"Been there with the Feds."

"Yeah?"

"Yeah. They take charge. Start from scratch like anything you did investigating was wrong or a waste of time. They don't tell you anything...share anything. And they put you down every chance they get with their not-so-subtle wisecracks. As soon as you think I'm acting like a Fed, kick me in the ass and throw me in the water." Ben took a deep breath. He extended his hand.

Gamos took it, then both detectives walked toward the beach. Gamos finally answered Ben's question. "What do I make of him? He's kind of a free spirit...living off his daddy's bucks. They were more than forty years apart. My guess is they didn't see the world exactly the same way."

"If we didn't have another victim, I'd be on him day and night. You know if either Churchwell has some connection with the second victim...even a remote one?"

"Don't think so...but we haven't completely checked that out yet. Remember...the second one's only a few days old. But we did background the other guy in the bar fight. Not a local...just a mainlander on vacation. A thirty-something who thinks he still a twenty-something. Waiting at the local soda shop for the guys to show up...and the guys are long gone."

The sound of the crashing surf worked its course through the trees. The warm wind picked up blowing some sand into little funnel clouds that danced around the *pili* grass. Palms fronds clapped and clattered, and ironwood branches creaked and groaned. Ben watched a large frigatebird flying against the wind, barely inching forward. He wondered what prize was worth such an expenditure of energy. He wondered if he and Gamos really had a truce or if he'd need to keep dangling the threat of going to the Chief.

They walked another few paces before Ben asked, "This is the path Eros followed?"

"Yeah…he headed straight down the driveway, then angled toward the stream. Followed it for another hundred yards beyond the property toward the beach. Stopped where the stream meets the beach, went a few yards in both directions, then just barked at the water."

"Let's have a look."

The path along the stream was filled with depressions, non-descript footprints in the soft, white sand. Ben guessed a lot of locals came and swam here when the ocean wasn't too rough. Squat pines, branches intertwined, lined the trail, as did a few tall palms, and farther back on each side dense ironwoods, which covered much of the forest floor in darkness. Every now and then the bulbous trunk of a huge palm crowded the pathway. Suddenly, the wind died down to a whisper. The heavy surf thundered just ahead, and looking up, Ben now saw an assemblage of great frigatebirds kiting on wingspans that reached eight feet. He felt dizzy watching them circle about.

Two-thirds of the way to the beach, they stopped. Nothing of particular interest there, except for a two-foot waterfall, which effectively marked the beginning of deeper water. Gamos commented on the freshwater stream. He explained there were many streams along the North Shore, runoff from Mount Wai'ale'ale, the wettest spot on earth, which received between four- and five-hundred inches of rainfall each year. Wai'ale'ale literally means *overflowing water.*

Ben thought this would be a good spot to tie up a small boat. "Eros didn't stop here…even for a second?"

Gamos shook his head.

Ben gestured toward the ocean and the two detectives left the stream bank, cut across a patch of sand and knee-high grass, then trudged across the beach toward the ocean. Evidence of footprints disappeared, both the high tide and wind saw to that. Ben stopped a few yards short of the water, standing on a two-foot rise that marked where the surf sank its jaws and stole the sand.

"Right here?" Ben shouted to be heard above a crashing wave.

Gamos nodded, sparing his voice. He came closer.

"Mooring a boat right here isn't too smart," Ben said. To him, the undertow looked like it could rip your teeth out.

"It would be more logical to come in along the stream, but Eros wouldn't move from this spot. The surf's usually rough here, like now, but sometimes it's calm. If you knew what you were doing you could get a Catamaran or a Zodiac raft in here. Only something small could navigate the stream, and something small would be a problem to keep afloat out there...especially leaving with an extra passenger...dead weight at that."

Ben thought about a story his grandmother told him. A ghost story of the night marchers. Hadn't she said the seas calmed during the full moon, when some night marchers, the spirits of warriors returning home by canoe, came ashore?

"McMillen?"

Ben gave Gamos a thoughtful look. "What was the moon like that night?"

"Don't know...s'pose we can check. Why?"

Ben wasn't going to explain his thoughts on night marchers to Gamos. "Just thought it would be pretty difficult maneuvering a boat through the reef and rocks without some light."

"You know, maybe it could have been something small...like a two-man outrigger...it's small but stable with that runner."

"You think he dumped the body farther out and paddled home?"

"Something like that," Gamos answered.

"Let's get going." Ben was thinking, then smiling.

"What?"

"Maybe we *should* bring Eros out here again."

Gamos replied, "I thought we agreed there's no scent left."

"Not for that. Put a sign on Churchwell that says I HATE ERNIE...maybe Eros would get his attention and he'd get serious."

They laughed.

"Let's check out the second M.P.," said Ben, referring to the second victim.

"McMillen, I'm telling you...they're missing, but they're bodies."

▼▲▼

The drive farther west along King Kūhiō Highway took them past Princeville, a golf resort community situated on a relatively flat parcel of land, wedged between the hundred-foot cliffs of the northern coastline and Hanalei Valley. Surrounding the lush fairways, sandy white bunkers, and velvet-like greens, were rows of wood and stucco condos, a small shopping center—a mixture of retail shops and commercial offices, mainly vacation rental companies. Beyond to the west, overlooking the great crescent bay, itself, two resort hotels, the Hanalei Bay Resort and the Princeville Hotel—the latter structure stepping down the rugged cliffs to the bay below.

Mauka, inland, deep green taro fields choked the Hanalei River basin, stretching to the foot of the mountains, the front ridge brown and deep green, and farther inland, the highland rose into a dense vale of tumbling dark clouds, the kind mid-westerners call snow clouds. Hawaiians named them *aokū*, rain clouds, or *kōkōli'i*, black clouds.

Abruptly, the road seemed to end, but a diamond-shaped, yellow road sign understated the one-hundred-eighty degree turn with a simple arrow arching left and a 15 mph speed limit that should have been underlined and exclamation-pointed. The sign didn't warn of the steep drop to the Hanalei valley floor either. Ben noticed that most sections of the guardrail had more car paint than Maaco.

Detective Gamos eased around the curve and coasted downhill.

Along the Hanalei River, Ben saw dozens of white egret, some searching the shallows for small fish, others perched in the tangle of trees that lined the far bank. At the bottom of the steep grade was another one-hundred-eighty degree turn, this one across a one-lane trestle bridge. When they crossed the river, Gamos commented that there was a herd of buffalo in one of the pastures just beyond the bridge. He pointed, Ben looked, saw maybe twenty big brown shapes. One turned and stared at the two detectives.

"What are they doing here?" Ben asked, a little bit incredulous.

"They're no different. Liked it when they visited...decided to stay."

The small town of Hanalei lay ahead. The Hanalei Dolphin restaurant was on the right, sitting on the west bank of the river, just as the waterway turned north and joined the bay. Farther up, a few stores, the busy Ching Young shopping center, several cozy restaurants, a couple of kayak and canoe rental places, Captain Zodiac tours, Mahikoa's Hanalei Bay Inn—the only real place to rent a room—then the Hanalei School, and the Post Office. Less than thirty seconds later they were headed out of town.

For the next ten minutes they drove along the winding North Shore road, through thick vegetation and steep *pali* to the left, past clusters of beach homes on stilts, catching glimpses of the ocean to the right. They crossed three one-lane bridges, drove by several beaches, each with more warning signs—HIGH SURF and DANGEROUS UNDERTOW. They crossed the Wainiha Stream and soon after a ninety-degree bend in the road, they came upon a pair of one-lane bridges at right angles with one another, precisely where another small river bisected the roadway in two spots. When they crossed the first bridge, Gamos slowed, then carefully left the road, ignoring the second bridge, and entered a dirt driveway.

Gamos pulled up to a chain link gate and turned off the engine. "We have to walk the rest of the way."

The size of the beach home surprised Ben. It was set on a grassy knoll surrounded by tall trees, beyond was a long winding path through a fairly wide valley that lead into the mountains. Ben assumed there were several trails back there for hiking, something he loved to do.

The house was two stories tall with a verandah that encircled all but one side. The driveway, sand and finely crushed black lava, was lined thick with hibiscus on one side, close-cropped Bermuda grass on the other. Deep ruts filled with rainwater made it necessary for them to forego walking up the driveway.

They ascended the front steps and ducked the crime scene tape hung across the verandah's front two columns.

Gamos added, "Samuel Frobert gave a lot to charity, the schools, museums, but like many who call themselves philanthropists, he took a lot, too. I think you can trace his roots back to the overthrow of the Queen."

Ben looked hard at Gamos. "Where'd you find out that?"

"Local paper covering his disappearance."

"Same guy I'm supposed to be careful with?"

"Same one." Gamos extracted a key and unlocked the front door. He stepped inside first, held the door for Ben, who noticed a crime scene warning stapled to the front door jam.

The front foyer was large and gave a magnificent view of the garden in back. Downstairs were the kitchen, a dining room that easily handled an enormous *koa* table, a formal living room with a fireplace opening into which Gamos's Explorer would fit, a library filled with books and a heavy mahogany desk that seemed to sink into a thick Oriental rug. At the end of a hallway and down a few steps, quarters for live-in help. The windows in every room went almost floor to ceiling, affording great views of the cliffs, the garden, and the stream.

Upstairs there were six bedrooms and four full bathrooms. Ben went through all but the master bedroom quickly. Saving the master for last, he now stood at the foot of the king bed. While Gamos seated himself on the window sill, Ben examined the bed sheets. The white top sheet was bunched at the bottom of the bed. It looked like someone pushed it there with his feet. The bottom sheet had a two-foot hole in the center, a ring of black and a wider ring of brown. The mattress cover, which showed through the hole, was brown, as well, but looked more like a water stain than evidence of a fire. Ben remembered the mattress at Churchwell's showed no brown. He didn't know what to make of that, except maybe Churchwell's mattress was made from different fabric. Or maybe, the first fire was put out more quickly. A thin cotton blanket hung over the bed's bottom rail.

Sarcastically, Gamos asked, "Fireball?"

Ben ignored Gamos's tone. "This looks strange…it's basically the same size as the other one. In fact, maybe the exact size as the other one. Got a tape measure?"

Gamos reached into his pants pocket, extracted a measure, and tossed it to Ben.

Two feet across top to bottom and left to right. "Same size." Ben raised his head, thinking, then leaned forward to examine the wall above the bed, which caught his eye. "Look at this."

Detective Gamos got up and approached the bed.

Ben pointed. There were two hooks, small, screwed into the ceiling, each a couple of inches from the wall and about three feet apart. On one hook there was a knotted piece of translucent string, light fishing line probably. The line had been snapped.

"It's in the report."

"But what hung here?" Ben studied the wall again, trying to gage the size of what once was suspended there, having trouble because of the patch of sunlight that illuminated the wall. He looked toward the window and saw there were no curtains or blinds, but spied a bi-fold Japanese screen in the corner of the room.

"Get that screen and put it in front of the window sill…to block the light."

"Sure."

Now a slightly darker shape was revealed. Ben estimated it to be four feet by five.

Gamos ventured a guess. "Another quilt?"

"Doubt it. Not how you'd typically hang a quilt and the hooks are too small. Something lighter." Ben had a bad feeling. For the first time it really sank in…The stolen wall hangings somehow elevated the intent of the crime in Ben's mind to revenge and murder. What was taken might not be valuable, but they were significant, pointed to a motive he believed.

Kidnapped?…but there'd been no ransom demand. And these guys had the money. Gamos was right. Missing bodies, not missing persons.

Outside again, Ben and Gamos walked back along the driveway, crossed the road and followed the path to the ocean, which Gamos said Eros followed. The wind seemed cold here, and Ben felt goose bumps—locals called it *chicken skin.* For some reason his mouth became dry and he noticed Gamos wetting his lips.

Ben remembered his grandmother used to say when that happened 'that you passed the recent path of a ghost.' He had an uneasy feeling inside.

They stopped by the second bridge, the one crossing the stream where it entered Frobert's property, and Ben knelt to observe underneath the structure. Although there were several pipes hung parallel to the water that minimized the clearance, there was still room for a small craft to pass. Ben asked if anyone checked for scrapping underneath the bridge.

Gamos said they had. Nothing. Undisturbed slimy moss and snails. He added that he thought the boat had been beached much farther up, since Eros hadn't hesitated by the bridge.

The sandy trail to the beach was lumpy with old footprints, mottled from the rain. Looking over his shoulder, Ben could not see much of Frobert's house. The Ironwood trees and thick pandanus blocked most of the view.

A hundred feet from the ocean, Gamos pointed to the spot where Eros stopped. He said they'd searched the path and surrounding area on hands and knees, but found no evidence. Said there were no close-by neighbors, but they interviewed a few people at the other end of the beach two days before, the day after Frobert disappeared. None of them was there much past sunset, when it was assumed the crime took place. Also, those who frequented this beach saw nothing in the last few days that aroused suspicion.

Ben nodded and headed for the ocean. He wanted to see what the sea looked like beyond the mouth of the stream.

Nearing the water, Ben spotted a man sitting on a smooth lava rock, facing the ocean, legs crossed, flicking small stones into the surf. Several brown noddy arrived and soared overhead, probably thinking the stones were small fish. The man turned and looked at the detectives long before Ben would have guessed he could have heard them approaching.

Like he'd been waiting for them. Or waiting for someone.

Chapter 6

The detectives walked along the beach toward the man on the rock. Ben watched him rise, pick up what appeared to be a black notebook, and slip his feet into his flip-flops. The man jumped over a small tide pool that separated him from the beach, then waved to the two detectives as he approached them.

Gamos said, "That didn't take long…"

"Who is he?"

"It's Ray Kuali'i. He's the reporter. Works for *The Garden Island*."

New-looking aloha shirt, light gray pleated Dockers with cuffs, brown braided belt cinched tightly, four inches of the tip hanging straight down, and sun glasses bouncing on his chest, dangling from lime-colored Croakies. Kuali'i appeared to be about Ben's height, five-ten, his hair was black, longish and straight, parted in the middle.

"Aloha, Detective Gamos," he greeted, climbing up the small hill carved into the wet sand by the surf's strong undertow. He nodded to Ben, extended his hand, and said, "Aloha, Ray Kuali'i."

Ben shook the reporter's hand and introduced himself. He left off the detective and the Kona part.

"You new?…haven't seen you around."

Gamos answered, "He's on loan to us for a while."

Ben watched as the reporter's eyes darted back and forth as if he were trying to intercept their brain waves. Moments later, he raised his eyebrows as things apparently clicked into place.

Kuali'i smiled and said, "McMillen…Ben McMillen…so…I'm not the only one who thinks we have a serial killer here. Followed your case a few years ago…nice work."

"We have two missing people…that's all." Ben looked beyond Ray Kuali'i and saw a wave forming, which seemed much bigger than those that preceded it. "I think we should move back." Ben pointed and began to back-step.

Gamos and the reporter followed him…they needed no coaxing. A rogue wave was something no Islander ignored.

The giant breaker crashed just beyond the sculpted sand rise, then spread across the lumpy dry sand like a lava flow on fast-forward. The detectives ran. Kuali'i laughed and trudged through the surging water. The three men were wet to their ankles when the water began to recede. Gurgling bubbles in the sand gave evidence of hundreds of burrowing sand crabs, *ōhiki.*

"Should be wearing flip-flops," Kuali'i said, laughing when they reached dry sand. He became serious quickly. "So what's the deal?"

Ben looked at Gamos. He expected his new partner to explain this right from the start. He felt the reporter's eyes. *Wait much longer to answer and this guy will just suspect more.* "My role is to interpret the Hawaiiana clues."

"C'mon, McMillen. There are people here who can do that."

Ben countered quickly. "Not with a policeman's slant on it."

Gamos said. "Look, Ray. We've got two missing people and some clues that seem like they were conjured up from the past. We've only got one Hawaiian detective and he's so fresh out of school, he only gets assigned purse snatchers for now…and Ben was available. Nothing out of the ordinary here."

Ben relaxed a bit.

"A cop saying 'nothing out of the ordinary here'…is like a salesman saying 'no problem.'"

Gamos countered. "Like a reporter saying 'sure…it's off the record.'"

Kuali'i gave him a sour frown.

Ben ignored the banter and checked his watch. He was surprised it was already four o'clock. Then he looked up and concentrated on Kuali'i until the reporter returned his stare. Ben thought that maybe it wouldn't hurt to spend some time with him—see what he knows.

"Tell you what. We've got to head back, check out a few things at the station, then I'm going to drop off my stuff…and go for a run. How about we meet you someplace after seven for dinner. Sound okay, Mike?"

Gamos gave Ben a pensive look. Then his face muscles relaxed a bit and he said, "Count me out. Family tonight…meet the teacher."

"Okay if I go alone?"

"Fine. Just make sure he picks up the check."

"Okay, Ray. You pick the place."

"Where you staying?"

"B and B…in Wailua."

"Got a car?"

"Uh huh."

"Thai?"

"Didn't bring one."

The reporter snorted. "Thai food?"

Ben smirked.

Kuali'i nodded. "Guess you're quicker than I thought. Meet you at The King and I on Kūhiō…Waipouli Plaza…say…seven-fifteen or so. I have a seven o'clock deadline."

"You writing this up?"

"Kona cop comes to the rescue. Must be a story in there somewhere."

"No serial killer stuff," instructed Gamos.

Hands up, looking defenseless. "Who me? Just kidding…I'll wait 'til there's another development. Writing about Hawaiian Sovereignty this week. See you later." The reporter trudged up the beach, headed for the trail to the plantation house.

Just before Kuali'i was out of earshot, Ben called out above the noise of the surf, "Hey!"

The reporter stopped and looked over his shoulder.

"Why were you here?"

The reporter cupped his hands around his mouth and shouted, "Just like you…looking for clues."

Walking back up the path, Ben asked, "Tell me about him."

"Like what?"

"Do you trust him?"

"Sure. His reporting is strictly factual. Doesn't jump the gun. The only thing controversial he writes is that sovereignty stuff."

"What about this serial killer stuff?"

"You think he's jumping the gun? I don't."

Ben let it go. When they reached the path, he asked. "He for or against?"

"Huh?"

"Sovereignty."

"Actually, he writes about both sides, but I think he's for. His family goes way back. What about you?"

Ben didn't feel comfortable answering questions about Hawaiian Sovereignty. It bought him back to his feeling that he was becoming less Hawaiian over time. Sovereignty…so many questions, different factions with different proposals. "I feel strongly about the customs. And I know a little about Hawai'i Homelands. But sovereignty…don't know how practical that is. I guess I need some time to think about it."

"No offense, but don't waste your time…it'll never happen."

Ben didn't show it, but he took offense. Truce on…truce off.

▼▲▼

Ben dropped his bags onto the bed, then arched his back and stretched until his shoulders cracked. He walked back to the door, shut it, clicked on the ceiling fan, turning the dial to HIGH, and started to undress.

The rented room on Haleilio was small but had a nice view of Nounou Mountain, known now as Sleeping Giant, the place where a mythical tyrant chief met his death in battle. The furniture was old and simple, but the mattress tested firm, and that was all that really mattered. He'd be there a week, he hoped, no more, and only use the room to sleep and shower. He expected to be working long days from now on. Part to solve the crime quickly, part because he wanted to be back home to get ready for the Ironman. His plan for the upcoming three weeks was intensive training with the help of a few days off from work. Given his current circumstances, he'd have to push that back a week. That made him uneasy—only a week to recover and get ready for the big day. But just then he felt an emptiness in his stomach, a guilty feeling. What he'd thought about missing first was training…not Lisa.

Her willingness to meet him more than half-way scared him. And now, for the first time, he thought he realized why. He finally admitted to himself that it bothered him that he was less than three-quarters Hawaiian—that if you looked at his name on a piece of paper you probably assumed he was of Scottish descent. And by marrying Lisa, their children would be less than half Hawaiian. That he would be responsible for letting his family's heritage slip away, like too many others had before him. Were your bloodlines more important than what you believed in? Was it your blood that made you Hawaiian or was it how you carried yourself and how you embraced the culture and customs? Could he push away someone he'd spent more than three years with? Was he trying to repair the past when who he was and where he came from didn't matter to him? Was he consumed with changing that…when he halfheartedly listened to his grandmother's teachings?

He sighed deeply. This was too much to unravel now. When he got back, he and Lisa would talk about it. Best to speak his mind and tell the truth and not delay the confrontation any longer. This wasn't something he could solve without her. This wasn't a case. There was no perp trying to deceive him. He could tell Lisa the complete truth and receive the same from her in return.

Shaking his head, he forced himself back to thinking about the Ironman.

After finally *finishing* the grueling race the year before, his desire to improve his time became a compulsion. He trained hard for the past five months. With the exception of Sunday, he ran ten to twelve miles each morning, biked forty miles each night after work, and followed each session with a half mile swim in the ocean.

He could swim here, and run, but he didn't think it appropriate to bring his bike, given the circumstances. Unfortunately, the bike segment was where he could make up the most time. His goal was five hours on the bike, a pace of twenty-two miles per hour. Not easy pumping through the barren lava fields where the black heat poured over the highway, and where the treacherous winds of the Kohala Coast pushed the bike and rider sideways. And if there was no cloud cover…your lungs simply fried.

Ben unzipped his sports duffel, took out his running shoes, shorts, an oversized cotton tank top, which proudly boasted *Ironman Finisher,* then dug around until he found a pair of ankle socks. He dressed quickly, looked at his watch, five thirty-five, and calculated that he could run about ten miles and not be late for dinner with the reporter.

After only stretching his leg and back muscles for a few minutes, Ben clambered down the stairs, and shortly was on Haleilio Road headed for Kūhiō Highway. Soon he joined the rush hour traffic headed north toward Waipouli and Kapa'a. He easily out-paced the cars, realizing, with no alternative roads south to Līhu'e and north to Hanalei, that the busy connected towns of Waipouli and Kapa'a were to be forever bottlenecks of the north-south traffic flow, unless the highway underwent some serious widening. But right now, traffic inched forward like a stubborn lava flow trying to claim a hill.

Before checking into the B & B, Ben bought a map of Kaua'i and found, much to his pleasure, what appeared to be a ten mile loop that surrounded his present living quarters. The path followed the Kūhiō Highway for about two miles along the coast, went *makua* on 581 curving around the Nounou Ridge for five miles, then down 580 along the Wailua River and back to Kūhiō Highway for the final three miles.

The route promised to be scenic and quiet once he left the highway. The elevation gain was about eight hundred feet, nothing compared to the Saturday morning assault up the hillside back home. The section around the mountain and the stretch along the river, good places to think about what might have happened to the two victims.

There was little wind, the sky was filled with friendly clouds, and the sun sat just above the mountains to the west. Perfect for running. Ben passed the Sheraton Coconut Beach Hotel, a few of the landmark's coconut palms now nothing but stately trunks, old victims of Hurricane Iniki. He ran by two women joggers who must have thought he was showing off as he dashed by, but probably realized he wasn't as he continued the pace until he was out of sight.

Gliding now, running easily.

Turning inland on 581, Ben finally put the distractions of traffic and people behind, and, beginning the first climb toward the Sleeping Giant, the disappearance of the two landowners came center stage. First, Gamos said there was no obvious connection between the two men, other than they were wealthy. They were still checking, but what had Gamos said later on the way back to the station? 'Probably on the same page in the social register.' He filed that away for later.

Both times the police dog traced the scent of the attacker to the sea, or at least close to it. So what kind of boat had the perp employed? Had he dumped the victims at sea like Gamos believed? Or had he kidnapped them? There were no ransom demands, so what was the motive? If he didn't dispose of them at sea, where did he take them? That one held many possibilities. Ben thought about the Nā Pali Coast, the sea caves, the ancient valleys, *heiau* sites, where the old Hawaiians prayed and gave sacrifice…there was Alakai'i Swamp, the massive bog that covered an enormous remote area east of Waimea Canyon, much of it mud that sucked up hikers to their knees. Could Eros find anyone in there? Could he even walk? He laughed to himself as he pictured Eros strapped to a helicopter's rescue harness, skimming along inches from the ground, sniffing the swamp for the scent of Frobert and Churchwell. Ben shook his head.

After the initial steep climb, which accounted for most of the altitude he would gain, Ben began to run easily, the burning sensation in his calves and quads gradually left. He thanked his Saturday morning routine for that.

When the road turned south behind the ridge where the tyrant 'Aikanaka slept, Ben checked his watch, saw he slipped off his pace a bit, and lengthened his stride. Ahead, the black asphalt seemed level, though the road curved and dipped more than he liked and did a pretty good job of hiding on-coming cars. There was no shoulder to speak of, just the drainage ditch, steep, rocky and covered with weeds. He remembered the last time he'd fallen and received nasty cuts and a bruise on his left knee and burning scrapes on his palms and left shoulder. Kept him from training for a week. He certainly couldn't afford that now.

The sun touched the mountains to the west. A yellowish-orange glow spread across the mountain tops making them seem much closer than they were. And seconds later the sun disappeared, twilight set in, and the sky became layers of salmon, pink, and deep purple.

He was behind Nounou Mountain now. Deep shadows crept across the road and Ben began sweating and shivering at the same time. Up ahead there were headlights weaving in and out of his vision. He thought of his mesh reflector vest. Not much good to him still jammed into an end pocket of his duffel bag.

What was the significance of the quilt taken from Churchwell, the first victim? What hung in Frobert's bedroom? Those hooks weren't heavy-duty. Something nylon? The only lightweight thing that shape he could think of was a flag—a flag in a bedroom? He doubted that. Was there a connection to what was taken or had the attacker simply used whatever was handy to wrap the body? Okay—time to face the mystical part, the connection to the sorcerer *kahuna*. He thought about the burned sheets, perfect circles. Who deemed them fireballs first? There were no witnesses, no one saw a fireball, or whatever it was, hurled. So who came up with that? Lots of ways someone could burn a round hole in a bed sheet. Forget fireballs, look at the evidence. The fact that someone sought to make it look like a *kahuna* did it was what was important. Ben tried to remember what a fish hook symbolized. Was it just a calling card, or was there something in Hawaiian custom or folklore about that? When he neared the end of 581, Ben thought of his grandmother once more. He was sorry now, was for a long time, that he didn't spend more time with her, listened more carefully, asked better questions. He thought about how frustrating it must have been for her to live her last years on the mainland, away from her native land, ironically, because she, a healer, became too ill to care for herself. Living with her daughter, Ben's mother, slipping slowly away from them, coming back for short periods, but finally falling into the permanent grasp of Alzheimer's.

All he could recall was that there were all kinds of fish hooks. No matter how hard he tried to remember, he couldn't place a single story his grandmother related dealing with fish hooks. Maybe if he could identify which kind these were, for catching what fish, there'd be a clue. Subtle markings or how the hooks were carved might point to a clan, to a village, to a location. Did the perp live nearby? Was it his homeland? His ancestors homeland? There was the Kona Historical Society on the Big Island with all sorts of helpful, knowledgeable people. There must be a similar group here. He made a mental note to make that his first priority in the morning. That and the 'social register.'

Turning left, the road plunged downhill almost immediately through a neighborhood of small homes. There were banana trees, hibiscus, plumeria, palms, and large ferns whose shadows danced in the wind. He was drenched with cold sweat and his neck was stiff. He rolled it side-to-side and almost lost his balance.

Ben caught a glimpse of the ocean turning black with the eastern sky, then looked over his shoulder and saw the purple and yellow glow against the fading mountains. His breathing was more labored now, his shins feeling the small sharp pings that always accompanied a long downhill stretch. Ben wiped the clammy perspiration from his forehead.

Highway 580 led back to Wailua, meandering downhill between the north fork of the Wailua River and 'Opaepa'a Stream. Along the Wailua River to his right, it was noisy with deep-throated water fowl and the high-pitched jabbering of the small birds that gathered each evening in the trees to exchange news of the day's events. A few cars passed, their headlights blinding him temporarily and forced him to slow down.

In the deepening dusk, he saw several Hawai'i Visitor Bureau signs, a full-dress warrior, marking points of historical interest. Ben was amazed how much this short stretch of highway offered. Several *heiau*, petroglyph fields, and the Bell Stones. He'd heard of the Bell Stones and barely made them out in the dim light. Two huge boulders that were pounded whenever a royal birth took place. Apparently, the sound could be heard for miles throughout the valley.

Ahead the lights of the cars on Kūhiō Highway. A mile farther. He was more tired than usual and his shins hurt badly. This was a beautiful run, but far too hilly and the side of the road was uneven. Without his vest he was almost invisible but because of the worn and rutted road shoulders, Ben had to stay on the asphalt much too close to traffic. With only half a mile to go, a car came right at him. Ben jumped onto the rocky shoulder, felt a rush of air as the vehicle passed, stumbled when he stepped into a hole, but recovered and returned to the roadway, after checking the oncoming traffic. Something bothered him more than usual about this close encounter. Soon he realized what it was. The car's lights weren't on. He looked over his shoulder. The pavement in front of the car now was illuminated.

Asshole.

Turning left onto the Kūhiō Highway, pain not withstanding, he pumped his legs and arms and finished with his traditional kick, hot, sweaty, starved, and wishing he were home.

▼▲▼

The King and I, in Waipouli Plaza, was small, about twenty tables, most of them for two. The decor, red carpet and walls of pink paint above waist-high wood paneling, needed some serious help, but the smells coming from the kitchen told Ben he'd like the place.

About a half dozen tables were occupied. Ben looked around, didn't spot the reporter, and approached one of the waiters.

"I'm meeting someone. No smoking," Ben pointed, "maybe that back corner."

A waiter, college age, dressed in khaki Dockers, loafers, no socks, long-sleeve white button-down shirt, and surprisingly, wearing a narrow flower print tie, led the way.

Ben sat and accepted a menu. He said, "If you weren't working here, would you be wearing that?"

The waiter laughed, showing a wide space between his front teeth. "Good for you. Not many people get it." He smartly tightened the knot of his tie. "Drink?…while you're waiting."

"Beck's."

"Light or dark or…," he smirked, "…lite-light."

"Light as in not dark," Ben said.

The waiter winked. "Be right back."

Ben looked around, spied several wood carvings on the walls, also Far Eastern paintings, and hung in the corners of the dining area were woven planters filled with orchids that appeared in desperate need of some humidity. Ben glanced at his watch. He was fifteen minutes late and he wondered if Ray Kuali'i would show.

The waiter, whose name was Dave, arrived with Ben's beer and a suggestion that Ben try the *ono* with peanut sauce. Then added that he'd be back when the other party arrived.

Ben, thinking about the time, realized the man he was waiting for was Hawaiian as well. Seven-fifteen between two Hawaiians could mean seven-thirty, maybe even eight. So he sipped his Beck's, tried stretching his aching calf muscles by flexing his ankles, and arched his back. He played with the wet rings his beer glass made on the glass covered table, shifted uncomfortably in his chair a few times, watched the ceiling fans for a few minutes, then began an inventory of the other diners.

Ten minutes later, Ray Kuali'i came strolling his way, big smile, hair slicked back wet, wearing the same clothes he wore that afternoon, sun glasses, still dangling from their lime leash hanging around his neck.

"Sorry, I'm late."

"Don't worry...Hawai'i time."

"No...don't subscribe to that. The article took a little longer that I thought."

The waiter appeared and the reporter pointed to Ben's beer. Dave then asked Ben if he wanted another. He nodded.

When the waiter left, Ben folded his arms across his chest. "Sovereignty a big issue here?"

Ray eyed him carefully, a small frown developed. "How much Hawaiian are you?"

"Nearly three-quarters." Ben ran his hand through his hair, then rubbed the back of his neck. The base of his neck was the other thing that hurt beside his shins and calves.

Dave was back, placed down the bottles of Beck's, and waited.

Ray looked at Ben. "Mind if I order for both of us?"

Ben indicated that was fine.

"Spring rolls, crispy noodles with bean spouts, shrimp Phad Thai, and barbecue chicken strips."

Dave grinned, apparently showing his approval, and headed for the kitchen.

Ray Kuali'i turned his attention back to Ben. "Three-quarters, huh. I'm pure except for a great-grandfather. Yeah, sovereignty's a big issue here. Interesting, too. There's some who want the whole State back. You need a copy of *Hāloa*...local sovereignty magazine...and maybe we get you to a Ka Lāhui Hawai'i meeting. I'm surprised you're not more in tune with the Movement."

"The Big Island has other native problems. That geothermal mess just drags on in the courts, and there's been rumor of a space launch facility at South Point..."

"This afternoon you mentioned Hawaiian Homelands...that's part of it."

Ben leaned forward. "That's probably a good compromise if it were run honestly."

Ray Kuali'i laughed. "That'll run honestly when there's no more money to be made from it."

Ben took a sip of beer. "Sovereignty is…well, it doesn't seem practical."

The reporter gave him a look and a shoulder shrug that said 'don't give up so easily.' "Some think that. But remember…Hawai'i is the only country…Kingdom actually…the only one where the United States overthrew the government. And only about a hundred years after it fought for its own independence. Short-term memory."

"You sound rather committed."

"Just reporting the facts."

Ben's back felt stiff so he slid back into his chair until he was sitting straight up. "I see." He arched his back and brought his shoulders together and held the position for a while. Sleeping Giant conquered him.

"Hey, we can talk about Hawaiian Sovereignty for hours, but aren't you interested in the disappearing landowners?"

The way Kuali'i phrased that—disappearing landowners—seemed strange to Ben. It kind of smacked of another sovereignty statement. Ben stared at the reporter for a few seconds, trying to look behind his gray eyes.

Spring rolls came then and put the conversation about the case on hold while Kuali'i explained how to eat them.

"Take a spring roll and a mint leaf and a cucumber slice, roll them up in the lettuce leaf, then dip it in the sesame sauce."

Ben did. He had to admit this was the best spring roll he ever ate.

During the consumption of the rest of the meal, the reporter's view of the case didn't reveal anything new to Ben. Ray Kuali'i merely rehashed the facts.

Hot tea came. Ben decided it was time to probe deeper.

"Tell me what *you* think…what *you* believe."

Ray held up his cup, watched the steam rise, said plainly, "They're dead."

"Not kidnapped?"

"Who'd pay to have them returned? Frobert lives alone…the next generation runs the business. They don't listen to him…they don't need him. Churchwell's son's a goof-ball, who was waiting for the old man to die. The other family members are probably just like Frobert's."

"What about Churchwell's son…he a suspect?" Ben asked.

Kuali'i's eyes narrowed. "I've read the reports. He was on O'ahu that night."

"Could have had it done."

Frustration and impatience filled the reporter's expression at the same time. "C'mon, McMillen...Churchwell's son has no motive to kill Frobert, too. We got a serial killer here. That's why they brought you in."

Ben decided not to contest what the reporter said. Kuali'i was smart. "I guess I should have asked you before, if this was off the record."

Kuali'i smiled, "Too late."

Ben pursed his lips.

"Just kidding. Off the record for tonight. Starting tomorrow, it's everyone for himself."

Ben nodded. *Might as well find out what I can now, then.* "Serial killer?...or a pro with a motive?"

"Ah...good question."

"Got a good answer?"

"Nope."

"You said 'two landowners'...why'd you classify them as that?"

"Because that's what they were."

"There a sovereignty angle to this?"

"Hey...now that's an interesting idea."

You've been thinking of tying the two stories together all along.

Nodding, Kuali'i said, "I know what you're thinking. And you're right."

CHAPTER 7

The moon, low in the west, a descending three-quarter crescent, appeared twice its normal size. The Milky Way, thirty degrees above the horizon spanning the cloudless eastern sky, was brighter than usual, the Sagittarius Arm alive with the glow of distant fireballs. And the ocean was restless, white-capped waves surged onto the empty beach, carving away the sand, carrying the coral and lava crystals out to sea for the commencement of the annual winter washing.

The wind was steady but light at Ka'iwa Point, which overlooked Lāwa'i Bay. The beach below was dark and still except for two silhouetted figures, walking slowly, hand-in-hand. When they reached the mouth of Lāwa'i Stream, they stopped and kissed, talked for a few minutes, then kissed again. The woman turned and left, looking over her shoulder once. She headed back along the beach, up a small incline where the sand ended and the rippled lava began, skirting tide pools and jagged crevices where the black scavenger crabs, *'a'ama*, were on night patrol. Climbing barefoot through the soft *pili* grass, the woman looked toward the sky. The abundance of stars held her gaze for a long time while she thought about the man with whom she had fallen in love. The man who lived on the old sugar cane plantation, the largest single parcel of land on the South Shore, vast, rich acreage—family holdings for a hundred years.

Funny though, the man she was married to probably had a bigger fortune.

This new man's virility surprised her. Her husband was no match for the wealthy descendant of the plantation. Actually, it was hard for her to compare her husband's prowess in bed with anyone. It was many years since they slept together. And years before that since they were intimate. And to think she was only forty-one.

After slipping on her shoes, the woman climbed up the compacted earth driveway that curved around the eastern side of Lāwa'i Bay. She found the small gap in the lava wall that enabled her to by-pass the padlocked chain-link gate. Then she walked along the red dirt cane road that mostly ran parallel to the driveway and finally reached the outer gate, which was locked as well. She went around the gate, stepped over a pile of lava rocks and headed for her rental car. She'd parked a half mile down Lāwa'i Road, at the far end of the parking lot at Spouting Horn, where the giant blowhole spewed water high into the air and made an eerie sound, which she imagined to be like the wailing of ghosts, or the death call of a beached whale.

The woman started the engine, turned on the lights, sighed, and headed back to her room at the Hyatt a few miles away, where in an adjoining room, her husband would be sound asleep.

Charles Bowden III, barefoot, walked along Lāwa'i Stream, kicking at the glazed sand, crunchy from a light shower hours before. He thought about the woman he'd met in Kōloa Town two days before. Knowing then that his flowing blonde hair, deeply tanned face, multi-colored T-shirt and baggy Nautica shorts, gave the impression that he was closer to forty than sixty. And aware, at six-four, with large, strong hands, and a most beguiling stare, that most women, married or not, wondered what it would be like to be held in his muscular arms. This woman was no different than the scores of others, except that from first eye contact she couldn't stop wetting her lips. At the time, he remembered joking to himself that 'this one is simply starved.'

He laughed quietly now as he crossed the narrow stream and headed up the great expanse of lawn behind the old plantation house. He was proud of himself. He'd come three times that night and he was sure she'd been right there with him each time.

Bowden arched his back, then touched his toes, noticing there was a small roll of fat around his stomach. He pinched his hip to measure. Much harder to stay trim these days. More hours, less results. He got into bed, pulled the covers over his naked body, smelled the fresh scent of sandalwood soap as the motion of the sheets created a small wind, then reached and turned off the bed lamp, checking the time just before he did. Two-thirty. Grinning to himself, glad that he could sleep late.

He was asleep within minutes. But his slumber wouldn't last long.

▼▲▼

The floating torches came up from the stream. A procession of light flickering through the palm trees, gray smoke curling upward into the fronds, sparks and loose glowing embers floating in the wind, rising as if they were to join the stars in the sky. A single cloud obscured the moon and somewhere in the distance a dog howled and Charles Bowden sat up in bed, mouth agape, chest pounding, without a clue why he awakened so abruptly. He looked at the clock. It glowed 3:35 and slowly Bowden lay down his head on the soft satin pillow. He concentrated on breathing slowly.

Over the expansive lawn, past a small stand of guava trees, the torches came. Near the Gazebo behind the sprawling estate home the procession halted, torches to the ground, extinguished one by one. Then a single night marcher continued toward the plantation house, opened a screen door that led into the *lānai*, and disappeared inside.

Ten minutes later, the night marcher emerged carrying Charles Bowden over his left shoulder. The marcher was hunched under the weight of his victim, struggling to stand upright. He came away from the house, bent carefully, removed his hand from the victim's torso, reached into the binding of his *malo*, and lighted his torch. Then he seemingly passed the torch along to the others. When all the torches were lighted, he raised his torch, straightened best he could, and carried his burden back down the lawn, losing his balance once, but regaining it quickly, and followed the stream to the bay.

The woman with whom Bowden made love had returned, and now she saw the torch light and quickly ran for cover. She found a small bush and ducked behind it, just pulling her suitcase next to her as the torch light passed within twenty feet. Squatting, her heart pounded as she slowly pivoted on her toes and watched as the man retreated. He went no more than another thirty feet, when he stumbled down the embankment of the stream. At once the torches fell in unison into the water and were extinguished with a hiss. She heard him curse, and, without the benefit of the torch light, she barely made out that he was balancing something on his shoulder, using both hands to hold it in place. After a few sidesteps, he straightened, walked a little farther, bent slowly and reached into the water and retrieved what looked like a long stick. Then, with much effort, like a weight lifter bringing the bar to his chest before the actual press, he rose once more, made a grunting noise, and slowly staggered toward the beach. It was then, when the moon came from behind a cloud, that she got a better look at him. He appeared to be wearing a loin cloth. But when her eyes made their way to his head, she gasped. His head was large and round. She was scared and only her confusion prevented panic. She noticed he seemed to be wearing wristlets and anklets. She thought of the dancers she'd watched perform in the Kiahuna Shopping Center. They wore anklets and wristlets made from ferns. Was this nothing more than some Hawaiian ritual? But what was he carrying on his shoulder—one of those large gourd drums? Where had the torches gone? She took a deep breath and felt less afraid.

Her first instinct was to run to the house and report to her lover what she had seen. But she was curious and convinced herself that the man had no expectation of being observed in such a remote location so early in the morning. There was no chance he'd notice her, if she was careful. So she left her suitcase behind the small bush and followed. The possibility that she was witness to a secret ceremony of some sort, excited her. She smiled to herself, wondering if, after you were unfaithful for the first time, you had a different, more cavalier attitude toward life's dangers.

The night marcher crossed the beach, angling toward the western end of the small crescent. The sand made the going difficult and he had to stop. He let his load roll from his shoulder onto the sand, and rested, kneeling with his palms on his thighs and his head down.

The woman watched from behind the short palms that lined the rear of the beach. She decided that crossing the sand was too risky. She thought that the man might hear her because the waves, surging wildly hours before, now only trickled ashore.

Once more the man lifted his burden. He struggled harder this time, obviously worn and tired. He continued to walk to the far end of the bay. The woman followed along, ducking behind palm trees, making some noise as she brushed against the fronds, but it was indistinguishable from what the night breeze created.

Finally, the night marcher reached his destination. He slid the bundle off his shoulder, inching it forward until it gently dropped to the sand next to a large palm tree. Then he let go of the pole he carried. He looked around and sank to the sand, resting his shoulders against the trunk of the giant tree. His head was back and he breathed heavily. After a few minutes, he stood and grabbed for a rope that was tied around the trunk of the palm. He began pulling. He still wore the large helmet, although it appeared to be brown now that the torches were extinguished.

Clouds drifted across the moon and the woman smelled a hint of fresh rain on the way. Once more she felt her heart racing. Looking toward the bay, she could see nothing, but could hear something pushing against the water. Then she thought she saw a glint of something metal. When she heard something scrape across the sand, the man stopped pulling. She knew it was some kind of a boat, but she still couldn't see very well. She watched as the man loaded the heavy bundle onto the boat, and finally, the long pole.

For the first time, the idea that the heavy bundle might contain a body crossed her mind, and it was a split second later, when the woman saw an arm slip out of a rolled blanket, that she turned and ran. Luckily for her, the night marcher already was pushing the small outrigger canoe into the water, making enough noise himself that he couldn't hear her trampling through the sand and fallen palm fronds. He couldn't hear the frightened squeals that escaped from her throat. Now she only worried about distance not noise.

The woman turned just once and saw the lines of the canoe disappear around the western point. Her screams echoed along the cliffs, sounding like a frantic tropicbird.

Beth ran along the stream, came to the sloping back lawn, and scrambled up. Her lungs burned, her thoughts a tangled mess of mixed messages. One minute she envisioned waking Charles and being safe in his arms, the next she was thinking of returning to the Hyatt, slipping into her room, and making believe nothing happened. It never occurred to her that the arm she saw might belong to her lover. Perhaps she blocked out that possibility.

And once again the moon reappeared from the veil of clouds and the shadows of the huge house reached out across the wide lawn. A thin mist fell.

At the back door she smelled smoke. It was strong here and Beth stood, a little afraid to enter, and looked around. When she didn't see or hear anything, she tried the door. The handle moved easily, so she twisted it slowly, and opened the door. She stepped inside. The burning smell intensified. Beth called out. But Charles didn't answer. She ran to the front of the house, knocking over a small table, took the stair steps two at a time, and reached the master bedroom. The door was open. The large Queen Anne's bed squarely in front of her. Moonlight filtered into the room between the cracks of open louvers. Beth brought her hand to her mouth, biting her knuckle. The scream just wouldn't come. The center of the bed was burned, faint traces of a glowing circle marked the spot. She took a step forward. Unknowingly, she kicked something that skittered along the plank floor in the direction of the bed. That small noise made her ears ring and her mouth completely dry.

Beth couldn't call out his name. All she thought of was the dangling arm.

▼▲▼

The Zodiac sped west. The night marcher had secured the two-person outrigger canoe across the bow, and now he stood nervously at the helm, racing to beat the sunrise, cursing that Bowden spent so long with the woman. He wondered about her. To the best of his knowledge Bowden had no steady girlfriend. He wondered if this one would come back the next day. If she would be the one to discover he was missing, would go up to his bedroom and find the circle of fire and the necklace.

Flat out he was doing 25 nauts—near top speed for a Zodiac when only two were aboard. The weight of the outrigger preventing better. It was less than an hour to the remote valleys of the Nā Pali Coast. And although he'd known the bays and coves of western Kaua'i since boyhood, he was glad to have the moon as a companion. Guiding the craft through the reef in the dark was dangerous. He was thankful it stopped raining, but he knew rain showers along the south shore were like ghosts. They came out of nowhere and disappeared just as quickly.

Around the southwestern side of the Island. The low lurking shape of Ni'ihau, the Forbidden Island, was barely visible to his left. Barking Sands was ahead to his right. He headed another five degrees west, staying away from the shoreline just in case the Army, whose Pacific Missile Facility was the sole tenant of Barking Sands, had any boats in the water. He couldn't be stopped and he knew he wouldn't be able to outrun them. Dressed the way he was, he surely didn't look like a fisherman, at least not one from the present. And Bowden didn't quite resemble a fish, past or present.

Half an hour later, an hour before sunrise, the night marcher carried his victim ashore. He dropped Bowden unceremoniously onto the sand and went back to the Zodiac, took the fifty-pound anchor, and secured it between two shore rocks. Then, after checking his watch, he returned to his victim.

After a series of slow, deep breaths and a look toward the heavens, he bent once more, lifted the body onto his shoulder and began the long trek into the remote valley tucked into the Nā Pali Coast. This one was the most difficult. The previous victims each weighed less than a hundred and fifty. This one was like carrying a pig to the *imu*.

Chapter 8

Just when the sun popped above the calm Pacific, Ben, already dressed for a workout, came charging down the stairs, athletic bag in hand, and headed for his rental. The engine idled roughly. Ben let the wipers cruise through the condensation on the windshield and snapped his seat belt in place. He was anxious to get started, but the rental car wasn't. Even with Ben leaning forward, foot to the floorboard, the car slowly chugged down Haleilio to the highway. Reaching Highway 56, he turned right toward Līhu'e, swinging the sun visor against the side window to block the bright sunlight. Finally, something seemed to clear the gas line and the car zipped ahead.

Traffic was light and he made Līhu'e in fifteen minutes. He continued south of town until he reached the Kukui Grove Shopping Center. Turning left, Ben found Kukui Grove Street, and pulled up in front of the Kaua'i Athletic Club. He was surprised to see so many cars parked there at six-thirty.

He paid the weekly fee, was handed a towel and a key for a locker, and headed for the row of Lifecycle machines. Nodding at two men on exercise bikes, Ben dropped his athletic bag, looped the towel around his neck, and mounted the remaining machine. Familiar with the Lifecycle, he selected a program of steep uphill and downhill sections, like those on the Kohala Coast, site of the Ironman bike component. After setting the timer for an hour, he arched his back and rolled his shoulders for a while, then slipped his feet into the pedal straps. Soon he was 'gliding along' while he watched an early morning aerobics class to pass the time. The rear view of the instructor proved to be the most entertaining.

After a few minutes, he sensed someone watching him and he turned to his right.

"You're truckin', man."

"I do a lot of bike work."

The man next to Ben was short, maybe five-six, appeared to weigh close to two-hundred. He was solid like he'd been working out for a long time, barrel chest, huge arms—he looked like the local softball slugger. Ben thought he was mainly Hawaiian blood.

The man then eyed Ben's legs. "No kiddin'…your calves are like rocks."

Ben shrugged his shoulders and said, "Nice place."

"Yeah," said the man. "Come here every other day during the week for a couple of hours. Sometimes on the weekend, if I can make it." He looked at the Lifecycle console for a few seconds, apparently to check his time.

"Whaddaya do?" asked Ben.

"Construction work…work for the County. You?"

"Work for the County, too. Big Island."

"Vacation?"

"Haven't had one of those in awhile. Just helping the local Police Department."

"You a cop?"

"Detective." Ben leaned right, kept peddling, and extended his hand. "Ben McMillen."

"Glad to meetcha, Ben. Gus Ka'aka'anui."

They talked for another twenty minutes, when Gus's Lifecycle beeper sounded. He stopped peddling, said he'd see Ben later, and headed for the free weights. Ben wondered what it would be like to have job you didn't have to take home and you didn't have to sleep with. And without gristly images waking you all the time.

Half an hour later, Ben showered and dressed. He felt refreshed as he left the locker room. While returning his locker key at the front desk, he spotted Gus, waved, and pushed through the front door.

▼▲▼

Ben parked near the evidence containers. The police station was busy. Officers showing up for the day shift, patrol cars returning from the night shift. He got out and spotted Ernie Dumas walking toward the kennel. Eros was by his side.

"Hey, Ernie."

Ernie turned and waited.

Ben saw Ernie say something to Eros. The dog seemed to relax and Ben figured he'd been told 'just family.'

"Howzit going?" the patrolman asked.

"Nothing so far. Had a question, though."

"Eros...*mai.*"

Ben recognized the Hawaiian word for *come.*

"Can't miss the shift meeting...we'll talk about it on the way."

When they reached the kennel, Ben asked, "How does Eros differentiate between two scents presented at the same time?...Like the perp carrying the victim."

"Good question. These dogs are trained to follow the strongest scent. Sometimes that's not so easy. But take the Frobert case. The perp's scent was much stronger on the necklace although he had contact with the victim's clothing.

"By the way, since the necklace was no problem for Eros...he zeroed in on it right away...it tells us something else. The necklace must have been worn by the attacker, not simply carried in a pocket. So the perp enhanced the scent with perspiration, body oils...even after shave, if he used it. That mixture of scents to Eros is like a fingerprint to us." The patrolman paused. "I guess him wearing it adds to the craziness, huh?"

Ernie unlocked the padlock with a key that hung from his belt, opened the gate, and Eros scampered inside. Eros sat immediately when Ernie gestured him to do so. After the padlock was secure, Ernie said 'aloha,' and Eros barked once.

Continuing inside, Ernie took up where he left off. "Eros followed Frobert's scent straight to the water. Never hesitated. Means the intruder and victim never separated, otherwise Eros would have detected the scents diverging, checked both, then would have continued tracking Frobert."

"Doesn't the rain wash out the scent?" asked Ben, when they entered the station.

They walked into the Squad Room when the Patrol Sergeant said in a loud voice, "We'll be a few minutes late beginning. Hold tight."

Ernie and Ben sat. Ben looked around for Mike Gamos. Didn't see him.

"Rain's a problem, but you have to remember what kind of nose we're dealing with here. Forty to fifty times keener than a human nose and with a much wider range. It's almost as if things we can't smell at all have the odor of grilled Maui onions to a dog. But the real trick is to start with an item with a very strong scent. That's why for the victim we picked out a shirt from the laundry not the closet or dresser drawers. Otherwise Eros would be leading us to the laundry room all the time. Little joke, but you get my point."

"Dumas…McMillen." It was the Patrol Sergeant. "Chief's office…on the double!"

Chief Johnson was seated at his desk, leaning back in his chair, arms folded across his chest. His expression was grim.

Detective Gamos was on the window sill. Like the chief, his arms were folded across his chest and his face bore an angry expression. He nodded to Ben and Ernie.

"Listen to this," the Chief said. He leaned forward and started a tape recorder. "Came in about ten minutes ago."

Ben expected to hear the perp's voice.

It was a woman's voice, soft and shaky.

'You have to go to Charles Bowden's home. He's missing…and… and…there's been a *fire* in his bedroom.' A second female voice asked, 'Who is this? Where are you calling from?' A few clicks followed, then dial-tone.

The Chief spoke. "Bowden lives on a huge estate in Poi'pū, just past Spouting Horn. Mike knows where it is. I want the three of you and the dog down there right away. There's a uniform from Waimea on his way to secure. And Forensics is out that way working on a two-car head-on…at the Kōloa turn-off. Pick up one of them." He paused. "Call me right away after you've done the prelim."

Ben said, "So this one came in 9-1-1."

"Yeah." Chief Johnson answered.

Ben wondered if the perp worked alone. Maybe he had a female accomplice. Or maybe it was the perp disguising his voice as that of a woman. Wouldn't be the first time.

Chief Johnson urged, "Go…go…"

The detectives and Patrolman Dumas hurried out.

Heading for the parking lot, Ben wasn't thinking whether they had a third victim, he knew they did. His thoughts were focused on the number of anonymous calls associated with the case, including the one suggesting that he be brought in. He wondered if they were missing something there. Voice analysis would be good if they had the previous calls on tape. But they didn't. Only the last one.

Gamos's Explorer was in for repairs so they took a patrol car. Ben, riding shotgun, wasn't used to riding in a speeding patrol car—he couldn't recall one high-speed chase he'd ever been on. His right hand was firmly attached to the molded interior panel and his right foot applied constant pressure to the floor.

Cars pulled off onto the soft grassy shoulders on both sides as they headed south on Kaumuali'i Highway. Ernie Dumas was close behind, portable blue strobe flashing atop his station wagon. For just a second, Ben grinned, wondering if Eros had his seat belt on.

"Guess it's another."

Gamos gritted his teeth and gave the steering wheel a few punches with the side of his fist.

Ben asked, "These guys are all from families that go way back?"

"Yeah...descendants of landowners...big plantations."

"Great...probably every Hawaiian has a motive."

Gamos took his eye off the road for a second and gave Ben a quizzical look. "This one could just be a domestic quarrel. Maybe the lady caller did it. You remember that woman who said her kids were kidnapped? Turned out she drowned them. More and more of that happening. Spouses, parents...now they're the prime suspects."

"She said there was a fire. How much does the public know? What exactly has Kuali'i written so far. I keep forgetting to check." Just then he remembered that he needed to find out the location of the Kaua'i Historical Society.

"He's written that...*kahuna* magic stuff...fireballs. Just a little on the landowner connection, but I think this one will change that, if that's what it is."

"It is. Hey! Up ahead!"

Gamos braked, flicked off the siren, but left his overhead flashers and emergency blinkers on, then carefully came to a stop on the right shoulder.

"Jesus," Ben whistled softly.

The accident scene ahead was as bad as he'd witnessed. The car closest to them seemed to have swallowed the front-end of the other car. Actually, the wreck looked like a stretch limo with two rear ends. The middle of the tangled mess resembled the destruction caused by a car bomb. Ben experienced one of those. First year as a Kona detective—pipe bomb placed there by an angry army vet, a munitions expert, who thought the victim was fooling around with his wife. Killed the intended victim's teen-age son.

"No front seat survivors in this one." Detective Gamos sighed.

Ben looked into the rearview mirror. Dumas pulled up in back.

One of the Forensic Team looked up, said a few words to the other technician, then gathered some things from the top of the trunk of one of the wrecked cars, and placed them into a black duffel bag marked LAB in yellow on the side. He walked quickly toward them.

"Pretty gruesome," Gamos said when the Forensic man got close.

"Got that right, Mike. Guess it's lucky it was just the two of them. Nobody would have survived this one."

The Forensic man opened the rear door and hopped in. Gamos drove around the accident scene. Dumas's station wagon followed. Ben saw the entire mid-section of the wreck was covered in blood and his stomach churned. It was hard for him to swallow.

"Kev…this is Ben McMillen. Kevin Thompson."

Ben turned around, offered his hand, which Kevin shook.

"Got some more witchcraft, I hear."

"Careful…Ben's a little sensitive about this."

Ben remained silent. Thinking.

"Where we going?" Kevin asked.

"You know Charles Bowden?" asked Gamos.

"The guy who owns all the land just west of Spouting Horn?"

Gamos filled in Kevin.

"Anonymous call, huh?"

Ben focused on that for a while, separating it from the other calls.

Gamos had told him that Bowden was rich, unmarried, a womanizer. Ben wondered if the woman just might have a jealous husband who found out that his wife toured old plantation houses at night. If it weren't for her comment about the fire, he'd probably think that this might be an unrelated incident. But then he remembered Tobi's advice. 'Except for O'ahu, any two murders that happen close together are most likely connected.' Did she call right away? Meaning she found him early this morning. Or did she find him last night and waited awhile, unsure what to do? Found him last night. Last night fit the pattern. So she has something to hide, like a husband, but didn't think about 9-1-1 recording the call. Did she witness anything? He hoped so.

Left on Highway 520, Maluhia Road. *Maluhia* meant peaceful. Hardly today.

Under the archway of eucalyptus they followed Maluhia Road, which cut across the cane fields that made Kōloa a prosperous town for nearly a hundred years until the early '60s. Shortly, they reached the center of Kōloa itself. A quick right, then left, a few stores, more cane fields, an intersecting cane road marked private where they turned right. The red dust from the patrol car obliterated any view of Dumas's trailing station wagon.

They followed the bumpy road through more cane for almost two miles—the last part ran parallel to the end of Lāwa'i Road, past a black iron gate supported by brick columns on each side, then a winding plunge downhill. Gamos explained they were on a cliff and the house, a hundred feet below, fronted the beach and the bay. He said it was probably the most idyllic spot on the Island.

Ben commented that he was surprised to see cactus, which grew between the cane road and the paved road. "Seen a few on the Big Island...but where it seemed to be much drier than here...farther from the sea."

Gamos told him the cactus grew on the South Shore, especially around Po'ipū and along Waimea Canyon Road. "These are a little different. Plan to stay away from them...sea urchins may be poisonous, but these here...you'll be finding hairy stickers in you for years...like they grow on you. Much better than Rogaine."

Ben liked Gamos's sense of humor. Was glad that the other detective seemed to have accepted him, but like Tobi warned, 'keep your eyes open.' Ben cast Gamos a sideways glance.

After a wedge of thick vegetation that separated two sections of sugar cane, Gamos took a hard left and crossed a stream via a narrow one-lane wooden bridge. They entered a sanctuary of sorts, where lush fruit trees lined the road and the narrow stream widened considerably to form a pond. On a protected upslope next to the pond, was a huge mansion, much bigger than the homes owned by the other victims. A true plantation home.

At the top of the driveway, a uniform patrolman stood by a parked patrol car, hands shading his eyes.

Eros appeared anxious as he was led from the station wagon, but he didn't bark. The patrolman, Henry Lopez, eyed Eros warily.

Ben was the first to speak. "You been inside?"

"Yessir."

Gamos said, "Henry, this is Ben McMillen. We're partners on this one."

Ben continued after shaking Patrolman Lopez's hand. "Anyone else around?"

"No, sir."

Kevin, carrying his duffel, headed up the front steps. He had donned Latex booties and gloves and tied string tied around the sole of each booty to distinguish his foot impressions from others to be found. He handed three pair of booties to Gamos and some lengths of string.

Gamos said, squeezing Lopez's shoulder, "Keep an eye out here." He tugged on the booties and tied the strings around each foot.

So did Ben and Ernie.

"Let's go."

"Gloves?" Ben asked.

Gamos said, "I hate those things. Just don't touch anything Kevin hasn't bagged."

They mounted the stairs and had no trouble finding Bowden's bedroom. There was no sign of blood anywhere. But the smell of smoke was still fairly strong.

The mattress had the same blackened circle, about two-feet across. The bed sheet and blanket were burned through, dark fibers, looking like curled eyelashes, formed a near perfect circle. A light brown ring surrounded the charred circle. The outside edges resembled a giant dried sunflower.

Ben could hear everyone breathing. He could almost hear them thinking. *Is it black magic?* He stepped back from the large four-poster bed and scanned each post. No necklace. He searched the floor for the fish hook necklace. So did the others.

Eros started whining.

Ernie Dumas said, "He can sense we're going to need him soon."

Ben dropped to his knees and looked under the bed. "There it is!"

They let Kevin crawl underneath and retrieve it. When he came out, he held it carefully, looped around his thumb and forefinger. The fish hook was secured tightly and knotted at the top. Ben wondered if they could identify the knot and perhaps that would hold a clue for them. Kevin squashed that thought when he remarked that the knot was a simple square-knot. The clasp, like the others, appeared to be fashioned from a small piece of bone, rectangular in shape, hole in the center where the cord passed through and was knotted. When turned, the bone clasp fit sideways through a small loop on the other end of the braided cord. Kevin gave Ernie a pair of gloves. When Ernie had them on, Kevin handed him the necklace.

Ernie held the fish hook necklace in front of Eros. The tracking dog stretched his neck and sniffed. The dog's nose followed the boar's hair cord entirely around, lingering at the clasp, then digesting the scent of the hook itself.

"*Ho'omo'o.*"

Eros began to 'follow the course.'

Ben, Ernie, and Gamos followed the tracking dog.

Kevin remained behind to search and dust the bedroom and take samples from the sheets.

Eros came down the stairs, veered right, went through the dining room and into the screened *lānai,* then scratched at a set of double doors. Ernie took out a pencil and pushed against the top of the latch handle. It released and the door swung open. Eros bounded through, nose to the ground.

Across the wide manicured lawn. Along the stream.

Ben could hear the ocean surf breaking over the far edge of the reef in the bay. He marveled at the pace Eros maintained. Although there were fruit trees everywhere, a meandering, layered garden filled with exotic flowers and small shrubs, pools with carp, the police dog was locked onto a single scent and followed it. A hundred yards farther, the stream narrowed just before it carved a fairly wide curved channel into the beach and connected with the sea. Immediately, Eros turned to the right, broke into a run, kicking up sand, heading for the far end of the protected cove. Detective Gamos and Eros's handler ran, too. Ben yelled for them to keep off to the side. "In case there are footprints."

And soon they saw that there were…lots of them—all fresh. All barefoot.

Eros stopped at the water's edge. Then he backtracked and headed for a single tall palm. He raised up and clawed at the tree trunk, then returned to the water, barking, looking expectantly at Ernie.

"Same as before," Ernie said, a little out of breath.

Ben examined the tree bark. Below waist level there were many small fibers. Above, where the trunk began to narrow, was a thin line where there weren't as many fragments of bark. Like something smoothed them away. His eyes followed the path from the palm to the water. Ten yards from the tree there were a few smooth channels resembling thin bike tire marks.

Ben said, "Tied up a boat here." Then he duck-walked a few paces from the tree. There was another depression in the sand. It was about six-feet long, the size and shape of a broom handle. There were small ropelike markings at the edges. Most mystifying were five holes in the sand along the length of the depression. They seemed about equal distance from each other. "I wonder what made this."

No one offered a guess.

Ben stood, stared at the strange imprint, then blew out his breath. He brushed some loose sand from his pants, then walked back up the beach toward the footprints.

Gamos, wiping his brow, joined him. There were two sets of footprints in the sand, right next to those Eros made. Even where the sand was soft it was clear that one set headed to the house, one back to the water. Down nearer the water, where the sand was firm, the prints looked like the same person made them with two exceptions.

Ben wet his lips. "See how deep these are compared to the others on the way up. And look how he's scuffling along coming back."

"Carried off…another victim." Gamos knelt in the sand and stared off toward the water.

"Describe Bowden. I mean how big is he?" Ben asked.

Gamos said, "Big…well over six-feet, I guess. Never talked to him, but saw him some."

"Our kidnapper must be strong…" Ben's voice faded. He also looked out to sea and followed a course west.

Fanning out, they found another set of prints nearer the grass bluff that separated the beach and the front lawn, but the wind feathered away much of their shape.

Ernie, the Belgian Shepherd at his side, suggested it was time to give Eros an article of Bowden's clothing.

Gamos said he'd stay and look around for more clues.

Finding no laundry basket or clothes hamper, they gave Eros a whiff of a nightshirt that they found hanging in Bowden's closet. It looked recently worn, hanging off center on its hanger, unbuttoned and wrinkled. Eros stayed close to the bed for a few seconds, then moved over to the window and put his front paws on the sill. He sniffed between the louvers. Then, he left the room, but this time into the adjoining bathroom. Then back out and down the stairs.

Eros followed the path through the garden, across the broad lawn, keeping close to the footpath next to the left bank of the stream. But suddenly, the Belgian Shepherd stopped, walked ahead, then came back. A few cautious steps into the undergrowth. Then he came back to the path. Finally, he turned and looked at Ernie.

Ben saw the dog's narrowed brow. Ben shook his head in admiration. The dog thought just like a human.

Eros barked several times.

"He's confused. Like the trail goes two…"

Eros bounded off into the undergrowth. They had trouble keeping up with him and both men nearly tripped over some ground-clinging vine. Suddenly, the dog stopped by a clump of small bushes. Excited, nose hooked onto something as his body pivoted around the spot.

Gamos heard the commotion and high-stepped over the small shrubs.

Ben arrived first. He saw the suitcase and gulped. He let out a low, long sigh and thought—*Too small to hold a body…*then he shuddered, as if trying to shed his next thought…*unless it's a child…or it's been dismembered.*

Chapter 9

The suitcase was made from soft green canvas with tan leather reinforcing the corners. The handle was two strips of canvas with a leather grip, which snapped around the two straps. It looked new. There was no luggage ID tag.

Looking around at the ground, Ben saw flattened *pili* grass and depressions in the course sand-lava mixture, but nothing that could be cast into usable footprints. Gamos said he'd get Kevin and hurried toward the path that led back to the plantation house.

Ernie, stroking the back of Eros's head, said, "Never heard of a kidnap victim packing. Whaddaya think's inside?"

"Usually, I'd say money or drugs…what I don't understand is why Eros tracked the intruder to the beach, but left the trail and came here for the victim." Ben dropped to one knee and examined the ground more carefully, hoping to find another clue. He looked up after a few seconds. "You got the nightshirt with you?"

Ernie extracted it from a pouch he wore around his shoulder.

Ben took the garment and sniffed the front. Nothing special that he could pick up. He looked at Eros, who seemed intrigued with a human looking for a scent. Then Ben sniffed the collar. There was something…to him it smelled like perfume. Not a man's cologne, though he was no expert, but stronger, sweeter, like something a woman might wear. Ben stood. "Any chance…I mean, what if there's the scent of two people on a garment? How's he distinguish the two?"

Ernie screwed up his face. "He goes for the stronger."

"You seem hesitant."

"I was trying to think if it's ever happened. You mean two people wearing something recently without it being washed?"

"Ernie…never heard of a woman sleeping over, then wearing the man's shirt afterward?"

Ernie smiled. "My wife wears mine every Sunday morning."

"So…what part of the night shirt did you give Eros to smell?"

"The collar…that's where the body oils have the most contact."

Ben handed the night shirt to Ernie. "Smell the collar, then the front."

Ernie sniffed. His eyebrows raised. "Collar's cologne or perfume, front's kind of…nothing."

"Have Eros smell the chest area."

The tracking dog took the scent, sniffed the ground, made a small circle near the shrubs, but came back and stood in front of his handler.

"He can't find it."

"Let's take him back to the trail and have him smell again."

"Eros…*mai.*"

They walked back to the trail. Ernie presented the front of the night shirt. Eros started up the path, then turned and suddenly bounded down the path, headed for the beach.

"Two people wore that night shirt. I'd say our victim had a lady friend. I'd say that's her suitcase we found…why it's over there, I have no idea." Ben thought for a few seconds. "Ernie, you follow Eros. I'll stay with the suitcase and wait for Mike and Kevin."

Ernie took off down the path.

Ben stared at the suitcase. *The lady who called in the tip…she saw the whole thing!*

A minute later Gamos and Kevin came down the trail. They left the sandy path, cut through an opening in the lowland shrubs, and joined Ben. In the distance Ben could hear Eros barking. He was sure it was by the huge palm at the water's edge.

She saw it happen. Maybe…maybe she's married and having an affair with Bowden. She can't come forward. The suitcase? It's hers…she's leaving her husband…but why's the suitcase here?

Ben turned and looked up the driveway that connected with Lāwa'i Road, wondering if she lived close by, maybe in one of the houses on Lāwa'i Road. She could have walked two miles. Then he had another thought. She could have driven and parked her car in one of the condo lots, or maybe somewhere along Lāwa'i Road.

Ben then related his theory after explaining the perfume on the night shirt. He also suggested that the set of footprints along the bluff belonged to the woman.

Gamos seemed convinced.

It took ten minutes for Kevin to examine the area and dust the suitcase. He ignored the handle, where'd there'd be many overlapping prints. When he was done, he took out a small tool to spring the lock. Ben asked him to lift the suitcase first. Light, he commented. Which meant to Ben that she could have parked at least a mile away. He didn't think she lived close by. Didn't even believe that she was a local. Inside were women's clothes, toiletries, but no papers, no keys…no airline tickets. No ID.

Ernie came through the woods, Eros by his side. "Ended at the same spot as before."

Ben pursed his lips, then looked at Gamos. "What exactly did she say on the phone?"

"You have to go to Charles Bowden's house. He's missing and there's been a fire in his bedroom."

Now everyone was standing, thinking, looking around as if he half expected to find the woman watching them from some other vantage point.

The Forensic man broke the silence. "I'm going back up to the house. I'll send these prints to Honolulu." Kevin looked at Detective Gamos, who nodded, then the Forensic man hurried away.

"Well, Ben?" Gamos asked.

Ben wondered if this was a challenge or was Gamos looking for direction. *A challenge seems more likely.* Ben turned to Ernie. "Can Eros track the woman back where she came from?"

"Maybe, I think she's been all over. If your theory is right, she's been inside the house, maybe twice last night, wearing the night shirt, coming back later with the suitcase. Along here, watching the intruder…" He stopped and looked East, over his shoulder, at the dirt road on the ridge. He shook his head. "Most likely, if she came on foot, she'd come from over there, down Lāwa'i Road, near where we came in. The other way in seems like a rough go…no matter how light the suitcase is."

Ben's eyes followed the winding road to the top of the ridge.

"Mike. What's up that way?"

Gamos looked up at the ridge. "More cane fields and a dirt road that runs parallel to the one we came in on. Then Spouting Horn…a blow-hole, then some houses, condos, smaller hotels, and the Hyatt Resort. Golf course beyond that."

Ben had hunch she was a tourist. The contents of the suitcase were high-end and some of the clothing seemed southwestern to him, although he supposed you might buy those things in Honolulu. "I hope Eros can narrow this down for us. Let him go."

"We're going to move from here…too many conflicting scents. Wait here while I get Eros started."

About fifty feet away from the clump of shrubs, Ernie had Eros sniff the suitcase. The tracking dog didn't react at first. Then he turned and walked toward the beach but in the direction opposite of where the other scent led him. Eros stopped, nose close to the sand, then slowly climbed the small incline to the ridge, which led up the cliff and ran parallel to the cane road.

"He's going back out…toward Spouting Horn, "Ernie said.

The scent ended just beyond the first gate in the cane field. It ended because a half mile away, field workers were burning cane and the trade winds blew the thick earthy smell their way. Eros couldn't handle it. He looked up at Ernie, an almost apologetic look in his eyes. Ernie patted the dog's head.

Ben's hands went to his hips. Frustration was setting in. Here he was standing amidst the trails of cane smoke, eyes stinging, realizing that without the woman's phone call, they wouldn't have found out about Bowden's disappearance for days. They weren't closing in on the killer, or whatever he was…they were choking on his dust and smoke.

"Mike, how about if you and Ernie take Eros and try to pick up the scent somewhere on the way back to Spouting Horn, past where they're burning. I don't think she's a local, but maybe you'll get to where she parked her car, or a hotel. Then at least you'll have a starting point to ask questions. It must have been late, but maybe somebody saw her. Talk to those cane workers…they probably work for Bowden."

Gamos asked, "And you…?"

"Is there a Historical Society in town?"

Gamos made a slight frown and hesitated a little. "Kaua'i Museum on Rice Street…they don't call it the Historical Society, but the director, Beverly D'marco, she's the historian."

"I'm going to take the necklace to the museum. Maybe the director can point me somewhere. Maybe she can explain the connection among the victims and some of this fireball stuff...Back to Bowden...while you're after the woman's trail, see if you can get another detective to go through his personal stuff...check book, address book, bills...then have him ask around town who's he's been seen with recently...like lady friends. I'm sure everyone knows him."

"Knows him...this'll send the rumor mill spinning. They'll be carving up his land in their minds once they get wind of this."

And Ben thought about that. Is the killer seeking revenge or is he after the land? His thoughts went back to last year's geothermal case—to the attorney who manipulated the land deals knowing precisely where the money would be made.

Gamos tossed him the patrol car keys. But Ben was so absorbed, they sailed right past his head.

▼▲▼

The Kaua'i Museum on Rice Street was not too far from Police Headquarters. The two-story main building had a Greco-Roman facade, and until 1970, housed the Līhu'e Library. Inside, the gallery floors held exhibits of Hawaiian heritage and art. Beyond a small courtyard to the left of the main structure was the William Hyde Rice Building, which depicted the history of the Island's development.

There was a receptionist sitting at a large oak desk in the main foyer. She directed Ben to an office across the lobby. There, wearing faded jeans, purple tank top underneath an over-sized light blue work shirt, was Beverly D'marco, the museum's director. With bare feet on her desk, crossed at the ankles, and her long thin frame angled back in an old, but well-padded swivel chair, Beverly's gaze burned a hole into the large book wedged into her lap. She didn't notice him at all.

Ben cleared his throat.

She looked up and smiled broadly.

Her smile won Ben over immediately. He extended his hand, which she leaned forward to shake.

"I'm Ben McMillen. I'm a detective with Kona on special assignment here."

"Beverly D'marco."

Ben nodded. He guessed by her dark eyes and thick black hair that the woman was part Hawaiian. He assumed there was some Portuguese there, as well. "I have some questions you may be able to help me with."

"Sure," she swung around, dropped her feet to the floor, hefted the big book onto her desk with a thud. She found her flip flops without looking down, slipped them onto her feet, then shimmied up into her chair, "have a seat."

Ben slid a stiff-looking chair closer to her desk and sat. "Have you read anything about the two men who are missing from the North Shore?"

"Samuel Frobert and Walter Churchwell. Of course…it's been in the paper, plus there's been a lot of talk."

"Talk?"

Beverly stared at him for a while. Then she asked, "How much Hawaiian are you?"

She was the second person to ask him that in two days. "About three-quarters."

"I'm half. Have you lived here all your life?"

"Just the last six years."

"You weren't born here?" Her expression somewhat incredulous.

"My father married my mother here, she's pure. Then he got a job in California. I was born in Pasadena." The woman seemed to want more and Ben felt compelled to give it. "A few years after college, a friend convinced me to move to the Big Island. We started out as patrolmen." The thought of Harry Dag Dag, his friend, his old partner, made him swallow hard, made that queasy feeling come back. A lump sat uncomfortably in his throat and the hairs on his neck felt like small electric prods. He guessed he would never get over what Harry did and what had happened to him.

The museum director leaned forward and closed the old book she'd been reading. She rested her elbows on the desk. "Men like that…people talk about. I just was surprised you don't know more about them."

Ben remained silent, crossed his arms.

"They are from old families. The Froberts and Churchwells…their families go far back…to the sugar cane days, the real sugar cane days…when it was the entire economy. They were, are…" she paused, eyes looking upward, seemingly deciding their current status. "…were large, large landowners. Did you know that more than fifty percent of Kaua'i is privately held by the descendants of five or six families? Guess you know none of them is Hawaiian."

Ben sensed this was a woman who could help, but a woman who wanted to understand who he was and what he believed before she shared anything. So he offered what made him most proud to be Hawaiian. "My grandmother was a *kahuna lapa 'au*. She lived the last five years of her life with us in California. She told me much about how our ancestors lived. I may not have listened as much as I should have, but some. And now…her memory, being here…seeing what goes on…it's made me want to know more. So I understand what you're saying and even though I'm a police officer and work for the County and that usually means protecting the big developers' interests, I'm not like that. I try to do what is fair, and when what is fair is hard to determine, I tend to side with my heritage and that's *not* off the record."

"Prepared speech?"

"From now on."

Beverly gave him a smile. "I work for the county, too. Think about wanting to preserve the remains of the ancestors, yet having a job here, where we are supposed to teach by displaying the past. Do I accept artifacts from various sources and display them here, or should I find out where and to whom they really belong and return them?"

She paused, fingering the spine of the large book on her desk, then continued. "So you want to know what I've heard about the fish hook necklaces and the *kahuna* magic and what I think about these big powerful landowners who claim to be philanthropists?"

Ben arched his back and smiled. "Especially the last part."

"Do *you* think they're dead?" asked the museum director.

"I do now."

"Now? What changed your mind?"

Ben wondered if he should trust this woman to keep things to herself. She said herself that there's a lot of talk. Then again, it wasn't fair to hide the latest development, as long as nothing he said jeopardized the investigation—people should know to be careful. "There is another man missing…gone."

Beverly sat upright and she seemed to stop breathing, but she gestured for him to go on.

"I just came from there. I guess now that there's three I have a hard time believing that the perpetrator would be holding three men captive. That's harder than it sounds, especially if you're trying to keep them alive for any period of time."

Now Beverly's right hand was at her mouth. She dropped the hand to her chest. Slowly it came out, a statement not a question. "They *are* dead."

Ben cocked his head and gave her an inquisitive look.

"Just a bad feeling. And, like you said, the other alternative doesn't make sense. May I ask who?"

"You need to keep this to yourself until you see it or hear it elsewhere."

A serious expression clouded her face and she softly said 'okay.'

"Charles Bowden." He expected her to gasp. But all she did was nod and she kept nodding for a few seconds. Ben took out his note pad. "Let's start with the three men and leave the black magic for last."

The woman closed her eyes and pinched her nose, something Ben realized he did as well when confronted with something that was hard to deal with. It helped him to concentrate. Sometimes it warded off the beginning of a headache.

Beverly rubbed her forehead, then took a deep breath and folded her hands in her lap. "Okay. All three families are extremely wealthy. Like their counterparts on O'ahu and the other Islands, they do a lot of good. Sponsor museums," her palms opened and extended upward, "schools, festivals, donations to libraries, the community college…they all benefit. But also there are development deals, and hardly ever do they give back to the people the one thing that is most valuable. The land. No land…no self-determination."

Ben leaned backward and arched his back. *Hawaiian Sovereignty again.*

Beverly continued for fifteen minutes, devoting equal time to each of the missing men. Each was the main inheritor of vast land holdings, land that used to grow sugar cane, and to the best of her knowledge, only the Bowden land still was actively farmed. Frobert's cane interest was small and rumor was that his family soon would develop that parcel of land. Charles Bowden was the youngest landowner by almost twenty years. She added, that except for Bowden, attorneys and the adult children took care of the family business…mostly real estate development and utilities.

When she finished, Ben said, "This is extremely confidential, but we suspect a woman saw what happened to Bowden. Do you know who she might be?"

Just then the receptionist appeared at the office door.

"Bev. Your eleven's here."

"Thanks, Margo. Ask him to look around. I think I'll be another few minutes here."

Margo nodded and left.

"What were you asking?"

Ben arched his back again, this time it cracked rather loudly.

The director cringed as if she shared his pain.

"Nothing like sleeping in your own bed," he said. "I wondered if you might know Bowden's most recent companion."

"Nicely put. No…but how come you don't…if a woman told you…"

"She called in a tip. Wouldn't leave her name…wasn't on more than ten seconds…. I suspect she might have a husband."

"I see. Well, I have no idea who it might be." A glance at the wall clock.

"Just five minutes more," Ben said.

Beverly slumped back into her chair.

"The fish hooks…I have one here." He dug the newest one from his pocket and placed the sealed plastic bag on her desk. "What can you tell me about it?"

The museum director picked it up and studied it for a few seconds. "Probably made from whale bone…could be shark's tooth. Looks old, I mean authentic…rough spots, not symmetric, made with the tools of old."

"Anything else? Like is there anything significant in its size or shape."

"Were they all like this?"

"Basically."

Beverly yawned. "Excuse me. Tired, not the company."

Ben gave her a slight grin.

"Just like fish hooks today. They're fashioned based on the size of the fish you're after and the shape of the mouth. We have a few on exhibit here, some copies for sale in the gift shop, although they aren't like this one. There's a collector in…Hanalei, I think…who might be able to help you. I'll have to look for his name." She eyed the wall clock.

"You can call me at the station later."

"Fine."

"Anything else?" she asked as she stood.

Ben got up. "Yeah…the fireballs."

"You mean the night marchers?"

Ben gave her a long hard stare. Then he gestured for her to sit. She didn't.

"What do you know about night marchers?" he asked.

"That a couple who live near the Churchwell place reported seeing them."

"Really? On the night he disappeared?"

She nodded slowly, her tongue making a complete circle along her lips.

This time it was Ben who pinched his nose and closed his eyes. Before he could ask his next question, Beverly spoke.

"I hear about them all the time from people who live in the forests near the mountains and others nearby the ocean. Legend says there are three kinds. Some are the ghosts of people who lived in the area who just want to walk the old trails. Others are from farther away, maybe even another Island, but that is rare. They have something to tell their *'ohana*, some family matter that is bothering them, or maybe they just want to visit. But the last kind are the black magic makers, the ones who seek out someone who has wronged them in the natural life. These, sometimes, are the *kāhuna* who can conjure up black magic. And they are the fireball throwers.

"A woman who lives near Churchwell's home said she and her husband were net fishing for mullet…before dawn's best for that. They were near the trees at the edge of the sand, folding their nets. They saw a procession of torches marching up the beach in the direction of the house. Came pretty close to them."

"And?"

"That's it…that's all they saw. They left immediately and hurried home to pray."

"They saw marchers?"

"They saw torches, but only one marcher."

"So you knew of this and didn't report it?"

Beverly snorted. "After I read about Churchwell's disappearance, I went to the station and saw the detective in charge, Mike Gamos."

"You did? What did he do?"

"He took my statement…and he was laughing on the inside the whole time. Maybe you'd better ask yourself why he didn't tell you about me, first. You see, I thought he'd sent you to follow-up. I should have known better about him. But, at least now I know for sure that you came on your own."

Chapter 10

Ben walked back to the station, knowing now that the connection was wealthy landowners, or at least their descendants. And the motive was pretty clear to him as well, although he didn't want to believe it, and wasn't quite ready to share it. Revenge, strange as it sounded, pay back for the annexation of the Hawaiian Kingdom, when the land and power shifted to the American sugar cane growers and the Hawaiian people began to lose what all people prize most, self-determination.

Crossing Umi Street, thinking about what he knew about the overthrow of Queen Lili'uokalani, Ben spied an empty bench in Līhu'e Park and headed for it. He sat with his arms out, resting them along the top of the bench.

For years, back then, the wealthy American plantation owners desired control of Hawai'i. They wanted power over the sugar cane market and dominion of the rich farmlands. Finally, five powerful landowners, with the help of the U.S. military, overthrew the Queen in a bloodless coup. The Queen, knowing that a group of civilian agents with the support of the local British Military attempted such an uprising in 1843, only to have the British Government restore power to the monarchy and discipline the revolutionaries, assumed the same thing would happen again. So she didn't resist, feeling she could appeal to Washington. But there was no savior this time. And although actual Annexation didn't take place for another five years, much of the Crown Lands and the Hawaiian Government Lands made its way into American control.

Ben knew there were many Hawaiians who felt strongly about this illegal act. Some called for reparations, some for the return of the monarchy. He knew a Constitution for a Hawaiian Nation was drafted. He didn't know much about the different organizations with plans for Hawaiian Sovereignty, only that there were quite a few, and that they had support on every Island. And if he remembered correctly, Kaua'i was the hotbed.

It started to rain, so Ben got up and headed across the park to POLICE HQ. Steam rose from the pavement not unlike the anger that boiled inside him.

Three victims, so many potential suspects. A man with Hawaiian blood behind it all. That made it Ben's blood as well.

Inside the station, he picked up his messages—one from Tobi, one from the woman officer in Juvenile Aid about Loki, Ray Ahuna's son. He thought of calling Lisa. Then he thought about Beverly D'marco. Suddenly, there was tightness in his chest. It was difficult to swallow and even harder to wet his lips. For the first time since being with Lisa he felt an attraction to another woman. A woman who seemed more like him. Hawaiian blood—and a strong feeling for Hawaiian culture, customs and birthright, and the same conflict between what was law and what was right when the two didn't mesh. He wondered if the museum director was thinking of him right now rather than paying attention to her eleven o'clock appointment. Was she as incensed as he about the implications of the three disappearances? Although he never really gave the sovereignty movement more than a passing thought, it had his attention now. These crimes would be a serious setback to those who stood for self-determination.

Although he wanted this case solved quickly, Ben realized that he dreaded going home. Wondered if he really could express his feelings to Lisa. It was one thing if you sensed your partner wasn't happy either. But if it was just you…

A cold sweat covered Ben's forehead and neck. He could feel his pulse racing, pumping in his neck like when he ran uphill against the wind. He exhaled deeply as if he could expel the feeling of guilt and catch his breath, then headed for the bathroom to wash away the imaginary dirt on his hands.

Ten minutes later he found Chief Johnson in the Squad Room talking with one of the other detectives. The Chief held up his hand, fingers stiff and extended, indicating that he would be another five minutes. Ben nodded and with his eyes gestured that he'd wait for him in the Chief's office. He got some coffee and found an empty desk with a phone.

He got Tobi right away.

"How is it going?" Tobi asked.

"Not good. I just came from the scene of a third disappearance. Wealthy landowner…fish hook necklace…two-foot circle burned into the bed…that's the pattern."

"Witnesses?"

Ben swung his feet around, lifted one onto the desk, then crossed it with the other. "None on the second. An older couple who were fishing the reef at night say they saw night marchers walking up the beach near the first victim's house."

"Night marchers…you mean…?"

"They say they saw a procession of lights…torches. One marcher, I mean one man…who knows what they saw? They say the marcher came from the sea and went inland along a trail that passes the victim's house."

"And?"

"They ran home to pray. The latest one happened last night or early this morning. A woman called it in anonymously. Said a man was missing and there had been a fire in his bedroom." Ben explained what they'd found, and based on the tracking dog, what he'd surmised happened. He described the victims together for Tobi but didn't get into his theory of vengeance for the overthrow of the Hawaiian Kingdom. And he didn't relate the size of their landholdings. There was silence on the other end. "Tobi?"

"Maybe someone wants their land."

That seemed uncanny to Ben, that Tobi had focused on the land issue so quickly. "How? There must be relatives…trusts, wills."

"Maybe the victims would not sell…maybe their relatives will. Maybe a relative is helping things along."

Ben took a deep breath. Tobi's approval of his theory was important to him, so he decided to bring it up since Tobi's comments leaned in that direction. "I think maybe it has something to do with the overthrow of the Hawaiian Kingdom…someone's getting back for what happened a hundred years ago."

"Continue."

A small smile crossed Ben's face as he visualized Tobi with a pensive expression, then he saw Chief Johnson pass, headed for his office, and he knew he had to hurry. "You know the clues are all old…fireballs, fish hooks…and an old Hawaiian quilt was taken from one victim."

"Someone doing it the old way…hurling fireballs?"

"Something like that…copying that scenario anyhow. But the thing is…is that there seems to be so much talk of Hawaiian Sovereignty here. It's much further along here than at home. I think someone's avenging the overthrow of the

Kingdom. Getting back at the descendants who wrongly prospered from what happened back then."

"And you think you will find the victims in the water below the leaping point?"

Although he thought Tobi was making a joke, Ben's mind raced trying to think where *leina a ka 'uhane* was—the leaping point on Kaua'i, where the spirits of the dead jumped from the cliffs to join their ancestors in the nether world. He guessed it had to be somewhere off the Nā Pali Coast. "You don't buy it?"

"Actually, I do. Someone who wishes he could live in the past. Living in another world is what psychopaths and serial killers are about."

Ben felt better. "Thanks. I have to go. I'll call you tomorrow. Say…what's the latest on Ray Ahuna?"

"He pleaded 'no contest.' I think the judge will be fairly lenient."

"Jail time?"

"Yes…Federal crime…a simple burglary would have given us more leeway."

"I understand." Ben asked about Julie Washburn.

"Not here…I think she called to let you know everything with the boy is okay."

"Good."

"Oh, Ben…go by the airport…after five. I sent your bike."

"Thanks, Tobi…but does that mean you think I'll be here for a while?"

"Means I have sent you your place where you do your best thinking."

"A long bike ride…"

"Sounds like the longer the better."

Nodding to himself. "Yeah."

"Ben…have you called Lisa?"

"She okay?"

"I assume so…but call."

"I will."

Dry mouth. *How'd he know?*

"I was on the phone with Tobi." Ben pulled a chair closer to the Chief's desk and sat.

"How is he?" asked Chief Johnson. He walked around his desk and chose to sit on the window sill.

"He's fine. Just brought him up to date."

"Detective Gamos will be here shortly. They were able to pick up the trail again…just up wind of the cane fires. Led them to the parking lot at Spouting

Horn. Our mystery woman must have parked there. So, between you and me…what do you think's going on?"

"How much has Mike told you?" Ben closed his eyes. It was barely noon and he was worn out.

"Everything that you found down there. So…what do you think?"

When Ben opened his eyes, he saw the Chief looking at him mindfully.

"I think she was leaving her husband…or boyfriend…for Bowden. If she was unattached, she'd have driven to his home. If it was a date…say a one-nighter, she'd have brought a lot less. This is a reasonably big suitcase, not an overnight bag. She was in the house earlier with Bowden and later she returned. She stumbled on our night marcher carrying a body to the beach and found Bowden was gone."

"Night marcher?"

"Hawaiian ghost…what the couple described seeing at Churchwell's."

"Yeah, I guess I've heard those stories before. So now you're convinced there's a murderer?"

"Yeah."

"So this woman left someone for Bowden and had no part in the disappearance."

Ben nodded. "She wouldn't have tipped us."

"Same woman?"

"Explains the anonymous call…the husband's still in the dark and she has nowhere to go now. She's trapped…must be scared. Wouldn't surprise me if she's already made up some excuse for her husband and flew back to the mainland."

The Chief raked his crewcut a few times.

Ben decided to share his speculation on the motive. He exhaled slowly. "The connection is their families. Their land holdings. What their families had to do with the overthrow of the Queen.

Chief's Johnson's brow rolled into deep furrows.

"Somebody's taken the Sovereignty Movement a little too far. But that's the motive. And he's compelled to seek his revenge like it would have been done in times of old…using whatever folklore and mythology seems wildest to him. At least that's my take on it."

Chief Johnson stood, walked over to his other window, placed his hands onto his hips. Then he turned and faced Ben. "No offense, Ben…but…well, let me just say it straight. Do you think if you weren't Hawaiian, you'd have some other theory? I mean…night marchers, fireballs, overthrow of the Queen,

Sovereignty…maybe, well, maybe it's something that you'd like to believe, something that intrigues you."

Ben inhaled slowly through his nose, pursed his lips, hiding lower teeth biting into his upper lip. He was furious, but knew better than to show it. Only when he tasted blood, did he relax his jaw. "You brought me here to help with the Hawaiian slant to all this, Chief…as well as my experience dealing with a serial killer, but I'm not here because I'm hung up on black magic. What I'm saying is that someone is avenging what happened in the past. He's probably Hawaiian. The amount of publicity sovereignty's gotten has stirred him up, made him snap. Probably, if you go back, you'll find his family was cheated out of their land, what he considers his birthright. A serial killer has mental and reality problems. He takes action when something that has festered inside for a long time is brought to the surface by some triggering mechanism. The Sovereignty Movement, in this case, as it gained momentum, could have set him off. I'd say he's trying to seek revenge in the way it would have been done in times of old. Fireballs…ghosts. Night marchers carrying off the evil people. But keep this in mind…I'm probably the last person who wants to arrest someone who's willing to die for Sovereignty. So I'm not influenced by anything other than the facts. If anything, I wish there was another motive…almost any other motive."

"Sorry."

Ben waved off the apology, but he was still angry and frustrated. This was the last time he'd work with another jurisdiction. He felt out-of-place. He had doubts of most everyone he'd met. Churchwell's son was a loser, Gamos still hadn't completely convinced him that he was willing to work as partners, especially having held back his interview with Beverly D'marco about what the old couple had seen, and Chief Johnson, well, he just seemed so different from Tobi, that Ben wondered how the two possibly could be friends. Patrolman Dumas and Eros the only exceptions. Given his new mixed feelings about Lisa, he even doubted himself.

"If that's it, where's he taking them…and has he killed them?"

"Sorry…"

The Chief gave him a grim look. "I asked…"

"I heard," Ben rasped. He swallowed. "When I first got here I felt…no body…no murder. Now I'm not so sure. Three prisoners are too much to care for. Granted, the victims could have been drugged or knocked unconscious…but the boat trip, wherever he took them, would be a lot easier if the victims were dead."

"Where?"

"Could be the *leina a ka 'uhane*, the leaping place. You know what that is?"

"That's one I missed." The Chief re-took his chair.

Ben felt his teeth grinding and stopped. "It's the place where the spirit of a dead person leaps to join its ancestors in the afterlife. Each Island has one. On the Big Island it's La Kae, South Point."

Chief Johnson cleared his throat, then swallowed like it hurt. "And here?"

"Don't know. Probably the Nā Pali Coast...But I'll find out. He could also take them to his family's land. Or to the site of an old village. Actually, the leaping place might not be right...it's where the spirit gets its reward. Don't think our night marcher is going to reward these people."

The Chief seemed to be daydreaming now. Hardly above a whisper, he said, "Sure would like to find the woman."

"I don't think she's going to be much help unless she saw the boat leave. If we knew what kind he used and what direction he headed...that'd be useful."

There was a short rap on the door. Ben heard Detective Gamos's voice before he could turn around. "Gonna be a long case."

"Ben and I were just theorizing here, Mike. Whatcha got? Christ! What happened to you?"

Mike Gamos walked by Ben and sat on the vacant window sill, back against the corner of the frame. He looked tired, his hair was slicked back, and his clothes were wrinkled. Ben noticed the mud on his shoes and on the cuffs of his pants. And he smelled like a smokehouse, and not one of hickory or mesquite.

"That lady...she led us on one helluva pig hunt through the cane field. Water spraying to control the fire, fuckin' wind came up big time, smoke in my eyes...I'm gonna smell like barbecued cow manure for a week...red mud puddles everywhere. Whoever called Hawai'i paradise didn't slop through burned cane fields...that's for sure. Don't know why she didn't just walk along the paved road. The cane road almost runs right next to it."

Ben was amused—it broke some of his tension—thinking Gamos did indeed look like he'd been hunting *pua'a* in the rain forest, but he held his smile, still bothered that Gamos didn't tell him of Beverly D'marco's visit to HQ.

Gamos frowned and feigned a snarl. He continued, "Then it started to rain and Eros had trouble. We decided to cut across the cane field to Spouting Horn, since that was the logical way she'd gone. Got stuck in the mud." Suddenly, he laughed. "Ernie had to carry Eros, then he lost his shoes. Mud sucked them right up."

The Chief smiled, but it was obvious he was really thinking about what Ben said.

"Anyhow, Eros picked up the scent in the parking lot. At the far end. But there's no tire marks…the rain. After that, he just walked around in circles. End of trail…"

Chief Johnson subconsciously cut him off, asking Ben to explain his theory to Gamos. Ben did and he watched Gamos carefully when he reached the part about avenging the Queen's overthrow.

Gamos squinted and stared at him. "So long ago…?"

"Sovereignty is getting so much press these days, you'd be surprised how many younger Hawaiians are resentful." A few minutes later Ben ended with the landowner theory.

Gamos's face was neutral.

"To a psycho, vengeance grows stronger with time…it never gets cold, only hotter 'til it boils over." Ben let that sink in, then switched topics. "Anything from the cane workers?"

"Nada. Of course they know who Bowden is…they work for some company he owns. I talked with the supervisor, said Bowden didn't get involved with the day-to-day operation at all. Hadn't seen him in a week or so. No idea who the woman is. Said, 'Who can keep track?'"

"So what's next?" asked the Chief, who looked at his watch. "I've got a meeting with the Mayor in fifteen minutes. She's not gonna like hearing that Bowden's the third victim. What do I tell her our plan of action is?"

"Did you get DeLuca to go down to the Bowden place?" Gamos asked.

The Chief answered, "Just talked with him. He's on his way. He'll follow up what he finds there."

Gamos looked at Ben. "If your theory's correct, don't think the woman will be too much help."

Ben said, "I agree, but if we find her, she may at least be able to describe the boat and which way he headed. But I think she may have gone home by now…I would."

"If she did, we lost her. I'd like to assume for a day or so that she's still here."

"Game plan, gentlemen?"

Gamos cleared his throat. "We can't have Eros sniffing all the tourists at Po'ipū."

The Chief smirked.

"We'll go through her suitcase. Maybe there's something we can trace. In the meantime, I'll have a few Uniforms check with hotel and condo security people. Maybe they saw somebody leave early, before dawn."

"Try valet parking," Ben suggested.

"Only got that at the Hyatt, I think," Gamos said, "but worth a try."

Ben added, "We should check out who the next possible victims are. Warn them, maybe even put some surveillance on their homes for the next week. Then we look for the victims. That's where the clues are."

Gamos said sarcastically, "I guess if we find all the victims together, we can wait for our perp to come to us?"

"Just what I want to tell the Mayor."

"Seriously," said Gamos, "Where do we look for the bodies? I still think they're at sea. We've already alerted the Coast Guard and the fishing fleet to be on the lookout."

"And the tourist boat excursions," the Chief added.

Ben shook his head. "I think he used a boat because the place isn't accessible by land. Some remote valley along Nā Pali...that seem logical?"

"Could be, or Alaka'i Swamp, both with a million possible hiding places...and dangerous to boot." Gamos looked at the mud on his pants with disgust.

"Maybe the fish hooks point to a fishing village. Maybe if they're for a certain kind of fish, we can find out where the fish are."

"The fish are everywhere."

"Not every species. Beverly at the museum said there's a guy in Hanalei who collects fish hooks. Maybe he can help us."

"I'm changing clothes first," Gamos said.

Chief Johnson stood, checked his back pocket. Then grabbed his keys from his desk. "Keep me posted." The Chief grabbed a vinyl-covered notepad and left.

Gamos said he'd get Forensic to go through the woman's suitcase and see if anything could be traced locally. Maybe a shopkeeper would remember the woman, have a credit card slip. With that they might get her hotel. He told Ben he'd meet him in ten minutes in the Squad Room and departed, making wet sounds as he squeaked down the hallway.

And Ben sat back down and wondered who they were really up against. He pictured a big Hawaiian man, scowling face, not unlike the images of the carved statues he'd seen at the Temple of Refuge in Kealakekua, but this guy with a necklace in one hand and fire in the other.

Ben looked into the eyes of the imaginary chiseled face.

Why do this? Why do you have to be Hawaiian?

Chapter 11

Gamos stuck his head into the Squad Room.

Ben got up and said, "Let's go over to the museum. Maybe we can determine who's next."

They signed out. Outside, they spotted Ernie. He was inside the kennel giving Eros a bath.

Gamos yelled to him, "Hey…Ernie…find your shoes?"

Ernie gave him a disgusted look, then waved them away.

The detectives came around the building and halted immediately when they saw Ray Kūali'i leaning against a blue Camaro. Neither said anything.

The reporter walked toward them. "Aloha. Hear we got another one."

Ben didn't like glib people, especially when the subject was about a serious crime.

Gamos asked, "Ray, how'd you find out?"

"All the guys inside are talking about it. What can you tell me? Who was it? Nobody would tell me who."

Ben put his hands on his hips. He didn't want the reporter following them to the museum. But he did want to give him something to write about. Ben was a strong believer that you printed as much as you could when you had someone out there who might be a threat to others. He wanted people to take precautions. It was important that what was printed was accurate. Maybe you held back a few key clues so you could eliminate crank callers easier, but you let the rest go. At least that was the policy in Kona. Here…

"His name is Charles Bowden," Ben stated.

"Bowden! The Bowden estate in Po'ipū?"

"The same," affirmed Gamos.

"Jeez, he isn't like the others. I'm mean he's younger…he isn't of their generation…is he?"

Ben walked behind Gamos and whispered. "Don't tell him anything about the woman caller." Then he continued over to a patrol car parked next to the blue Camaro and leaned against the side door. He thought about Bowden. Had Ray Kuali'i inferred that there was an older surviving member of the family? He asked Kuali'i about that.

"I don't know."

"What *do* you know about Bowden?"

The reporter said, after extracting a small notepad from his back pocket, "Never met him. Only know what everybody on the Islands knows…about his family."

Ben turned to Gamos. "You think his father's alive?"

Gamos hesitated, then shook his head. "No…he's it, I think."

The reporter pressed closer. "So…how about it?…what happened?"

Gamos explained what happened. He left out the part about the woman witness who possibly was the caller, as well.

Ray Kūali'i asked the inevitable. "Who discovered he was missing?"

Ben stepped in. "We did."

"How?"

"Next question."

"So you're protecting a witness."

"We didn't say that."

Kuali'i seemed a little put off, but he took a deep breath and seemed to relax. "Okay…okay. Didn't expect you to answer that one. Fish hook necklace?"

Ben nodded.

"Burnt bed sheet?"

Ben said there was.

"Another wealthy landowner, huh? Ready to admit to a serial killer, or do you think we just have an aggressive real estate developer?"

Ben pushed himself away from the patrol car door. "That's all we have now. Got to go, Ray."

The reporter stood his ground.

Gamos said, "See you, Ray."

Kuali'i smirked and closed his notepad. "Guess I'll just have to go down there and snoop around. Be nice if you guys would make it easier for me…just…"

Ben finished it for him. "What?…give you a badge."

The reporter grinned, wet his lips. "Say, McMillen...thought I might interest you in attending a Sovereignty meeting."

"When?"

"Tomorrow at eleven."

"Where?"

"At the Community College...Student Center dining room...in the back. Might be enlightening."

"I'll think about it."

"Hey...if the killer, kidnapper, whatever he is, is after the big landowners, maybe you'll find him there. Plenty of people who've had it with the *haole* plantation people will be there." With that, Kūali'i said he had a story to check out and strolled away.

Ben sighed, a little frustrated, a little confused, but glad Kūali'i wasn't tagging along. "That guy's a little too glib for me."

Gamos said, "How 'bout we get something to eat before we check out the museum? I ate breakfast at five...I'm starved."

"Why so early?"

"Couldn't sleep. We live next to a dog who barks at his echo."

Ben laughed, picturing the scene. "No ordinance?"

"Not out where I live. Gonna take that dog fishing one day...see if he can bark underwater with a shark chomping on his ass. C'mon."

▼▲▼

The two detectives sat on squat, four-legged wooden stools at an orange Formica counter inside the vestige Hamura Saimin restaurant on Kress Street, a short distance from the station. They were spooning and chop-sticking their way through giant steaming bowls of the Saimin Special—strips of chicken, pork, and fish, with noodles, sliced hard-boiled egg, won tons, and local vegetables in a broth with thick, translucent oily bubbles like those found inside a golden lava lamp. Gamos drowned his in Red Devil hot sauce. Ben took the high road and ate his the way it was served.

Gamos finished with a belch befitting the size of the Saimin bowl. Ben, used to his training diet of yogurt and banana lunches, stopped halfway when his eyeballs felt like they were floating in soup. The thick oily broth that remained in his bowl reminded Ben to pick up his bike at the airport. He needed a long hard ride to work off the fat calories in this one. He bet the Saimin Special was a two-hundred-grammer.

They walked back along Rice Street. Ben figured he waited long enough and asked Gamos about the museum director's report concerning the couple who supposedly saw the night marchers near Churchwell's at the time of his disappearance. Gamos related what happened, that yes, he'd taken it lightly, but checked it out, and didn't mentioned it because the couple seemed confused—one marcher and five or six torches. He added that it wasn't the first time these two reported night marchers. Ben accepted that. He thought of suggesting that Gamos apologize to the museum director and explain himself, but he didn't.

They hopped up the steps to the museum and finding the receptionist's desk unattended, headed for the back office where Ben met with Beverly D'marco earlier. Her office door was open but she was not there.

They looked for her, first trying the gift shop, then back to the lobby, where they found the receptionist returning to her desk. She informed them that Bev just left for lunch and wouldn't be back for another hour.

"Maybe you can help us." Ben introduced Detective Gamos. "When I was here this morning, Beverly and I discussed some of the Island's large landowners, you know, back from the sugar cane days. We have some more questions for her, but in the meantime, can Detective Gamos and I look through what you've got on them?"

The receptionist, a dark-haired woman, no more than twenty, smiled. "I can show you where to look. Follow me." She opened her desk drawer, took out a small sign folded into a tent, and placed it at the head of her desk. It said—BE RIGHT BACK. She led them to a long narrow L-shaped room just behind the gift shop. The walls were covered with built-in shelves, each crammed with oversized books and journals, as well as the inventory of Hawaiiana books sold in the shop. Running her finger along a row of books near the back of the room, she finally extracted a huge volume with a faded green cover. It was about an inch thick, pages edged in red. A velvet ribbon marked someone's place. After paging through the middle sections of the book, the receptionist took the volume to a small table near the back of the room. She pointed proudly. "Here's the section. And there's an exhibit covering some of this in the Rice building next door."

"Mahalo…?"

"Kim."

"Mahalo, Kim."

"I'll tell Bev where you are when she gets back."

"Thanks, again."

They found references to more than a dozen names from the period surrounding the overthrow of Queen Lili'uokalani. Although in one context or another, Ben had heard many of the names before, most from families he connected with other Islands, only the name Bowden was recognizable as it pertained to their case.

Gamos continued reading as Ben looked out of the side window, which gave a view of the cluster of County buildings and part of Līhu'e Park across 'Eīwa Street. In a low voice, half day-dreaming, he said, "We're going to have to wait for Beverly to sort this out."

Gamos turned the page and exclaimed excitedly, "Here we go!"

The detectives hunched over the small table. The chart on the page looked like a road map someone drew just for them. It listed only the descendants to whom the land holdings passed.

Major Landholding Families of Kaua'i County
Controlling Interests (as of January—1987)

Gatston		Churchwell		Bowden	
J. McAllister (1851–1908)	M. Wordsworth (1860–1899)	D. Chadsworthy (1843–1904)	M. Caldwell (1855–1927)	G. Bowden (1865–1940)	K. Lansing (1873–1955)
J. Gatston II (1892–1966)	D. McAllister (1888–1941)	L. Churchwell (1878–1943)	M. Chadsworthy (1882–1954)	P. Bowden (1903–1977)	N. Winthrop (1908–)
J. Gatston III (1921–)	V. Byrd (1924–1981)	W. Churchwell (1915–)	B. B. Ellison (1920–1959)	C. Bowden (1935–)	---------------

Frobert		Klocke		Crowley	
W.W. Shaw (1862–1929)	L. Dunsberry (1866–1904)	J. Collingswood (1857–1932)	P. George (1859–1938)	H. Hartshorn (1861–1937)	C. Williamson (1861–1960)
N. Frobert (1890–1956)	F. Shaw (1893–1951)	S.A. Klocke (1875–1946)	S. Collingswood (1880–1954)	A. Mums (1894–1965)	M. Hartshorn (1900–1982)
S. Frobert (1917–)	D. Wittingham (1915–1984)	S. Klocke* (1912–)	G. Wilson (1920–1982)	C. Crowley (1929–)	F. Mums (1918–1983)

* Divorced 1955

The living descendants were all men. Three were missing, presumed dead. Ben checked that Charles Bowden was the last survivor of his family and found that he was. The remaining descendants of the original landowners were J. Gatston III, S. Klocke, and C. Crowley. Three people who had to be warned. Three people who may be able to shed some light on what happened to Frobert, Churchwell, and Bowden.

Beverly D'marco came back to her office at one-thirty. The detectives were waiting for her, sitting on a small wooden bench in the courtyard, watching the lobby in the main building through an open doorway. They got up and walked inside as soon as they saw her.

"Did I keep you waiting long?"

"Not at all. Kim was very helpful and we found what we were looking for. But we do have some more questions."

It was then that Beverly recognized Detective Gamos.

Ben noticed her smile wane.

"Ms. D'marco…I want to apologize for making you feel uncomfortable when you came to the station. I didn't take you seriously, and I apologize." Gamos wet his lips and swallowed.

"A bit rehearsed."

"Means I wanted to get it right."

The museum director let a small smile form on her lips. "I just want you to know I've heard many stories that are much stranger than someone seeing night marchers. And they come from people I've known all my life. I trust them. I take them seriously."

The Līhu'e detective nodded.

Ben thought about the transition Gamos appeared to have gone through. It did see somewhat rehearsed to him as well. Not just this word play with Beverly, but his whole attitude toward getting help from an outsider. Maybe Gamos realized the sooner the case was solved, the sooner the Kona detective would be on a plane headed home. But, no matter what, Ben still didn't like having him as a partner. This ordeal gave him a better appreciation for Cooper and Ha'aino, partners he could trust with anything. Then Ben noticed Gamos's clenched fist behind his back.

Beverly sighed, stared at him a few seconds more, then her smile returned. "So…how can I help you two?" she asked, gesturing for them to follow her into her office.

Inside and standing, as Beverly sat, Ben brought out his notepad, flipped back several of the pages, then handed the pad to her. "We want to find these three men. Do you know their first names and where they live?"

"I see you found the remaining three families. I was going to suggest you talk with them, except for Stephen Klocke...he passed away last May. John Gatston lives in Waimea. Charlton Crowley in Kapahi. Be nice to him...he's been ill."

Ben began to ask where Kapahi was but Gamos quickly said, "In the hills above Kapa'a."

Ben rubbed his temple. "Stephen Klocke..."

"Kloc-kee," Beverly corrected.

"How did he die?"

"Cancer. He was sick a long time."

"What happened to his land?" asked Ben.

"It's a mess. He and his wife had three children. They divorced a long time ago. She's dead now, but she had remarried. She had two step-children. They're all fighting over the land."

"Are they local?"

"I think the step-children live in Los Angeles. Of *his* three children, one hasn't been heard from in years, the other two live on O'ahu."

Ben didn't think they were at risk, but he wanted to talk with them anyhow. "How can we get their names and addresses?"

Beverly handed back Ben's notebook. "You can try their attorney, I suppose. I think you'll have to call the District Court in Honolulu...that's where the law suit is being heard. As far as John Gatston and Carlton Crowley are concerned, they're in the phone book...or you can ask when you get to Waimea and Kapahi."

Ben checked his watch. One-forty. Friday or not, there was still a lot to do. "Different subject. Let's talk about the Sovereignty Movement...the groups here on Kaua'i."

"Who put you on to that?" she asked.

Gamos, whose face was red and perspiring, "Ray Kuali'i."

"Good old Ray."

"You know him?"

"Sure...we went to high school together," Beverly answered. "We even went out a few times back then. He's been writing about Hawaiian Sovereignty for a while." She took a deep breath, then reached into her desk drawer, brought out a roll of Life Savers, curled back the paper, and offered them. Ben took one. Gamos shook his head. Beverly plopped one into her mouth and placed the roll into the crease of an open book on her desk. "There are groups on every Island who want reparations for what happened in 1893. They meet among themselves, they create proposals for the Federal Government, even work with several world-wide organizations that lobby for the rights of indigenous people, including the United Nations. Some demand the land be returned to its rightful owners, some are less ambitious...they just want some money. One group here, Ka Lāhui Hawai'i, The Hawaiian Nation, is one of the more vocal. They propose a Nation-to-Nation arrangement with the United States...like the Iroquois have. Did you know the Iroquois are represented in the United Nations? Have their own passports?"

Mike Gamos stood and headed for the doorway. "Be back in a few minutes." He was breathing slowly but deeply.

"What's the matter?" Ben asked.

"I don't feel well."

Beverly told him where the bathrooms were, but he was gone before she finished.

"Shouldn't have eaten the whole bowl of Saimin." Ben said.

"Where'd you go?"

"Hamura, I think it's called."

"He ate the Special? All of it?"

Ben smacked his lips. "Yup and with plenty of hot sauce."

Beverly laughed. "*E 'ao lū'au a kualima*! You understand Hawaiian?"

"A little...something about offering something to the gods."

"Very good. 'Offer young taro leaves to the gods five times.' When someone has made a mistake this offering was made to rectify it. It was also made sometimes when someone was sick. I think both apply to Detective Gamos." She pointed toward the bathroom. "Might have to charge him rent."

"While we're waiting for Mike to offer his leaves," he paused while Beverly grinned, "are there other groups besides Ka Lāhui Hawai'i?"

"Here?"

"Yeah."

"There's a meeting tomorrow at the college. I heard they're trying to bring several groups together, maybe work out a joint platform or something."

"Ray Kuali'i already invited me."

"So go." She paused, thinking. "You think it might be a member, don't you?"

"I hope not."

"Me, too. So far there's been little violence...nothing serious...some squatters on O'ahu, a little pushing and shoving."

Ben stared out of the window into the courtyard. He wondered if she noticed how he looked at her. Her hair was so shiny and her dark eyes intrigued him. He had to swallow before he could speak. Still looking outside, he asked, "Do you know of anyone who's an expert on night marchers?"

"There's one man. His name is Nelson Ala'ipaleile. He teaches at the Community College. He's writing a book on that…ghost stories, sorcerers. So go tomorrow. You can net several fish with one throw."

"How's that?"

"You think your…perp, is that the slang…?"

Ben turned to her and nodded.

"…might be there, right?" She didn't wait for an answer. "And Nelson Ala'ipaleile works there…you can learn a little about Sovereignty."

Ben jotted down the teacher's name after asking Bev to spell it.

"And one other thing…I think Nelson's a Ka Lāhui Hawai'i member, too."

CHAPTER 12

With Gamos headed home sick, Ben enlisted Ernie Dumas to cover and asked him to coordinate the activities surrounding the woman caller. He then decided the Community College professor could wait until the next day—right after the sovereignty meeting. Just a hunch, but he felt he'd see or hear something there that would advance the case and perhaps enable him to better question the professor.

He called the expert on Hawaiian fish hooks in Hanalei and found out from the man's wife that he was lecturing in Oregon. She promised to have him call as soon as she talked with him. Next on his list was the landowner who passed away the previous Spring. Ben asked one of the clerical staff to find the names, addresses, and telephone numbers of the children and step-children of Stephen Klocke. The clerk gave Ben a frown when all he could give her as a starting point was that they were involved in litigation in Honolulu District Court.

Those things out of the way, he went into an interview room and shut the door. He needed quiet, a place to think. Sitting in the only comfortable-looking chair, he got down to what was really important, interviewing, actually warning, the two remaining living descendants of Kaua'i's major landowners. John Gatston and Charlton Crowley. He also counted on the two having some information that would help. Surely they knew the victims. Any enemies of the victims might be theirs as well.

While trying to decide which of the landowners to visit first, Ben couldn't help thinking about the three missing men, still hanging onto the slim chance that they were alive, but finding it easy to visualize that they were buried somewhere in Kaua'i's interior, a burial that probably followed some ancient tradition in a place so remote even their bones might decompose before they were found. Without bodies or without catching the night marcher in the act, there would be no case.

Ben slumped backward in his chair and closed his eyes. Old burial rituals came to mind. Had the killer scraped clean the bodies, leaving only the bones to bury? Had he kept hair and fingernails? Maybe buried the remains in an ocean cave? In a crevice on the treacherous Nā Pali coast? What about in the deep valleys that time carved from the mountainous western coastline? Was this serial killer different than most? Maybe he had no conscious connection to the real world. Maybe his mind lived completely in the past. Was there a hermit of sorts living in the interior? One last vestige of a lost tribe.

He remembered the story of Ko'olau, a Waimea cowboy of the 1890s, who, along with his son, contracted Hansen's disease, leprosy. Rather than submit to exile on Moloka'i without his wife, who was free of the disease, he and several others with the same plight tried to hide from authorities in the Kalalau Valley. All were rounded up except for Ko'olau and his family. To survive, Ko'olau had to kill his friend, Deputy Sheriff Louis Stolz, whose job it was to capture him. After that, nearly one hundred policemen and soldiers came after him, which forced Ko'olau and his family to live a life similar to the Hawaiian outcasts of old. He hid in the valley for two years, living off the land, outrunning the pursuers, before he and his son succumbed to the dreaded disease. His wife, Pi'ilani, faithful to the end, finally emerged from the valley and returned to Waimea.

No, that wasn't possible. This wasn't a cannibal lurking for hikers in the jungle. This was a man who had specific targets. He was just making it look like old *kahuna* black magic.

Ben considered that the killer might have used a Zodiac, a large reinforced rubber raft that sightseeing companies used to reach the remote beaches, sea caves, and valleys of the famed Nā Pali Coast. He began to wonder, if instead, the killer's compulsion with the past led him to employ an outrigger canoe.

He shook his head, realizing his imagination wasn't going to solve this.

Soon Ben was back on Highway 50. Fifteen minutes later he passed the turnoff to Kōloa and continued west. This was new territory for him. To his right, *mauka*, was thick vegetation framed by purple mountains. Dark clouds smothered the slick mountain peaks. Black streaks of rain at the higher elevations fed hundreds of waterfalls. It all looked pre-historic. He almost expected to come across a T-Rex hitching a ride to Jurassic Park.

Makai there were cane fields wedged into the forest, but no mountains, only the sense of a slow, gradual decline to the sea. The ocean, itself, was obscured from his vantage point. So was the Bowden estate, and, he wondered, where was the woman who discovered Bowden's disappearance? Had she left the Island? Did she leave with her husband? Or was she sitting on a lounge chair right now, sipping a Mai Tai, smiling on the outside, shaking like an earthquake on the inside? Maybe they'd get a seismic reading and that would pinpoint her location.

Windows rolled down, left hand holding the line of the roof, his arm feeling the warmth of the sun, Ben's mind now focused on the night marcher. Even though he thought he convinced himself that the abducted victims were dead, he kept wondering if they were alive. Time to decide one way or the other.

It seemed much too difficult for the night marcher to keep so many prisoners captive. To keep them alive he'd have to feed them. To keep them from escaping or making noise, he'd have to guard them. So, were there two night marchers? The couple in Hanalei said they saw a procession of torches. Only one marcher, but who knew what they really saw as frightened as they were. Maybe that was it. If this was indeed a plot to avenge the overthrow of the Hawaiian Kingdom in the name of Sovereignty, then maybe these were kidnappings carried out by a band of rebels. After all, was this no different than the geothermal drilling issue he became involved with? An organized group trying to prevent something, or better described, trying to make things go back to the way they were—a pristine rainforest, with resources one chose carefully, never taking more than what was needed. Or in this case, something bigger, the return of the Hawaiian Kingdom to the Hawaiian people. But the geothermal opposition was right. Ben was on their side. And they hadn't become violent. Quite the opposite...the other side had.

Ben grabbed the steering wheel with his left hand and rubbed his temples with the thumb and forefinger of the right. He wondered why more and more each case brought with it a major issue, whether it be social, political, or environmental. Were his ancestors punishing him for his earlier apathy? He smiled, thinking Tobi would suggest that maybe it was not punishment, but trust. Maybe the ancestors were counting on him.

Dead or alive—he couldn't decide.

So now he had to figure out if the 'night marcher' the couple saw had a partner. Or partners? The real question—a madman, or a mob?

Approaching Hanapēpē, a small town halfway between Kōloa and Waimea, the ocean became visible, close to shore it was light blue and sparkled in the sunlight, farther out it became dark blue, almost black. About two hundred yards out, Ben saw a line of white surf atop huge waves, which seemed to be breaking apart prematurely. The foam gave an impression of an imaginary shoreline, although in reality, this simply marked the edge of the reef.

Highway 50 continued west and slightly north, and Ben continued thinking about the case.

Okay…what if a band of activists planned this? What could they gain? When you held someone for ransom, you wanted money. Money is portable and easy to hide. There's a chance of getting away. So was this about money, or the principle of Sovereignty? Ben believed it was about Sovereignty, about getting even. And in his heart, he had a hard time believing that some renegade band of Hawaiians involved in the Sovereignty Movement existed. Was there a Hawaiian Militia? Not that he'd heard about. From what he read and saw on television, many Sovereignty proponents were older Hawaiians and the younger ones weren't rebels, since from early in their youth the elders taught them respect for the culture. He concluded the night marcher was working alone, a man who became possessed with revenge. And Ben knew, that somewhere in the man's past, actually in his family's past, one or all of the five *haole* families took his family's land. He convinced himself that the torches were held by a single person. A person using some device, whose impression they found in the wet sand at the Bowden crime site. That explained the long pole shape and the five evenly spaced attachments. He felt better thinking one crazy person wouldn't be as organized as a group. He was wrong.

Waimea, not to be confused with Waimea on the Big Island, sat on a flat sandy stretch overlooking the Pacific and the Island of Ni'ihau to the southwest, and guarded the entrance to rugged Waimea Canyon behind, to the north. The wind blew so strongly here that Ben's hands ached holding the steering wheel straight by applying pressure from the right.

He spied a Chevron gas station situated where Highway 50 and Waimea Road intersected at angles. He looked into his rearview mirror as he signaled, turned left, drove past the two gas pumps, and pulled up in front of the station. A boy, no more than sixteen, approached from the lift bay. He greeted Ben and asked if he needed gas.

"No. Directions. Trying to find John Gatston's place."

The boy straightened, seemingly out of respect for the wealthy man's name, wiped his hands with a red rag that hung from his thick black belt. He pointed in the direction Ben had come. "The river you crossed…he lives about three-quarters of a mile up there on the other side…it's the only house. But I don't think he's there now."

"Why's that?"

"This time of year he goes to New Zealand. He owns a ranch there. Usually goes right after Labor day until the end of February."

"I see," said Ben, a little disappointed because he wanted to talk with Gatston, not just to warn him, but to see if the landowner could provide any useful information. But he was also relieved that the man was safe. "Who takes care of his place when he's gone?"

The boy, about Ben's height, skinny, cocked his head. "Can I ask who's asking?"

Ben smiled, extended his hand and answered, "Ben McMillen. I'm a detective from the Big Island. I'm working on a case here. Just wanted to ask Mr. Gatston a few questions. Believe me, he's not the bad guy, and neither am I."

The boy's tongue hung on his lips and he said nothing.

Ben took out his shield and offered it.

The boy examined the badge. "Okay."

"What's your name?"

"Johnny Panui."

"Buy you a Coke, Johnny?"

The boy grinned. "Get 'em for free. Buy you one?"

"Sure."

At Coke machine Johnny selected a key from a big chrome ring attached to one of his belt loops.

Ben asked, "So…who takes care of his place?"

"A friend of mine, Pete, is like the gardener, but the caretaker is a guy named Teroro Sapulu, and there's a woman who cooks for Mr. Gatston, but she's new and I don't know her name. I think she lives in Hanapēpē." He handed a Coke to Ben.

Ben held the cold can against his brow, then rolled it across the back of his neck. "What kind of man is he?"

Both popped their tabs and took long, noisy gulps.

"Mr. Gatston?"

Ben nodded.

"I like him. He's friendly."

"When's the last time you saw him?"

The boy looked at the ground for a few seconds. "Guess a couple of days before he left. He was with Teroro, across the street, shopping."

"And that was just before Labor Day?"

"Uh huh."

Ben realized there wasn't much else the boy could help with. "Well, thanks for the Coke. I'll see if I can find the caretaker. What's he look like?"

"Big guy…strong. Ever see the TV show *Byrds of Paradise*?"

"Couple of times."

"He looks like the handyman the schoolmaster took in…'cept he's Samoan."

Ben was nodding.

"The guy on TV was real friendly. Teroro seems more like a bodyguard to me. Doesn't smile much…kinda glares at you."

"Why would Mr. Gatston need a bodyguard?"

Obviously unaware of the recent disappearances, the boy answered, "Why would anyone around here?"

Ben crossed back over the Waimea River as instructed, turned left onto a narrow dirt road, and headed inland and upland. Soon he was a hundred feet above the river bed. The road followed the canyon wall to a fork where the Waimea snaked to the left into Waimea Canyon and the Mākaweli River went right and quickly disappeared from view behind the trees. Right there, the road ended abruptly at a narrow, triangular-shaped metal gate that blocked a dirt driveway. A sign hung from two wires. It said—PRIVATE KEEP OUT—KAPU. Thick, twisted *kiawe* shrubs flanked both sides of the gate.

Ben stopped and got out, swung the gate open, got back in his car and drove through, stopped, got out and closed the gate, then continued up the dirt trail. The Mākaweli River appeared again, narrow here, more like a stream. The bumpy dirt drive wound for a quarter-mile before forming a wide loop in front of the Gatston plantation house, which sat on a wide plateau, surrounded by a grid of cane fields, some sections brown and dead, some new with foot-high shoots, and some so thick and green and tall that Ben had the urge to find a hideaway and go to sleep.

The house resembled that of the last victim, two-storied, white stucco, wood trim, enough windows to create the impression of many rooms, chimneys at each end of the structure, and a wide verandah encircling the home. The grounds near the house were beautifully landscaped—rock gardens, a long row of yellow and white *hau*, hibiscus that went from front to back and disappeared into the only section of forest amidst the sugar cane. There were native and exotic fruit trees, even a pond fed by a man-made tributary from the river. He could see the metal wheel of a shut-off dam where the river fed the pond. The scents from the flowers were strong, but pleasant, reminding Ben of Tobi's Japanese garden.

There was a large separate barn about fifty yards from the house. Ben parked, turned off the engine, and got out. Right away, he heard a noise coming from the barn's interior, something like the pounding of metal, though muffled, and he walked over to investigate.

The barn was old, graying *koa* plank siding, but the roof was relatively new and the structure, unlike most old barns Ben had seen, didn't look like it leaned to one side or that the roof sagged in the middle. A split-rail fence formed a small corral on the right side of the barn. One barn door was shut, the other open about a third of the way. The sound of a hammer against metal was more persistent now. Peering inside, Ben's eyes were surprised by a bright emergency light that hung above a workbench. The pounding stopped. He could see a big man at the workbench, holding a mallet, straightening up, and he guessed looking in his direction. Then the odor hit him. If outside was Eden, the inside of the barn was Hell, but at least the smell wasn't that of a decomposing corpse. Ben breathed through his mouth.

"Who are you?" a deep voice asked.

"Ben McMillen. I'm a detective working out of Līhu'e."

The man approached, still holding the mallet. "Whaddaya want?"

Ben decided to play it as if he didn't know John Gatston was gone. "Looking for John Gatston."

He heard the man snort.

"Is he around?"

"He's in New Zealand for the winter." The man came forward until he was a few feet from Ben.

"Who are *you*?" Ben asked, as he glanced side to side.

The big man hesitated for a few seconds, then shifted the mallet to his left hand, and offered his right. "Teroro."

Ben felt the man's strong grip and wondered how long he intended to hold it.

Teroro let go.

"When did Mr. Gatston leave?"

"Two weeks ago."

The air was hot and oppressive, although just then a strong breeze came up, but that only made Ben aware of a pile of manure heaped into a stall on the opposite side of the barn, which made the initial stench seem almost bearable.

"Mind if we talk outside? It's a bit stuffy in here."

Teroro laughed. "Never worked on a farm, huh?"

Before Ben turned to go outside, his eyes focused on the workbench. In a large vise was a pitch fork. Ben glanced at the caretaker for a second and saw that he was watching him.

The Samoan didn't say anything.

Something told Ben he shouldn't be inside a dark enclosure with this man for a second longer, and he headed out of the barn, walking briskly.

Outside, leaning on the corral fence, the section shaded by a lone monkeypod tree, Ben sized up the caretaker who just closed the barn door.

Dark gleaming skin, actually it had a reddish tint as if the Samoan rubbed his body in Kaua'i's volcanic red earth. Both his arms and face completely hairless. His black hair was short and greasy-looking. Teroro was at least six-three and probably over two-hundred and fifty pounds. His blue jeans, held up with dark blue suspenders, were tattered and almost black where they bunched up just above his bare feet. His faded yellow T-shirt, several sizes too small, pinched his upper arms accentuating their girth, and left a six-inch swatch of bare belly showing, including the top of a heavy scar that seemed to run down his right leg.

And Johnny Panui was right. Teroro had a deadly glare.

"Got a lot to do. Wha chu want?"

Ben decided to test him. "I just wanted to let Mr. Gatston know that two well-to-do landowners on the North Shore disappeared, and now another one who lived not far from Kōloa is missing. I just wanted to tell him that he should be careful."

Teroro's glare softened into a puzzled look. "Whaddaya mean disappeared?… missing?"

"We suspect foul play."

The caretaker remained silent but staring.

"We're trying to warn large, well-established landowners whose families go back to the early plantation days. Not to alarm them, but…"

"Who in Kōloa?…you mean like Mr. Bowden?"

Ben froze for a second, then instinctively braced himself against the fence. He didn't say anything, just cocked his head and stared intently at the caretaker.

Suddenly, the intimidating Samoan took on the look of a nervous schoolboy. "Hey, wait a minute. If I guessed…that's what it was…a guess. Mr. Gatston and Mr. Bowden are friends. They have dinner together sometimes. When he's here, Mr. Gatston treats him like a son." Teroro slapped his hands together, brushing the dust and dirt away. Then his right toes wriggled in the dirt. "Honest…it was a guess. Was it him?"

Ben wondered if he was too anxious to come up with a suspect. He knew he was now making Teroro more nervous than Teroro made him. It felt good to be in control again. "Look…I'll lay it on the line with you…someone out there has a grudge that goes back a long way. May not be recent, probably something that happened to his family, but he's going after the large landholders. Bowden's the third to disappear. Whether that means kidnapped or murdered, I don't know. But John Gatston is a potential victim."

The big man was putty now, his face covered with perspiration.

Ben watched as the caretaker wet his lips. "Notice anything strange around here in the last month?"

"It ain't me."

"Didn't say it was." Ben didn't think the caretaker had a motive, although he was big enough to carry Bowden. Ben looked at Teroro's bare feet. Thought about getting a cast made of his footprint, but realized the footprints going to Bowden's house from where the boat was tied up were nowhere near that large. "So…you see or hear anything out of the ordinary since Mr. Gatston left?"

"No. It's quiet out here. Nothing's happened."

"Where do you live?" asked Ben.

Teroro pointed behind the plantation home. "Back there…there's a cabin."

"How about the main house…when's the last time you were in there?"

Teroro narrowed his eyes and responded. "This mornin'…I go in everyday. I'm supposed to."

"Mind if we take a look around now?"

Inside Ben found nothing unusual. Gatston's bedroom was neat and clean, bed made. He asked where the laundry was. Teroro said there was none. Nothing dirty, the woman who cooked and cleaned washed everything after Gatston left. Ben asked where the clean towels and sheets were kept. Teroro showed him. No clues there, sheets had a pattern, but it wasn't of the burned hole variety. The caretaker gave Ben the cleaning woman's name. She lived in Waimea, not Hanapēpē like the boy in the gas station thought.

After determining that the landowner was scheduled to call on Monday, Ben told Teroro to have Gatston call him at Līhu'e headquarters. "Tell him right away."

They shook hands and Ben left, thinking about the pitch fork. Letting his mind wander a bit, wondering if when he found the victims their bodies would show puncture wounds grouped in fours. And maybe not quite in line after one of the tines struck bone. But something told him, besides the caretaker's foot size that he wasn't the one. The couple who claimed to see a night marcher surely would have made reference to the man's size if he were as big as Teroro. Just in case, he was going to have someone ask them about that.

Ben found Maria Zafirides, the woman who cooked and cleaned for John Gatston. She was scared of Ben, but very respectful at the same time. She told him the only unusual thing that happened was Mr. Gatston gave her an extra week's pay before he'd left.

'Does he want it back?' she asked him.

Just south of Līhu'e on his drive back, Ben glanced at his watch. It was almost three-thirty, plenty of time to check out the Carlton Crowley residence before meeting the five-forty arrival of the flight carrying his bike.

Forty minutes later, Ben's car slowed to a crawl just before Wailua. Ahead was the almost continuous day-time traffic jam that plagued the stretch of Highway 56 between Waipouli and Kapa'a. Fifty feet in front of him was Highway 580, which followed the Wailua River inland, the same road he ran along two days before when circling Sleeping Giant Mountain. He saw a gap in the on-coming traffic, crossed the double-yellow, and turned left onto 580 just as the light changed from yellow to red. He hoped that he could connect with a road that would take him to Kapahi without having to rejoin Highway 56. About five minutes later, turning off 580 onto Kamala, then right on 'Olohena, he was winding his way closer to the mountainous backdrop where the small town of Kapahi was located.

In town, he spied a Postal Service Jeep pulled off to the side next to a gang of mailboxes. The postwoman gave Ben directions to the Crowley farm, as she called it. Ten minutes later he stopped in front of a dirt road marked PRIVATE. Slowly, avoiding the deep puddles, Ben crawled along the one-lane entranceway, admiring the low flowering scrubs and tall trees that lined the drive. After a quarter of a mile, the road widened, a white board fence joined him on both sides, the shrubs thinned, and he came to a circular driveway and a beautiful plantation home, which seemed much newer than those of the other victims, including a blue-green tile roof hardly faded from the sun. On the front porch were two people, a woman he gauged to be about forty, and an older man, with a full head of silver hair, combed straight back, rocking slowly in a rocking chair. A Golden Retriever puppy curled up on his lap asleep.

The woman waved.

Ben parked the car under the shade of a tree, got out, and approached the house. He noticed how much cooler it was at this elevation. Bundles of light gray clouds ringed the mountain tops behind the house. The relief from the hot sun of Waimea was welcome. His shirt, stuck firmly to his back during the ride up, now billowed in the breeze.

"Aloha...what can we do for you?" the woman asked.

She looked part-Hawaiian, and on closer inspection was probably nearer fifty than forty. She wore a floral print wrapped around her body, exposing her shoulders and arms. Ben knew it was one of those pieces of material that could be worn a half dozen ways that Lisa liked to wear. How anyone ever folded and twisted and turned the material so it wouldn't fall off, was beyond Ben.

The man, Ben guessed, was Carlton Crowley. Crowley was staring ahead, not quite looking in his direction. Reading glasses hung tucked into the breast pocket of a plain tan work shirt buttoned at the collar. A book, open and upside down, sat on a small table next to the rocking chair. A glass of what appeared to be lemonade sat sweating next to the book. The man smiled, but it seemed strained and gave his face a contorted look. He nervously stroked the golden retriever puppy's head with his right hand. His left hand sat limp on his thigh, bent at a right angle to his wrist, fingers curled, but not moving at all. There was a plain golden wedding band on his ring finger.

"Aloha. I'm Ben McMillen." He didn't want to alarm them by saying he was a detective, but couldn't think of anything else to say to describe himself. "It's beautiful...real peaceful up here." He saw the woman's eyes narrow, although the old man hardly reacted. He'd run out of small talk. Looking at the woman, "I'm from Kona. I'm working with the Līhu'e police on a case and I need to talk with you about it."

"The police?" The woman shifted in the cushioned chair, uncrossed her legs, and re-crossed them. "Is something wrong?"

Ben cleared his throat, looked at the old man, and asked, "Are you Carlton Crowley?"

The old man's eyes showed some life. His head came forward slightly.

"He is," said the woman, "please don't frighten him...he had a stroke two summers ago and another one a few months back." She smiled at the man in the rocking chair and patted his thigh.

"Oh...I'm sorry, ma'am. I just came up here to ask you to be careful. I don't want to upset you, but...several long-time landowners have disappeared recently, and we suspect foul play. I don't know exactly how to explain it, and I know it sounds strange, but it seems as if someone is intent on doing some harm to the families who controlled most of the land here just after the overthrow of the Hawaiian Kingdom." He saw the old man's body tremble. Ben gave the woman an apologetic look, thinking he was too blunt.

"What do you mean disappeared?" she asked.

"Can I ask who you are?"

"I'm his daughter. My name is Mary Rice. I came to live with him after the first stroke."

Ben nodded.

"Who disappeared?"

"Do you know Charles Bowden, Walter Churchwell, and Samuel Frobert."

"I know them, certainly. How awful. When did this happen? We don't get a newspaper."

Carlton Crowley slowly turned his head and stared at his daughter, then lifted his eyes and focused on Ben. "Wha…wha happ-end to th…them?"

Ben looked at Mary.

"Tell us."

Ben explained what he thought happened to the previous victims. He talked slowly. Crowley didn't react much at the mention of fireballs and the fish hook necklaces. Ben told them that the other major landowner, John Gatston, was safe, spending the winter in New Zealand.

"Have you noticed anything strange around here? Heard noises at night? Seen anyone? Had any visitors…someone you weren't expecting."

Mary clasped her hands in her lap. "No…nothing. Like you said, it's very peaceful up here."

"We can post a patrolman out here at night if you'd like. There's no telling how long it will take to catch who's responsible."

"No…we'll be all right. My husband's coming back tomorrow. He's been on O'ahu for a few days."

Ben took out his card, made sure it was one on which he'd written the Līhu'e station number, and handed it to Mary. "If you change your mind, call right away. You don't have to get me necessarily. Just explain who you are and what I offered. I'll let them know about you as soon as I get back."

"Ben…you left something out, didn't you? Something you didn't want to tell us."

"No…not really."

"You just asked if we'd seen anything strange. What were you hoping we'd say?"

"Well…at least at one abduction scene, some neighbors said they saw…said they saw night marchers."

"Night marchers! Are they sure?" She seemed to be intrigued at the thought.

"Who can be sure about that?" answered Ben, trying to gauge the excitement in her voice.

Mary asked, "What did they see?"

"They said it was a procession of torches walking from the water to the house where Walter Churchwell lived."

"Poor soul…They saw the marchers?"

"One marcher and a procession of the torches. He decided not to talk about his theory that the marcher carried a pipe or stick of some sort with torches attached. For the first time he envisioned a length of PVC with holes drilled along the top. "They ran home immediately, scared."

"Night marchers are serious. My mother told me about night marchers and I believe in them."

"If I were you, I'd take the precaution of having a policeman watch your house. This is not a night marcher. It's someone with a lot of problems and my guess is that he thinks the major landowners, your family included, have done something wrong."

She stared beyond Ben, down the mountainside toward the distant ocean. Mary Rice was silent.

Suddenly, the old plantation owner came to life. He struggled to sit upright. "Ahh…night mar-chers," said Crowley. "Bad…bad things hap…hap-pen to p…people who…who en-count-ter night mar-chers."

Ben felt a shiver go up his spine as he watched the old man nodding and his hand trembling uncontrollably.

Suddenly the sleeping puppy jumped off Crowley's lap and ran to the side of the house and disappeared from sight.

Even Mary seemed a bit startled.

"Night mar-chers," Crowley repeated. "B…b…bad things."

Right then Ben knew that Mary Rice was holding something back. He decided to post a patrolman. Why did she refuse? "A few more questions."

Mary Rice stood and bent over her father. "Not now, it's time for his nap. Don't worry about us."

"But…"

She led her father inside. At the screen door, she looked over her shoulder and mouthed, 'Not now.'

▼▲▼

Later that night, sitting on the edge of the *lānai*, crashing surf and jagged cliffs emerged in Ben's thoughts. He pictured the remote canyons and undiscovered bogs in the great Alaka'i Swamp, and saw corpses being thrown from helicopters, remains that quickly disappeared into the pre-historic muck. He thought about the long periods of rain and how, in just a few days, the terrain would be repainted, plants would double in size, body parts would badly decompose, and flash floods would carve out rivers and disperse tissue fragments into oblivion. All the evidence, the whole mess naturally distributed in a lost world. His mind peered beneath the turbulence of the waterfalls where he saw shimmering ghost-like images pinned between the rocks. Following the foot trails between old villages, he visualized a clearing and a pack of wild boar ripping apart the flesh of a body staked to the ground or of one they dug up from a shallow grave to finish off.

There seemed to be no peaceful way to die in the wilds of Kaua'i, but thousands of ways to disappear.

Slowly he rose, opened the screen slider and stepped inside. He spied his bike at the foot of his bed. The flight hadn't damaged anything, but still he knew he would spend a couple of hours aligning the wheels, fiddling with the shifter, and cleaning the chain.

First, he sat by the phone and called Lisa. She wasn't home. He left a message. Hanging up, he felt guilty that he was relieved that she was out.

Hours later, bike assembled and fine-tuned, he shuffled off to bed, too tired to shower, too lazy to turn off the light. Maybe a little afraid of the dark as well.

▼▲▼

When the moon finally knifed through the heavy cloud cover, the stream by which the night marcher sat came alive, bubbling with light, like a sorcerer's caldron boiling with black magic. He reached into the folds of his *malo* and extracted a necklace. Raising it skyward, finger and thumb holding the braided loop, he was mesmerized by the image of the moon which fit perfectly into the curve of the ancient fish hook. Just then a new wind came ashore, caught the fish hook and swung it back and forth ever so slightly, but enough to have an hypnotic effect. The night marcher closed his eyes and thought about Charlton

Crowley. He felt a little sorry for the old man. He thought about the fire and the disabling stroke that followed. No one should be put through this twice, but he couldn't change that now. After all, Crowley's family took much, much more than it gave. It was up to him to balance it out. His thoughts shifted to the Kona detective. Nodding to himself, realizing that McMillen was closing in.

Time to scare him. Time to leave a calling card a little closer to home. He wondered, in the end, if he'd have to *take* him as well.

CHAPTER 13

He woke to knocking.

When he opened the door to this room, the woman who owned the bed and breakfast told him there was a call for him. Ben noticed her examining his room and he guessed, from the look on her face, that she wondered why he'd slept in his clothes.

"What time is it?"

"Almost 8:30. Breakfast is over, but I saved some for you." Gloria Mendonca gave him a doubting look.

"Mahalo…I'll be right down after I take the call."

She forced a smile and turned for the stairs, tightening her apron strings as she walked.

Ben went to the head of the hallway, sat uncomfortably on the tiny chair by the tiny phone stand, and picked up the receiver. "Hello."

"Thought you were an early riser."

"How you feeling?"

"Stomach's not so good. Doctor says I've got an ulcer. I guess I knew it all along…but, you know…thought it'd get better by itself."

"Not if you polish off a couple of Saimin Specials every week." Ben felt his stubble, then sniffed his underarm. He presumed the landlady categorized him as 'hard-boiled' by now.

"Look, I'm gonna be in bed a few days…Chief doesn't have another partner for you, unless you really want one. He's down a couple of detectives…but you can use Ernie if you want. Ernie's a good investigator by the way. He's not just a dog handler."

"Ernie sounds fine and I already had him help me with something yesterday."

"He told me."

"He find out anything about the woman who was with Bowden?"

"Nothing. None of the night people at the Hyatt saw anything that'd help. There's a few people who were off who worked the night Bowden disappeared. Ernie'll follow up with those."

"What about the guy checking out Bowden?"

"Nothing there. No big withdrawals, nothing left behind by the woman other than her suitcase, which is definitely mainland stuff. How 'bout you?"

Ben told him about the visit to Gatston and Crowley. "Feel sorry for the Crowley guy. You can tell there's a sharp mind trapped somewhere inside there." Ben thought about the old man's comment on night marchers. It still gave him the chills. "I'm gonna see what I can find out at the Sovereignty meeting, plus there's a professor at the Community College who might be able to help. Seems he's an expert on night marchers."

Gamos coughed and groaned and Ben could sense that it was painful.

"If you're willing, I bet I can find out some Hawaiian cure that'll have you up and around in no time."

"It works on Portuguese?"

"Maybe not ugly ones."

"Call me tonight."

"Try to get some rest."

"Yeah, right. Remember, I live next door to a dog who barks at his echo."

"Got a Hawaiian cure for that, too. I hear they're tasty after they've been wrapped in banana leaves and smoked for a few hours."

There was a long pause. "I guess we didn't start out so good, you and me."

"I understand…it's OK now. Let me get to work., I'm late enough already."

Ben shaved, showered, dressed, and had his hand on the doorknob, when he recoiled. He had to force himself to exhale. Hanging from the knob was a fish hook necklace. He had been half asleep when he went out before to answer the phone. Had the necklace been there then, meaning it had been left during the night, or had all this happened within the last five minutes? He couldn't remember seeing it, but he wasn't sure. Once over his initial shock, he bent closer to examine the it. The necklace was just like the others. Realizing he may have wasted precious time, he spun around and ran to the *lānai* and scanned the rear of the property. No cars speeding away, no one on foot running. Ben came back inside. He told himself he had to act like a detective now, not a victim. Carefully, applying pressure with the backs of his hands so as not to cover any fresh prints, he managed to twist the doorknob and open the door. He looked at the area in the hallway in front of the door but saw nothing out-of-the-ordinary, although he didn't expect to see sand or traces of dirt standout on the well-worn carpet. Bounding down the stairs, he came out the front door and scanned the small parking area and the front yards of the houses on either side of the B & B. Nothing. Nobody.

He went back inside to the phone and called HQ and asked for Ernie Dumas first.

Ernie and Eros arrived in a half hour. Eros sniffed the necklace, then crossed the room and went out onto the *lānai*. Barking loudly along the railing on the left next to the house, seeming frustrated that he couldn't jump down. Ernie had to drag him away to lead him downstairs and out back. Once there the tracking dog followed a trail that led to a side street. He stopped at the curb and barked some more.

"Sorry, Ben."

Ben nodded and patted Ernie on the back.

Twenty minutes later Kevin and his partner arrived, searched Ben's room, dusted for prints, and bagged the necklace. Now they were outside checking the grounds.

Ben and Ernie were out front by Ernie's car. They just finished talking with Gloria Mendonca who said she was up since five-thirty No noise woke her, that's when she got up whenever there were guests.

Ben realized it didn't matter. How the killer got into his room was easy. Rethinking the events, Ben was pretty sure that he had paid little attention to the doorknob when he went for Gamos's call. He sort of remembered seeing something, but it had registered as a DO NOT DISTURB sign you'd find in a hotel doorknob. Even though the B & B had none of those—that's what his sleepy mind recorded. He was exhausted the night before, so not hearing the nighttime intruder didn't surprise him. Why the perp came was easy, too. To make him think about who was being hunted and who was the hunter. Now Ben knew how vulnerable he was. Given that, the remaining two landowners wouldn't have a chance except that one was in New Zealand and, thankfully, he had a patrolman watching the Crowley estate from dusk until dawn. But was that enough?

Kevin came around to the car. "Nothing anywhere. Not even ladder impressions next to the *lānai*. Don't know how he got up there, 'cept maybe with a rope. Maybe he's a mountain climber…or an experienced hiker." He shrugged.

"Doesn't matter," Ben said. He thought for a few seconds, then said that he'd write up the report, spend a little more time with Mrs. Mendonca, then head out to the sovereignty meeting. He asked Ernie to keep working on locating the woman caller and to follow up any leads uncovered from Bowden's personal effects.

"Also, set up a twenty-four-hour watch schedule on the Crowley place."

"You be okay?"

"Don't worry about me, Ernie. I'll be fine."

"I haven't seen you with a weapon…need to borrow one."

"No, I have one."

At home.

Chapter 14

He ate breakfast in the kitchen. Gloria told him a different version of the story of Sleeping Giant Mountain while she rinsed the breakfast dishes and placed them into the dishwasher. Before that, he questioned her again, but she simply had nothing to add. Now she wanted to talk, probably thought she was safer with a detective there, apparently not making the connection that the only reason there was an intruder was *because* of her house guest.

She said there were many Sleeping Giant stories, but this one was her favorite.

"One day a small boy caught a small fish. But when he brought it home, the fish demanded to be fed. So the boy gave it some *poi*. But the more the fish ate, the more food it wanted. Soon the fish grew into a giant fish, and still wanting more, was fed by the villagers, because now the task was more than a single small boy could handle. The fish turned into a boy, and the boy into a giant, still demanding more food. The villagers were consumed with the task. Finally, one of the young girls in the village sang until the giant went to sleep, where he has remained resting to this day."

Ben joked with Gloria, asking for more *poi*. It helped to relieve some of the tension he felt.

After wolfing down a stack of three pancakes, a big glass of guava juice, and a cup of coffee, Ben accepted a second cup and leaned back, admiring the mountain view from the huge window behind the sink.

"Breakfast was great, Mrs. Mendonca...and the coffee...it's better than Kona."

"Probably is Kona," she said, laughing quietly, then asked Ben to call her Gloria. She reached and opened a cupboard door, took out a brown and white tin, and read the label. "Kona." She held it up for him. "But you're right, it's called Kaua'i Pie...Kona coffee, chocolate, macadamia nut, and coconut flavor. It's Lappert's, brewed in Hanapēpē." She paused. "Detective McMillen?"

"Ben. What is it?"

"Can I ask you about your case?"

Normally, he would have said no, but given the morning's events, he said, "Go ahead."

"This man who was here...Well, I read some things in the morning paper and the article said that the three people who disappeared were from old *haole* families. It said the men might be victims of revenge against people, descendants, I guess, who got their land because of the overthrow of the Queen..."

"...and mentioned a Kona detective was helping on the case."

Gloria nodded.

"Would you feel better if we had a patrolman watch your house?"

She hesitated, but not long. "Oh, no. I just want to understand."

Ben wondered what Ray Kuali'i's next column would contain. He planned to ask him this morning at the Sovereignty meeting. He was beginning to worry that maybe he'd been a little too forthright with the reporter. "It didn't mention me by name, did it?"

"No, but Detective Gamos told me a little about you before he rented the room."

"Well...that's the angle we're working on. What's bothering you? There's something else, isn't there?"

The landlady turned off the water, wiped her hands on her apron, faced him, then leaned against the sink. "My mother used to work for one of the *haole* families."

Ben lowered his coffee cup and raised his eyebrows. "Which one?"

"The Crowleys...up the hill." She gestured to the kitchen window, moving her hand up and over Sleeping Giant Mountain.

"I was just there yesterday. They're okay. Did you know about Mr. Crowley's stroke?"

Gloria lowered her head for a second. When she raised it her eyes were glassy. "He's a nice man. My mother took me up there sometimes. Mr. Crowley let me ride his horse."

"His daughter moved in to take care of him. I had a patrolman watch them last night. And we're going to have someone there around the clock. The daughter…

"You mean Mary?"

"Yes. She said her husband would be back today." Ben drank some coffee. "They'll be okay…and I plan to go back."

"I haven't been there in a long time. Is the house rebuilt?"

Ben remembered it looked new…he thought maybe the new roof just made it seem so. "Yes…what happened? Iniki?"

"More coffee?"

Hands up. "No, thanks."

Gloria came and sat with Ben at the table. She folded her hands on the table. "No, not the hurricane. Two years ago there was a fire. I heard the police thought it was arson. They never caught anyone. Right after that Mr. Crowley got sick. He was sick a short time…then he had his stroke." She appeared to be reminiscing. "I should go there and see him."

"I think he'd like that."

Gloria wiped her eyes and smiled.

"Let me ask you something. Are you part Hawaiian?"

She held up her hand, thumb and finger slightly separated. "Just a little…one grandmother. A grin, "…my *kupuna wahine*."

Ben rested his hands, also folding them on the table, thinking for a while about his *kupuna wahine*. Her resting place on the western slope of Haleakalā came to mind. He easily pictured the lava rock wall above the fern-covered crevice where her remains were hidden, wrapped in a traditional sennit casket, *'aha*, made from coconut husk, human hair, and the intestines of animals. He saw himself sitting on the lava wall, talking with her, apologizing for not having spent more time with her when her spirit and body were one.

The sun went behind a cloud and brought him back. Mrs. Mendonca smiled at him.

"Mr. Crowley didn't say anything until I was about to leave. I wasn't sure he was following the conversation, but Mary and I were talking about night marchers," Ben waited for a reaction and got a small one as Mrs. Mendonca raised her eyes and stared directly into his for a second, "and Mr. Crowley said…'Bad things happen to people who encounter night marchers.' You know any reason he'd say that?"

The woman was silent a long time. She stared again at the mountain that filled the kitchen window.

Ben could sense she was bringing something forward. He cleared his throat. The noise seemed to snap Gloria out of her trance.

"This may sound strange, unless you believe in night marchers...but I understand Mr. Crowley told the police he saw night marchers that night...with torches. He said they set fire to his house."

Ben thought about his conversation with Mary Rice. The day before she probed for something he'd left out. But when she got him to tell her about the night marchers that were reported at the site of one of the disappearances, she didn't mentioned the fire, didn't mentioned her father's statement to the police. Hadn't said anything at all after her father spoke of 'bad things' happening when night marchers come, except to whisper 'Not now.' He needed to talk with Mary Rice again, and soon.

He looked at Mrs. Mendonca. Her face was blank, her eyes unblinking, staring over his left shoulder as if he wasn't there. Something from her past, perhaps the horse rides, perhaps thoughts of playing with Mary, maybe night marchers. What ever it was, it completely occupied her mind.

▼▲▼

It was a quarter to eleven when Ben turned off Kaumuali'i Highway and drove into the parking lot of Kaua'i Community College. He parked in the last row of empty spaces and checked that he had his note pad. Two prolonged rings of a loud buzzer vibrated off the campus buildings. Soon the walkways between the buildings were filled with students, some headed for their next class, others for the parking lot.

"Hey, Ben."

It was Ray Kuali'i. "Glad you could make it. You ever attend anything like this back home?"

"Not a sovereignty meeting, but an anti-geothermal rally."

"Well, those against geothermal have made some progress...maybe we'll make some here." Ray Kuali'i put his hand on Ben's shoulder and gently pushed him toward the rear of the small campus. "C'mon, we'll miss the beginning."

They walked side by side and Kuali'i asked, "I suppose by now you see the pattern? Have you warned the other landowner?" The reporter cleared his throat.

Ben stopped and gave the reporter an angry look. "You been following me?"

"Hey, man...no way. It's logical, that's all."

Ben thought for a few seconds, then decided to expound a bit with the reporter. Maybe getting the potential victims' names in the paper might discourage or, at least delay, the night marcher. Give them time to find the him first.

Ben sighed. "Yeah…it is. Gatston's safe…he spends the winter in New Zealand. I talked with Crowley's daughter. They seem okay. Thanks for not naming me in the article, but can I ask you to tone it down a little."

"Scaring people?"

"If it were random, I wouldn't have said a thing. But when you know the targets…"

Kuali'i changed the subject. "Too bad about the old man. Don't know him, but people seem to like him."

"What do you know about the fire?"

"Only what I read," he said smiling, then added, "…didn't cover it."

"Tell me what you read."

The reporter explained that it happened almost two years before. No one was hurt. Arson was suspected—a torch was found near the rear of the property. There were no prints on it and no one was ever arrested.

"A torch?"

"Two years ago, though. Never heard a description of it. Just no prints."

"Are there any known arsonists around?" Ben asked. He added, "Crowley got any enemies?"

"I think they found one, an arsonist, that is, on O'ahu but he had an alibi. As far as enemies go, everybody has them, but I don't know of anyone who's had a run-in with Crowley. In fact, I think he's probably the most decent of the bunch."

Ben inquired, "What makes you say that?"

"You hear more about what he gives than what he takes. But, maybe he's a quiet taker."

Ben made a mental note of the torch, thinking someone should have told him about that.

They entered the Campus Center. Ben asked how long the meeting would last.

"Anywhere from thirty minutes to three hours. Depends how feisty Auntie Marguerite is feeling."

The dining room was filled. All the folding chairs were taken, so Ben and Ray Kuali'i went to the right side of the room and leaned against the wall. Although three windows on the left side of the dining room were open, the room was already stuffy and hot. Ben saw Kuali'i open another button at the top of his aloha shirt and Ben did the same. The odor of sweat and stale coffee hung in the air reminding Ben of the holding cells at Kona HQ.

On stage—a temporary eighteen-inch platform covered with green carpet—were six folding chairs and a speaker's podium with a drooping microphone. Three women were seated as were two men. One woman, who Ben assumed was Auntie Marguerite, stood at the podium and appeared to be ready to begin. She was a heavy Hawaiian woman with gray hair braided into two longish pigtails that rested on her shoulders. A pink hibiscus was tucked just above her left ear. She wore a colorful red and yellow *mu'umu'u* and a ti *lei* hung around her neck. Even from Ben's vantage point he could see the *lei* was wet and made dark green stains on the Auntie's garment.

One of the women seated on the stage caught Ben's attention. She was considerably older than anyone else, thin, and her hands, which were folded in her lap, trembled. She seemed to be staring at him. Ben pushed off the wall and went to the drinking fountain, watching the woman out of the corner of his eye. He took a long drink before walking back to his place next to Kuali'i. The old woman's eyes appeared to follow him the entire time.

"Who is that woman on stage?...the old one."

"Auntie Marguerite's mother. Why?"

"What's her name?"

"It's a long one...Kelikoa'elakauaikekai Pahanui. Her first name means 'rain sparkling on the sea.' People call her Keliko. She's the Island's authority on *hula*."

Ben had seen or heard the name before, the shorter version, but he couldn't make the connection now.

Ray looked at the old woman. "She's smiling at us." Ray waved. "She doesn't speak much now, but much of what she thinks and feels is what Auntie Marguerite says."

Auntie Marguerite cleared her throat, stepped up to the microphone, choking the base with a fleshy hand and offered a loud 'Aloha,' which sent an accompanying squealing noise through the wall speakers.

The crowd responded with an 'aloha' and clapping.

Ray took out a large black notebook, then a mechanical pencil from his shirt pocket, and gave the eraser tip two pushes with his thumb.

When the applause died out, Auntie Marguerite began. "I want to welcome all of you and say *mahalo* for coming." She waited for the crowd's murmuring to subside. "Ka Lāhui Hawai'i—Kaua'i has always stood at the forefront of the

Sovereignty Movement. But now we face a serious problem and I think it is our responsibility to make the initial move."

The room was completely silent. Ben could sense the feeling of excitement. He glanced at Keliko Pahanui, but the old woman stared intently at her daughter now. Ben noticed her hands trembled worse than before.

"We set a deadline for Sovereignty. It was January, 1993...a hundred years since our land was taken. That day came and passed. No Sovereignty. We drafted a new Constitution, but so have others. Our plan is different from other plans. Maybe our plan is the best. Maybe not."

There was some grumbling and a few shouts from the audience, but it became quiet quickly.

"And that is the problem. How can we expect the Federal Government and the United Nations and the people of the world to take us seriously when the Hawaiian people are divided in their quest for self-determination. Ten years ago there were six or seven groups kindling the fires of freedom. Five years ago there were twice as many and the fire began to burn. Now there are so many pro-Sovereignty organizations that we now have our own committee just to keep track of the other organizations."

There was brief laughter, but Auntie Marguerite's angry stare made the crowd realize this was not intended to be a joke.

"And now the fire we lit burns out of control. And when the fire has consumed everything, it will go out forever and we will have nothing."

Ray Kuali'i wrote furiously.

For some reason Ben felt ashamed. Here was maybe the greatest challenge to the survival of the Hawaiian culture and he was a bystander and worse, on a mission that might set the Movement back years. What if the killer was an important person in the Movement?

"So now we must follow a different course. We must persuade our fellow Sovereignty groups that we each need to modify our position. We must come up with a plan we can all agree upon. It means compromise. It means we have to choose one goal whether it be Nation-to-Nation, or Nation-within-a-Nation, or something else. But we can't continue to have different objectives and we can't continue to argue with one another."

Ray Kuali'i leaned toward Ben and whispered into his ear. "See the guy leaning in the doorway...wearing the white golf shirt and baggy shorts?"

Ben nodded.

"That's Nelson Ala'ipaleile…you should talk with him. He teaches history here and sponsors the school's archeology club. He might be able to shed some light on your case. He knows a lot about night marchers."

Ben eyed the man and thought that he looked more like a student than a professor. He appeared to be about Ben's height, maybe a little taller and no more than twenty-five or so. Ben's visualization of the man who headed the Archeology Club included gray hair, hunched shoulders, a man probably sixty years old, and without eyeglasses because he'd lost them.

"Beverly D'marco already suggested it. I was going to look for him after this was over."

"Interesting guy."

Ben asked, "You and he friends?"

"Not really…interviewed him once when the *ka'ai* were stolen from the Bishop museum."

Ben gave the reporter an inquisitive look.

"You must know about it."

"I remember reading something…on O'ahu?"

Kuali'i seemed a little frustrated, like every Hawaiian should be aware of this. He gave Ben a pensive look. "Supposedly they were the remains of Liloa and Lono'ikamakahiki…rulers in the 15th or 16th century…preserved in coconut fiber caskets. Stolen by a living descendant, so they claim. Anyhow, with Nelson in charge of the Archeology Club…I thought he might have some local story that fit the Star-Bulletin article we were going to reprint. He gave me a good sidebar…"

Kuali'i's attention went back to Auntie Marguerite.

"And so…as the spokesperson for Ka Lāhui Hawai'i—Kaua'i…I want you to take some time and talk with your *'ohana*, and your friends here and on other Islands, and also try to learn about what other groups are about and come back to our next meeting and tell me what you have decided and what you think is best.

"I can tell you this. I contacted Ka Pā Kankau and the people of the Round Table and Nā 'Ōiwi o Hawai'i and The Office of Hawaiian Affairs, and even the United Church of Christ, with whom you know we've had major confrontations. I asked them all to think of compromise. I told them we are willing to compromise. I told them there would be no Hawaiian Sovereignty ever…if we didn't join forces now and come forward with a unified plan. I asked them to meet with their people just as we have done today. That is all I have to say. Are there any questions?"

There were many and Auntie Marguerite patiently answered them.

Finally, twenty minutes later, she said, "If that's it, let me remind you to pick up the literature on the back tables. There are copies of the Constitution. There are policy statements and proposals of the other major sovereignty movements. There's some things from the Indian Nations. Pay careful attention to what they have accomplished. They faced much the same problem as we do today. Very few made it work."

A man in the audience stood and shouted, "Not the same at all!...there is desert and dust on their lands...there's a fortune on ours. And that by itself makes our task much harder!"

The crowd became noisy, shouting, and pointing fingers in the air.

Auntie Marguerite did nothing to quiet them.

Ben looked at Kuali'i. "He's right."

The reporter, watching the audience, said, "I know."

After a minute the crowd suddenly became still.

Auntie Marguerite whispered one last thing. "Our task *is* much harder."

Everyone heard her. There was no applause, just eerie silence, as if the members of Ka Lāhui Hawai'i—Kaua'i finally realized the real meaning of self-determination.

Ben didn't know what to think, other than he, too, had much to come to terms with. What would Tobi say if he told him he joined the Sovereignty Movement? *What would Lisa say?* He thought about her compromise and felt maybe he should make one as well. Maybe what you believed in and how you acted on those principles was more important. And the mixture of your blood not so significant. He was back to that dilemma.

But also he had a case to solve. He checked his watch—almost noon.

Kuali'i was excited. "This is some story."

"I just hope that the leaders can work out their agendas. It's the power struggle among them...that will be the problem...not the members, not the average citizen."

The reporter snickered. "Thought you'd say that. Sort of like Kamehameha trying to unify the Islands all over again. What is yours and what is mine?"

"...then there's the white man's money." Ben shook his head.

Now as people crowded the tables in the rear of the dining room, Ben saw the professor turn and leave.

Ben pushed off the wall. "Later."

Ray Kuali'i gave him a mock salute, closed his notebook, and hurried away.

Ben headed for the exit. He glanced over his shoulder toward the stage, looking for Auntie Marguerite's mother. He didn't see her, so he hurried after Nelson Ala'ipaleile.

Outside, the sun was bright and men on tractors mowed the grass. Others trimmed plumeria and carried yellowed palm fronds to a large trash bin on wheels. There was a clean, sweet smell in the air and Ben was weary enough to want to sit on one of the benches and just watch the gardening crew. He yawned until his jawed cracked.

At first he couldn't spot the professor. He trotted down the walkway, dodging through and around the members of Ka Lāhui Hawai'i, finally taking a path across the fresh-cut grass. After jogging fifty yards, he saw Nelson Ala'ipaleile walking briskly along the cement walk, loose docksiders clapping against his heels. The professor was at the bottom of the walkway, headed for a group of buildings on the left, before Ben was within shouting distance.

"Professor, wait up."

Ala'ipaleile stopped and turned.

Right away, Ben noticed the huge bulges in the professor's calves. Much bigger than his own, of which he was a little self-conscious. Ride a bike and run enough and your calf muscles resembled flat stones about four inches around and at least an inch thick. But Nelson Ala'ipaleile's calves were those of a pure biker, someone who did a hundred miles or more a week. His calf muscles had muscles, looking like a second layer three inches around.

Ben extended his hand and at the same time decided that he wasn't going to use Ray Kuali'i's name as a reference, either with the professor, or anyone else, reasoning he get more information if people didn't think their comments and answers would end up in print. Also, he wasn't going to give the reporter any more information, at least nothing of significance. He didn't want Kuali'i investigating on his own, possibly ruining the case, maybe getting hurt in the process.

"My name's Ben McMillen. Beverly D'marco at the Kaua'i Museum thought you might be able to help me."

Nelson took Ben's hand and gave it a single half-hearted jerk. "With what?"

"I'm a detective with Kona, but I'm helping on a case here. Talk here?..." Ben gestured toward a bench under a small stand of trees, "...or your office?"

"Let's go to my office...I need to check on something."

They walked quickly across the campus. Ben asked Nelson what he'd thought of the meeting and the compromise proposal. That was enough to get the professor talking the rest of the way.

The professor offered a seat to Ben and walked around behind his desk.

"Just a second."

Nelson Ala'ipaleile sat on the edge of his desk with his back to Ben, facing the PC on his credenza. He leaned forward and struck a key. On the screen a new window appeared. Ben watched him maneuver his mouse, scanning what appeared to be e-mail messages. The professor stopped at one, read it, then hit another key, and the e-mail window disappeared. Then he turned around and sat.

"Okay. What can I help you with?"

Ben liked the professor, maybe he was influenced by the fact that the teacher was a biker. He decided to share whatever he needed to and to come right to the point.

"You know about the landowners who disappeared?"

The professor said he heard a little, but hadn't read a newspaper in awhile.

"We don't know if they're still alive or being held somewhere. The evidence suggests one perpetrator and the evidence points to some very strange things. Old Hawaiian practices."

Nelson's interest seemed to increase. He had been semi-reclined in his chair, hands behind his head, showing reasonable biceps and triceps. But when Ben mentioned there were strange things surrounding the case, the professor unfolded his arms, lifted himself up and back against his chair, and folded his arms across his chest. "Strange Hawaiian practices…like…?"

"Black magic, *kāhuna* sorcery…fireballs to be specific, and a report of night marchers."

Sounding both pleased and excited, "Yeah?"

Ben gave him a firm stare.

The professor realized his mistake and lowered his eyebrows and pursed his lips. "I'm sorry some people have been kidnapped, but this is the kind of stuff I research. I'm writing a book on night marchers…but you know that. That's why Beverly sent you. Tell me about the fireballs. Did anyone see them?"

"You mean flying through the air?" asked Ben.

"Yes."

"I don't think so. The evidence was indoors. The traces of fire were circular, found right in the middle of the victims' beds. I'm just assuming someone copied the old fireball legends from what I saw of the physical evidence and of the report of night marchers…well, they saw floating torches…one person…coming from the beach to the house."

"How'd you get from burned sheets to fireballs, then?"

"Traces of lava rock in the burned spots."

"Interesting. So you think someone is playing the role of a *kahuna ʻanāʻanā*?"

"That's what I think, a sorcerer." Ben took a quick look around the professor's office. At least some of the stereotype was intact. The place was jammed with books and stacks of paper and there were at least a dozen dusty carrousels of 35mm slides.

"I know where everything is," Nelson said smirking.

"Then mind telling me where the victims are?" Ben said with a feigned expectant look.

Nelson became serious. "Well, you've said most of it. I know enough from my research that many of the *kāhuna* tricks were no different than what a good magician can do today. It's slight of hand, it's having knowledge about how something works, understanding the relationships in nature, being clever. It's about building credibility over time and getting your audience to focus their attention where you want them focused...away from what you're really doing."

Ben arched his back. The chair, a cheap secretary's model, was extremely uncomfortable. He decided to stand up and stretch. He walked over to a tall book shelf and leaned against it. "What about leaving a fish hook necklace by the victim's bed?"

"An old one?...was it carved from whale bone or shark's tooth?"

Ben reached into his pocket, extracted a small plastic bag, and tossed it to the professor.

"Can I take it out?" he asked.

"It's been dusted...sure."

The professor unzipped the bag and let the necklace fall into his palm. Then he held the necklace by it's clasp.

"The necklace itself is not old. It's boar's hair, braided. The clasp is ivory, not old either. But the fish hook looks authentic. I'd have to test it. Actually I have dozens just like it. You find them all the time along the Nā Pali Coast, if you know where to dig. Most are made from whale bone and shark's teeth. *Makau* is the word for fish hook. There are hundreds of kinds. For catching sharks, eel, crab, small fish, big fish, double barbs. Hundreds. Some made from bone, mother of pearl, and smooth stones, used as lures...didn't have Reynolds Wrap in those days. This one's good-sized and has a good-sized barb. It's for a big fish like an *ulua*. There was one at every crime scene?"

"Same as that...same size, same shape."

"But not exactly the same."

"I didn't examine them in detail. I guess if they're authentic, like you say, then there's bound to be some differences. But they all looked like that. So…out of the hundreds he could have left, is there any significance to that one? Did it have any symbolic meaning long ago?"

"The fish hook, by itself, no. But a *kahuna* who was an expert at fishing would wear a fishhook necklace. Maybe your man is a fisherman."

"You mean maybe his ancestors were."

Nelson Ala'ipaleile nodded, then added that the man could still be a fisherman today.

"You happen to notice any of yours missing?"

"Like I said…I have dozens…should have said hundreds. I'd never know. But…I do have three or four that are very rare. I'd know if they were gone. But, they're much larger than this one you showed me. More than twice the size."

"And what were they used for?"

"Reef shark."

Ben gathered that in, then thought about the fish hook expert in Hanalei. "Do you know Burgess Panui?"

"Sure. He might be able to give you more…like what region or village used this kind of hook…maybe not every village fished for *ulua*, though they *are* pretty common. Maybe there's a telltale marking on them…a clan marking, but I don't see anything. Burgess would be better."

Ben thought about his next question. "Okay, now how would *you* tie night marchers into this?"

"How much do you know about them?" The professor checked his watch.

"Some." Ben quickly stated that he knew of three kinds—spirits of people who had lived in the area, relatives visiting family members, and those who marched to avenge something wrong that was done to them in the physical life.

"You said the victims were rich landowners. I assume you mean they inherited the land…few people can afford to purchase vast amounts of land today. You're talking about original landowners."

Ben nodded but thought to himself…*that's the problem. Hawaiians back then had no concept of land ownership. The land belonged to the gods. So when outsiders offered worldly goods for land, Hawaiians thought they were getting gifts in exchange for something they did not own.*

"Well, you know how the original landowners got their holdings, maybe that's why they have disappeared. Night marchers were sent to get them."

"Are you saying that tongue-in-cheek or do *you* believe in night marchers?"

"That's like asking if I believe in God. Of course I do. But the real question is whether God created man, or was it the other way around?"

Ben didn't like hearing that, but the man had a point.

The professor continued. "I believe that many Hawaiians do. My book has many references, many accounts of strange things, some stranger than you have here. But, being realistic, I think you have someone re-enacting, playing out the way it might have happened in the past."

Ben walked to the window and stared out at the campus and the mountain beyond.

Nelson swiveled his chair to face Ben. "That's Kilohana Crater. There's a dead giant inside."

"And a sleeping one in Kapa'a."

"The Island's filled with them."

"One last question…if you were the night marcher responsible for this, where would you take the victims?"

Nelson got up, took two books from his desk. "Kind of a strange question, don't you think?"

Ben grinned. "Nothing personal. You're the archeologist. You know most of the remote places on the Island, right? So where would be a good hiding place, keeping the evidence in mind? Where do you go to complete the fantasy of avenging your ancestors?"

"Well if you weren't going to complete the re-enactment, just want to get rid of the bodies, then I'd say the Alaka'i Swamp or the ocean…but if you were set in the ways of the past…an old fishing village."

"Nā Pali Coast?"

"Yeah, that sounds about right."

"How many are there?"

"Five or six."

"What's the best way to get there?"

"For you?…Police helicopter."

Ben thought about the night marcher. "It seems each time he leaves by sea. A Zodiac?"

"Probably."

Just then, Ben remembered something else. "What about the leaping place?"

"Polihale…?"

"Where's Polihale?"

"Just beyond Barking Sands. Why there?"

Ben said, "Maybe he threw them off the cliff."

"Polihale's a hell of climb, let alone carrying a body. But he'd never send a *haole* he killed to join his own Hawaiian ancestors."

"You're right, if he's Hawaiian. But if he wasn't..."

Nelson's hands surrendered. "You lost me...if he's not Hawaiian, then none of this makes sense."

"Unless he's really clever...any chance you'd come along with me?"

"To the fishing villages? When? No. No. I can't right now...I've got too much going on. But I'll bring over a map with the spots marked for you and I'm sure you can get one of the Zodiac tours to help out. They know the territory." He looked at his watch again. "Got a class. Anything else?"

"Guess not."

Nelson grabbed his backpack from the floor and waited for Ben to make a move for the door.

Ben pushed himself off the window sill. "Recommend a good bike route?"

The professor grinned. "The calves don't lie, do they? How experienced are you?"

"I've done two Ironmans."

Nelson's face showed he was impressed. "Then try Waimea Canyon Road, if you have a few hours."

"What's the elevation gain?"

"To the end...four thousand feet. But it's a real charge coming back down."

Back in the parking lot, sitting in his car, Ben revisited the thought he had back in the professor's office. What if it wasn't a Hawaiian? What if someone wanted to make the disappearances look like something the Sovereignty Movement was behind? Be a good way to set the movement back. Following that logic, what about someone against sovereignty? Ben saw how ridiculously hard that scenario would be to track down. Those against the Movement probably out-numbered those for by five to one.

Just what he needed...another angle with many more suspects.

CHAPTER 15

By the time Ben ate lunch and got back to the Līhu'e Station, Nelson Ala'ipaleile already dropped off a topo of the Nā Pali Coast. Ben carried the map back to the office that the detectives shared, stacked the folders, memos, and notepads off to one corner of Mike Gamos's desk, and unrolled and spread out the relief map. He used two coffee mugs, a tape dispenser, and a stapler to hold down the curled edges.

Five beaches were marked in red, each clearly annotated with information about the landing area, and directions to old villages and farming areas where someone living in the past might be drawn. In the area inland from each beach there were a few blue circles penciled in. Looking closely at the small print, Ben saw that the circles marked the location of caves and bogs. He guessed that it was the professor's way of indicating where someone might hide a victim. Ben thought it all seemed pretty macabre and also intriguing that the professor put all of this together so quickly, especially when he said he had a class to teach. But he realized the stereotype probably was pretty accurate. The professor's office looked like a war zone, but his research was most likely meticulous.

He took out his notebook and jotted down the map locations. One caught his attention. A place called the Valley of the Lost Tribe. It was beyond the southern end of the Kalalau Trail, and according to the land features depicted on the topo, eight rugged miles north of Polihale, the leaping place, putting it in that region of coastline where the only access was by water. Chances of meeting campers or hikers as you brought a Zodiac and a body ashore were pretty small.

After picturing the scene over and over, Ben's thoughts turned to the fish hook he found on his door. He was somewhat surprised that he was able to keep it out of his mind for most of the day. Putting his feet up, he leaned back in his chair and went through a list of everyone who knew he was working the case. His brows furrowed and a half scowl formed around his mouth. First, he eliminated everyone on the police force, including Gamos, although there was still something about him that didn't sit right, his turning hot and cold.

Mrs. Mendonca—he shook his head no. Beverly D'marco—no way. That left the caretaker, professor, and the reporter. He grinned. Saying those three to himself sounded like a bad title for a movie.

Gatston's caretaker, Teroro, though fearsome at first, genuinely appeared upset about Bowden's disappearance. Ben saw no motive there, not for killing all the landowners, anyhow. And the large man wasn't a Hawaiian. Although the professor provided so much information in such a short period of time, Ben had a good feeling about the man. Maybe he was prejudiced a little, Ala'ipaleile being a bike rider. But there was the fact that he was an officer of Ka Lāhui Hawai'i. Ben decided his background should be checked. Since he wasn't highest on Ben's list, he decided to give that chore to Ernie.

Then there was Ray Kuali'i. Ever since their first meeting by the beach near the second victim's home, Ben wondered about the reporter. Tobi didn't believe in coincidences. They were there investigating, likewise the reporter, so he said. The man seemed so sure of himself, glib, just short of arrogant. Being a reporter, he had access to information. He'd know all about the landowners, the succession of the land holdings. He could sway public opinion, give the crimes any slant he liked. He was the one Ben decided to check out himself. And just in case, he wasn't going to tell anyone about it. Probably a long shot, but that's all he had and deep down inside, he wasn't sure who he could trust.

He thought again about the necklace on his door knob, frustrated that the night marcher had been a few feet away and he had been asleep.

It was two-thirty. Ben eyed the phone. He thought for a few minutes what he would say. He took a deep breath as he called Lisa. She answered on the first ring, hardly giving him a chance to exhale.

"Nice of you to remember me," she said.

"Sorry. It's not going well. Guess you figured that much out by now." Ben brought her up to date. Told her he hoped to be back in a week. She said she could come for a few days, but Ben told her he'd rather wrap up the case and come home. Lisa said Julie Washburn from JS called about Loki. She'd forgotten Ben was on Kaua'i. Loki was placed in a foster home not too far from where he and his father had lived. He was going to school.

"I bought him a few things to wear and brought them down to Julie. She said he feels much better about himself."

Ben felt badly. This was not a relationship you threw away. "That was nice of you. What about his father?"

"He gets sentenced in two weeks. I know Tobi's trying to help."

"So how's the new job?"

"I'm learning that people are wary of me. You know, there seem to be so many non-Hawaiians who are experts on Hawai'i."

Ben found himself nodding.

"I want people to believe I care...I don't want them to think I got this job because I'm white. And on the other hand, I'm not going to defend myself with 'but I live with a Hawaiian.' They should judge me on face value."

"I understand." Ben thought for a second. "The best advice my grandmother gave me was 'to be a good teller, you have to be a good listener first.' Show people you can do that. But remember one thing as you approach this...and don't take offense...you can never *be* Hawaiian or *think* like a Hawaiian. All you can do is try to do a good job."

"You sound...a little angry."

"No. All I'm saying is don't believe that by being close to someone else's culture that it can become your culture."

There was a strange silence between them, then Ben said, "I miss you."

"I miss you, too."

Ben felt uncomfortable. "Look, I've really got to go." I'll try to call every day from now on."

"Okay. Be careful."

"I will."

After he hung up, Ben's heart hammered against his chest.

Next Ben called Kona HQ. Tobi was out, so was Jack. He asked for the Chief's assistant, Millie Kalehuna.

"Aloha, *keiki*."

"Aloha, Millie.

"How's it going?"

"Slow...very slow. I think I understand the motive, and we know the potential victims, but there are no clues to the ID of the kidnapper, killer, whatever he is, and...we haven't found any of the victims."

"You think they're alive?"

Ben blew out his breath. "Kind of hard to imagine. Do you know where Tobi is?"

"No, but I can ask Joyce."

Ben said, "That's okay, I'll ask her. But I wanted to ask you about a cure."

"Are you sick?"

He detected a little worry in her voice. Ben knew he was her favorite. She treated him as one of her children. "My temporary partner here…he's got an ulcer."

"That didn't take long."

"Funny."

Millie laughed. "Okay. Write this down."

Ben dug out his notepad.

"You wash an *'olena* root, pound it, and extract the juice. Have him take one tablespoon twice daily, before breakfast and before dinner."

"Where do I find *'olena*?"

"It's turmeric. But you need the root. Find a Chinese grocery, they'll have it. If not, call me. I'll send some."

"Mahalo. See you soon. Next week, I hope. Let me have Joyce."

"Be careful."

Joyce Ah Sing, the Kona detectives' secretary, said Tobi was in Hilo for the day. Jack was out questioning somebody.

Ben gave her an update, then he asked, "Remember the guy you used to date who moved to Hanalei and became a guide or something?"

"Sure. Bill Gleason."

"You know the name of his place?" he asked.

"That was five years ago."

"Bill Gleason, though."

"Yup."

"Okay. Any messages?"

"Nothing important. The bank manager called to say thanks. Danny Mitchell wanted to know about fishing. Nothing else. Jack and Ha'aino took the rest."

"Okay."

"Want Tobi to call you?"

"I'll call him. Don't know where I'll be."

"About time for a cell phone. You know, we give them out for free."

"Never got around to it, but yeah, you're right. First thing, when I get back."

"It's not like carrying a gun, you know."

Ben smiled. "Get me one and leave it on my desk."

Ben said good-bye and hung up.

He spied a Rolodex on Gamos's desk. Found his home number there. He spoke with Mike's wife. Mike was sleeping. Ben offered the Hawaiian remedy, which she said she would try. Ben didn't think she would.

Ten to three. Dark a little after seven. He needed a bike ride. A long one, his own Hawaiian remedy and like Tobi said, the place where he did his best thinking.

Before he left, he looked up Bill Gleason in the phone book. He called. The recording said the phone was disconnected. He called a GTE operator, identified himself, and asked if she had an unlisted number for Bill Gleason. She did not.

Ben figured a Zodiac tour captain would have to do.

▼▲▼

Only because he felt confident there would be no other victims, Ben decided to leave early. Plus the ride up Waimea Canyon would give him a chance to think about the perpetrator and the location of the victims. He wasn't sure, but maybe he'd stop along the way and look down on the Nā Pali Coast. Maybe something he saw would inspire him.

He'd raced back to his room, slipped into his riding gear, then with bungee cords borrowed from Gloria Mendonca, he fastened the Trek to the roof of his car, and left for the South Shore and Waimea Canyon.

Forty minutes later he pulled into the gas station where he'd met Bobby Panui the day before. The boy wasn't there, but the man working now said Ben could leave his car there.

When the man asked if he was going up the canyon road and was given a nod, he reminded Ben that it got dark around seven-fifteen. "Your bike and outfit say you're good, but you better be…patches of fog appear without warning. It's two and a half hours to the end, all uphill, and maybe forty-five minutes down. Don't wanna be caught up there in the dark. It's black as hell. Gets cold, too."

Ben checked his watch. It was four-ten. He slipped on his windbreaker and tied the bottom drawstring tightly around his waist.

"To be safe…turn around by six-fifteen," the man offered.

Ben thanked him, guided his bike shoes into their tracks, and locked them in place as he leaned against his car, smacked the top of his helmet with his left hand, and with a right-handed push off the rearview mirror and he was on his way.

The first quarter mile through Waimea was easy and the road freshly paved. Then, just as he began a long, looping one-eighty-degree stretch, the flat, sandy surroundings gave way to the upslope, which marked the beginning of the west face of Waimea Canyon. Before too long, Ben was out of his seat, churning his legs, passing a sign that told him he was a hundred feet above sea level. It was then he realized he should have warmed up and stretched.

It was hard to think about the case while concentrating on the winding road and occasional traffic. Passing a marker at the five-hundred-foot level, Ben came to a relatively level stretch where he was able to sit and enjoy the view as he peddled. To his right, Waimea River sparkled in the late afternoon sun. Ahead and right, was the beginning of Waimea Canyon, a giant gorge of pastel layers of compressed limestone rock. Ben looked over his left shoulder and saw the backside of the Nā Pali Coast, jagged cliffs and deep valleys and a rolling layer of clouds that moved through the peaks like a parade of ghosts. Farther out, he could see the Pacific, a flat faded blue from this distance, only interrupted by the Island of Ni'ihau, the last bastion of Hawaiian life the way it was many years before. You got the sense that beyond Ni'ihau was the end of the world.

And Ben thought—Maybe the inhabitants of Ni'ihau should be asked how to structure the Sovereign Nation. Then again, they might have trouble dealing with the concept. It's harder for someone with freedom to define it than for someone who's lost it or never had it.

The road became steeper and Ben raised from his seat again, leaned forward, and pushed against gravity. His cheeks filled with air as he exhaled. The only thing he tried to think about was how easy it would be on the return.

An hour and forty-minutes later, he reached a place called Kukui. It was three-thousand feet above sea level and every muscle in his legs, arms, and back burned with exhaustion. Ben pulled off to the side of the road and coasted toward a large tree, slowed to the point where he was barely able to balance, then leaned toward the trunk and reached out to brace himself. He was breathing hard as he painfully jerked his feet free of their bindings and got off the Trek. His legs were unsteady for a few seconds, but he managed to start walking, drawing the tension from his leg muscles, arching his back and slowly moving his head from side to side, listening to the cartilage in his neck crack. Next time he needed to get away, he'd find a calm bay and float on his back. He crossed the road and placed one foot on the guard rail and looked down along the intimidating coastline. He wasn't going to get any clues from this vantage point. A few minutes later he walked back to his bike uninspired.

Riding again, after the rest, he felt better knowing the remainder of the way to the end of the road at Pu'u o Kila Lookout was about twelve miles and only another thousand feet elevation gain. He figured he could do that in forty-five minutes. And if the man at the gas station was right, and the return trip, all downhill, was forty-five minutes, he'd be back to Waimea by seven-fifteen. With a Nike nylon jacket, sporting three strategically placed pairs of silver reflector material, stowed in the small pouch under his seat, he wasn't worried about riding the last five miles in the dark.

Finding some rhythm, remaining seated since the incline was gradual and he was in a low gear, Ben kept looking to the west. The Nā Pali Coast. He knew that each of the five locations that the professor marked lay along this stretch, though they were three miles west and almost three-quarters of a mile down. He tried to picture the perpetrator steering a Zodiac rubber raft, powered by twin outboard engines, riding the waves with his victim aboard. In his mind he envisioned the victim wrapped in something and lashed to the bow. But lifeless.

He thought about the fireballs. Did he have to use the quilt? the other wall hanging, a flag, whatever it was?...to put out the fire. Had the victims been burned? There was no trace of burned flesh in the lab report. The victims probably were subdued and moved away from the bed. Then the fireball, a symbol of the past, deposited on the bed. A hot lava rock dropped there for a few seconds. That made sense. But how do you carry a hot lava rock?...and a torch, or torches?...and a body?

So if he killed them, how did he do it? And where? And the thought of the Valley of the Lost Tribe came to him again. The name was compelling. It was easy to envision the killer being drawn there.

At Pu'u o Kila Ben got off his bike and leaned it against the timbered stairway that led to the lookout. There was only one car in the parking lot—two other people at the lookout. Ben nodded to them, then walked to the northwest corner of the platform and tried to guess where the Valley of the Lost Tribe was. Looking over the Kalalau Valley somehow he knew they were down there.

Monday he would go. And take Ernie and Eros and camping equipment, because they weren't coming back until they found the landowners.

For the first time, on the first steep downgrade, Ben squeezed the right brake grip, which controlled the back brakes. The brake cable was loose, so extended he hardly slowed. He tested the front brakes and found them better, but nowhere how he'd set them up. He knew right away the man who left the necklace didn't just slip in and out of his room. He couldn't believe he'd slept through that. And he couldn't remember a time when he'd forgotten to test the brakes right at the start of his ride.

He fought back a little panic. He didn't want to hit the front brake with any real force—maybe the cable would disconnect. Better to have some small measure of slowing than none at all. Worse yet, coming down hard in a last ditch effort to stop might mean catapulting over the front and crashing if the brake did hold. He thought he could manage the steep grade if he milked the brake and reduced his speed by weaving slightly, the way a slalom skier navigates down hill. Plus, this late, there shouldn't be many cars. From the ride up, he knew there was a level spot a few miles ahead, where he could slow down and stop without too much difficulty. A few adjustments with the tools he kept in a zippered pouch underneath the saddle would solve the problem. He reached back and felt for the pouch. It was there. He shook it. The tools didn't jingle—he squeezed the pouch and discovered the small case was empty.

The alternatives now where to apply the front brakes, and see if they held. If they did, he was in for a very long walk back, unless the cars he hoped weren't around in numbers, were. And if the front brakes didn't hold, then the only thing he could try was taking off his nylon wind breaker and jamming it into the wheel. But doing that with one hand and preparing for a possible crash with the other…well, he didn't like the odds. Foremost in his mind was that crashing probably meant no Ironman.

The first mile went so well, Ben quickly became confident. His speed was twenty—he could manage that. The first ninety-degree turn coupled with a ten-degree downgrade ended his euphoria. The guardrails whizzed by. The slalom plan was worthless. Ben's arms ached from holding the handle grips so tightly. The digital readout displayed his speed as thirty-five.

Whirling down, almost felt like free-fall. Then the fog rolled in and the mist made the pavement slick. He had no choice but to apply more brake pressure. He did it slowly and evenly, and the pads barely held against the tire. He took a another glance at his Avocet, quickly removed his right hand off the grip and pressed a button on the multi-function device, which changed the readout from *mph* to elapsed time. He had twenty more minutes until Waimea. Maybe a little less due to his speed. He was glad he had new tires, the fresh tread held the wet road. And soon he felt more comfortable, knowing how much in advance of a turn to start banking, and judging the line to follow coming out of the curve. The fog only allowed him to see about a hundred feet ahead, but that was enough.

The only thing he feared now were blinding headlights. Waimea was a road for tourists and none should be headed up the canyon this close to dusk.

But could someone coming down see him in time? Would he even know if a vehicle was behind him?

Luck was with him. A few miles later he saw the hazy lights of Waimea. The mist turned into a steady rain, but he'd already reached the flatland. He could smell the ocean and breathed in the sour salty smell like it was pure, sweet oxygen. Breathing came a little easier.

His thoughts switched from the reporter to the professor. Anyone could have dismantled or loosened his brake cables, but most likely only a serious bike rider could do so quickly and quietly, while the intended accident victim slept a few feet away. And who suggested Waimea Canyon, where you never braked going up, but desperately depended on braking most of the way down? Nelson Ala'ipaleile.

Sonnufabitch.

Ben raised his fist. He wanted the night marcher. And as he unclenched his fist, he realized his jaw was so tightly clenched that it took the rest of the way back to his car before he could open his mouth wide enough to speak.

"Sonnufabitch."

▼▲▼

"'Bout to send the police up for you."

Ben smiled at the man who worked at the gas station. "Wasn't so bad."

The man shrugged as he watched Ben lift his Trek onto the car's roof. Then he came over and held the bike as Ben secured it with the bungee cords.

Ben thanked him, glanced at his watch, which reminded him how hungry he was. "Recommend a good place to eat?"

"Where you headed?"

"Back to Kapa'a."

"You look like you could use a good steak. In Kāleheo, about ten minutes…Camp House Grill. Blue building, *mauka*, can't miss it."

Ben thanked him, climbed into his car, eased carefully into the seat, and hoped the Camp House Grill had chicken or fish. He hadn't eaten red meat in years. The thought of trying to digest a cow was about as appealing as another bike trip up Waimea Canyon Road.

He also hoped they had well-padded chairs and he hoped he didn't smell to badly. The bike trip certainly hadn't afforded him much time to think about the case. So now, as he drove to Kāleheo, two faces played in his mind. The reporter's and the professor's. He wondered why the reporter's just wouldn't fade away.

▼▲▼

At precisely midnight, a torch ignited. Then another...and another...five in all, five in a row. The procession began.

A gust of wind came down the mountainside just then and extinguished two of the flames. The procession stopped and the three remaining torches were lowered to the ground as if the night marchers now sat. The middle torch seemed to drift backward, dipped to light the trailing two torches, then returned to its place in the middle. Rising, the five lighted torches proceeded along the narrow trail that followed the Kapa'a Stream just to the south of the Keālia Forest Preserve. Through the mix of ironwood, guava, swamp mahogany, and silk oak, past the sleeping white flowers of the bindweed. Into a flat area at the rear of a plantation estate the torches came, weaving their way around the mass of long tangled limbs of *hau* and then a cropping of *hala*, whose above-ground root systems cast eerie spiderlike shadows across the moonlit pathway. The rich smell of damp earth and exposed roots filled the night air.

Ahead, the re-built plantation home.

Above, the descending half moon of Lā'au Pau—the twentieth day of the Lunar month—slid behind a large, slowly drifting cloud.

The sleeping golden retriever puppy didn't wake, but Mary Rice did. She heard footsteps approaching the rear of the house, just beyond her open second story bedroom window. Her first thought was that it was her husband, who called earlier to say he would be very late, assuming he could get a private plane to fly him over from O'ahu. If not, he'd be there the next day. But, Mary wondered, why would he be approaching from the rear of the house? Had she heard his car? She couldn't remember.

She donned her nightgown and walked quietly to the window and hid behind the curtain as it danced in the breeze. What she saw took her breath away and her hands covered her mouth.

Night Marchers walking along the back path. Five torches. She screamed and screamed and the procession of light halted.

For a full ten seconds she felt that the marchers were looking up at her. Then, the torches turned and walked away, headed toward the spiderlike *hala* and the twisted shadows of the *hau*, and disappeared into the forest.

Mary ran to her father's room, but slowed as she neared his bedroom door. She heard the puppy struggling up the stairs. Soon he was at her feet, whining and rubbing against her legs. He barked sharply twice, but she ignored him and reached out for the door knob. It turned easily and the door opened without a sound.

And fast asleep in his bed was Carlton Crowley, his contorted left hand on his stomach, the usually trembling right hand still, at ease in the sanctuary of sleep.

The puppy tried to enter the room, but Mary scooped him up, hefted him against her chest, and closed the bedroom door. She descended the stairs, followed the hallway back into the kitchen, and placed the puppy on the pile of six pillows that made up his bed.

He watched her for a few seconds, then lowered his head.

Heart still pounding, mouth dry as sand, she continued on to the back door and looked out. Far away, almost at the end of the clearing, she saw a small flicker of light for an instant, then it was gone. She stood there thinking for a while. Thinking about the other landowners. Thinking about the detective from Kona. She thought about what she'd seen. Five torches but only the shadow of one man. And when they, or he, turned to leave, the torches seemed to have pivoted around him, the two end ones moving more quickly than the two that flanked the center. Only when she convinced herself that the night marchers wouldn't return, did she go back up to bed, but she couldn't fall asleep. A sliver of moonlight illuminated the phone and she stared at it for a long time. The only thing that kept her from calling the police was something in the back of her mind. Something she didn't want to believe, but couldn't forget.

The night of the fire two years before, she had been at home on O'ahu. Alone. Her husband had been on Kaua'i, on business.

He had called her to say he had to stay another day.

Patrolman Dizon returned to his post at the bottom of the driveway that led up to the Crowley estate. He just finished eating a sandwich in his car, which was parked three hundred yards down the road around the bend, so the daughter wouldn't see it, because Detective McMillen told him that she refused police protection. All he'd heard was the running stream that gurgled and splashed not ten feet from his car.

So now he sipped coffee and watched the house, completely unaware that the watching was done for the evening.

Chapter 16

It was a day when the flowers didn't smell so sweet, when the song of the birds seemed mournful, when the ocean appeared flat and lifeless.

▼▲▼

The night before they camped in the Kalalau Valley—two couples in their late twenties. They explored the Nā Pali Coast a half dozen times before, always hiking the Kalalau Trail, spending a night or two, depending on how *crowded* the campsites were, in each of the primary valleys—Hanakāpīʻai, Hanakoa, and Kalalau. This time, for a change, they decided to make it a kayak trip, entering the ocean at Kēʻē Beach, staying close to shore, exploring sea caves in the mornings, picking the prime secluded campsites just after lunch time, when the campers from the night before packed and left, and hours before the new arrivals from the adjoining valleys would come. That left the afternoons for exploring the valleys, walking deep into the forest along the stream beds, by the terraces of the old villages. They searched for hidden *heiau*, found fish ponds and taro paddies. It was a chance to see the remote spots they simply were too tired to seek out on previous trips, when hiking the Kalalau Trail, itself, sapped all their energy.

September was a good time to kayak, the summer surf still calm, less breakers, more rolling swells, plenty of green sea turtles to play with, and dolphins who leaped about. They'd been out a week now, enjoying the adventure immensely, and they weren't expecting any trouble.

That was yesterday.

Now, with tents folded, compacted tightly into unbelievably small nylon cases, food—in waterproof bags—and water stowed under the two seats in each kayak, backpacks with clothes and cooking utensils wedged into each narrow bow, the adventurers shoved off. They paddled smoothly around the rock slide that jutted into the water and followed the coastline west and south.

They spent the morning exploring a chain of sea caves and a *heiau* that wasn't on their topo, before finally reaching Honopū Valley, also known as The Valley of the Lost Tribe, around one o'clock.

Naki, the unofficial guide, was born on Kaua'i and hiked and camped much of the Nā Pali Coast with his father and older brother since the age of six. He scouted the beach. Julia, Naki's constant companion, fixed lunch, while Carrie and Todd erected the tents. Usually, they secured the kayaks to the tent poles, as much as they resented having to do it, but here, in Honopū Valley, it seemed unnecessary. They found no campers when they arrived and no footprints in the sand. The valley was narrow and not as interesting as Kalalau, or Awa'awapuhi and Nu'alolo 'Āina and Nu'alolo Kai beyond. The main reason they chose Honopū was that they expected to be alone.

After lunch they collected and sealed the trash in a plastic bag, then spent fifteen minutes soaking string with a strong insecticide, tying the saturated cord to each sack of food and to the garbage container, then hung the three pieces well off the ground on a tree branch, spacing the bundles far from the tree trunk, presenting the ants and cockroaches with an insurmountable task, impossible as long as they coated the string every eight hours. Next, they sorted through their backpacks and re-packed, taking snacks, flashlights, knives, insect repellent, sun block, a compass, a topo map of the valley, and a fifty-foot coil of orange nylon rope. Another ten minutes was spent making sturdy walking sticks from recently fallen tree limbs, applying sun block, strapping water bottles to their belts. They headed for the valley interior, first up a stretch of sand dunes, then along a shallow stream, Naki in the lead, followed by Julia, Carrie, and Todd.

▼▲▼

Ben was furious. After calling Mary Rice to schedule another interview, then meeting with Officer Santos Dizon, he'd pieced together how Carlton Crowley and his daughter were left unprotected and how they missed the opportunity to catch the night marcher. His anger barely diminished as he drove to Kapahi, third in the caravan of police vehicles headed for the Crowley estate. What bothered him most was that Mary Rice hadn't reported the incident. On the phone her shaken voice led him to ask what had happened. Only then did she talk about it—briefly, a few clipped sentences. He had to get to the bottom of that—what she was reluntant to tell even though her father's safety was at stake. Ben knew it had to do with the fire.

Ernie Dumas and Eros were in the first car, along with Officer Dizon, who sat sullen in the back seat. The Forensic Team, Kevin Thompson and his partner Julian Dee, followed in their army green station wagon. Although Ben could see that the two men from Forensic were talking animatedly, his thoughts had nothing to do with them. He was thinking about the night marcher, trying to measure the strength of the man's compulsion, wondering how he would react to being discovered. With John Gatston in New Zealand, Crowley was the only remaining target. Almost all serial killers were thwarted on one or two occasions as they hunted, sometimes scared off by the victim's screaming, other times a third party inadvertently showed up, and sometimes it just didn't feel right, and the killer simply retreated for the time being. Some other demon having filtered into his mind.

But this was different. There was no finding a different victim. Now for sure, he knew they knew his next victim.

When would the night marcher return? Ben knew it would be soon because there was nothing random about his vengeance, the trigger for him had gone off, and unlike most other pathological murderers, he didn't need another jolt before each killing. What Ben wondered now was, would the night marcher change his method? Would he panic? Would he do something out-of-character? He hoped not.

Up the red dirt driveway, dust flying to the sides like the wake of a speedboat, the three cars sped. When they pulled up in front of the Crowley house, Mary Rice was standing on the verandah, her hands clasped and held in front of her chest. Ben looked at the rocking chair, expecting to see Carlton Crowley. The empty chair moved slightly in the cool mountain breeze.

Mary came down from the front porch. She seemed a little overwhelmed to see so many policemen, but what seemed to worry her most was Eros. She hardly took her eyes off the dog.

Ben got out, clipped a portable two-way radio to his belt, then closed the car door. "Where's your father?" he asked.

"Resting in his bedroom. Please don't talk about this in front of him. He doesn't know."

"Mary, this is Officer Ernie Dumas."

"Ma'am."

Ben looked around for Officer Dizon, saw him still seated in the back seat of Ernie's station wagon and decided to let him stay there. "Ernie's the dog's handler. Eros is a tracking dog. He's provided us with some valuable clues."

"He looks…"

Ernie stepped forward. "He's just anxious, Ma'am. He knows he's at a crime scene. Here…" He put his hand on Mary's shoulder, then spoke to Eros. "*'Ohana*, Eros. *'Ohana*."

Eros stopped staring at Mary. The wooded area behind the house now had his attention.

Ben turned in that direction and saw a bright red northern cardinal flying from limb to limb. He turned back to Mary Rice.

Mary didn't say anything but gave Ben a timid look.

Ben pointed to the two men gathering equipment from the other station wagon. "Kevin and Julian are with Forensic." Ben took a deep breath. "I want you to show us where you saw the night marcher and explain exactly what he did."

"From where I saw him?"

"You and I will do that after. Right now show us where he was."

Mary led them around to the rear of the plantation home and walked along a narrow worn path in the tall grass to a spot about a hundred feet from the house.

"This is were he stopped. I saw him coming up from there." She looked ahead toward the thick forest and pointed. Then she turned and pointed to a second story window at the left corner of the house. "That's where I was. I started to scream."

"What did he do?"

"He stared at me for a minute, then he turned around and walked away."

"He didn't run?"

"No, he walked."

"And it was just him?"

"Yes. But there were five torches. When he turned they all swung around at the same time, like they were connected."

Ben tired to imagine the scene. He hadn't shared his guess about this with anyone, but did so now. "Could it have been a pipe of some sort, with the torches fastened along the length?"

Mary Rice said, "The torches seemed to float. I guess the pipe could have been painted black."

Ben nodded, then said, "Okay, Ernie. See if Eros can pick up anything."

Ernie gave Eros a command and the tracking dog sniffed the ground, walking a few feet in every direction. Then Eros began down the path. When it seemed as if the dog was sure he was locked onto a scent, he turned and barked once at his handler.

"He's got it." Ernie looked toward the forest. "Could be I'm in for a long hike. I'll radio you every five minutes or so."

"Fine."

Without instruction from Ben, the Forensic Team, one on each side of the path, started looking for evidence.

"Let's go back to the house," Ben said to Mary.

They stood side by side in front of her bedroom window on the second floor, watching Kevin and Julian scouring the ground along the path for clues.

The bedroom was large, at least twenty by thirty. A queen-sized canopy bed and a heavy low dresser were dwarfed by the baby grand piano that stood near the front window. The piano sparkled and smelled of fresh polish.

"The other patrolman, the one you didn't introduce, he looked like he'd done something wrong. He was supposed to be here last night, wasn't he?"

Ben looked at her. "He was here. I decided to put someone outside until your husband got home. He went to his car for a sandwich. By chance, I believe, the marcher came when the officer was gone."

Mary wet her lips.

Ben leaned against the wall and said, "Tell me about the fire."

"You know about that?"

"You should have told me before. When I found out that, that's when I posted a guard."

Mary Rice sat on her bed and explained. "It was two years ago. The fire started in my father's bedroom. He smoked then…we thought he'd fallen asleep. He managed to get out, but that section of the house was destroyed. It took the Fire Department half an hour to get here." She shrugged her shoulders.

"He lived alone then?"

Mary said he had.

"Who called it in if he fell asleep?"

Mary stammered, "Well…he…he did…"

"…so he hadn't fallen asleep?"

She sighed heavily as she played with the tassels on a pillow cover.

Ben stated, "I heard the police thought it might have been arson."

Mary looked at Ben for a long time. "The Fire Investigator thought something was thrown through the window. Apparently all the panes exploded out, except one."

"Something?"

"He guessed a rock wrapped inside something burning."

"Okay…the truth. Why didn't you tell me when I was here before?"

"I was afraid it would give my father another stroke. He gets so agitated when the fire comes up. You saw him when you mentioned night marchers. The doctor said the next stroke would…"

Ben pushed off of the wall. "And nothing ever came of it? They didn't find any other evidence?"

Mary shook her head.

He bit his lip while staring across the room. "Where were you when it happened?"

"I lived on O'ahu."

"Were you married?"

"What are you getting at?"

"Nothing…just curious."

Mary got up and walked over to the piano. She sat on the bench, thumbed through the songbook that was open on the wooden music rest.

Ben came over to the window next to the piano.

"Where's your husband? He make it back?"

Softly, "No…not until tonight."

There was a strange silence between them.

Mary turned finally, and said, "What are you thinking?"

Ben's lips made a small smacking sound before he spoke. He knew he did that often when he was preparing to skirt the truth. "I was just wondering if the night marcher might have gone away after what happened here two years ago. It would explain the gap."

"And my husband?"

Certainly a background check was in order, although he wouldn't tell Mary about it unless he found something or it led to a question he thought only she could answer. But would she? His reverie was interrupted when Ernie's voice came across the portable radiophone. "Came to a stream, we're following it downstream. Ten-four."

"Ten-four."

Ben felt Mary's eyes on him. He looked at her, still thinking that she knew much more about the fire than she led him to believe. He wondered if maybe she wasn't on O'ahu that night two years before. Had she seen a night marcher then as well? Or maybe she was at home…and her husband wasn't.

So maybe she wonders about her husband, too. It'd be a hard thing for her to admit.

…or she's just scared. Maybe she believes in ghosts.

▼▲▼

The cliffs on either side rose several thousand feet. From a distance the *pali* seemed cloaked in a green veil, picturesque and peaceful, but as the hikers moved deeper into the valley and closer to the steep rock formations, the curtain of trees and giant plants, thick vines and spongy mosses, gave the valley walls a dangerous, pre-historic, foreboding look. The smell here was strong of rotting wood, yet there was an underlying sweet smell, a mixture of the varieties of flowers and plants blended into a single fragrance. And still farther into the Valley of the Lost Tribe, the sunlight became more muted and there was no wind, which made sweat and grime cling to their skin. It was only two o'clock, yet it seemed like dusk, long shadows fell over the path, smiles disappeared from the clammy faces of the four friends.

"Footing's slippery here," Naki called out. "Careful."

The drizzle started the second they reached the top of the dunes back near the campsite. The mist made everything slick—the compressed dirt path, the logs they used to crossed over mud puddles, the beds of leaves of the guava trees and pandanus, especially the mosses that seemed to grow everywhere.

"How far are we going?" asked Julia, wiping her forehead with the base of her palm.

"Can't go much farther," answered Naki. "It gets pretty steep up here. I'd like to show you guys the waterfall. It's carved a crack into the rocks wide enough to squeeze into. It's a blast."

"What if we get stuck?"

"You won't get stuck." Naki turned and looked for Carrie and Todd. They had fallen back about a hundred feet, but they seemed all right.

Up ahead they came upon a large patch of tree ferns, which glistened in the light rain. The ferns were about three feet high, bright green, and delicately fluttered in the subtle breeze. It was hard to see the path because the ferns formed a miniature canopy over the forest floor. The sound of the waterfall could be heard in the distance.

"I'm cold," said Julia.

"Put on your sweatshirt," Naki offered.

They continued walking as Julia let the left strap of her backpack fall to the crook of her arm, then she removed it with her right hand, and swung the backpack around. Still walking, she pulled back the Velcro flap and dug inside for her sweatshirt.

Naki spied a patch of taro. Without turning he said, "Bet you these were planted a long time ago."

Just beyond the taro there was a huge fallen tree that bridged a swampy pool. Naki stopped and turned. "We have to cross the tree trunk to get to the waterfall. It's muck all along here, but usually drier at the other end of the log," he said to Julia, who finally extracted her sweatshirt.

Julia dropped her backpack and put on her sweatshirt while they waited for Carrie and Todd to catch up. When the other two hikers joined them, Naki told them about the waterfall and explained that they had to walk across the tree trunk to get there.

He warned, "Be careful…it may be wide, but it's covered with moss."

Using his right hand, he grabbed onto a nearby branch and hoisted himself up onto the large tree trunk. Then he turned to help Julia. Once she was up, he held onto an overhead vine and told her to scoot by so he could help Carrie and Todd.

Julia held her backpack by the straps in one hand. She should have been wearing it. She was almost on the other side of Naki when she slipped. Naki turned and reached for her, but too late.

"Ayyyyy," she yelled as she fell, dropping her pack, landing on her back, arms high in the air. Her feet soon disappeared into the bog.

"Julia!" screamed Carrie.

Todd rushed to the edge of the muddy pool.

"You okay?" shouted Naki, who scrambled to the end of the tree trunk and jumped onto the firmer footpath.

Naki threw his backpack to the ground and knelt over it, frantically pulling everything out until he found the coil of nylon rope.

"I can't move and I think I'm sinking!" Julia shouted.

Naki yelled to her. "We'll get you out. It's not quicksand…you won't sink."

Todd retrieved Julia's backpack and handed it to Carrie. He leaned forward and tried to reach Julia. He couldn't get closer than a few feet of her outstretched hand.

Naki came to the edge of the bog. He'd fashioned the end of the rope into a lasso. "Here." He threw the rope toward Julia and she caught it. "Just put it over your head, then around your chest and under your arms."

Julia did it. She seemed relieved. "I'm so glad we brought the rope."

Naki and Todd took hold and pulled. Julia's body raised a few inches but no farther.

"God…I'm stuck. My legs are caught on something."

"Can you move them?" cried Naki.

"No…no!"

Julia, "Oh, Julia!" Carrie began to cry.

"Julia, listen…can you feel from which direction you're being held?" Naki asked.

She sobbed, "I think it's my right foot." She sank lower into the swampy pool.

"But from where?…farther out or from the side?…or the back?"

"Pull again…I…I can't tell. But hurry, I feel like I'm sinking!"

They pulled.

"From the right side! From the right side!"

"Can you twist your ankle left?" Todd asked.

"No! Please…get me out! I'm sinking!"

Naki shouted to her, "Take it easy…it's not quicksand. There's no quicksand anywhere around here…we'll get you out, but quit moving around, you're making it harder."

Carrie tried to calm her friend. "You'll be okay, Julia. Just relax. We'll get you out."

Naki said to Todd, "It's probably a tree branch that's got her…might be wedged up against a rock. Let's try pulling from the side."

Todd said under his breath, hardly moving his lips, "What if it's a tree root?"

Naki glared and said, "Then I'll go back and get that big serrated knife and we'll cut the damn thing in half."

"Naki!"

They quickly side-stepped to the right, careful not to get too close to the edge of the bog and pulled. Nothing happened right away, but when Naki stepped onto a rock and had better footing and they pulled from a slightly upward angle, Julia's body began to emerge.

"That's it! That's it! I felt it come apart."

Naki smiled at her and he and Todd pulled her out.

And when her legs were almost clear of the swamp, Julia reached down to free herself from the thing around her foot. When she grabbed it, and saw it, her face froze in horror. Julia screamed and screamed and didn't stop. The whole valley echoed with her terrified voice. For what had held her foot was not a branch. It was a person's arm, partially decomposed, the soft, mushy crook of the arm wrapped around her ankle. Ripped tendons and blood vessels and rubbery flesh hung from the torn appendage.

The others stood frozen, mouths agape.

Julia screamed until she lost her voice.

▼▲▼

At four, when Officer Dumas and Eros were more than two miles away from the plantation home and the Forensic Team gathered shreds of burnt cloth, presumably from the night marcher's torches, the telephone rang at the Crowley home and Mary Rice excused herself to answer it.

Ben was about to ask her if she new Ray Kuali'I or Nelson Ala'ipaleile. He went over the phrasing of his questions carefully in his mind, not wanting to lead her on. He wanted the truth, but he wanted it to come freely. He knew she had much more to tell. But no matter what she said with regard to his two suspects, Ben was headed to find the professor as soon as they wrapped things up here.

Mary Rice returned and said the call was for Ben.

He followed her into the library and picked up the receiver and listened to Chief Johnson tell him of a Zodiac touring the western coast seeing four frantic campers waving and shouting. Then he told Ben what the four people hiking in The Valley of the Lost Tribe discovered. Ben closed his eyes. He felt sick to his stomach.

▼▲▼

It was a day when you realized you had grown up much too soon. When you wondered if you could face tomorrow.

A day when you wished you were still small enough to carry.

Chapter 17

The helicopter swung around the last jutting cliff before Honopū Valley. Ben saw three Zodiacs just beyond the waterline, looking like a small pod of beached whales. Farther back, near the base of the large sand dunes, was another helicopter, a large white and orange Coast Guard rescue craft, large rotors still and sagging. He could make out police officers carrying things over the sand dunes, but they disappeared into the valley before he could determine what they were carrying.

The pilot sent a quick radio message to the Coast Guard helicopter, then notified Ben and the others that they were going to land. He pointed to a spot about a hundred yards from the other helicopter.

During the descent, Ben wondered again how he'd guessed that the night marcher chose The Valley of the Lost Tribe. It bothered him from the minute they'd lifted off from Līhu'e Airport. He assumed all three men were there, but so far all the information they had was from that first report of a single body. And as the giant rotors brought up a storm of sand, he realized the body didn't necessarily have to be that of one of the landowners, although, to him, that possibility was unlikely.

They were told it was a man's body and a quick check of Kaua'i's Missing Ps for the last month yielded a single person. A woman in her early twenties.

They made a soft landing and waited for the pilot to signal that it was okay to get out. The glass doors opened and Ben, Ernie Dumas, Eros, Kevin, and Julian scrambled out—the men duck-walked away from the helicopter and Eros crawled, mimicking Ernie's squat stance.

Ben looked out to sea briefly, then checked his watch. It was almost five-fifteen, only two hours more of light.

Ernie said to Ben, pointing, "That's my sergeant, Vic Medeiros."

Patrol Sergeant Victor Medeiros walked toward them. He stopped, knelt in front of Eros, and stroked the dog's chest.

Eros licked the sergeant's face.

Ernie whispered to Ben, "He handled Eros before his promotion."

Medeiros straightened and offered his hand to Ben. "McMillen, we haven't met…Vic Medeiros."

They grasped hands, Ben said, "Thanks for loaning me Ernie."

Medeiros waved him off.

"What do you have, so far?"

"Not pretty and not easy. I ordered in some night lights from the highway crews." The sergeant gestured to the dune and Ben could see that the police officers carried long poles and black boxes and portable Honda generators. "The Chief wants us here until we've recovered everything. Shit…he even sent tents and supplies."

Ben nodded and gestured for the sergeant to continue.

"Just a few body parts. We have to hook 'em with poles and pull them out of the swamp. We have two right arms, so there's at least that many. Thank God the bog's not that big."

Ben turned to Kevin and Julian. "You guys start along the beach…check the tide pools first, then work your way back to the swamp. How far back is it, Vic?"

"About a quarter mile…maybe a little more."

"Okay if I give Ernie and Eros…"

"Hey…it's your case…they work for you on this one."

Ben thanked him and told Ernie to take Eros back to the swamp. "Let him smell the fish hook necklace and see what happens. My guess is the rain and wind have taken their toll…you may just be along for the ride."

"I understand," said Ernie. "Eros, *mai.*"

To the sergeant, "Where are the hikers?"

Vic Medeiros pointed to the far end of the beach, where Ben hadn't looked before. Sheltered against the rocks were two brightly colored tents, one orange, one lime-green. Ben saw two people sitting on a piece of driftwood and another one who looked like he was trying to get a fire going.

"Where's the girl who fell in…take her to the hospital?"

Vic answered, "Nope. She said she was okay. Wanted to stay with the others. When we got here, she'd bathed and changed clothes. She's upset, but nothing wrong physically. You go talk with them. I'll be back by the operation. See you there."

"Thanks, Sarg."

By the time Ben reached the hikers, the beach fire was going.

"Are you guys okay?"

The young man who started the fire said they were. "Just a little shaken up, that's all."

"I'm Ben."

"I'm Naki."

Carrie and Todd introduced themselves.

Naki added, "Julia, she's the one who fell in…she's sleeping." He pointed to the orange tent.

"You guys saw it all?"

"Uh huh," nodded Naki.

"Let her sleep, then. Tell me what happened."

Naki assumed the spokesperson's role and described the entire ordeal.

"Then what?"

"We helped Julia back here, and while she bathed in the ocean, we spotted a Zodiac heading back to Hanalei. We flagged them down. If we missed them, might have been tomorrow morning. He had to leave us to use his radio…to get around the northern cliffs. He came back with the police, though, along with two other Zodiacs."

Ben was quiet.

Todd said, "If Julia hadn't fallen in, you might never have found the body."

Ben took a deep breath. "How long have you been out here?"

Carrie said, "A week."

"Here?"

"No, we've been kayaking along the coast. Just got to Honopū today."

"See anything out of the ordinary?" Ben frowned, shaking his head. "Sorry…besides what you found in the swamp."

The hikers each smiled weakly.

"No," answered Naki. "Like what?"

"Like flaming torches moving around at night."

Carrie huddled closer to Todd.

They shook their heads, eyes wide open, mouths agape, like he was telling ghost stories around the campfire.

"Late at night…see anyone? Hear any boats?"

They hadn't.

Ben stood, jotted down their names and addresses. He asked them if they were going to stay.

Naki said, "It's up to Julia...but if we do, we'll probably go on to the next valley...it's a little too spooky here."

Then Todd asked, "Can you tell us what this is about? The other cop wouldn't."

"Some people have disappeared...we believed they were taken here...somewhere along the coast."

"You mean there's more."

"Maybe...but if there are, they're all back there. You won't be finding..."

Carrie and Todd nodded solemnly.

Naki played with the beach fire, head down.

Ben told them to get some rest.

"Are you guys gonna be here all night?" asked Carrie.

"I expect so." He could tell from her expression that she felt a little safer. "You need anything at all, or if Julia changes her mind about staying, we'll be happy to help. We can fly you out of here, probably strap your kayaks," he pointed to them, "to the chopper."

"Mahalo, we'll see," Carrie said. "I think we'll be okay."

When Ben came upon the swamp, dusk was setting in and the scene looked like a Hollywood set on a night shoot. A half dozen gigantic floodlights beamed down onto the murky pool of mud and slime. Generators hummed incessantly. An orange Coast Guard life raft seemed stuck in the muck near a large fallen tree. It was a temporary repository for body parts as two police officers, who stood on the edge of the bog, legs sunken to the knees, systematically dragged long aluminum poles back and forth along the bottom. *Snagged* along the bottom described their actions better than *dragged*, as the bog was filled will rotted roots, tree limbs, and rocks from landslides long ago. There were many false alarms.

Sergeant Medeiros stood next to the fallen tree, looking like a film director, hands on his hips when they weren't pointing to the next section of swamp to be searched. Several officers, covered in yellow plastic suits and black gloves, each wearing a mask over his nose and mouth, were sorting body parts on three white body bags, fully unzipped, laid out in a row. The body bag closest to Ben was almost complete. It was a gristly sight, puffy legs and arms, all were ripped from their sockets, the torso, black and blue and green, swollen as well, but showing no signs of major wounds. The victim's head was another story. It appeared that the entire left side of the skull was exposed, caved in. Ben assumed that was the cause of death, repeated blows to the head with a heavy object. He envisioned a sledge hammer, not a lava rock, something with a handle for leverage to create such force. The other open bags contained body parts as well, a few appendages, one head, but no torsos, as yet.

Two strange images came to Ben. First, an about-to-be-born infant floating in a sack of amniotic fluid, but not looking hopeful about the next phase of life, looking fearful and unsure. The beginning. Then the vision of a full-grown human in a transparent body bag, surrounded by puddles of brackish swamp water, arms and legs twisted and torn, the victim of life's battles of which being bludgeoned to death was the last. The end.

Although, as Ben shivered and his shoulders rose as if to protect his neck from the cold, he had to admit that even his ancestors punished transgressors of the *kapu* system with fatal blows to the head.

The noise of the cliff birds brought him out of his reverie. He couldn't see them, but envisioned them perched in small crevices, watching the floodlighted scene below.

A short woman, wearing khaki pants and a long sleeve white shirt, latex gloves, and a wide-brim hat, knelt next to the second collection of body parts, examining the remains. Here there was a head and an arm and a leg. The woman was measuring the depression on the left side of the second victim's face.

Sergeant Medeiros said to Ben, "Medical Examiner…Doc Brundy.

The doctor kept to her work and Ben figured it would be better to question her later, after everything was recovered.

"Find out anything new from the hikers?" asked Medeiros.

"No…they fell into this…a million to one."

The sergeant nodded, then eyed the pond. "Getting pretty gruesome. The men think they're down there whole, but the mud's so thick and the bodies so soft, when they hook something and try to bring it to the surface, it comes apart. We're matching them best we can for now by their clothes." He paused and looked up at the moon, which was a faint slice overhead. "Chief Johnson said there'd be three."

"Right." Ben rubbed his chin, then looked back toward the beach and saw the Forensic team slowly working their way back to the swamp. When he passed them before they hadn't found anything. Now he saw they had flashlights out. They wouldn't find much that way, but even if they covered another fifty feet in the dark, it would be fifty less to cover in the morning. "Where's Ernie?"

Medeiros pointed deeper into the valley. "When Ernie presented Eros with the necklace, I'll be damned if he didn't pick up something…led Ernie across the tree and toward the cliffs. I sent two officers with them."

Ben thought about the fact that the last disappearance was five days before. The scent should be gone. "Means he must have been here recently…"

Sergeant Medeiros slowly lifted his head and looked around the valley walls. His expression thoughtful, eyes unblinking. He pulled his damp shirt away from his chest.

Ben also peered into the gathering dark, wondering as Medeiros probably was if the murderer was up there somewhere, watching with macabre fascination. Once more Ben felt goose bumps on his neck and arms.

The Captain asked, "You ever see anything like this?"

"Not while I was awake."

Medeiros solemnly nodded, probably thinking about his own nightmares. "Think he comes back here…I mean without a body…just to…you know, guys like this are drawn to it…they want to relive it."

Ben wet his lips, then rubbed his arms. "Could be. Could be that he doesn't kill them right away."

"Tortures them?"

"Who knows, but there don't seem to be any burns or bruises on the remains…except, of course, the crushed skull on the first recovery. But maybe he just leaves them tied up for a while…lets the roaches and ants drive them crazy."

Both men heard the vacuum sound of something breaking the grasp of the mud. Something big.

"Jesus!" said one of the officers who was dragging the bottom of the swamp. He threw his pole onto dry ground and went to help the man who hooked the body now suspended near the surface. They struggled to the rescue raft, carrying a corpse only missing a leg.

This body wasn't bloated as much as the other recovered body parts. Ben knew from the man's size and his hair that he was staring at the remains of Charles Bowden. "Bowden," he said softly.

The sergeant took out a small notepad and wrote.

It was dark now and the cries of the cliff-dwelling birds rang out louder, echoing deep into the valley. Ben thought for them this must be getting better than the filming of Jurassic Park.

"Think I'll see what Ernie's got. You have a flashlight I can borrow?"

The sergeant called to one of the patrolmen, who had helped carry the corpse of Charles Bowden to the third body bag.

The officer came over and handed his flashlight to Ben. "Middle's off, up is narrow, back is wide beam."

"Thanks."

"Take this," Medeiros said. He gave Ben his two-way radio. "Be careful."

Ben hooked the radio to his belt, then climbed onto the fallen tree trunk, shined the broad light from his feet along the length of the log, then slowly back. Pointing the flashlight down, switching to the narrow beam, he placed his left foot forward. Then the right, carefully, at first, then realizing the tree trunk was pretty wide, that walking it wasn't too difficult as long as you stayed cleared of the patches of moss, he quickly crossed. At the end, he shined the light down to the ground, satisfied himself that it was solid earth, jumped off, switched to the wide beam, and headed off along the trail.

Five minutes later he spotted flashlight beams off to his right and about one hundred and fifty feet above the valley floor. He was glad they were flashlights and not torches.

He heard Eros bark. Then it was silent except for the birds, whose shrill shrieks resumed when the echo of Eros's barking faded into the night.

The trail forked and Ben took the right. Soon the footing became slippery with moss covered rocks, bulging roots, and slick banana leaves. Ben shined his light upward and saw at least two dozen banana trees. He knew he was headed for a *heiau* or a terrace where villagers once lived and farmed.

The trail consisted of many switch-backs, each no longer than thirty feet. Directly above, he could see the beams of light from the flashlights, which, for the most part, remained in one spot. When he was within a hundred feet, Eros started barking. He heard Ernie's voice. Ben shouted back and hurried up the remaining three switch-backs. The trail led to the base of a platform about twenty by forty feet. The sides were made of piled lava rocks, black but scarred with white circles, resembling the skin of a humpback whale, pocked with a colony of barnacles. The surface of the platform was dirt, compacted and smooth, except for one spot, where a six-foot wide circular depression sank a foot into the ground.

"Glad it's you," said Ernie. "Look at this."

Ben nodded to the two policemen, who were seated on a lava rock wall, each paying more attention to the bananas they ate than Ben. Eros was pacing along the perimeter of the structure.

"What'd you find?"

Ernie held up an evidence bag and shined his light against it.

It took Ben's eyes a few seconds to adjust, but soon he saw the fish hook necklace.

Before he could comment, Ernie handed the plastic bag to Ben, and promptly took out another one. "That's the one we brought. This...we found here...in there."

The second bag contained another fish hook necklace.

Ben followed Ernie's flashlight beam to the round depression on the ground.

Ben asked, "Footprints?"

"We made it up here at dusk. Didn't see any. Besides...it rains here every-day...the clouds are low, sometimes they choke the valley with fog and mist for hours."

"Eros came straight here?"

"Yeah."

"How old do you think the scent is?"

"Day or two, no more."

"So he came back."

"Maybe it's part of his ritual. Maybe he didn't kill Bowden until yesterday."

Ben told Ernie they recovered Bowden's body and added that he wasn't in as bad shape as what was recovered previously. Then he turned to the two officers. "You guys go back and show the Forensic guys the way up here."

After they left, Ernie asked Ben what he thought the lava rock structure was.

"Probably a family *heiau*..." and as his voice trailed away, he wondered if there was another reason why the killer was there four days after taking Charles Bowden. Maybe to bury someone else. Not Gatston, not Crowley. Was there another tier of intended victims in the family tree?

All along Ben knew it was probable that they wouldn't find out about each disappearance right after it happened, but a few days later. Maybe even a week or more.

They passed the Forensic team and the two officers on their way back to the swamp. In the distance the brilliantly lighted scene around the bog seemed more surreal than before. When they reached the giant tree trunk, Eros jumped up and dashed across. Ernie and Ben took their time. Ben jumped off the tree trunk. He noticed the medical examiner talking with Sergeant Medeiros. Ben and Ernie joined them.

"Ben, this is Doc Brundy."

Ben eyed her slime-covered gloved hands and nodded, saving a handshake for another time. "Doc."

The Medical Examiner was no more than five-two, overweight, her face was red with tiny blood vessels, which seemed magnified by the glare of the floodlights. Her hat hung from a cord and covered her neck and back. A wet mess of plastered hair snaked across her scalp and forehead. And she had a huge mole at the top left-center of her forehead, the kind that Ben always wondered why people didn't just have removed.

Ben looked at the body bags. The first bag was zipped shut. The second corpse was still missing a left arm, and Bowden, laying in the third bag, was without his left leg.

"What do you have?"

"This is preliminary. All three suffered blunt force trauma left side…severe cranial damage. I estimate there were multiple blows to each. Can't determine trace evidence out here, especially with all the mud and moss and infestation lodged in the trauma areas. I do think the victims were on their sides when they were struck. And on something firm, but not a rock. There's damage on the opposite side of the skull, smaller, like it absorbed a lot of the force of the blows. Did find some wood splinters there."

"Time of death?" asked Ben.

"You a comedian?"

"Uh…no…I…"

"Save it, just yanking you." She smiled.

Ben added crooked teeth to her description.

"Can't pinpoint it quite yet, but they were in the swamp for varying times. One, I'd say about ten to fourteen days. Another, about a week, maybe more. The last one, he was far younger by the way, maybe three to five days."

Ben recited the three men's ages. "These bodies close to that?"

"Sounds about right," said Brundy.

"Another arm!" came a shout.

Ben turned and saw an arm, more bloated and seemingly more blackened than the other recovered appendages, caught on the hook of the officer's pole. He watched as the policeman swung the arm around and lowered it into the rescue raft. Then, another officer carefully picked up the arm—water ran out of the shoulder joint—and carried the appendage to the body bag in the middle. He placed it where the corpse's right arm should have been.

The Medical Examiner, Ben, and Sergeant Medeiros walked over. Ben looked over his shoulder and saw Ernie sitting on a rock, petting Eros between the ears, the dog handler's eyes vacant. He had seen enough.

They formed a small circle around the second victim. Ben wondered if it was Frobert or Churchwell. The Medical Examiner bent and studied the arm for a few seconds.

Prematurely, Ben thought, Dr. Brundy stood, her left hand cupped and held closely to her mouth, but not touching. She took a deep breath, looked at Medeiros for a long time, then slowly shifted to Ben. "You see it?"

Ben, who studied the doctor's expression for a few seconds, knelt and examined the arm. His eyes traveled from the torn shoulder joint, to the swollen elbow, to the twisted wrist, which took his breath away for a few seconds, then to the bloated hand and the fingers, where the skin separated and curled away from the fingernails.

"Shit!" Ben exclaimed, then looked at Doc Brundy for confirmation.

"What? What?" the Patrol Sergeant implored.

The Medical Examiner nodded and said plainly, "The forearm's twisted a hundred and eighty degrees...the palm's facing out. It's a left arm."

Rarely do three corpses have four left arms, even when night marchers are involved.

Chapter 18

By one in the morning the four corpses were recovered and transported to the Coast Guard helicopter. Right after the rescue helicopter departed with the Medical Examiner on board, Ben worked out a plan with Patrol Sergeant Medeiros.

It was agreed there was no access to the valley from the cliffs surrounding it. The beach was the only way in. So when the Forensic team finished, four officers were to remain behind, positioned on top of the sand dune at the extreme northeastern end of the valley, obscured from view by rocks and a stand of palms, posing as campers if they were discovered.

The hikers, who found the first body part, agreed to leave in the morning. They promised not to talk about their episode. Naki said they'd be home in three days and that he'd be at his house in Wainiha with Julie and could reach the others if need be.

Chief Johnson was contacted. He reported that four men were watching the Crowley estate. Since Crowley was safe, he told Ben to go back to Gatston's place and get dental records.

Ben spent a half hour with one of the Zodiac captains learning all he could about inflatable craft. Most important, he determined there were a dozen on the Island. Captain Zodiac, where the man Ben interviewed worked, was the Island's largest Nā Pali excursion tour operator. They had ten rafts, four that were in use, six were undergoing standard maintenance—usually, they never had more than six operating at one time. Captain Zodiac was located in Hanalei, the maintenance boat shed was at Wai'oli Beach Park at the far western end of Hanalei by the mouth of the Wai'oli Stream. Fairly close to the Churchwell and Frobert homes.

The other commercial Zodiac was owned by Nā Pali Explorer, which operated out of Kīkīaola Harbor, mid-way between Waimea and Kekaha on Kaua'i's southwestern coast. Close enough to Bowden's plantation and less than two miles from Gatston's. Nā Pali Explorer's Zodiac was Hurricane class, twenty-six feet bow to stern, eight-foot beam, with a fiberglass bottom that made beach landings much easier. Ben learned it was powered by twin 140 hp Johnsons and could reach The Valley of the Lost Tribe in an hour from Kekaha. If the load was two people, and not a tour group of eight and a captain, the time was cut to forty minutes. After the Captain Zodiac driver described the fuel capacity and other facts, Ben was convinced the killer used a Zodiac. And then, when he was told that the only other Zodiac on the Island was donated by Captain Zodiac to the Community College for 'field' trips, Ben began to think about Nelson Ala'ipaleile.

He thanked the Zodiac captain, then walked the beach and found Ernie Dumas asleep under a palm with Eros laying next to him in a pose that was best described as Sphinxlike, motionless but eyes fully open and shoulders up.

In a soft voice, Ben said, "*'Ohana.*"

He heard Ernie laugh, then saw him rise to his elbows.

"Ready to go?"

Ben took a last look at the valley. "Guess so."

They crossed the beach, heading for the helicopter that brought them, and awoke the pilot, who was sleeping across the rear seats. The pilot said he'd be ready in a few minutes, walked to the ocean, scooped some sea water, washed his face, trotted back, and hopped aboard. He went over the flight checklist as the rotors came up to full speed. Then he tucked the clipboard under his seat, signaled thumbs up, and they lifted off, skimming the water, rising slowly, banking slightly to port in a steep climb. Rising over the valley, Ben tried to get a glimpse of the bog, but in the early morning dark all he saw was the reflection of the quarter moon dancing off the rocks in a nearby stream.

They rose over the *pali*, across Waimea Canyon, then made a straight line for Līhu'e Airport, and landed twenty-five minutes later. The airport resembled a ghost town. Now, to Ben, everything was ghosts.

Ben's plan—to his room to sleep for a few hours, then to Līhu'e Community College. He wasn't sure how he'd handle the professor. Confront him, or scare him into making a mistake. Right now he had no proof, just circumstantial stuff, not anything you could classify as evidence. Hunches, educated guesses, gut feel.

After that…if he hadn't arrested Ala'ipaleile, to Waimea, to see if it was possible to contact Gatston in New Zealand. If not, then tracking down his dental records.

Sleep did not come easily. Only thoughts of the fourth victim did.

▼▲▼

At 6:45 a.m., Ben awoke to a pounding sound on his door. He jerked up, not remembering where he was. Then he heard Mike Gamos's voice urging him to 'wake up.'

He got out of bed, slipped into his pants, then opened the door.

Gamos was all smiles.

"Feeling better?"

"Yeah., but you look like shit." Gamos came in and sat on the chair by the window. "That Hawaiian remedy really worked."

Ben gave him a wry look.

"Didn't think I'd try it, did you?"

"Not really."

"On the way here the Chief filled me in about last night, but not much else. Where to first?"

"We're going to find Nelson Ala'ipaleile."

Gamos looked puzzled.

"The professor at Līhu'e CC." Ben told him about his conversation with the professor, the fish hook collection, the suggestion of the bike route, and the sabotage to his brakes. Then his theory on accessing the Valley of the Lost Tribe by Zodiac. "I found out a few hours ago the Community College has a Zodiac."

"They do? So he's our prime suspect…"

Ben put on his socks and shoes and hunted for a clean shirt. "I think so. But we have to careful with him…it's circumstantial…we make him nervous, maybe he slips up. But if nothing pans out there, we're going to Gatston's place again, look around more carefully."

"Chief said Gatston was in New Zealand. He thinks it's someone else."

"I didn't see Gatston off, did you?"

"Okay…we'll check it out. Then what?"

"If we still have 'then what' after that, we're in trouble…means there's a lot more potential victims."

"From that chart we read at the museum?"

"No. Those are the five families who divided the major holdings. What we'd have if the killer's pattern isn't confined to them, are all the families who received any land. And my guest is that there were quite a few. Just means the killer is working from the top down."

Gloria Mendonca fixed breakfast to go—scrambled eggs with bits of Portuguese sausage tucked into a pocket pita and a Thermos of coffee.

They drove down to Kūhiō Highway, sun directly in their eyes, and turned right. Traffic was light and there were puddles everywhere. Gamos commented that it rained hard in the early morning, even thought he'd heard thunder. Through a mouthful of egg and pita, Ben said he hadn't heard a thing. They stopped by the station for a few minutes, Gamos wanted to change into his 'work' shoes, and Ben called the Medical Examiner. Doc Brundy came to the phone, let Ben know in no uncertain terms that she hadn't slept. She confirmed her preliminary finding that each death was the result of several massive blows to the head. She extracted bits of black rock from each wound.

"You mean beaten with a lava rock?"

"Exactly. And with more time, I might even be able to tell you from what part of the Island the rocks came."

"Rocks? Different rocks, or a single weapon made from one?" Ben asked.

"I think different. So far I haven't found any blood that's been mixed with the other victims. But it's hard to tell with a rock…different wound sizes don't necessarily mean a different weapon. You can hold the same rock a number of ways."

"Any burn marks around the head wounds?"

"Waiting for you to ask that. Yeah, there were. But they came from sticking something like a lighted torch into the fracture. Found pieces of cloth…old cloth…like tapa."

The bile rose in Ben's throat.

"You still there?"

Ben swallowed carefully, the taste in his throat horrible.

"Never heard of a cop passing out over the phone, usually they gotta be here to see it before they keel over."

Ben composed himself. He wasn't going to explain to her that it was the tie to his Hawaiian heritage that made him sick to his stomach. "What about a more exact time of death?"

"Working on that now. Be a day or so before I have that. Assuming I don't sleep."

Ben suggested she take a few hours off, to which she mumbled something he couldn't understand. "Anything else?"

Doc Brundy answered, "Yeah. The last body we found, the one we didn't expect…I'm pretty positive that it was the first one dumped there. The body was underwater at least two weeks. If you remember…most of the skin on the face already separated from the facial bones and we didn't recover much of it. You won't ID number four from his face. So anyway, if it helps your case, number four was probably the first one murdered."

"OK. Thanks." The conversation ended with Ben saying he'd call back that afternoon.

Mike Gamos came up from the basement locker room, just as Ben came out of the bathroom, and they signed out. Ben related his conversation with Doc Brundy as they headed for the car.

The building marked Staff I was unlit inside and the door locked. Gamos remarked that it wasn't eight yet. Both of them leaned against the stucco wall that faced north, keeping the bright sunlight out of their eyes. They talked about Gamos's ulcer.

After a minute, Ben was about to suggest that he wait for the professor and Gamos check with administration for Nelson Ala'ipaleile's schedule, when a tall bearded man approached. He carried a brown satchel in one hand and a stack of bulging manila folders in the other.

"Good mornin'. Waiting for me?"

Gamos straightened and introduced himself and Ben.

"Jack Biggins, teach botany and some chem."

Ben said, "Nelson Ala'ipaleile's been helping us with a case. We have a few more questions for him."

"Oh. Sorry to disappoint you, but I don't think he'll be in this week. He's taking the archeology club on a dig."

Gamos asked, "Have they left already?"

"Not sure. Check inside with administration. They'll know his schedule."

The detectives thanked him and started to leave, when Ben stopped and asked, "Maybe you can help with something else."

The teacher finished unlocking the front door, pocketed his keys, then turned around. "If I can."

"We're interested in the college's Zodiac…still have it?"

"Sure."

"Who uses it?"

"Who doesn't?"

Not the answer Ben hoped for. He gestured for Biggins to embellish.

"Just about every science department does. I do, Biology does, Nelson, Hawaiian Studies..."

"And where do you take it?"

"Me?"

"Everybody."

"Wailua River, the reefs along the southeastern shore, Nā Pali, Waimea River, Hanalei, just about everywhere."

"Would Nelson have it for the dig?"

"Depends where he's taking them. If it's Nā Pali, then obviously he'll need the Zodiac."

"Okay, thanks."

Biggins nodded, checked his pocket for his keys, and proceeded inside.

The detectives headed across the walkway to the Learning Resource Center, which housed Administration. The wet grass shined in the morning sunlight. Ben spotted the gardeners again, this time raking flower beds.

The office was lighted and the door open. Three people were inside. When the detectives approached the counter, one of the women got up from her desk and greeted them. She appeared to be no older than twenty, petite, big smile, and Ben thought probably a mixture of Japanese and Hawaiian.

Ben waited as Mike Gamos introduced them. Then Gamos asked Nelson Ala'ipaleile's schedule. The woman went to another desk and checked a thick set of papers on a clipboard.

"He's taking eight students on a dig."

"Where?" asked Ben.

"Miloli'i Valley and Nu'alolo Kai."

"Not Honopū...The Valley of the Lost Tribe?"

"Not according to this."

"When do they leave?"

"They're leaving this afternoon...says here, at three," she looked beyond Ben and frowned.

Ben looked over his shoulder and saw a student take a seat. His hair was long and stiff, his denim shorts were ragged, the front pocket liners showed, the tank top he wore had a big hole in the front and was dirty. The student's book bag looked like he'd dragged it through a cane field during fire and rain.

Ben smiled to himself, then turned his attention to the woman. "Does Ala'ipaleile have any classes this morning?"

She walked to another desk, opened a loose-leaf notebook, flipped through the first few pages, then dragged her finger down the page of a chart in a plastic protective cover. "None today."

"Any idea where he is?"

"Probably at home." She shrugged.

"Can we have his address?"

The woman gave him a discerning look. "I want to help you," she said, "but I have to check. Just a minute, okay?"

She went into an office, spoke with another woman. This woman, heavy, in her fifties, thick black hair with prominent gray streaks, shifted to her left, and looked through the glass at them.

Ben heard the first woman say 'police detectives.'

Shortly, both women emerged from the office, the older one in the lead. "Is there any problem?"

Ben answered, "No…Nelson's helping us on a case…we just have some very important questions to ask him."

"I see. Well, Professor Ala'ipaleile lives in Lāwa'i, on Kōloa Road…just a little south of Kaumuali'i Highway."

Mike Gamos stepped forward, "If we miss him, will they be leaving for the dig from here?"

"Yes. They take the school van and the rubber raft."

"And the raft is where?"

The young woman chimed in and told them it was behind the Campus Center at the end of the parking lot.

Ben said, "Mahalo."

The young woman said, "*He hale kou.*"

He smiled and nodded. There was no Hawaiian equivalent for 'your welcome.' *He hale kou*, meant 'you have a house'—you are always welcome here.

When they were outside Gamos asked, "His house?"

Ben nodded.

They drove twenty mph over the speed limit, zipping past the Kōloa turnoff. Near the intersection of 50 and 530 in Lāwa'i, Gamos pointed out that Ala'ipaleile lived just down the road.

The professor's house, which was white with a black shingle roof, was perched on top of a hill, barely visible from the road. They parked at the bottom of Ala'ipaleile's steep driveway, blocking the exit, and walked up. The driveway, red dirt and some crushed rock, snaked through banana and guava trees. On level ground, at the top of the driveway, they found no car. No tire marks, either. Just puddles and yellow leaves. There was no answer to Ben's knock on the front door, then he tried the handle, found it unlocked, opened the door a crack, and called out for the professor. No one appeared to be home. Gamos said he'd make a quick check around back. While he did, Ben peered inside, but he decided not to enter.

Gamos came back a few minutes later, held his palms out and up and suggested they try again on the way back from Gatston's.

Ben radioed in and asked for a uniform patrol to watch the professor's house. He was told there wasn't anyone available. With the stakeout in the western valley, and a bad traffic accident just north of Līhuʻe, they were down to clerks only. Ben asked for someone to go there later, when things were back to normal.

The dispatcher asked him to define 'normal.'

Speeding through Kalāheo and Hanapēpē, soon they were a few miles from the dirt road next to the Waimea River. The discussion focused mainly on the fourth body. They had no choice but to hope that the fourth set of remains belonged to Gatston. If the killer's pattern wasn't bound to the original five families…

Ben pointed and Gamos turned right, leaving the paved highway. The rain made the dirt road barely passable. Gamos kept the left wheel on the right edge of the road while the right side of the car skirted the fringe of the cane field, where the plants weren't as high nor as thick. Ben knew if there were remnants of old cane, chopped down low to the ground, that a blowout was a strong possibility. A blown tire would cost them valuable time.

"Got a spare?"

Gamos grinned, "Yeah, but it's flat."

Up from sea level, climbing onto the plateau above the river, several white egret drifted inland along the banks, some braking to perch in the trees, which in turn, seemed to encourage a few resting egret to take flight. Quite comically, the arriving birds appeared to be bumping those roosting to flight.

The sun was bright now and the Waimea River glimmered. In places it sparkled so much that it was impossible to look at the water for more than a few seconds. At a crest in the road, where the view was unobstructed in all directions except west, Ben saw there was but a single cloud. Looking below, he followed its huge shadow as it floated across the cane fields.

"Gonna be a hot one," said Gamos.

Downhill for a mile, then the fork in the river, and at last, the Gatston triangular PRIVATE PROPERTY sign on the narrow metal gate.

Ben got out, swung open the gate, let Gamos through, then closed the entry. Driving up to the main house, Ben answered questions about his last visit, saving his description of Teroro for last. Gamos asked if the caretaker was a suspect.

"Don't think so."

"What if Gatston's body is number four?"

Nothing from Ben but a long deep sigh, reminding himself that number four was number one.

They parked, got out, and headed for the barn.

Ben shouted the caretaker's name. There was no answer. Together they slid open the barn door and were immediately hit by the smell of manure.

He saw Gamos cover his nose and mouth.

"Sorry, should have warned you."

"Jeeez. Is there a body in here?"

Horrified at that thought, Ben admitted it had come to mind on his first visit. But he made a basic mistake—believed Gatston was in New Zealand, just because he was told that.

After opening the barn doors and latching them completely back, they found a shovel and a pitchfork and went through the piles of straw and dung in the stalls. Sweat soaked their clothes. The smell made them gage and cough, but they found no body. Ben climbed up the ladder to the loft. There was nothing there either.

Outside, they leaned against the corral fence.

Ben snorted when he asked Gamos if this was a bad as the cane field fire.

"Much worse."

Ben spied a water pump.

Gamos saw it, too.

Both raced for it.

After soaking themselves and resting for a few minutes, Ben suggested searching for Teroro at his cabin. They followed the path behind the house, which headed in the direction that Teroro indicated when Ben asked him on his first visit 'where do you live?' The trail was smooth and dry, no trees nearby, plenty of sunshine. There a refreshing wind and the sun felt hot on Ben's neck and shoulders—his clothes were almost dry. The path made a wide, looping turn west, then headed directly to the river. Ahead in a grove of trees, and almost hidden among them, was a modest plank cabin. It appeared to be in good shape, maybe thirty feet long and twenty feet deep, with a door in the center and two flanking windows midway to the corners.

"Teroro." Ben waited. He called it again. Still no answer.

Gamos said, "Let's have a look inside...if it's unlocked."

Although Ben knew it was wrong, an illegal search of the caretaker's cabin didn't seem as bad as entering the professor's house without a search warrant. He could rationalize it any number of ways—he wasn't positive this was the caretaker's cabin, the suspicion of foul play...but he didn't feel good about it.

There was one wooden step, on which Gamos stood as he pounded against the door. Then he pulled on the latch and the door opened. Ben followed him inside. It was dark, but after a few seconds their eyes adjusted and they began to look around. The cabin had three rooms. In the front open area was the living room and kitchen. A small table that would be a squeeze to fit four divided the kitchen and living room. An archway in the center led to a small hallway and a back door. Off the hallway to the left was a long narrow bedroom. The bathroom was to the right.

"Let's just give it a quick once-over." Ben added, "You take what's back here, I'll take the front."

Ben headed for the kitchen, opened the refrigerator, checked the freezer, found nothing out of the ordinary. Shook his head then, wondering what made him go there first. Checking the cabinets, the only thing he found a bit strange was a stuffed toy bear. He couldn't figure that out at all. Gamos came in then.

"Nothing much back there...wish my place was this uncluttered."

They looked around the living room, taking more time on a set of bookshelves, but found nothing that raised suspicion.

Ben showed Gamos the stuffed teddy bear.

"Maybe it's a present for someone."

"First thing I thought of is maybe he kidnapped a child," Ben said, embarrassed that he'd even had that thought.

"You need a vacation."

Suddenly, the room became darker.

With only that warning, a voice bellowed, "What are you doing in here?"

Ben spun around, saw Teroro standing in the doorway. Quickly, he said, "Teroro, it's me, Ben McMillen. We were looking for you."

"You have no right to be in here, man."

"This is my partner, Detective Gamos."

"Why are you here?"

Teroro was wearing khaki pants rolled up just below his knees, no shirt, his feet were bare, and he was carrying a fishing pole. A woven basket on a long leather strap hung around his neck, right shoulder to opposite hip.

"You're right we shouldn't have come inside, but we have reason to believe Mr. Gatston isn't in New Zealand…we have to check it out."

"What?" said the caretaker as he stepped inside. "Whaddaya mean?"

Ben said, "You said he'd call today. Did he?"

"No," the Samoan said in a softer voice.

Ben looked for a telephone. He didn't see one.

Teroro picked up on that. "The phone's in the main house." Teroro walked by them, leaned the fishing pole in a corner of the kitchen, lifted the basket over his head, and placed it in the sink. Then he let out a deep breath but didn't say anything.

Gamos asked, "Did *you* take him to the airport?"

"No…he called a taxi."

"How come?"

"I had to be somewhere else that day."

"Where?"

"Hey…bruddah…you can check it out."

Ben stepped in. "Listen Teroro, we found a fourth body…we expected three, just like you and I discussed. The other two possibilities are Mr. Gatston and another landowner. The other guy is okay. Get what we're saying?"

"Look…check it out, okay? I'm telling ya the truth."

"Let's go to the main house and make some calls."

"Fine with me, bruddah."

Ben heard something under the Samoan's breath. Probably the Samoan version of 'Fuck you'. He didn't blame him.

They called the taxi company—a place called Al's on Po'ipū Road. The dispatcher checked the log from two weeks ago and found that when the taxi showed up no one was home.

Ben asked, "What time?"

"Two…says here, passenger had a four o'clock flight to Honolulu. My driver waited for a half hour, then came back. We called from here, too. Nobody home."

Ben hung up and related what the dispatcher said.

Teroro said, "Call the Outreach Program."

Ben looked at the caretaker.

"I'm a Big Brother. I spend every Wednesday with a boy from Hanamā'ula. Go ahead…check it out."

Ben stared at the Samoan for a few seconds, waiting to see what his expression revealed. When Teroro didn't blink and his jaw remained firm, Ben picked up the phone and asked the number.

He verified Teroro was a Big Brother, got the family's phone number, called, spoke with the mother. Ben kept saying 'uh huh…uh huh…' Finally, he replaced the phone. He turned to Teroro. "We owe you an apology."

"She told you we went fishing, then to McDonald's…then brought home ice cream, huh, brah?"

"Said we were sorry." Ben walked over and gave him his hand.

Teroro hesitated, but then they slapped palms.

Gamos cleared his throat. "So what happened to Mr. Gatston? How'd he get to the airport? Did he get to the airport?" He looked at the caretaker.

Teroro shook his head. "Don't figure." His eyes focused on the wall clock for a few seconds, then he brushed by Ben and picked up the phone. He dialed.

Ben saw him start with 0-1-1 and presumed that he was calling New Zealand. The sound coming from the receiver was easy to hear. A few clicks, then static, finally an unfamiliar-sounding ring.

While the phone rang repeatedly, Ben asked, "Exactly where are you calling?"

"A ranch outside of Coromandel."

"Is he alone?"

"No." Finally, Teroro hung up.

Gamos asked Ben, "You checked upstairs last time?"

Ben nodded. Then to Teroro, "Any other building on the property?"

"There's another cabin way back…and a boat house down by the river."

"Mr. Gatston ever sleep in either?"

Teroro's eyes narrowed at the question, then he scratched his chin. "Not the cabin…it's in bad shape…hasn't been used in…" He shook his head. "Boat house, maybe…but he never stayed there. Took him out on the boat fishing." After thinking for a few more seconds, Teroro added, "There's a bed there and a kitchen."

Ben was thinking about the ocean and the river that dumped into it, and the Zodiac. The boat house fit. "When I was here before, you said you saw him the day before he left."

"Sure…went into town together for some stuff he needed."

So why would John Gatston sleep there the night before he was leaving for New Zealand?

Eyes up and darting back and forth, as if he was trying to visualize something, the caretaker finally stopped moving his eyes and gasped, "Oh, no!…" He slumped into a chair and buried his face in his hands.

"Teroro?"

The caretaker's head lifted. His eyes were red and teary. "Once he slept there, after his granddaughter died…she drowned in the river. The family trip was canceled."

"Family trip?"

"For the winter…to New…" Teroro swallowed the rest.

The boat house was situated about a half mile north of Teroro's cabin, at a spot where the land sloped downward and formed a valley only a hundred feet above the river. Teroro took them down a trail where flat stepping stones were layered into the cliff and where sections of a sturdy metal handrail were cemented into the ground along the steepest parts of the pathway.

At the bottom, Ben saw a row boat attached to a short dock. The river was low and the opposite bank was exposed more than four feet. A single white egret perched on the boat house roof, but took flight when the detectives and the caretaker approached the last stepping stone. Down near the river, where the wind didn't reach, the smell was earthy and stale and with a hint of sulfur, not unlike the scent in the lava tubes on the Big Island, where another case once led Ben.

The boat house itself was strange-looking. The back was about a story-and-a-half high, the roof angled from there to the front. It gave the impression that the back half of the boat house had been sheared off.

Teroro stopped at the doorway, then after a few seconds, stepped to the side. He turned around and a fearful look filled his large face.

Ben stepped up, pulled the latch, pushed open the door. The smell was mainly mildew and musty, but hidden in the air was the slightest hint of smoke. He gave Gamos a knowing look, then stepped inside and Gamos followed.

They went past the small kitchen, nothing seemed disturbed. The bedroom was a loft, tucked into the high back wall. Gamos found a pull-cord for the ladder and gave it a yank. The ladder slowly creaked it's way down. He pictured Gatston hearing that noise, waking. What had the old man thought as he first glimpsed the night marcher's head rising above the stairwell?

Ben went up first. When his eyes reached just above the level of the bed, he saw the brownish hole on the bed sheet. He climbed up, gave Gamos a hand.

Gamos pointed to a bare spot over the bed. Two nails, slightly angled, five feet apart, were driven into the wood.

Gamos fished out a small plastic zip-lock bag and a pencil, and handed the pencil to Ben.

Ben bent, looked under the bed and used the pencil to pick up the necklace. When he got to his feet, both detectives examined the necklace. It only took a few seconds to verify that it looked the same as the others. Ben dropped it into the plastic bag that Gamos held.

Outside, Ben asked Teroro what had hung over the bed.

Teroro's was stone-faced. "A British Flag," he said.

Chapter 19

They waited for an officer from Waimea to arrive and for the Forensic Team, who, by this time, must have been thinking of relocating to one of the Northwestern atolls, as far away from the Kona detective as they could get.

Ben decided it didn't make any sense to have Ernie and Eros on the scene—they knew the scenario and the trail was weeks old. After telling Teroro he'd have to come to Līhuʻe to identify John Gatston's remains, the detectives got into Gamos's car. After the engine caught, Ben said one more thing to the caretaker. "Bring the name of his dentist with you."

Teroro nodded as he stared at the ground.

Ben knew Teroro knew it wasn't the remains he would try to identify, only patches of clothing.

Gamos seemed to be in no hurry. Ben saw his partner rubbing his stomach. He guessed the ulcer flared up again.

"You okay?"

Gamos took a deep breath. "At least it isn't another set of landowners."

"Who knows. Maybe after Crowley, he has plans for the others. But he's definitely going to try Crowley again…and soon."

"We've got that covered. Now what?"

"We're going back to Alaʻipaleile's place." Ben picked up the radiophone. "I'm going to have someone watch the college's Zodiac and detain him in case we miss him."

"Good idea." Mike Gamos slowly inhaled and exhaled.

"You didn't answer me before."

"It hurts a little. Guess it's time for more *'olena* root."

"You up for this?"

"I'll be okay." Gamos started the engine, backed up, then headed down to the driveway.

Ben pressed the TRANSMIT button. "Two-four-one here."

"HQ here. Why haven't you answered before? Chief wants you in here right away. He's on his way over."

"What's up?" asked Ben, leaning forward.

"Lady called...read about the other vics...she's coming in."

"What lady?"

"Lady who called in the Bowden tip."

The car's acceleration pushed Ben back in his seat before he could speak.

"You hear me?" asked the dispatcher.

"What about Ala'ipaleile?" Gamos asked Ben.

Ben answered the dispatcher. "On our way...but get a patrolman out to the Community College and tell him nobody leaves with the Zodiac. If Nelson Ala'ipaleile shows up, I want him brought in. Understand?"

"Who?"

Ben repeated the name. "He's a teacher there, scheduled to take a class on a field trip this afternoon. He's going to take the Zodiac raft and the school's van. He doesn't go, he comes in."

"Describe him."

Ben did.

"Gotcha."

Ben signed off and looked at his partner. "Faster."

▼▲▼

Her name was Elizabeth Weston. She preferred to be called Beth. She was dressed in a long skirt, sleeveless knit shirt, wore bracelets on both arms plus an expensive watch. Her hair was short, blonde, and seemed like she could shake her head, wet or dry, and her hair would fall neatly into place.

Sitting in Chief Johnson's office, Beth Weston seemed remarkably calm, nothing like the person with the wavering voice who'd left the anonymous message several days before. But while Ben watched her carefully, he could see the canvas of her shoes stretching as she wriggled her toes. She swallowed more often than she blinked.

Chief Johnson told the detectives that he hadn't questioned her yet. "I just got back."

He turned to her and said, "Okay, Mrs. Weston…from the top…and don't leave anything out…every detail is important."

She told them she met Charles Bowden in the Kiahuna Plantation Shopping Center. They made eye contact several times—outside an art gallery, inside another one, outside Crazy Shirts. While she stood outside Roy's reading the dinner menu, he introduced himself and asked if she'd join him for a drink. They sat in Roy's bar and talked for two hours.

"I had to leave because my husband would be getting back from golf."

Ben asked, "What day was this?"

"Monday…the twelfth."

"Two days before…"

She nodded, her eyes now unblinking.

Ben stole a glance at Gamos. The Līhuʻe detective breathed slowly. Perspiration formed above his lip and by the sides of his eyes. His right hand rested on his stomach.

Beth explained she went back to the shopping center the next day. So had he. They made plans to meet. That night she left her room at midnight. She added with some embarrassment, "We have separate rooms, Philip and I." Bowden waited for her in the parking lot, the one away from the main entrance to the Hyatt, on the west end. They went back to his plantation home.

Ben shifted in his seat, eyed her feet, her toes were still at it. "That was Tuesday, early Wednesday?"

"Yes."

"And your husband doesn't suspect anything."

"Heavens no!"

"Go on."

"He…well…after…he asked me to come back Wednesday night."

Gamos sat forward, both hands on his abdomen. "This is the night…?"

Beth nodded. "But the phone rang after eleven…just as I was about to get out of bed. It rang in my husband's room. I was scared it was Charles, that the hotel connected him with the wrong room, but it was one of my husband's London partners. They talked for almost an hour. I didn't get out until twelve-thirty." She stopped and asked for some water.

Gamos got up and left.

Ben stood as well. "Two-minute break."

The Chief gave him a sour look like he didn't want to be left alone with the woman.

Ben walked down the corridor, turned left, saw Gamos coming out of the break room with a cup of water and told him he'd be right back. Gamos gave him a weak smile.

Ben headed for the detectives' office. Ernie Dumas was there hunched over a keyboard. He looked up. "Heard about Gatston…scent's too old, huh?"

"Right. Can you do a few things for me?"

"Sure."

"Call the M.E. and see if she has anything else."

Ernie nodded.

"Also, have Churchwell's and Frobert's remains been ID'd?"

"Working on it. Nobody home at Churchwell's…can't find the son. One of Frobert's daughters will be here tomorrow, but I also have a neighbor of his who agreed to come down."

"You check if the neighbor saw or heard anything?"

"He was home, but asleep. Besides, he lives a quarter mile away past a bend in the road. And he had trouble hearing me on the phone."

Ben placed the backs of his hands on his lower back and arched, holding that position for several seconds. "There's a guy named Teroro…caretaker at Gatston's place. He'll be here in awhile. He'll ID Gatston's clothes if he can. He's supposed to bring the name of Gatston's dentist."

"Okay."

"There's a woman in with us and the Chief…"

"I know."

"Have her ID Bowden when we're done. I can tell by her composure that she hasn't done it yet."

"Got it."

"Oh…you know who's out at the college watching the Zodiac?"

"Yeah…Patrolman Dizon."

"He's on days now?"

"He's a good cop, Ben. You were a little hard on him before."

Ben was still bitter about the blown stakeout at the Crowley place. "Maybe I was…just contact him…make sure he's knows Ala'ipaleile is not to leave no matter what. And let him know he may be dangerous and not to trust him about anything…not 'can I go to bathroom, first,'…nothing. Better yet, send him some backup right now. Also, keep trying Ala'ipaleile's house…if he answers…hang up and come find me right away."

Ben sank into his seat and gestured for Beth Weston to continue.

"I got there at one."

"Exactly?"

"Maybe one-fifteen…"

Gamos, who sat upright, appearing as if his ulcer quieted, asked, "You took your car?"

"Yes."

"Which way did you go…Lāwa'i Road?" Ben inquired.

"No. When I came back later I went that way…"

"So you left and returned?"

"Yes."

"Sorry, go on."

"There's a road that comes from the highway in Lāwa'i. That's how Charles took me the first night. He also showed me what used to be the main way in, but he keeps the gates on that road permanently locked. Otherwise he said he gets too many trespassers continuing on from Spouting Horn."

"Okay." Ben glanced at his watch and thought about Nelson Ala'ipaleile, wondering where he was if he wasn't home or at the school.

"I was there about an hour and a half…we talked a lot…after…you know. I don't know what came over me…but I started thinking about leaving my husband." She took a sip of water. "I left…maybe two-thirty…little after, walked to the car, drove back to the hotel, and laid awake in bed for an hour. Then I decided I'd had enough." Right then her voice raised and she leaned forward. "Ten years of being ignored. My schedule set for me. My monthly allowance. Charity work that he picked out. Christ!…usually I was the only woman on the committee…and it was for some dumb golf outing." She was breathing hard now, her nostrils flared like those of a snake ready to spew its venom. "I packed…I packed my things." She gulped some water, then blew out a deep breath. "I took the rental car and parked it at Spouting Horn. Then I walked down the road, went around the gates and…when I got within maybe a hundred feet of the stream, that's when I…that's when I saw the flames."

"That's a long walk, Mrs. Weston," the Chief said.

"Not if you're running away from Mr. Weston. No distance is too far." She grinned, seemed like she felt a little liberated.

Ben remembered his first case as a Kona detective. Husband said his wife was missing. Ben found her in a few days. She told him 'the only thing missing was her husband missing the point.'

Chief Johnson dragged his hand across his crew cut, then said, "Go slowly now, Ma'am…try to remember everything. What time was this?"

"After four…I left the Hyatt at three-fifteen…quarter after four or so…I wasn't planning on coming back for the car. I thought it would make it harder for my husband to find me if I left it there."

The Chief's eyebrows raised, inviting her to continue.

"I saw a man…"

Ben interrupted, moved to the edge of his chair, "Only one man?"

"Just one. He was walking along the path to the beach…the path along the stream. He was carrying a body…" Her shoulders sagged and tears formed in her eyes.

"Please go on…" Ben urged.

"A…a body wrapped in a blanket. I mean…at the time I didn't know it was a body…I thought he was carrying…I don't know. I thought it was a Hawaiian ritual of some sort."

"Why?"

"There were five torches…" She paused as if she expected to be interrupted again.

"…they were attached somehow to a long pole." She explained how the man dropped them into the stream. "He had trouble seeing in the dark, especially with that helmet on."

"What?" said the Chief.

Ben came forward in his chair. "Describe it."

"It looked like a pumpkin…in the light it was orange and big and there was some kind of stuff hanging from the bottom."

Ben said in a barely audible voice, "A carved-out gourd with tapa strips hanging down. A canoeman's helmet." He stood up. "Describe the guy."

She looked up at him and her voice caught in her throat. He realized standing over her was too intimidating, so he sat back down.

She gathered her composure. "It's kind of hard. I mean it was very dark except around the torches, and they made a glare and there was smoke."

Ben stared at her. They locked eyes. He knew the frustration showed in his face. "How tall…what kind of build did he have?"

"Very tall, a regular build."

What the hell is a regular build? "Wait a minute. Very tall because of the helmet?"

"I guess…I suppose I really don't know. There were some kind of plants or leaves sticking out of the top of it. That made him seem taller, I suppose. And I was crouching, so he looked very big to me. I'm sorry, but I was scared and...and mesmerized at the same time."

"Was he built like Bowden, big, strong?"

"I don't know, but he struggled carrying Cha...he had a difficult time walking, but he made it, so I guess he was pretty strong."

"A guess on his age?"

She shook her head.

Ben let out his breath. He didn't try to hide his exasperation. "Go on with your story...I mean your account of what your saw."

She bit her lip and narrowed her eyes. "You try describing someone under those circumstances...I didn't know what was going on. I certainly wasn't thinking I was witness to a murder." She huffed and turned to the Chief, her back to Ben.

"Like I said, I thought it was some kind of ceremony." Beth Weston's fingers scratched at the molding on the Chief's desk. "Then he carried poor Charles off to the other end of the beach."

Ben's mind drifted and the woman's voice faded away for him. He pictured an old outrigger canoe and helmeted warriors crossing the channel between O'ahu and Kaua'i. Big orange gourds with overlapping figure-eight circles cut out for the eyes. Dyed black inside so the only thing that you could see were the flames from the torches reflected in the warriors' eyes. Tapa strips hung from the bottoms of the gourds, each streaked with the markings of the clan. Ben's thoughts moved from the warriors paddling across the water to Charles Bowden, a man so full of himself that Ben easily pictured Bowden laughing at the intruder, challenging him, then shrinking into a corner when he realized what he was up against. Then he imagined the horrible scene for the other victims, much older men, much more frail. He saw their faces and their demise, one by one.

Finally, he envisioned Carlton Crowley underneath his bed covers, an old Hawaiian quilt held under his chin with his usable hand, though it shook like his other. Grasping the quilt as if it would protect him from what was coming down the hallway toward his bedroom. Ben could hear him repeating—'Bad things.'

Ben came back to the present, the woman's words a bit louder and clearer, but his mind still was occupied with the remaining living landowner. The other four lived by the sea. How was the night marcher planning to disappear with Crowley who lived at the base of a mountain, far away from any navigable stream? How was he going to do that? Unless he planned to break with the past. Cheat a little. Park a car nearby. Then drive to the Wailua River where he'd hidden the powered raft.

"Go on, Ma'am," Chief Johnson said softly.

Ben eyes focused on Beth Weston. He wasn't sure he wanted to hear more. He knew the Chief didn't. And Gamos sat there obviously deep in thought, perhaps believing in things he never thought were possible.

Beth Weston finished her story. Then Gamos escorted her out, nodding at Ben, knowing he wanted her to ID Bowden.

Chief Johnson excused himself, so Ben sat alone in the Chief's office for a long time. Alone except for the image of Crowley's terrified face, which wouldn't go away. Ben had a bad feeling that Nelson Ala'ipaleile had it all figured out.

Chapter 20

The rest of Beth Weston's story was pretty much what they expected, except Ben hoped she'd heard the engine of a Zodiac, instead she described what he believed was an outrigger canoe. He couldn't believe the murderer would take the fantasy to that level. A quarter of the way around the Island in a canoe? That would take four hours or more. The risk of exposure was too great. Plus it didn't make sense in Bowden's case where they had a reliable time-frame for the killing. In a canoe, the second half of that excursion to the western coast happened after dawn. Not likely.

After Gamos escorted the woman to an interview room to write up her official statement before being asked to ID the remains, Ben got up to find the Chief. They nearly collided in the doorway. Ben asked the Chief how long it would take to get a search warrant.

"For where…?"

Ben told him and they argued.

The Chief didn't like it, not enough hard evidence, but finally relented.

"I need it in an hour."

"You ever get one that quickly back home?"

"Nope."

Ben found Ernie still at his desk, phone tucked between his shoulder and chin. Ben could hear someone shouting on the other end. Ernie held up a finger, pressed his lips together, looked annoyed, rocking in his chair now, looking like a tiger ready to spring. Then he said, "Look Mr. Churchwell, I suggest you come down…if not we'll just have to come up there and drag your ass down…"

Ernie slammed down the phone.

"The S.O.B. hung up on me! You sure you have a suspect? I'd rather lock up that bastard."

Ben, without saying anything, slid into the chair at the desk next to Ernie's.

The patrolman let out his breath, stared at the wall for a few seconds, then composed himself with a deep sigh. "Churchwell's son doesn't want to come down."

"Why not?"

"At first he said 'what's the point.' Then it changes to 'he's too upset.'"

"Send someone up there."

"I'll send Eros." Ernie called out mockingly, "Eros, *'Ohana*...not!"

They shared a quick laugh.

"And Dizon?"

"Nobody's showed up...and he's real clear on what he's to do. Sergeant Medeiros sent a backup, too."

"Good." Ben looked at his watch. He wanted to get out to the professor's house right away and wondered how long Gamos would be taking the Weston woman's statement.

Ernie took a sip of coffee from a lop-sided mug with a heavy-looking handle.

When Ernie tilted it back, Ben could see a child's etching on the bottom. "I was thinking...wouldn't it save time to have Eros come along to Ala'ipaleile's place? If the professor's our man, won't Eros find the scent of the necklaces everywhere? Maybe lead us to a stash of them? We need some solid evidence."

"Sure."

Quick footsteps approached.

Mike Gamos walked in. "Ernie, you can take the Weston woman over to ID Bowden."

"Have a seat for a minute," Ben urged.

Gamos grabbed a wooden chair, turned it around, and straddled it.

"We have a lot to check out. Here's my suggestion. One of us has to find Nelson Ala'ipaleile. We've got the bodies to identify and the M.E. to talk with. And...we've got the last potential victim...Carlton Crowley. I know he's got something to tell us...if we can get him to communicate. Plus, I think his daughter knows more."

Gamos asked, "Like what?"

"It has something to do with the fire and her father's comments about night marchers." He told them what Crowley's daughter said about the how the fire started two years previously.

Gamos whistled. "I was working patrol at the time. Never heard anything about it."

"I think maybe our night marcher tried to get to Crowley back then. And that's an angle that might help us."

"You mean what was the perp doing for two years…why'd he wait so long to start again?"

Ben nodded. "Maybe, it's just that at first he wanted to scare Crowley…and possibly the others as well. But he lost his nerve. On the other hand, what if something else intervened? What if he was forced to wait? Maybe Crowley or his daughter can shed some light on that. I just have a feeling they know who's responsible. What I mean is…they know or know of the person who's responsible, but just haven't thought of him in that way. I'd start by asking them about the family history…in detail. Maybe they displaced some Hawaiian family long ago who didn't go so quietly. Maybe the reason everyone has such good things to say about Crowley is because he knows about something very wrong in his family's past, something that he's ashamed of and he's gone overboard trying to make amends all these years." Ben let that sink in with Gamos. "How do you want to divide this up?"

Gamos asked, "Does following up on the professor mean riding one of those rafts around the coast?"

"Only if he gets away."

"You can have the professor…" He pointed to his stomach.

"Okay. You stick with the bodies and Doc Brundy for a while. Then head up to Kapahi and see what you can get out of Mary Rice and her father."

Gamos agreed.

Ben then told Gamos about bringing Eros to Ala'ipaleile's place.

"Sounds good."

Ernie asked, "You guys think the killer's going to try again soon, don't you?"

Ben filled his cheeks, then let the air out slowly. "The compulsion for a serial killer gets stronger as he goes. And since ours has a specific target, the one he knows completes his mission…" *Does a serial killer ever complete his mission?*

"Maybe I'll stay at Crowley's tonight," Gamos said.

"Good idea. Don't let Mary Rice talk you out of it."

"No problem."

"And one other thing…" Ben said, "Mary's husband should be back by now. We really don't know anything about him."

"Suspect?"

"Let me put it this way. He wasn't with his wife this time when the night marcher came. Maybe he wasn't with her the night of the fire two years ago. It certainly explains why Mary Rice might have something to hide...or at least, something she's afraid to talk about. Maybe in her eyes...her husband's the suspect?"

▼▲▼

Ernie made a sharp turn off Highway 50 onto 530 and Eros whined as he lost his balance and fell from the back seat.

"Sorry, boy."

Ben glanced back and saw the tracking dog jump back onto the seat. "You're too valuable...you should be wearing your seat belt."

Eros hunkered down.

"Here we are," Ernie said, as they slowed and came abreast of a white mail box with the professor's name on it. "Where do you want me to park?"

Ben looked up the steep driveway. "You can go up."

Near the top, Ernie said, "Never saw anybody get a search warrant so fast."

"Chief needs this wrapped up quickly."

"Yeah, but to get one just on a 'who has access to a Zodiac theory and the stuff done in your room'...besides, you don't really think it's him, do you?"

"If it's not him, you don't want to hear my second choice."

"I don't?"

"Not quite yet."

Ernie seemed to be wondering if his second choice was the same as Ben's.

"You think the professor's family lost land?"

Ben didn't answer right away. Ernie didn't understand that every Hawaiian family lost land one way or another. He gave the patrolman a 'yes' and a quick nod.

The station wagon stopped and Eros got up and jumped through the open window. He sat next to the car.

Ben and Ernie got out and walked up the steep steps to the front door.

Ben knocked and waited. He knocked again, much louder this time. Then he tried the door. To his surprise it was locked.

"Damn! He's been here...it was unlocked before. Let's try the back."

Ernie to Eros, "*Mai.*"

They followed the driveway to the rear of the house. Ben pointed down and they skirted fresh tire marks, which lead to the back of the property. The tread marks ended just beyond the dirt in the tall grass, which was wet and bent where a car had been parked.

The backyard was small, crowded with exotic fruit trees. A rope hammock hung between two papaya trees and a green garden hose wound around a rusted wheelbarrow, the nozzle draped over the edge as if it were siphoning a drink. The grass was high, bending with the wind in the sunlight where the yard was dry, but still matted in the damp shadows of the foliage that bordered the rear of the property. Jutting into the yard was an addition to the house, a single story, one long window, about ten feet in length, the wood siding painted white like the front of the house, but the roof shingles were gray, not black like the main structure.

The rear door was on the side of the original house. Ben knocked repeatedly, shouted the professor's name, then tried the doorknob, which twisted easily, the door creaking as Ben carefully pushed against it.

Normally when you had a search warrant and no one answered, you were trained to assume that someone was there, hiding, waiting for an opportunity to bolt out another door, or worse, taking aim. And because of that, Ernie whispered for Eros to sit, then unsnapped the flap on his holster, and placed his hand by his side.

Ben turned when he heard Ernie draw his revolver. Ben put up his hand, then stepped inside. He stood silently in a small room observing a stacked washer and dryer, a basket of dirty clothes—mainly nylon shorts, tank tops, and Spandex biking suits. There was a separate pile of white ankle socks covered with a coarse spray of red earth.

"Let me go first, Ben," Ernie said.

"He's not home."

"This is a homicide investigation…I can't do it any different." Ernie held his gun in both hands, pointed at the ground. He told Eros to stay.

"Go 'head."

Ernie stepped up, peeked into the kitchen, darted inside, two hands on his weapon, sweeping the revolver left and right, then pointed it at a doorway, which led to the rest of the house.

Ben followed, ten feet behind. Thirty seconds later, Ernie was satisfied that Ala'ipaleile wasn't home.

"I'll get Eros."

Ben looked around the living room, then walked over to a nook where the professor had a desk. It was stacked with books and maps, which surrounded an old Dell PC. The keyboard sat on top of the computer, there was no room for it on the desk top. The mouse dangled from its cord, hanging over the computer screen.

Ben heard Ernie and Eros approach.

Ernie knelt in the center of the living room. From his breast pocket, he took out a small plastic Ziploc bag, opened it, reached inside, and carefully took out the fish hook necklace. He presented it to Eros. The dog sniffed the necklace, first the fish hook, then the braided boar's hair, then the ivory clasp.

Ben thought that Eros seemed to be going through the motions, as if he'd recognized the necklace.

Eros sniffed the hardwood floor, going plank to plank, then quickly left the living room and headed toward the bedroom.

Ben said, "His sense of smell must be like a hawk's vision."

"Let me put it this way. If a hawk was trained in a similar manner to the way Eros was, he could be taught to catch only white mice...even if he was starved and there were a hundred gray mice and only one white one. And he could spot the white one hiding in very deep *pili* grass from a half mile away."

"Your kids get to take Eros along on Easter egg hunts."

Ernie laughed. "Now there's an idea."

Eros was in the bedroom, in the closet. Then he retreated and went down the hallway, back toward the kitchen in the rear of the house. The tracking dog didn't go into the kitchen, however. Past the kitchen doorway, at the end of the hall, was another door. This door didn't match those in the rest of the house. It was newer, flush, with flat trim, and unpainted. It led to the addition. Eros pawed the door, turned and looked expectantly at his handler, then sniffed under the door jam.

Ernie opened the door and Eros leaped inside.

The room was the professor's workshop. The smell of bike oil was prevalent. Two overhead rows of fluorescent lighting, work benches on both sides running the length of the workshop. Along the back wall was another work bench, on top of it, clamped with two vises was a metallic silver Corima carbon bike frame, one Ben knew cost two thousand dollars, just for the frame, everything else, the gears, saddle, handle bars, brakes, and wheels were extra. The front wheel was in place, the rear wheel lay on the work bench, the gears and brakes were dismantled.

Ernie said, "Look at this!"

On the work bench along the right wall were hundreds of artifacts, most in divided plastic drawers with white labels adhered across the fronts. There were fish hooks, mother of pearl lures, stone spearheads, and tiny shells. On the table were calabashes, short wooden paddles that Ben knew were for beating tapa, other rounded grinding tools, brittle looking pieces of braided coconut husk, more shells and fish hooks. But nothing on a necklace.

Eros honed in on a cabinet.

"He's got something," said Ernie. He walked over to the cabinet, gave Eros a command, and Eros moved back.

Ben took a pair of latex gloves from his rear pocket and slipped them on. Then he stepped forward and pulled the door handle from the very top so he didn't smudge any prints. Obviously the professor's prints would be everywhere, but for some reason he also thought there might be others. The cabinet door swung open. Inside, on a shelf at eye level, were several fish hook necklaces that appeared to match those found at the crime scenes. Ben ignored them for the time being because something else caught his eye. He reached up to the next shelf and extracted a folded piece of material. It had a white canvas edging on one side that appeared yellowed with age. There was a single brass grommet in one corner of the material. Ben unfolded it. The design on the old material was unmistakable—a British Flag. His heart sank…he didn't want it to be the professor. Actually, he admitted to himself, he really didn't want the killer to be Hawaiian. Ben wondered, when they checked Ala'ipaleile's family background, which plantation owner's ancestors took the family's land. He had this feeling that it was Gatston or Crowley, for no matter what the killer's pattern, Ben knew the person central to the killer's thoughts would be the first victim or would be saved for last. The triggering event or the finale.

"It's him," said Ernie. "Jeeez."

Ben reached higher, to the top shelf, and brought down another piece of material, this one extremely heavy. It was a quilt. He carried it to the work bench where the racing bike was clamped and unfolded the old bed cover. He didn't need a yardstick to know it once hung over Churchwell's bed.

"Ernie…don't touch anything else. Go back to the kitchen, there's a wall phone. Call Chief Johnson and let him know what we found. Then call Gamos. And get Forensic down here. Get some back up to secure the house and yard. Get three more patrolmen out to the college. Have one watch the parking lot, put one in Staff Building #1, and have the third backup the men watching the Zodiac. And find out what kind of vehicle he drives and the same for the college van and send them out. Everyone approaches with caution. They only take him if there's no college kids with him. And make sure they take him alive."

Ernie hurried off, Eros by his side.

Ben sat on a stool, staring at the cabinet, then his gaze shifted to the work benches. He really didn't want to believe this, he liked Ala'ipaleile. He thought about the Sovereignty movement and how these murderous acts of vengeance would impact it all.

Staring at the ceiling, envisioning the Islands before the white man came, thinking about how quickly—just two hundred years—a single concept transformed Hawai'i into another battleground for wealth and power. The concept was the ownership of the land. Thinking about all the things his grandmother taught him, the one theme that seemed most important to her was that the old Hawaiians, like indigenous people everywhere, believed it was their responsibility to care for the land, not own it. The land belonged to the gods of nature, not those sent there to nurture it.

Another cabinet caught his eye.

He got up and walked toward the second cabinet. On top was a brownish-orange gourd with strips of dyed tapa attached around the base. He went back and got the stool he'd been sitting on, stepped up, and looked at the gourd closely without touching it. There was a hole in the top. He smelled inside. The odor reminded him of some of his well-worn workout caps. The smell of sweat permanently ingrained into the material. He leaned left and looked at the other side of the helmet. The figure-eight opening, though dark and empty, seemed to be staring at him. Ben's arms and neck got *chicken skin*.

He stepped down, but continued looking up at the canoeman's helmet. And then he spotted something else hanging on the wall behind the helmet. It was a pipe that first seemed like it was part of the plumbing, but it wasn't. It appeared to be made of iron and it just hung there not connected to anything. Ben took a closer look. The pipe was about fifteen feet long. It wasn't iron. Probably lightweight aluminum. He didn't reach for it, though—leave that for the forensic team.

The pipe was painted a flat black, and had five welded extensions of different heights equally spaced along the top. At the end of the extensions were what appeared to be pipe collars. Upon closer inspection he saw dark black stains on the collars, the kind flames made. Soot. At the center of the length of pipe was a black hand grip from a bike, sliced along the back, fitted over the tubing.

The night marcher's torches.

The device made one person appear as five.

Ernie came back, his voice excited. "You're not gonna believe this."

"Not Crowley!"

"No. Hanalei called...Ala'ipaleile took one of Captain Zodiac's rafts."

Ben closed his eyes, lowered his head, and pinched the bridge of his nose. "Stole it?"

"No...seems like they said he borrowed it. The students are with him. Chief's on the line...wants to talk to you."

Ben pointed to the helmet and the torch piping.

Ernie's jaw dropped and his eyes became huge circles, not unlike those carved into the canoeman's helmet.

Chapter 21

The game plan was set. Ben was in charge of finding and arresting Nelson Ala'ipaleile. Ernie and Eros were to go with him. Arrangements were made with the Zodiac tour company on the south shore—the day's tours were canceled and the Hurricane Zodiac and the firm's owner were waiting for them at Kīkīaloa Harbor, twenty minutes away from the professor's house. They decided against helicopter backup—the noise might serve to warn Ala'ipaleile. The Island tour operators, helicopter and sea craft, were contacted, none were allowed anywhere near Miloli'i or Nu'alolo Kai or Honopū. Backup would be four patrolmen with the Coast Guard coming from the North Shore.

Part two of the plan was to guard Carlton Crowley and his daughter. Ben and the Chief agreed that they should be moved to a safe location and Mike Gamos and a team of six officers, dressed as gardeners, would watch the estate.

Ben and Ernie left through the professor's kitchen. On the way out Ernie took one of Ala'ipaleile's tank tops from the laundry basket, put his nose to it and commented that 'they'd have him in no time.'

They waited outside in the shade for twenty minutes for someone to show to secure the house. Ben saw Ernie cleaning his sunglasses. He slipped his own out of his breast pocket and put them on. He hated spending the time waiting for the hand-off, but knew in the courtroom that the evidence chain was what every lawyer went after first. They had the LAPD to thank for that.

First to arrive were two Līhu'e patrolmen. Ben showed them the evidence, gave them instructions to relay to the Forensic Team, and was about to leave when Kevin and Julian pulled up the driveway.

Kevin yelled from an open window, "What do we got?"

Ben approached the crime scene vehicle. "This is the prime suspect's house. The stuff you want to look at is in the workshop. The Uniforms can show you...we gotta go."

Julian got out of the station wagon, then opened the rear door, and took out his dusting kit. When he shut the door, he gave Ben a sarcastic smile.

Kevin asked, "Can we bring the evidence in when we're done?"

"Absolutely."

"Have a nice day."

They made the harbor in under twenty minutes. The Hurricane Zodiac was tied to the dock, two men were loading what looked like mesh duffel bags and other gear aboard. One of the men, who wore khaki shorts and a white, three-quarter sleeve T-shirt, and a broad-billed cap with a back flap to protect his neck, stopped and watched them approach.

Ernie found a parking space in the shade and once again Eros jumped through the window.

They got out and hurried over to the dock.

The man in the white shirt said, "Guess you're the police."

Eros clearly was agitated and Ernie had difficulty keeping him still with just hand signals.

Ben introduced himself, Ernie, and finally Eros—Ernie had a tight hold on Eros's collar. He reached out with his free hand and placed it on the man's shoulder. "*'Ohana.*" Then he led Eros to the other man, who was seated on the side of the inflatable raft. Ernie smiled at him, put his arm around the man, and told Eros the man was also 'family.'

The man in the white shirt said he was John Tucker. "I'm your Captain...and I own the company." He then gestured to the man sitting on the raft.

"I'm Kupulau...Kip," the other man said. "Is he an attack dog?" Kip was a big Hawaiian, short bristled black hair, round face, wearing a yellow tank top that advertised THE EXPLORATION COMPANY, black shorts, no belt, and a pair of black flip flops, which were nearly worn thin.

"A tracker," answered Ernie, "but an attack dog when it comes to me."

"What's his name?"

"Eros."

Kip lowered his voice and said, "*'Ohana,* Eros...big-time *'ohana*!"

Ben asked, "How soon can we get underway?"

"All set…just gotta connect the gas lines." He handed caps to each of them. He didn't need to explain the effect of the burning rays of the sun reflecting off the water.

Ben liked the fact that the raft had the added protection of a thick plastic hull. The craft looked like a long rowboat with a rubber raft wedged inside. Two powerful Johnson Oceanrunner outboards provided the propulsion. Inside the raft, the Captain's wheel, port and starboard engine gauges, and throttles were mounted atop a waist-high housing centered near the stern. Under a protected plastic cover above the gauges were the ship-to-shore radio and the communication system for describing the sights to the tour passengers. The rest was pretty simple—storage areas, eight orange life preservers, coils of yellow nylon rope, a large built-in ice chest. Passengers sat on the raft's floor boards and held onto heavy-duty canvas handles attached to the inflatable's sides.

Right after they cleared the breakwater, the Zodiac owner said, "Might be a bit bumpy…lotta wind."

"I'm used to it," said Ben.

"Me too, and Eros loves it on the water," Ernie added.

John Tucker grinned. "Great…wanna keep the puppy happy."

The Captain took it up to full speed and Ben settled back and explained the plan to the crew. He had to shout over the engine noise and the wind. They would try Miloli'i first. Ben said that they would let Eros smell the suspect's clothing and he would be able to track him pretty quickly if he was there. If they had no luck, then Nu'alolo Kai was next. Ben thought he'd save mention of The Valley of The Lost Tribe for later.

"Why do you think he'll be in one of those two valleys?" John called out.

"He's on an…exploring trip with some of his students. They were planning to go to those two valleys and dig for artifacts. Not sure which one first. They left…probably within the last few hours so the trail will be fresh. What we've got to worry about is the safety of the students, first. Then we have to bring him in."

Ben saw the bright look on their faces. "I need you two to stay with the raft."

The Captain asked, "We know the terrain…we can help."

Ben pointed to Eros. "Besides…Police procedure…can't do it."

Kip, sitting on the port side, asked, "A teacher? What's he wanted for, anyhow, brah?"

"They didn't tell you?"

Both men shook their heads.

"Murder."

Ben expected a joke like 'guess we'll watch the raft,' but there was silence and serious expressions. He got up, steadied himself, walked forward, and sat next to Ernie. Eros was at the bow, tongue catching the salt spray, head cocked to the right as the broad sand stretch of Barking Sands flew by.

The wind picked up, maybe to twenty-five knots, and the bow began to lift out of the water every few seconds as they came across the inbound swells. Slower was much smoother, but Ben told Captain Tucker to 'let it out.' Behind the wide expanse of beach was the beginning of the *pali*, the jagged cliffs covered thickly in vegetation, which formed deep shadows as the trees and other scrubs folded into the steep valleys. The cliffs were topped with thick brush strokes of gray clouds that appeared laden with rain and ready to let go. But on the water, the sun baked their backs and arms. Only the speed of the craft, which churned up the ocean spray and made the wind seem much stronger, provided some relief.

When they angled north coming up to Polihale, the leaping place, the sand abruptly ended and the great cavernous walls of the Nā Pali Coast rose thousands of feet above the surging sea. The beach was now a moss-covered boulder field and the closeness of the ancient rock spires revealed that the seemingly soft velvet veil of vegetation as seen from a distance was actually a tangled web of twisted limbs and branches and chiseled stone. Hardly the place to rock climb, even without the gusting wind.

"Ben?"

"Yeah, Ernie?"

"I was thinking…since Ala'ipaleile left earlier than we thought he would, do you think he knows we suspect him?"

Ben checked that they were out of earshot of John and Kip. "It explains the borrowed Zodiac. Maybe he observed our stakeout of the school's raft. But I don't really think so, since he took the students with him."

"You sure?"

"Pretty."

"So then this is simply what it's supposed to be…a field trip for the class."

"Yeah."

"And if not?"

Ben moved over so his back fit more comfortably into the curve of the raft. "He leaves the students at Miloi'i or Nu'alolo Kai. Tells them to set up camp and he says he wants to scout out the next site. Then takes the raft and tries to get away."

"Off the Island?"

"That's one option. He's got more than a hundred miles of open sea to O'ahu...he better have a couple of extra gas tanks. But the Coast Guard will spot him and overtake him pretty easily, so I don't think he'll try that. Second...he forgets Crowley and plays out the end of his fantasy...in which case we won't find him at Miloi'i or Nu'alolo Kai, he'll return to The Valley of the Lost Tribe, I think. Maybe he'll hide, maybe he's ready to put up a fight, maybe he just ends it."

"You mean kills himself?"

Ben wasn't sure how that would play out. He couldn't remember having heard any stories about Hawaiians of old committing suicide. He assumed it happened. But did they jump to their deaths? Drink some poison? He looked at Ernie and shrugged his shoulders.

"What if he uses the students as hostages?"

"Not likely for a serial killer. So, let's hope we don't have to deal with that."

Eros came from the bow. He shook off the sea water, spraying Ben and Ernie, then sat next to his handler.

Ben licked his dry lips. They were crusted with salt. "Third option...he moors the raft somewhere along the Wailua River, drives the van to Kapahi, waits for midnight...early morning...and tries to get Crowley. If it weren't for the fact that Mike's up there and Crowley's not, he'd abduct him, kill him, drive back to the raft, and take the body to the swamp where he hid the others. And, of the three, that's the most likely, because there's a lot wrong with him, and he's compelled...he's so close to completing his mission. After that, he doesn't care what happens to himself. At least, I don't think so."

"But you think we'll find him with the students because he has no idea what we know?"

Staring inland, Ben added, but without breaking his gaze, "If they're with him, we just have to be extra careful." Ben's eyes narrowed and shifted to the raft's wake.

"What are you thinking about?" Ernie asked, as he stroked Eros under the chin.

Ben looked at Ernie. "I don't know...when I met him, I liked him...maybe because he bikes...maybe because...I guess it's just hard to imagine that anyone has done this. But it happens all too often."

Ben's old partner's face appeared like a apparition on the water. Ben tried to look away, but couldn't.

They heard John Tucker shout, "We're heading in."

Ben looked up. Ahead now was Miloli'i with a backdrop of fourteen-hundred-foot cliffs, parched by the sun, looking bleak and gray, nothing like the green slopes they'd first seen or those farther up the Nā Pali Coast.

The beach magically appeared, much smaller than Ben previously imagined. The Captain zigzagged a couple of times to avoid parts of the reef, which were just inches beneath the water, but he never let back on the throttle as they skimmed across the shallows. Just as Ben thought he heard sand scraping the hull, he saw John pull up the twin engines and they glided onto the beach.

"Don't see the other Zodiac," the raft owner stated.

They got out and stood on the wet sand.

There were no footprints that Ben could see. He listened. All he heard was the surf and the wind and the faint sounds of the cliff birds high above. His shirt billowed and a gust of wind forced him to take several steps forward.

Ernie took out the shirt he'd confiscated from the professor's laundry basket. He held it in front of Eros's nose. The tracking dog smelled for a few seconds, then walked along the shore line to the right. He kept his nose low to the ground and his eyes blinked continuously as sand blew across the beach.

"Wait here." Ernie followed Eros. Each time the Belgian Shepherd stopped, which was every twenty yards or so, Ernie offered the shirt again and urged the dog onward. At the western end of the beach, they turned around, Ernie jogged back with Eros closely by his side.

While they repeated the exercise heading to the east end of the beach, Ben walked up the sand along the stream and stood before Miloli'i Valley. The Captain and his mate soon joined him.

The cliffs along here were scorched dry from the constant sun. Whereas, farther east, toward Kalalau Valley there was sufficient rain—here, twenty inches a year was about all one could expect. There were pockets of green in the *pali*, but mostly gray rock, edges carved to sharp points by the immutable wind.

"Not here, Ben," the Captain said.

Ben turned and faced John Tucker.

"Although the wind and tide can erase footprints in an hour…," then he pointed to Ernie and the dog, "…I don't know what the wind does to a scent, but there's no raft. You don't get here any other way."

"Could you hide it?" asked Ben.

"Damn heavy," Kip interjected. "Maybe in a sea cave…but there are none big enough around here. Farther up, maybe…"

John Tucker knelt, grabbed a handful of sand, and let it trickle through his fingers, then watched as it was washed sideways by the wind. "Let's try Nu'alolo."

Ben looked east, saw Ernie and Eros running back. Just barely, he could tell, Ernie was shaking his head.

They shoved off, backing carefully through the reef into deeper water. Before John could throttle forward, they took a large wave broadside that drenched the raft and pushed them back closer to the sharp coral. Ben heard the fiberglass hull scrape against the rock.

John shouted, "That might have blown a hole in one of those soft bottom jobs." He gave Ben a smile, then slowly moved off the edge of the reef, made sure they had clearance, throttled the engines ahead quarter speed, then, after they rode a wave, pushed forward to half and then full speed, which sent them skimming across the water, whizzing by the cliffs that rose dizzily toward the sky. They ran along the coastline not more than fifty feet away from where the surf crashed against the rock wall. Only Kip sat on the inland side with his back toward the *pali*. Ben and Ernie copied Eros's crouch and hunkered down.

A short time later, just when Ben found a somewhat comfortable position to settle into against the side of the raft, they turned inland, and the engines slowed. He heard John Tucker yell, 'Makuaiki Point,' and saw him point to the large rock formation starboard. Ben raised himself on his elbows and saw another beach, this one surrounded by towering, sheer cliffs.

Kip came forward to get a better look at the reef. He signaled the Captain forward. Then he looked up and said to Ben and Ernie, "Up there...thirteen hundred feet...Kamaile Peak. It marks the path through the coral. The people who lived here long ago used it as a guide at night when they came back from fishing, when it is impossible to see the path through the reef."

"Look!" Ernie stood and pointed ahead.

A Zodiac on the sand.

"Looks like they're here," said Captain John.

Engines cut to a minimum, so there was less noise, the Captain steered the Hurricane Zodiac while Kip motioned which direction to turn. It took a few minutes before they neared the beach and the Captain cut the engines. But because they'd come in so slowly, they didn't have enough momentum to clear the water, so John ordered everyone out. They splashed knee deep along the side of the craft. Kip and Ben took lines and pulled the craft ashore, while Ernie and the

Captain pushed forward against the sides. All four fell to the sand. Eros ran for the other Zodiac, but braked and returned when Ernie shouted.

They rested only a short time. Ben was the first to get up. He walked to the other Zodiac, scanning the beach for footprints, hoping to find many. But there were none.

Soon at his side, John Tucker, said, "Told you…the wind."

The Zodiac was empty, nothing left behind to give evidence of the number of passengers. Thanks to the sun, there was no telling from the heat of the engine covers how long the raft had been beached.

Tucker said, "It's one of Captain Zodiac's."

From behind they heard Ernie shouting.

"He's got him!"

Eros was headed toward the eastern end of the beach, nose once again to the ground, nothing distracting him, except every ten seconds his head turned to make sure where his handler was.

Ben asked John, "What's up ahead?"

"There's an old Hawaiian settlement over there by Alapi'i Point. You said they were students on a dig…then I say they're at the old village."

Ben looked at the Captain for a few seconds. "Okay, you come with us. Kip, think you can yank something out of the other inflatable that'll keep it here."

"No sweat, brah."

"Then stay out of sight." With that Ben and John Tucker ran after Ernie, who walked briskly behind Eros. Ben shouted back, "If we're not back in a hour, Kip…go get help."

"If you're not back in hour, I'm coming after you!"

With the wind, nobody heard him.

Chapter 22

Behind the beach, clusters of *naupaka*—bright green, waist-high bushes with succulent leaves and small white flowers—covered the sandy soil. Eros followed the scent through the bushes, moving swiftly, having no trouble when the path forked, and wasn't fooled farther on when a small stream of rainwater runoff cut across the sand. The dog had to walk parallel to the rivulet for some distance before he picked up the professor's scent once again. Eros checked behind, making sure his handler was with him, then continued along deeper into the beach cover.

The three men walked briskly, Ernie in the lead, Ben last.

Ernie offered, "The scent's real fresh."

"This is the way to the old village...gotta be where they are," John Tucker added.

The loose footing caused Ben's shoes to slip sideways with every step. Soon his calves ached and he couldn't wait for firmer ground and respite from the bright sun. He wiped the perspiration from the back of his neck, wishing he had his fishing hat, the one with the white flap that hung from the back. Some water wouldn't be so bad, either. He pushed all that aside and concentrated on the terrain and thought about the questions he had for Nelson Ala'ipaleile. He wondered if the professor would put up a fight.

Mauka, Ben saw tall palms, sentinels of the beach, whose chattering fronds bent in the wind, and farther back an expanse of ironwood trees, whose needle-like leaves resembled those of a pine. Ahead was a ledge, where John Tucker said the old trail to Nu'alolo 'Aina began. He explained that this valley was divided by the cliff they saw. He said long ago, when both parts of the valley were settled, the natives on the land side, Nu'alolo 'Aina, grew taro, and those on the sea side, Nu'alolo Kai, fished. The two settlements constructed ladders made of braided coconut husks that enabled them to travel between the two valleys during the winter months, when travel by sea was too dangerous to trade goods.

Eros began whining when they came to the clearing that marked the beginning of the village site. Ben saw something moving through the brush ahead. They stopped, Ernie gave Eros a command that silenced the Belgian Shepherd, quickly he knelt next to the dog.

The Captain turned to Ben. "You see him?" he whispered.

Without looking at Tucker, Ben said softly, "Get down and stay here." Then Ben, back bent, ran ahead, past the Captain, past Ernie and Eros, until he reached the cover of a stone foundation. Peering over the top of the layered rocks and through the dense vegetation that surrounded this section of the old settlement, Ben saw the back and legs of a man wearing khaki shorts and a light blue, long-sleeve shirt. From the rear, only the man's bulging calves gave away his identity. And when the professor stepped onto higher ground and turned to go farther inland, Ben saw something on Ala'ipaleile's right shoulder. His heart sank. It was a person, head hanging down, and tied around the person's head was a bloody bandanna.

Then Ben saw a dangling arm and could make out the professor's right arm supporting the person's body.

Turning to look over his right shoulder, Ben gestured for the others to remain where they were, keep down, and keep quiet. He turned back to watch Ala'ipaleile, who trudged along the path ahead. Ben made his decision, stood up straight, and dashed for a nearby cluster of palms. He remained there for a few seconds, then darted behind a lava rock foundation. There was a second old *hale* foundation off to the left. Peeking out, he spotted the professor walking, though now, more slowly, the weight of the person across his shoulder obviously taking its toll.

Ben ran after Nelson Ala'ipaleile, closing quickly to about fifty feet. The professor stopped and rested, leaning his free shoulder against the trunk of a large palm. The next thing Ben witnessed confused him for a few seconds, but finally made him realize he might be in time. Ala'ipaleile seemed to be talking to the person he carried.

Ben wondered if it was Crowley—the weight of the person seemed right, but he could not see any of the person's facial features and the bandage about his head covered his hair. But how had he gotten to Crowley? Did that mean that

Gamos and the team of 'gardeners' had been infiltrated? Did it mean that they were…?

He scanned the terrain ahead and saw that the path through the old village wound left again and headed back toward the beach. Maybe he could cut across and get ahead of them.

When his eyes came back to where Ala'ipaleile and the person he carried had been resting, they were gone. Without hesitation, Ben cut back between the two *hale* foundations and ran as quietly as he could through the bushes. In no more than twenty seconds he found it, a place where the path came within fifty feet of the beach, although the area was so thickly vegetated, it was barely passable. He knifed through, scraping his arms and his face on the branches, fearing he made too much noise. But it was too late to worry about that. Soon he was on the beach, running parallel to the path, then he ducked to the right, through more heavy growth, and emerged back on the sandy trail, this time in front of the professor. He ran ahead, looking for a suitable place to hide, and found a spot where the path curved abruptly, heading inland once more. He crouched and waited, listening for footsteps. He looked ahead along the cliff, saw another lava foundation, and beyond, several more. There were more than a half dozen foundations of ancient home sites. Ben wondered if Ala'ipaleile was starting on a new burial ground. He thought about Ala'ipaleile's students and wondered where they were. Actually, he realized, he didn't know if there were students here. Maybe there was no dig, just an excuse to be to gone and to take the Zodiac. Or maybe the professor left them on another beach. Came here saying he was scouting a second site, when all along he'd come back to finish off his last victim, someone who'd been captive for days. Crowley? No. Then who?

His thoughts were interrupted by footsteps approaching. Dragging steps, moving slowly. Should be no trouble stopping him. Ben hoped he wasn't too late.

And when the light blue shirt came into view and then two dangling legs, Ben stepped out of his hiding place, ready to apprehend the professor if he made an attempt to run. He stood and came eye-to-eye with Nelson Ala'ipaleile.

"Christ!…McMillen. You scared the *shit* out of me. What the hell are you doing here? C'mon…help me. He's hurt…let's get him back to camp. Jesus! What are doing here? What's going on? C'mon, give me a hand, he's heavy."

Ben's mind said 'Huh? His mouth said nothing. He thought he saw the professor's eyes light up as if he suddenly remembered something. But before Ben could say anything, he, himself, was startled, and he took a couple of very quick steps backward when the head on the professor's shoulder raised and turned and asked groggily, "Are we there yet?"

Ben and the professor carried the injured student—each held a leg, lent a shoulder, and placed an arm around the boy's back for support. Ernie, John Tucker, and Eros followed closely, listening intently to Ala'ipaleile's explanation of what happened. When Ben asked about the Zodiac, Ala'ipaleile gave him a strange look, then unperturbed, explained that he had trouble starting the engine on the college's raft the night before and called a friend, a guy who did maintenance on Captain Zodiac's rafts, and asked if he could borrow one of the Zodiacs. Ala'ipaleile was so convincing that Ben guessed it was possible.

It wasn't until the campsite, when a half dozen colorful two-person tents came into sight, that Nelson Ala'ipaleile halted and looked Ben squarely in the eye.

"Wait a minute…you weren't looking for the people who disappeared…you were looking for me, weren't you?"

Ben, unblinking, said, "Maybe we still are."

The professor's smile widened and he laughed.

Without another word they walked toward camp and Ernie held onto Eros's collar as tightly as he could. He was having a difficult time convincing Eros that the man he had tracked so many times was off limits for the time being.

The campsite was on the side of the trail opposite a cluster of six old home sites. When they neared the remains of the first foundation, a girl who sat crossed-legged carefully brushing the earth spotted them and shouted to the other students.

"Rick's hurt!"

Brushes and mallets dropped. All the students came running.

Ben and the professor carefully placed Rick down in front of one of the tents. Someone brought a rolled sleeping bag and put it behind the boy's head.

"How do you feel, Rick?"

"A little dizzy, Nelson."

"Nauseated?"

"Not really…just a headache."

The professor gestured to one of the boys. "Pali, go back to the beach and pull up just one," he raised a single finger for emphasis, "small *naupaka*…make sure you get the root. And take a plastic bag and get some sea water."

The boy dashed off.

The girl who first saw them approach went over to Eros.

Ernie intercepted her. "Sorry, can't get too close to him. He's a police tracking dog."

"The police?" Her face wrinkled and she looked to Ala'ipaleile.

"These men are police officers. They're looking for the man who kidnapped the landowners you probably read about. They think the men might be held captive in one of the remote valleys. Detective McMillen, here," he nodded toward Ben, "has asked me to help, since I know the area so well."

Ben felt uncomfortable. He couldn't gauge whether Ala'ipaleile was genuinely surprised to see him, or if he was the calmest criminal he'd ever met. He remembered the other case involving a serial killer. There no tell-tale signs of 'the other personality.' Like the 'crazy switch' was turned off.

Ben looked at Ernie for a second. Then he turned to John Tucker. "Maybe you should go back and let Kip know we're okay. We'll be back there..." he checked his watch, more for effect than anything else because he had no idea what was going to happen. Would the professor convince him that he wasn't the killer? If not, would there be a struggle? He smiled to himself, thinking of Eros. The professor wasn't going to get away. "...say by one."

The Captain gave Ben a resigned look, then headed back down the path. He looked over his shoulder a few times, then disappeared around the bend near the beach.

"What happened, Rick?" asked another student.

The professor put his hand on Rick's shoulder. He faced the other students. "We were at the *ho'oulu'ai* I told you about, the *heiau* where *kāhuna* prayed for a good growing season. It was wet and Rick slipped off the rock platform and hit his head."

Ben's eyes, along with everyone else's, shifted to the injured student. He nodded, then grimaced. Softly, he said, "Slippery as hell."

The other students laughed when they saw him smile.

"I suggest you get back to your assignments. I'll tend to Rick. Go on."

After expressions of encouragement and 'hope you feel better,' the students returned to the dig.

Pali came running up the path, raising high a long *naupaka* root.

Ben watched in admiration as the professor prepared an old remedy and applied it to the open wound on the boy's head. He stripped the bark of the *naupaka* root, from a nearby backpack retrieved a plastic bag that Ben could tell contained sea salt, an ingredient in most Hawaiian cures, and in a wooden bowl pounded the root and the salt into a paste. He asked Pali to go farther up the trail, past the old settlement, explaining there was a small surviving patch of ti plants near the base of the cliff where water trickled down the side. He asked the student to pick a few of the larger plants for wrapping. When Pali returned a few minutes later, Ala'ipaleile cleaned Rick's wound with sea water, applied the paste over and around the afflicted area, and wrapped the boy's head in a band of ti leaves.

"Are you sure your stomach feels okay?"

"Uh huh."

"Okay…let's get you inside, the mosquitoes like *naupaka* root."

Ben helped Ala'ipaleile carry the student into the tent—the professor held the boy's shoulders and Ben his feet. Ernie held the tent flap.

When Nelson Ala'ipaleile emerged from the tent, he straightened and said, "Okay…let's talk." Without waiting, he walked away, headed up the path, past the remains of the village, until he reached the last rock foundation, far from his students. He sat on a flat rock.

They followed a short distance behind. Ben quietly warned Ernie that Ala'ipaleile might try to escape.

Ernie smirked.

"What makes you think it's me?"

"We found the bodies," Ben paused for reaction and got widened eyes, "right where you said they'd be."

"Which valley? Lost Tribe?"

Ben was silent. He wanted the professor to continue talking.

"Look, if you think I'm going to slip up…forget it…there's nothing to slip on. I didn't do it. If…"

"If what?" Ben asked.

The professor eyed Eros for a few seconds. "Nothing."

Ben had an idea. "We found *three* bodies in a swamp about a quarter of a mile from the beach in The Valley of the Lost Tribe." He waited for the professor to give him some indication that he wondered why they hadn't found the fourth, but there was nothing in the professor's expression that gave him away.

"I'm sorry they died, but this has nothing to do with me."

"We have to take you in."

The man's head jerked. "What for? Because I told you where they might be found? Fuck you, McMillen. I did exactly what you asked, and because I was right, I'm a suspect!"

Eros growled.

Ernie said something to the dog and he quieted.

Ben stood up and paced along the rock foundation. "Because we believe the only way for the killer to get the bodies from where they were taken to where they were found is by Zodiac."

Ala'ipaleile stared at Ben and wet his lips.

"Know how many Zodiacs there are on the Island?"

"No, but..."

"Captain Zodiac has ten. John Tucker, he has one, and guess what?...the college has the other. It may not be seaworthy today, but what about on the nights the landowners disappeared?"

"Look, McMillen..."

"There's more." Ben arched his back, giving the impression it ached, but actually he was making sure he could still feel his handcuffs wedged between his waistband and his back. After wearing them there for a while, he knew sometimes you lost the feeling of them, especially in the heat of a tropical valley, when a wet, sticky shirt was all you could feel. "So..." a long, frustrated sigh escaped, "when we found out the Community College had one, well...let's just say I wanted to talk with you. We went to your house...with a search warrant, by the way."

Ala'ipaleile stiffened hearing that. "You're serious, aren't you? So you searched my house?"

Ben snorted and shook his head. "There's more. We were in your workshop...we found..."

"...so you found fish hooks. I told you before I had ones like the one you showed me. I dig them up, remember? Hell, we can probably go find some right now." He stood.

"Sit down!"

Eros stood.

The professor sat.

Eros sat.

"We found things from the murdered men's homes."

"What?" Where? What did you find?"

Ben told him.

"I don't have things like that!" Ala'ipaleile moaned.

"I didn't make this up."

The professor stared at the ground, then picked up a small twig and began to draw an oval in the dirt.

Ben reached over and took the stick. He leaned over and scratched out fern plumes on top of the oval, tapa strips hanging from the bottom, and a sideways figure-eight opening for the eyes.

"Mind telling me why you drew that?" asked Ala'ipaleile.

"You have one of those helmets?"

"I did…don't suppose you'll believe if I tell you it was stolen?"

"When?"

"A few months ago."

"Report it?"

The professor just sighed.

"Well, who ever took it, seems to have put it back. How nice for you."

The professor's fists clenched, but only for a few seconds.

"One more thing, professor. Someone left a fish hook in the room where I'm staying. That same person loosened my brake cables. Did it while I was sleeping a few feet away. I'm a light sleeper. Think maybe the person who did it knows his way around bikes? Think if he wanted to get rid of me, make it appear like an accident, he might suggest a bike ride up Waimea Canyon, where you never brake? Except, of course, when you go back down, and loose brakes might mean crashing badly? Seems to me you recommended Waimea Canyon for a good ride. You remember that, don't you? A good ride for who?"

Ala'ipaleile looked him in the eye.

Ben expected to see hatred. It wasn't what he saw.

"I have to take you in, Nelson. I have to read you your rights."

In a low voice, the professor said, "Somebody has framed me."

Ernie, who sat transfixed all this time, got up and said, "C'mon…"

The professor looked at him, his expression seemed hopeful that maybe the other policeman would believe him. "I'm telling you…I didn't do this. Somebody set this up!" He looked at Ben again.

Ben now saw fear in the man's eyes, but something else was missing. He tried to get him to reach the brink of his personal abyss, to the hopeless feeling that it was over, to the point of no return when the other personality inside would explode from its evil hiding place. When the man would either lunge at them or break down and cry. But that look of a maniac, the glint in a demon's eye simply wasn't there.

Ben asked, "Who would want to frame you?"

"How the hell should I know! Jesus…" His hands covered his face.

"Talk, Nelson…Who? Why? Maybe someone against the Sovereignty Movement?"

The professor shook his head, his face still buried in his hands.

Ben looked at Ernie and shrugged.

Ernie mouthed, 'We should bring him in right now.'

Ben tried once more to raise the devil. He grabbed Ala'ipaleile by the shoulders and jerked him up. "Who stole your family's land?"

Calmly, Ala'ipaleile answered, "That bastard Bowden…"

Chapter 23

"Good work."

Ben, sitting in the Chief's office, stared out the window, silent.

"What's wrong?" asked Chief Johnson.

"I don't know…maybe I just don't want to believe it's him."

The Chief made two fists, pressed them against his desk, and stood. He walked over to the window and sat on the sill, purposely blocking Ben's view. Johnson said, "Listen, Ben…you knew going in the killer probably was Hawaiian, but that doesn't mean the whole Sovereignty thing is wrong…or dead."

Ben looked up. "Maybe that's bothering me a little, but…I don't know…"

"Just because you didn't catch him burying Crowley, doesn't mean he's innocent. You think the killer used a Zodiac, Ala'ipaleile has access to one, two, in fact. The killer mimicked night marchers, he's an expert on the topic. According to the Weston woman, the killer wore a…what did you call it?…a canoeman's helmet?…you found a helmet in his house, along with the things that were missing from the victim's houses. People saw torches…you found that piping concoction. You got more damn evidence for one case than we usually get for a dozen. C'mon…lighten up…you solved it."

Ben arched his back. Riding the Zodiac, hiking the valley, no sleep, and no exercise, made him stiff and tired. "Sometimes things seem a little too perfect."

"Christ! So what do you want to do now? Spend the rest of the week proving him not guilty?"

"What about a polygraph?"

"I don't believe this. Look, he refused…said he's innocent and he's not going to let some machine take advantage of his emotional state." The Chief scratched his scalp. "Maybe you should get some rest. It's nearly three-thirty. Knock off early. You, me, Gamos, and Patrolman Dumas...we'll go over it first thing in the morning. Arraignment's not 'til ten."

Ben got up, walked to the opposite side of the room, and leaned against the wall. Lips pursed, cheeks holding his breath. Then he let it out and asked, "Doc Brundy got anything new?"

"Yeah. Time of death coincides with the disappearances. Bodies ID'ed...needed dental records for Gatston. Go home."

"Where's Mike?"

"Gamos is on his way back from the Crowley place."

Ben's head jerked up.

"Don't worry...we're keeping two men up there and Crowley and his daughter and her husband are safe."

The fire at the Crowley estate, two years before, still bothered Ben. "I'm going to check on Forensics. If you see Mike, tell him I'm back there."

"You're starting to aggravate me. Go get some rest."

"Sorry. Soon."

Ben walked down the corridor to the Evidence Room. He thought about the professor just around the corner, locked in the padded holding cell. He thought about the students, whose field trip came to a most bizarre ending, having watched their mentor being led away by policemen, and themselves riding back with a big, burly stranger named Kip, who was instructed not to talk.

At least they didn't handcuff Ala'ipaleile, spared the students seeing that.

If he's innocent, why'd he say 'that bastard Bowden?'

Kevin Thompson was seated at his desk, chair angled back precariously, wedged awkwardly against the wall. A stack of forms covered his lap. His eyes were fixed onto the paper he held in his hands. When he saw Ben, his eyes narrowed.

"Please...not again."

Ben grinned. "We're not going anywhere. Do I look as bad as you?"

"And you probably don't smell better."

Ben took a chair, spun it around, and straddled it. "Whatcha got?"

"Necklaces match...same type of fish hook, same boar's hair, same ivory clasp. Churchwell's son identified the quilt. Man, what a piece of work he is. I kind of wish he were the perp." He leaned forward, bringing his chair with him. It hit the floor with a thump. "One of Frobert's friends recognized the British flag. Hey, want you to know...the guy said Frobert told him it was his grandfather's. Said it used to hang in ‘Iolani Palace. We found Gatston's flag at Ala‘ipaleile's place, as well."

Ben felt a bitter taste in his mouth. "What else?"

"No prints on that pipe setup or the helmet."

"None?"

Kevin shook his head. "Just like the necklaces. Might be able to get some off the flag, but we don't have the capability here to work with fabric very well. Have to send it to Honolulu…to the FBI lab."

Mike Gamos walked in, broad smile, hand extended. "Way to go, partner." When he saw Ben's expression, he said, "What I say wrong?"

"Nothing." Then Ben thanked Kevin, got up, and gestured for Gamos to follow him.

When they passed the Detectives' office, Gamos asked where they were going.

"For some fresh air. Let's go sit in the park." Ben put on his sunglasses.

"Huh?"

The sun was bright now, even though it poured for fifteen minutes just a half hour before. Steam rose from the puddled sidewalk and a fresh ozone smell filled the air. All around the ferns and torch ginger sparkled with raindrops reflecting the sunlight.

They walked along Umi until they found an empty park bench. Each detective brushed off the standing water with his hand before sitting.

"So why the long face?"

Ben's arms stretched along the back of the bench and he stared straight ahead. Gamos was at the other end, angled toward Ben, hands locked behind his head.

"Something's not right."

Gamos's shoulders slumped and his jaw held a heavy frown. He didn't say anything, he didn't have to.

"It seems too perfect to me."

"I don't understand. You found…"

"I know…I know what we found. The Chief and I have been through that." Ben took a deep breath. "Let me tell you what's bothering me and see if any of it makes sense."

"Go."

Ben rolled his head around his shoulders a few times. He felt his neck crack. "Let's start with Ala‘ipaleile. When we caught up with him, he didn't seem…well…guilty of anything. He was surprised to see me, but I think he figured I was just looking for the bodies like he and I'd discussed." Ben faced his partner. "You know about the injured student?"

"Chief told me the whole story."

"Well, that was all that seemed to be on his mind."

"Hey…all good criminals are great actors. It's pathological behavior…that's all."

Ben shook his head. "But after we took care of the boy…and I started to lay out what we found, he said he was framed."

"Wait a minute, Ben. Have you ever heard of a serial killer who had enough control of himself to actually frame someone in the process?"

Ben thought about that for a while. "Seems to me there are two types of serial killers. One has a vision of a victim…hair color, sex, size, profession…matches the description of someone who's burning in his brain, but it's random. He couldn't frame someone. But ours has a specific list…he's had to plan every killing…part of his plan could have been to frame someone. Maybe he doesn't want to get caught. What if the person's he's framing is really part of the list, too? Maybe not a landowner, but someone he wants to get even with, as well?"

Gamos leaned back, wrinkled his eyebrows, and his tongue rested between his lips. Then he rubbed his face like he was trying to erase his doubting expression.

Ben continued. "I really believe that if the killer finally got to Crowley, he'd stop. He's not like the stereotype serial killer who wants to get caught. This is more like how organized crime gets retribution…take out the people responsible and that's it. It's just business."

"I don't see it," Gamos said.

"I tried to get Ala'ipaleile to lose control. The last thing I asked him was who stole his family's land. He said 'that bastard Bowden.' If he didn't want to get caught yet, I don't think he'd slip up like that. You see, the professor has genuine bad feelings toward Bowden and maybe the others. His family's land *was* stolen. He belongs to the Sovereignty movement. He's a perfect candidate for a framing."

Gamos bent over, pulled at a blade of grass, broke it off, and sat back again, rolling the grass between his thumb and forefinger. "I suppose you've got more."

Ben smiled. "Yeah, I do. In fact, Kevin just gave it to me when you walked in. And this is something you'd wonder about, too."

"Don't hold out on me now."

"There were no fingerprints…not a one…not on the piping used to carry the torches, not on the helmet, and not on the necklaces."

"So he wiped them."

"What good does wiping them clean do if you keep them in your home?"

Gamos held his breath for a few seconds and let it out very slowly. Then his eyes searched out Ben's. They stared at each other for a long time.

Finally, Ben, hands now in front of him, palms out, said, "But if someone planted them there, then…"

"…son of a bitch…he'd have to wipe them clean."

"I don't think it's our professor, but I think I know how to find out who it is. C'mon."

"Whoa…where we going?"

"Just across the street."

The Kaua'i Museum was quiet. No one, except the receptionist, was in the main lobby. She recognized the two detectives right away and said that Beverly was around somewhere and offered to locate her.

Ben said, "That's okay, we'll find her."

They walked across the lobby to the rear and turned left. The museum director's door was open, but her desk chair was empty. Ben stuck his head inside, just in case she was standing by one of the bookshelves in the corners.

Ben looked at Gamos and shook his head.

"Let's try the room behind the gift shop," Gamos suggested.

When they didn't find her there and the person at the gift shop counter couldn't help, they retraced their steps across the lobby, and headed for the courtyard and the exhibits in the Rice building. Outside, the tiled patio that connected the two buildings was bathed in sunlight, although there were still numerous puddles of rainwater that collected near the edges of the protected walkway. A two-sided, yellow plastic tent-shaped sign warned CAUTION WET FLOOR.

The detectives skirted the water and entered the Rice building.

Ben pushed his sunglasses onto to the top of his head. Gamos hung his from the *V* at the top of his shirt. There was no sign of Beverly on the first floor, so they climbed the winding staircase. Ben stopped when one of the exhibits caught his eye.

The pictorial described the history of the sugar cane industry on the Island. Some of the wall space was dedicated to the growing and harvesting process, but what captured Ben's attention was another panel that showed the locations of the plantations and pictures of the landowners, names that now were eerily familiar to Ben, especially that of Henry Hartshorn, Carlton Crowley's grandfather.

Ben pointed to the typed paragraph beneath Hartshorn's photograph.

Mike Gamos stepped closer and read out loud. "Henry Hartshorn owned the largest plantation on Kaua'i around the turn of the century. It extended along the northeastern side of Kaua'i from Kumukumu to Anahola."

There were footsteps coming down the stairs, then a familiar voice. "Back again?"

Ben looked up. "Hi, Beverly. Can we talk with you for a minute?"

"Sure...let's go down to my office."

Mike Gamos nodded but didn't greet her.

Ben could tell there still was a little animosity between them.

When they emerged from the Rice building, Ben saw the clouds building up again. A fine mist fell. Looking north, dead ahead, over the fence that ran along the back of the courtyard, a large rainbow arched across the sky. If you believed Hawaiian legend, or at least one of the many myths concerning rainbows, a rainbow in your path when you were on a business journey was an omen of bad things to come. It was a warning to turn around and go home.

Gamos didn't catch Ben's hesitation, but Beverly D'marco did. She gave Ben a reassuring smile.

The rains came again, bouncing off the courtyard tiles like clear miniature marbles.

Beverly sat behind her desk. Gamos took a seat on the window sill that looked out onto the courtyard. The window was open and in the distance there was the distinct sound of car tires slicing through the rain soaked streets.

Ben chose to stand near the doorway, supporting his body by leaning on the built-in bookshelf that ran the length of the wall, realizing that if he sat, he might doze off. He fought off a yawn. This was a different tired feeling, not like the end of the triathlon where you felt like you've lost control of your muscles. This was like you had no muscles to control, no mental strength and no desire to think. After the triathlon you thought a lot, about where you could have done better, about how you would improve next year. Leaning there, facing the courtyard window, he asked his body for one last charge of adrenaline. He wanted to wrap this up by tomorrow and go home. He had some repair work to do on that front and he was without a clue about where to start. Every time he met with Beverly D'marco, he felt as if he were cheating on Lisa.

Gamos prodded him, "Ben?"

He cleared his mind and felt a surge of power, one last jolt to energize his questions. Taking a deep breath, Ben nodded to Gamos, arched his back, then slid to his right, away from an oversized book that jabbed into his back. First, he brought Beverly up to date from the third murder to Gatston, who'd really been the first, and last to the evidence against the professor.

She shook her head and continued to do so as his story implicated Nelson Ala'ipaleile. When he finished, she let out a sigh that could have extinguished a flaming torch.

"Now," Ben said, "…I don't think he did it."

Beverly stopped shaking her head and leaned forward, placing her clasped hands under her chin. She stared intently.

"So my question is…who has a motive to frame him? *or*…maybe better yet, who's exactly like him? That's it," now nodding himself, "that's really it. Who has the same set of circumstances as Ala'ipaleile?"

The museum director asked, "What do you mean?"

"Somebody set out to methodically kill the five major landowners…their descendants, that is. So we assumed that it has to be someone whose family lost their land around the time of the overthrow of Queen Lili'uokalani. The killer leaves a trail that fits his rage, but also one that fits the professor. All he has to do is plant the evidence, since everything coincides so perfectly, except he has to wipe his prints, and that's what doesn't fit. If you clean off the prints, you expect it to be found, so you don't hide it in your own house.

"While you both are thinking about that, I've got something else for you. I think that Crowley was the first victim."

Gamos clearly was puzzled.

"Not the first one to be murdered, but the first victim. Two years ago, his home was destroyed in a fire. When I first met him, he said 'bad things happen to people who encounter night marchers.' I think our night marcher did it. I think Crowley saw him that night. At that time…the night marcher looked for revenge, but hadn't yet progressed to murder. When Crowley had a stroke, I think our man felt satisfied, at least for a while. But over time the feeling came back to him. Unfortunately, maybe the growth in the Sovereignty movement refueled his anger.

"The exhibit in the other building said Crowley's grandfather's plantation extended from Kumukumu to Anahola. I say our killer's family is from there. So who lost his land to Crowley's grandfather? It starts with Crowley's family."

Beverly D'marco looked uneasy. Her eyes were empty. She was trancelike. Then she lowered her gaze to her desk, seemingly unaware that anyone else was present. One fist in front of her mouth, the other she kept clenching and unclenching.

"Bev? How 'bout it?"

Slowly she looked up at Ben.

He knew she knew who the killer was. Actually, he guessed she'd thought about it for a long time, only she refused to believe it. But now, with what he'd presented, she'd was able to fill in the rest, convince herself. How? He wasn't sure. But she knew.

Beverly D'marco cleared her throat. She looked at Ben. Then quick glance at Gamos, then back to Ben.

"Two years between Crowley's fire and the first killing." She paused, her eyes blinking rapidly as if that would erase what she knew. "I know someone who was away then, someone who was here when the fire happened, then went away until about three months ago."

"Who?"

The rain stopped and sunshine flooded the courtyard.

"His family was from Anahola. He lives in Kīlauea now."

"C'mon Bev, who?"

Now her expression was close to catatonic as she continued. "He and Nelson don't like each other, haven't ever since high school."

Ben watched her chest rise and fall with each breath, her mouth hung slightly open after she spoke. She reached across her desk and with her finger traced along the masthead of the local newspaper. And that triggered something for him. The newspaper.

Ben rested his head against the bookshelf and closed his eyes and tried to remember the exact phrase. 'Have you warned the other landowner?' Landowner…not landowners. At the time only one person knew that John Gatston wasn't in New Zealand, the person who killed him two weeks before and buried him in the swamp in The Valley of the Lost Tribe. He knew only Crowley remained alive.

Ray Kuali'i said that. Right before they entered the Sovereignty meeting. And a little while later, the reporter pointed out Ala'ipaleile. Urged Ben to talk with him. He set the plan in motion. Probably listened to their conversation outside the professor's office. Most likely was thrilled when the conversation turned to a good place for a bike ride.

Ben opened his eyes.

There was the sound of skidding flip-flops on the courtyard tile. The clatter of the plastic WET FLOOR sign. Someone cursing as he slipped and fell. Then quickly to his feet, eyes glazed with horror. It was Ray Kuali'i's face framed by the window, just above Gamos's left shoulder, staring directly at Ben.

Then Kuali'i turned and ran, vaulting the courtyard fence and disappearing on the other side.

Ben raced for the door, hearing Beverly D'marco, in a sorrowful tone, and obviously unaware of everything that was happening around her, saying softly, "Ray Kuali'i."

Chapter 24

Gamos, who was close behind, heard Ben yell for him to get his car and meet him at Kūhiō and Rice Street. The Līhu'e detective pivoted quickly and raced back to the station, trying to remember whether he left his keys in the ignition or on his desk. His head cocked left when heard the squeal of tires from the next block.

Ben charged up Rice Street, his head was turned to the right, hoping to get a glimpse of the speeding car that made the tires screech. Running toward the highway intersection where Rice ended, he thought about Ray Kuali'i. Although he didn't understand everything Beverly said, pieces of what she related helped him put together most of the mystery. What he really didn't grasp was the motive for Kuali'i's framing the professor. What was the rivalry between Nelson Ala'ipaleile and Ray Kuali'i? Was it theirs, or had some feud between their families existed all this time?

Besides Beverly's innocent attempt to help, it was the reporter who suggested he attend the Sovereignty meeting, knowing Ala'ipaleile would be there. Putting the two of them in contact. Kuali'i researched this well. Both families with stolen lands, imitating a night marcher when he knew the professor was an expert on the subject, even the Zodiac. But that left a question for Ben, how did the reporter get the school's Zodiac? Maybe it wasn't locked up that securely. Getting the schedule might not be hard, especially for a resourceful newspaper reporter. Plus, they probably knew him at the college, probably quite well. Maybe they even let him borrow it.

Rice Street ended just west of the museum at the highway—vehicles turned left for Kōloa and the south shore, right for Kapa'a. The traffic light was green and a steady stream of cars and trucks filed out of Līhu'e. Ben raced around the corner heading north following the sound of horns honking. He slowed when he saw a light blue Toyota pickup fishtail ahead and cut into the left lane even though there was hardly room. The pickup accelerated, weaved back to the right, then left again, and disappeared from view. But Ben got a good look at the driver—it was Ray Kuali'i right down to the lime green Croakies from which his sunglasses hung.

Ben dashed back to Rice and looked for Gamos's car. He didn't have to wait long as the detective's white Explorer, portable blue bubble strobe pulsing, raced up the street. Ben stepped into the right lane, held his detective's badge in the air and waved on-coming cars to the left. But there were still two cars at the light with no place to go. Ben was about to hold up the northbound cross traffic and wave through the cars blocking the right lane, when he saw Gamos's Explorer jump the curb and continue up the sidewalk. Gamos came to a screeching halt next to Ben, who yanked open the door, jumped inside, and shouted 'right' and pointed.

"Did I hear her right?...Kuali'i?"

Ben shifted and leaned against the door as he pulled out the radio transceiver from underneath him. "Yeah. I'll explain in a minute. Did you radio any roadblocks?"

Gamos floored the Explorer. "I let them know we'd be doing it."

Ben shouted into the radiophone.

A voice ordered, "Softer, McMillen."

"Sorry. We're in pursuit of Ray Kuali'i. He's headed north on Kūhiō. He might be armed. He's the serial killer."

"What?" said the dispatcher.

"Listen...get airport security. Be on the lookout for a late model light blue Toyota flatbed pickup. No license number. Kuali'i is...hell, tell them to get a bunch of *Garden Islands* from the newsstand and pass them out quickly. Kuali'i's picture's right with his column...page two, I think. Make sure every gate is covered. If he doubles back that way, he'll be at the airport in two or three minutes. Send four uniforms to the airport to assist whoever's already there."

Ben handed the transceiver to Gamos.

"Gamos, here. Also set up roadblocks along 56 before 580 and after 581. Then get back to me with how many other patrol are available. Ten-four."

They kept the channel open and heard the dispatcher order personnel in place. The security chief at the airport, just like the station dispatcher, said 'What?' when he was given the name of the fugitive.

They passed Highway 570, which led south and west to the airport.

"Turn?" asked Gamos.

Ben thought for a second. "Ahhh...no. Slow down, but I think he's headed north."

"Why? He can't get away."

"He's not trying to in that sense...the airport was just a precaution."

Gamos gave Ben a confused look, but didn't say anything.

They slowed, looked down 570, didn't spot the pickup or signs of cars that had veered out of the way.

Ben motioned for Gamos to step on it and they sped ahead.

When they had the left lane all to themselves, Gamos asked, "So where's he going?"

"He's going to end it."

"You mean Crowley?"

"Crowley's safe right? The Chief said..."

"Well..."

"Well what?"

"When you brought in Ala'ipaleile...we let them go back home."

"I know *that*. The Chief said you left two men there to guard them."

"To help them move back in...help with the old man 'til the end of their shift."

Ben eyed his watch. It was after four. "You mean they're gone now?"

"How long were they supposed to stay there?" Gamos sounded angry. "We thought Ala'ipaleile was the guy."

"Shit! Ben pushed the transceiver's send button. "Dispatch."

"Gotcha."

"Get somebody up to the Crowley place with backup and fill them in if they haven't already heard. And keep them there!"

"Ten-four."

"Wait...there's more. Any sign of Kuali'i at the airport?"

"None."

"See if you can get a chopper up...have it follow Kūhiō north."

"And you?"

"We're heading north...just turned at the light where 56 and 51 meet."

"Ten-four. Out."

Gamos drove the left lane, both hands tightly on the steering wheel. "We lose a lane just over the Wailua River...then it's a snail's pace. I think he'd be nuts to try Kapa'a traffic this time of day."

Ben checked his watch again. It was four-ten. "I wonder…when it starts backing up…if I get out and run…maybe he's only twenty or thirty cars up. Might catch him in a few minutes."

Gamos looked at him and gave him a wary look. "Nuts or not, he can't be going this way. Tell me…where do you think he's headed?"

The tension between them was gone. Ben realized it made no sense to keep Crowley under guard after Ala'ipaleile was jailed.

"Where, Ben?"

Ben didn't want to just say the Nā Pali Coast. "I bet he's got a Zodiac hidden somewhere along here…"

The dispatcher's voice interrupted. "We're getting the Princeville sub-station to help. They're gonna secure the Princeville Airport and set up a road block just east of Princeville. Called the Crowley place. Woman named Mary Rice answered. Said everything was okay. Ernie, the dog, and Dizon are on their way there. Nothing to report at the airport. Ernie wanted to know if he and Eros should be with you?"

"Not yet, I'll let him know. What about the helicopter?"

"Should be taking off 'bout now."

"Have him follow the coastline north."

"What's he looking for?"

"A late-model, light blue Toyota pickup on the highway or a Zodiac."

"You mean one of those motorized rubber rafts?"

"Exactly."

"Ten-four."

Gamos downshifted as traffic slowed. "You think he's going back to the swamp?"

"Either there…" It was coming to him. "…or…if he thinks it's the end…and he's still acting out his night marcher routine, he just might go to the leaping place."

"Where?"

"Polihale…the leaping point."

Gamos steered with one-hand. The other rubbed the stubble on his chin. "You know…he planned everything so well, maybe he's counting on us thinking he's headed for Nā Pali. Maybe he *is* trying to get away."

"He may be smart, but he's a psychopath, too. And that's the personality in charge now."

They swerved right and left, passing the early 'returning-home' traffic north. Gamos asked Ben to explain how he got Kuali'i from what the museum director was talking about. "I couldn't follow her."

"I didn't until she kept running her finger over the newspaper masthead. She was mesmerized by it. Then I just thought of something Kuali'i said a few days ago."

Gamos kept looking back and forth between the road and Ben. "Which was?"

"After Bowden…we were discussing the likelihood of the major landowners being the targets. He asked if I was going to warn the other landowner. He didn't say landowners. At that time, only the killer knew that Gatston was already dead. But I wouldn't have remembered it, at least not then, if Bev hadn't figured it out and become spellbound by the newspaper."

"What do you think he was doing there? Spying?"

"Sure…I think he wanted to know if we really bought into the professor. Hey…he could follow us almost anywhere we went, and then if we spotted him, he could just casually walk up and say he was looking for us. Just on the job, looking for a follow-up story.

"I'm sure he could hear everything standing out there in the courtyard…bet he was shocked when he heard Bev putting it together. Bet she's the only one he worried about all along…"

"You think maybe he was there because he was going to kill her?"

Ben hadn't thought of that. "I'm just glad it was wet and he slipped." He rubbed his temples. He felt like someone was slowly turning a vise around his head.

Gamos braked, downshifted, and cursed. Then he asked Ben, "You getting out?"

Ben leaned out of the window and tried to spot the light blue pickup.

The radio crackled. "Mike and Ben?"

"Here."

"Ray Kuali'i lives just beyond Kumukumu, in the hills, near the reservoir. He might be headed there."

"I know where it is," said Gamos.

"Princeville's on the move, be there in ten minutes. Can only send one man to Princeville Airport. Chopper's up, you might even see it pass you 'bout now. Wait!"

The detectives heard excited voices on another communications line.

"Guys…a uniform checking out a complaint at the College just radioed in…their Zodiac and van are missing."

"Ten-four." Ben took a deep breath.

Gamos shook his head. "Ray Kuali'i...never would have guessed."

The pounding in Ben's head increased. "Where's he got it?"

"Could be any place from here to...hell...anywhere along the coast."

"We have to get around the traffic."

Gamos needed no further urging. He signaled left, crossed the yellow line and headed the wrong way up the highway. Cars honked, some seemed determined to hold their ground, but the Explorer managed to carve a path that straddled the double yellow.

"There...look!" yelled Ben.

The chopper whizzed by at about five hundred feet, following the coastline north.

They came to the Wailua River and Gamos prepared to turn onto 580 at the light ahead.

Suddenly, Ben shouted again. "Down there! There he is!"

At the mouth of the Wailua River, a Zodiac streaked by, creating a huge wake as it veered sharply north just after it reached open water. Kuali'i was at the helm.

"What now?"

Ben picked up the radiophone. "We're getting on the chopper...then we're getting a Zodiac."

Gamos uttered, "Oh, no."

One section of Waipouli Plaza's parking lot was cleared of cars. The police helicopter set down, Ben and Mike Gamos hustled over to it, climbed in, buckled up, and held on when the craft rose and angled inland across the mountains, headed for Hanalei.

Ben contacted Captain Zodiac. Gamos held his stomach.

They determined that the best place to land was the beach at Hanalei Bay where the Captain Zodiac tour operators promised two crafts and crew ready to go. They decided against a single Zodiac for two reasons. If one broke down, they'd have a backup. More important, a Zodiac with five people, a Captain, himself and Gamos, and two Hanalei officers, would slow down the raft too much. Kuali'i could easily out distance them. It was decided Ben would go alone with one captain, while Gamos and the patrolmen would travel in the other craft. The helicopter would lead the chase, but most likely, if Ben's guess was right, it wouldn't be much help flushing out Kuali'i from some dense valley or from the tangled growth on a vertical cliff. In the end, that was going to take legwork.

And luck not to get killed in the process.

▼▲▼

He wondered how it went wrong, more than two years of meticulous planning, figuring out how to get even with the *haole* landowners who swindled his ancestors, and finding a way to implicate the man who always got the better of him.

Speeding along the northeastern coast, passing Kahala Point and Anahola, homeland of his great grandparents, his *kūpuna kuakahi,* he remembered the first time he fought Nelson Ala'ipaleile. It was in the fourth grade after school. He took a few pogs from a small boy in the second grade and when the boy tried to get them back, he bloodied his nose. Then Ala'ipaleile appeared, pinned him against the wall, and made him give back the cardboard bottle tops, embarrassing him in front of his friends, in front of the girl he liked so much. Next year, it was May Day, and the races, and he finished second to Ala'ipaleile in both the fifty- and one hundred-yard dashes. And the girl he liked starting paying more attention to the winner. All through high school it was the same thing, Nelson Ala'ipaleile came in first, and he, the loser, came in second. He decided then that one day he would get the better of Nelson Ala'ipaleile.

Even when he first heard about the movement for Sovereignty, and he showed up at one of the meetings, Ala'ipaleile was there. Not only that, he was friends with the founders, and Ala'ipaleile soon became the group's secretary. He was the journalist, what right did Ala'ipaleile have to take his job?

Kīlauea Lighthouse loomed ahead port-side. The sea cliffs were made from hundreds of layers of compressed lava, the edges jagged and cracked from eons of wind and rain. The craggy face was covered with a beard of mosses and lichen and twisted shrubs that somehow managed a precarious foothold on the rock wall. The sea, which pounded continuously at the base of the great *pali*, carved away much of the sea cliff's foundation. One day much of it would fall into the ocean. But what the cliffs lost, the reef would gain.

Everywhere seabirds nested. Red-footed bobby, great frigatebirds, red-tailed tropicbirds. They soared above the relentless surf, fishing, feeding, and fertilizing. There were so many birds that when Kuali'i passed below, the collective wingspans of the birds blocked out the sun.

Ray Kuali'i's thought of the Hartshorns, the people who separated his great grandfather from the land of his ancestors, to Carlton Crowley, the grandson, who eventually took over the sugar cane plantation and destroyed every last remnant of Hawaiian life as his ancestors knew it. He remembered a story of his ancestors, huddled together in a dark cave, the only place where it was safe for them to speak their native tongue. He pounded the pilot's console with his fist and cracked the plastic covering.

His mind went back to the time, two years before, when he finally decided he endured enough. Disguised as a night marcher, a canoeman, warrior of the seas, he'd torched Crowley's summer home, not to kill him, but to let him experience the agony of losing something dear. And after, when he took a reporter's job on O'ahu for the *Advertiser*, he was assigned to cover the Office of Hawaiian Affairs and the Sovereignty Movement. Sovereignty was on the minds of many Hawaiians and Ray Kuali'i was no exception. It was then, during his two years on O'ahu, that his idea of retribution began to germinate.

Like on O'ahu, where five *haole* men were mainly responsible for the overthrow of the Queen and the eventual redistribution of the land, Kaua'i's sugar cane lands became the domain of five families. Why not make them all pay? This time make Crowley last. Make him worry, make him fearful, as one by one his contemporaries disappeared, never to be found.

But that damned detective from Kona found them, found him. Should have run him off the road when he'd had the chance that first night. Should have really fucked up his bike, or better yet, when he struggled with the Waimea downhill, just run him off the road right there. Throw what was left of him over the cliff.

Princeville, perched high to his left, made him angry—look what they'd done to the land. Condos stacked upon condos. Golf courses and chemical fertilizers. His hand pushed against the throttle, but it already was as far forward as it could go. Kuali'i took a deep breath, inhaling the fresh salt air, and he smiled broadly. Framing Ala'ipaleile was the best part. The first time, two years before, dressing as a night marcher was a whim, something that came to him just days before the torching. But now, when he began with Churchwell, it was part of his plan. Make it look like Ala'ipaleile did it, get even with that son of a bitch. Ala'ipaleile's family lost their land in Lāwa'i to the Bowden family—and Charles Bowden was on the list. Nelson Ala'ipaleile, the great professor, writing about night marchers. Terrific. The professor's archeology club, that's what gave him the idea to bury the landowners in The Valley of the Lost Tribe. It was symbolic, but more important, it was a place that Ala'ipaleile visited many times before.

His mood changed and suddenly he was sad. He always thought he'd get away with killing the landowners. And when it all was done, he planned to write a column, condemning violence, yet sympathizing a little with Ala'ipaleile, telling his readers not to mistake the crazed actions of one man as being the mind set of the people behind Sovereignty. He had it all figured out. Now, he was on the run, the long run, the last run, and his column wouldn't be written. Would his actions destroy the very thing he hoped to help? No one would understand. What would they say about him?

When he neared Hanalei Bay, Beverly D'marco's pretty face appeared in his mind. The woman he loved all these years.

▼▲▼

The speeding Zodiac with the killer aboard flew across the far edge of Hanalei Bay, just when Ben, Mike Gamos, the Hanalei patrolmen, and the crew from Captain Zodiac were shoving off.

Ben had hoped they could intercept Kuali'i before he made it past the bay. Now they were faced with a chase, but Ben was pretty sure Kuali'i was headed one of two places—The Valley of the Lost Tribe or Polihale. If not, Ben didn't expect to lose him—Kuali'i was sure to run out of gas before they did.

The stolen Zodiac disappeared around Makahoa Point, the western boundary of Hanalei Bay. The two rubberized rafts raced in pursuit, but as the Zodiac with Ben and his Captain made the end of the bay, the second pursuit craft began falling behind. It had slightly smaller engines and carried twice as many passengers.

Then more bad news. A radio report from the helicopter pilot that he had a red light. As soon as they checked it out and had the problem repaired they'd catch up. He guessed it would take thirty to forty minutes.

Around the point, Ben spotted Kuali'i. He was about a half-mile ahead, following the coastline about a quarter-mile out. Ben was amazed that not once did the reporter, murderer, turn around to see where they were. It was like he had his mind set on a destination, and nothing else mattered. Maybe he hadn't seen them in the first place.

The sun was an hour from going down and it cast a path of light that looked like stepping stones across the water, as if Pele, the fire goddess, took a sliver of the sun, and hurled it like a flat skipping stone across the sea.

They passed Kē'ē Beach and veered to the southwest. The northern Nā Pali Coast appeared, rocky, yet lush, dangerous with sharp ridges and a mask of low clouds, but also kind of serene as the cliffs absorbed the fading sunlight.

"Where do you think he's headed?" the Captain asked Ben.

Ben told him his guesses, then inquired how long before they reached The Valley of the Lost Tribe.

"Huh?"

"Honopū Valley?"

"Oh. No more than twenty minutes."

"You have a flare gun aboard?"

"Yup."

"How accurate is it?"

The Captain, Herman Baker, answered, "What do you mean?"

"How close would we have to get to be able to hit the other Zodiac?"

"Gee…I don't know. When you shoot them up in the air, some kind of twist and spiral, like a rocket a little out of control. I think we'd have to be pretty close."

"Would it put a hole in it?"

"Sure…I think so…if we're close."

A few miles back Ben realized, or at least came to terms with the fact, that Ray Kuali'i was probably going to kill himself. He couldn't hope to hide in the valley for too long. But gauging from how he went about the murders, it seemed that he would act out something from the past. Long ago there were places of refuge—*heiau* where defeated warriors, the weak, and *kapu* breakers, those who broke the law, could seek safety. Usually those in need of sanctuary were closely pursued, just as Kuali'i was now, and barely made the haven, sometimes running with abandon across jagged lava fields, or by swimming in dangerous currents. It was the responsibility of the attendant *kahuna* to provide asylum, to begin a healing process that typically lasted one cycle of the moon.

Ben knew of one such famous place of refuge—Pu'uhonua O Honaunau, which meant 'temple of refuge of (the place called) Honaunau.' It wasn't far from where he lived, a few miles to the south, on a lava field by the sea. But he knew of no place of refuge on the Nā Pali coast, and really he didn't think Kuali'i to be consumed with the past to the point where he believed that somewhere along the great cliffs was a place of real salvation, that there was a savior priest waiting for him.

No, Kuali'i came to die.

The stolen craft maintained its lead over Ben's Zodiac, but the third craft began to drop far back.

They made Hanakāpīʻai Beach, then Waiahuakua Stream, Hanakoa Stream, then Manono Ridge, a series of sea caves where Kualiʻi could hide if he had a greater lead. Then past Kalalau Valley dotted with neon tents, and finally The Valley of the Lost Tribe. But the crazed reporter continued on.

Ben swallowed hard. *Polihale.*

Twenty minutes later they reached Makaha Point, having passed both valleys, Nuʻalolo Kai and Miloliʻi, where Ben pursued Nelson Alaʻipaleile just the day before. From there he could see the barren cliffs of western Kauaʻi. Beyond, a speck of yellowish-white, the beginning of Barking Sands Beach, and above that point, just a little north, Polihale, the place where one's spirit entered the world of its ancestors.

The sun sat suspended above the horizon, orange now, swollen, wavering like a desert mirage, waiting for some magic moment when it was time to sink into the sea, extinguished for another day. For Ray Kualiʻi, maybe extinguished forever.

Kualiʻi swerved sharply and headed toward shore, to the sliver of sand at the end of the beach, where the grains of coral sand disappeared into a field of moss-covered rocks and boulders. He sped inland, never cut his engine, and wedged into the beach with such force that he was thrown from the inflatable raft and landed on the beach. A few yards farther left and Kualiʻi would have collided with the rocks. He sat there.

Ben saw him sitting in the sand as if he were there simply to admire the setting sun. Kualiʻi rubbed his shoulder. He seemed to be staring at them.

"Hold on," the Captain shouted.

Ben grabbed the side of the raft and knelt. When they were fifty feet from shore, Kualiʻi sprang to his feet and began climbing over the rocks, slipping on the film of lichen with every step. He scrambled on all fours and finally made it to the base of the cliff. He paused at the base of the *pali* for a few seconds, then started to climb.

Ben looked at the cliff, which from a quarter mile out didn't appeared so treacherous, but close in, climbing it more than fifty feet up seemed impossible.

Ben took his eyes off of Kualiʻi when he heard the Zodiac scrape bottom. He turned and saw the Captain yank the engines free of the sand and they glided fairly smoothly onto the beach twenty feet to the right of the other craft.

Ben jumped out. "Stay here, make sure the other Zodiac sees us," he shouted to the Captain, and get the flare gun ready to signal the chopper when it shows.

Then he focused on capturing the man who ended the lives of the four landowners. Having seen Kuali'i stumble on the rocks, Ben walked carefully, bending, using his hands to feel his way across the slippery stones. When he reached the foot of the cliff, he heard the third Zodiac in the distance, looked out to sea, and saw the craft slow down, and began to turn in. He looked up and saw Kuali'i more than a hundred feet above, perched precariously on a small ledge, looking at his hands, looking down at him, rubbing his shoulder again, then standing and climbing higher.

Ben took a deep breath and began his ascent, wondering if it made sense. Kuali'i wasn't going to escape. The only reason for Ben to go after him was to talk him down, to convince him not to jump. Was he worth it? This man probably set the Sovereignty Movement back a hundred years to its beginning.

A small avalanche of rubble and rock clattered down the side of the cliff, missing Ben by a few feet. He grabbed a tree root, tested its strength, and hoisted himself higher. That's how he climbed, holding onto a root or a branch, or the jagged edge of the rock wall, foot after foot. Not once did he look down.

When he reached the spot a hundred feet up where Kuali'i first rested, he stopped and carefully twisted around to sit. While catching his breath, Ben examined his hands. His finger tips bled, so did his palms. One fingernail was torn so deeply that the raw skin underneath already oozed a yellowish film.

He looked up. The cliff seemed to disappear, and so had Kuali'i. Ben was frantic at first, thinking while he climbed straight up, Kuali'i angled left or right. What if there was a way out? A path to the top? Or a cave that sat far above the beach? What if it actually lead the reporter to safety? Ray Kuali'i was not someone to underestimate.

A shot echoed from below. Instinctively, Ben jerked back, but soon saw the grayish-white streaking plume of the flare knifing through the muted sunlight. A deep red explosion of burst above the beach about a hundred feet over his head. Then deep gray smoke drifted out to sea.

Soon after he heard the thumping noise of a helicopter. He couldn't see it, but from the sound of the rotating blades, he guessed it was at the top of the cliff, where he assumed the actual leaping place was located. Kuali'i's escape, at least from up there was blocked. Twisting around, slowly standing, feeling a little dizzy when he accidentally looked straight down for a second, Ben caught his balance and began climbing again.

Fifty feet higher he was out of breath, his hands ached, and he had a bad cramp in his left calf. He was at another flat spot where the face of the cliff was worn away, a nesting place described it best. He no longer heard the helicopter, but thought he'd subconsciously heard the engine gradually shut down. Looking up into the fading sunlight, he saw Kuali'i only thirty feet away. The murderer looked down at him. His face reflected all the anguish a face could hold.

"This is it, McMillen. Right here, this is it."

Ben slumped against the rock wall, breathed deeply but slowly. He wiped the sweat from his forehead with the back of his hand. He looked down at the beach and had the sensation he was falling forward. Ben pressed his body against the rock wall. His mouth was dry. He could hardly swallow. If he was going to talk Kuali'i down, he would be from here. He would climb no farther.

Ben looked down again and saw the patrolmen from Hanalei slugging through the sand, headed toward the campers and bathers, a quarter-mile away, who now were running toward Polihale, probably curious about the helicopter perched on the cliff and the beached Zodiacs. The black rubber hulks probably looked like a small pod of beached killer whales from that distance.

Gamos was by the rocks, looking up, shouting with his hands cupped to his mouth.

Ben couldn't hear him. He looked up at Kuali'i.

"Ray. What do you plan on doing?"

"Isn't it obvious," Kuali'i shouted, his right hand extended toward the sea.

The sun now began to melt into the horizon. Far to Ben's right, other campers, oblivious to the drama on Polihale, observed the sunset, some with cameras, some standing, some sitting with their arms holding their knees. A few children ran up to the water, then raced back as the waves approached. But the tide was low and the surf weak and the game didn't seem to have the same appeal that it must have had earlier in the day, for the children soon sat down and watched the end of the day with their parents.

"Ray..."

"Don't waste your words, Ben."

Kuali'i stood and took off his shirt.

Ben could see the fish hook necklace pressed against his chest.

"Ray...does Sovereignty really mean something to you?"

"It means more to me than to you."

"Did you really think killing those men would help?"

"Of course it helps...maybe in the future, others will think twice before they displace a nation."

Ben thought about what to say next. He didn't want it to end with Kuali'i leaping to his death. He wasn't sure why. Maybe it was that some of the truth would die as well and that it was important that the entire story be known.

Maybe the truth would help someone else. Maybe even help those seeking sovereignty, make them step back, make them willingly to compromise.

Ben tasted the salt on his lips as he tried to wet them. "I'm not here to lie to you. You'll probably go to jail for the rest of your life, but if sovereignty means as much to you as you say…"

Kuali'i sat back down and some rocks tumbled down the side of the cliff, bouncing against the face, setting off small rivers of gravel and stone that in turn set off more, like a chain reaction.

Ben coughed as the cloud of dust passed, then his foot slipped, and he slid forward. He reached for a skinny, gnarled tree trunk, but it snapped when he grabbed it. With his other hand he found a jagged rock, which held onto tightly even though it cut into his palm. But he stopped sliding. He was afraid to move.

Kuali'i laughed. "Care to join me?"

Ben slowly wiggled backward until he was pressed up against the face of the cliff.

Both men were quiet for a while.

Ben finally broke the silence. "I was saying, if…"

"What…come down? Turn myself in. Say I'm sorry so the Movement can go on. You suggesting a little damage control here? The damage was done a hundred years ago. No, it was done long before that, when we thought Captain Cook was a god.

"I'm an old Hawaiian now, Ben. Here I am at Polihale, ready to join my ancestors, I'm a spirit now. We shouldn't have to fight for sovereignty…people are born with it…it should never be taken away." His pants went next. Underneath he wore a *malo*, dyed with the markings of his clan.

Ben's stomach churned. He didn't kid himself. There wasn't much he could say or do now. But he had to try.

When the sun completely disappeared and twilight set in, Kuali'i got up and faced southwest toward the Island of Ni'ihau.

Ben could see that Kuali'i's eyes were closed. Ben got to his feet, reached for a thick root for support. This one held.

Get him talking…buy some time. "Ray…why The Valley of the Lost Tribe?"

Kuali'i told him.

Ben asked several more questions, stalling.

Kuali'i didn't answer.

Finally, there was silence between them.

After watching several brown noddy fly by, the reporter asked, "Ben…do me a favor?"

"Ray..."

"Will you do me a favor?"

"What?"

"Will you?"

"Yes."

"I do believe that what I did was for the good of the Sovereignty Movement...write it for me. Write my last column."

Ray Kuali'i opened his eyes and looked down at Ben and smiled. Then his head jerked and he pointed and exclaimed, "Look!"

Slowly, untrusting, Ben turned his head and looked down, then quickly back up at Kuali'i, saw he still pointed below. Ben peered down again into water near the fading shoreline.

"There...look there...they came!"

In the water, maybe twenty feet from shore, four dark green spots bobbed in the surf.

"Ben...just like they said...*honu*...my *'aumakua*, beckoning me to join them. Four of them."

Ben stared, almost in disbelief, because if there was one story that impressed him most of all his grandmother's stories, it was that when a person was to die, his *'aumakua*, the family guardian spirit, would give him the signal when it was time, would lead him to the leaping point for *leina a ka 'uhane*, 'the leap of the soul.'

When the heads of the four green turtles suddenly disappeared beneath the sea, Ben instinctively looked up and saw Ray Kuali'i jump. Ben leaned forward over the cliff, one hand desperately clutching the tree root, the other completely extended, stretching until his tendons felt as if they would rip. All he felt was the movement of air.

Ben pulled back and closed his eyes, and prayed that Kuali'i reached the water. Then he heard the sickening sound on the rocks below that he would remember the rest of his life.

Chapter 25

The helicopter floated down to the beach. What was left of Ray Kuali'i's body was wrapped in two blankets and carried from the rocks to the helicopter. And Ben finally made it down from Polihale after sitting there for a long time, removed from the scene below, thinking about simple things—sunrise, clouds drifting upslope, gentle rain, birds in pairs darting through the rainforest, blow holes, humpback whales caring for their young, the sound the surf made as it crashed against lava rock. Sunset.

It was dark now, except for the distant campfires that dotted Barking Sands, the campers returned to their campsites and only a large brown dog remained near, sitting on his haunches, watching the policemen load the night marcher's corpse onto the helicopter, then watching the man who now sat by the rocks—grabbing handfuls of sand, letting a small stream trickle from his fist, over and over again.

When the rotors began to spin, the dog jerked up and ran away, headed back down the beach to the glowing lights.

Mike Gamos came over to Ben.

"Ready to go?"

Ben let go of a handful of sand, looked up, rolled his neck back and forth across his shoulders, took in a deep breath, then let it out slowly. "I think I'll stay a while longer." He picked up more sand. "You go…I'll go back with the Zodiac…pick up the car…you go."

"The car's in Waipouli."

"I'll manage. I need some time."

The Līhu'e detective patted Ben on the shoulder and walked back to the helicopter.

Ben saw him talk with the pilot, then the two patrolmen, and finally, with the two men from Captain Zodiac. The patrolmen looked at Ben and saluted.

Ben threw a half-hearted salute back.

While the Zodiac captains made ready, one patrolman tied the stolen Zodiac to the stern of the one of the inflatables. Then his partner secured the engines so they would remain out of the water during the return trip. Leaving one Zodiac captain behind to wait for Ben, the policemen and other Captain shoved off and soon disappeared into the dark.

Gamos climbed aboard the helicopter, looked one last time at Ben, then signaled to the pilot. The giant bird lifted off the beach, sandblasting a small crater beneath its fuselage, rising slowly, straight up, higher, past Ray Kuali'i's leaping place, above the ridge, then banked inland, and thumped away into the night.

The remaining Zodiac captain asked Ben if he was ready.

Ben responded, "I'll be ready soon."

"I'll take a short walk down the beach." The Captain added nonchalantly, "But I would like to leave in fifteen minutes or so. This is my first time out here alone."

Ben gave him an incredulous look.

"I'm new…from Washington State. I know all about Zodiacs, driven them for years. We'll be okay as long as we stay far enough out…don't know where all the reefs are yet…like to get underway soon just in case the sky clouds up and hide the cliffs." The Nā Pali Coast rookie left.

Ben stood, went to the remaining Zodiac, leaned over the side, and found a bucket. Then he walked along the waterline—about twenty feet from the rocks where Ray Kuali'i's life ended. Ben filled the bucket with sea water, and when he brought the bucket up the metal handle dug into the deep cut on his palm and the sea water sloshed over the sides, the salt stinging the rest of his cuts and scrapes. He switched hands, walked up to the rocks to the spot where the reporter's body landed, and emptied the bucket, washing away some of the blood and tissue. Back to the water to refill the bucket. Back to the rocks. Again and again, until finally, although he could not see clearly in the dark, he felt all traces of what happened were gone.

▼▲▼

When they passed The Valley of the Lost Tribe, Ben began to think about what Ray Kuali'i said when he'd asked why he'd buried the landowners there.

'Because that's what we have become...a lost tribe.'

And something strange happened to him just then, a feeling of anger swept over him, he felt hot and cold at the same time, his fists clenched, teeth grinding until his jaw ached. He ignored the pain in his hands. For the first time he actually felt hatred for the *haole* plantation owners who overthrew the Queen, who ended the Hawaiian Kingdom, who'd taken the Crown lands. Suddenly he felt bound to the indigenous people of the Americas, pictured Cavalry charging an Indian village, shooting men and women as they fled, leaving children without parents to perish on the prairie; envisioned thickly clad hunters decimating walrus and seal and polar bear, leaving the Eskimo nothing to eat and nothing with which to shield themselves from the Arctic cold; saw Hawaiians huddled in Church hearing about the greatness of the Messiah, saw the suffering and death of people with no immunity to the white man's diseases, saw a population of proud people dwindle to almost nothing, the land erode, the plants and animals and birds endangered, remembered that his people had to practice their culture and speak their native language in secret for many, many years.

Unfortunately, now it seemed that only Hawaiians who were willing to become Americanized succeeded.

He wondered about the middle ground. Would that approach work, or do you really have to take a hard stance on Sovereignty? There was a lot at stake here.

The Zodiac churned on.

Above, the sky glowed with light from other worlds. Thousands of stars, constellations that gave meaning to Hawaiian life, distant fires that led the ancestors to their new home. The white veil of the Milky Way, the sky so thick with promise.

He saw a shooting star. His people called it *hōkūlele,* flying star.

Just before Kē'ē Beach, Ben realized this would be the last time he'd see the Nā Pali Coast for some time. In the dark, as they neared the point, he peered at the silhouette of the giant cliffs, barely making out the jagged peaks against the glow of the distant fires in the sky. He thought about all that happened on the ancient coastline, discovering the missing landowners, finding the fourth victim, tracking the professor, the rush of excitement when he spotted Ala'ipaleile carrying a body, the momentary relief when he discovered it only was an injured student. The helpless feeling as he reached in vain when Kuali'i leaped from Polihale.

Staring into the darkened cliffs, he thought he it was a dream. But it was there. He couldn't believe his eyes. Ben shouted for the Captain, pointed up to a procession of fire, torches marching, seemingly floating over the side of the *pali*. The flames flickered, the wind caught small embers and lifted them higher, then the marching stopped and the torches formed a circle.

"What do you make of that?" asked the rookie Captain.

"Pull up on the beach."

"We're going up there?" he asked.

"You stay with the Zodiac."

Ben jumped off the inflatable, landed a few feet short of the shore, and high-stepped through the water. He crossed the sand and found the trail along the rocks that would take him back to where he saw the torches.

For some reason he wasn't fearful, but that didn't stop his head from spinning. Could there be someone else impersonating night marchers? Was Ray Kuali'i protecting someone? Were there really night marchers? Crazy thoughts.

The path was uneven with imbedded rocks and protruding tree roots and Ben stumbled several times. To his right, he could see the faint white curl of the incoming waves, heard the water make a gurgling sound as it carved out trenches on the shore. He barely could see the Zodiac and the rookie Captain and they soon disappeared from view. Then, to his left, along the steady rise of rocks and ferns, he saw the white clapboard of a house and he wondered who lived there, wondered if there was an old man inside, descendant of a plantation owner. Cowering in his bed? Or was he already gone?

The *hala* and *kukui* trees blocked the view of the rest of the house and there didn't seem to be an entrance from the trail that led up there, so Ben continued on, going quickly now, his eyes completely adjusted to the dark, enabling him to see the roots and rocks. The trail made a sweeping turn left, rising a little, but gave no evidence that it led to the place where he'd seen the torches, high up, at a height he'd estimated at two or three hundred feet.

Then, on his left, was another pathway, steep and partially blocked with rocks. He paused, eyes squinting along each trail until the darkness cut off his vision. He took a deep breath and listened. There were faints sounds of a drum to his left. More important—there was an pale, orange light above the new pathway like that of a distant forest fire. So he climbed the new trail, around boulders, through a few flat areas of short grass, barely able to see the worn earth as his eyes adjusted more to the glow above than the darkness below. Ben followed the path more by the sound his shoes made than by sight. He was about halfway up now and when he looked over his shoulder, he saw the white foam of dozens of small waves as they rolled toward the shore. A line of clouds began to cover the band of the Milky Way and it became darker again.

He felt perspiration along his spine and on his forehead. Then he saw the flaming torches, and he slowed, catching his breath while he thought. Continuing as quietly as he could, walking on the grass, which bordered the pathway, remembering at that very instant that he'd taken off his handcuffs and tucked them into the crack between the hull and the side of the Zodiac, just after they'd left Barking Sands.

He heard chanting. A low droning call to the past.

The boulder field in front of him blocked his view now, but the smooth rocks shone with torch light and the voices became louder. It sounded like many people, not one night marcher, but it also sounded like women. He swallowed, licked his lips, and moved forward, using the boulders to shield his advance.

When he came to an opening between two large stones, he saw, about fifty feet ahead and maybe twenty feet higher up the side of the cliff, a large platform, not unlike those in the old village of Nu'alolo Kai, this one illuminated by the flames not flashlights. At the rear, several people sat. The chanting stopped. It was quiet. Then a woman shouted something and almost immediately Ben heard the upbeat sound of a gourd drum and the sound of feet, dancing feet. The drum pounded against the earth. He heard the swishing sound of ferns harmonious with the movements of five *hula* dancers, young girls, serious faces streaked with torch light.

Using the boulders for leverage, he squeezed through the narrow opening, climbed up a set of uneven stepping stones, and stood before the ceremony, hands on hips, breathing just as hard as he usually did after running ten miles. Would his mouth be dry forever?

The drumbeat stopped as did the song and the dancers stood still.

He heard a voice.

She said, "Aloha, Ben. Come…come sit by me."

He couldn't see who spoke, but he could tell from where the voice came. Walking up to the platform, he shielded his eyes from the flames, and peered at a person seated twenty feet away. Squinting, leaning forward, then quickly he straightened. It was the old woman from the Ka Lāhui Hawai'i meeting. The one on the stage. The woman who watched him then. Her voice sounded strong and young. He looked at her hands. They weren't trembling at all.

Looking in every direction after he ascended to the *hula* platform, he saw at least a dozen young girls. They were seated now along the other three sides of the *heiau.* Only the old woman sat on the far side. Her legs were crossed and she smiled and gestured for him to sit beside her.

When he was seated she asked, "Do you know where you are, Ben?"

"No…I don't." He swallowed and stared into her eyes.

Her face seemed remarkably smooth and wrinkle-free, her lips were painted white. Gray hair pulled back and held by a ring of hibiscus. A *maile lei* hung open around her neck, twisted fragrant leaves, shiny, dark vines that were associated with Laka, the goddess of *hula.*

"This is Ka Ulu a Paoa…birthplace of the *hula*…where my *kupuna wahine* learned *hula*, and my mother, and me. Where I teach these *kamali'i*, children."

"How do you know me?"

The old woman smiled.

Ben couldn't remember her name. He felt embarrassed. It was Ray Kuali'i who told him what her name was. He shivered. 'Chicken skin' covered his arms.

The woman took the blanket that protected the base of the drum from the ground and handed the cloak to him, gesturing for him to wrap it around his shoulders.

He was warmer now and he concentrated on her name. But it was no use.

The old woman said, "Tobi Otaki told me about you."

Ben's head jerked, and as it did, some of the girls laughed.

The woman smiled.

"Tobi?" Then he was drawn back almost two weeks, to the day he left for Kaua'i, and he remembered it. Ben lifted the blanket away from his left arm, reached into his back pants pocket, and took out his wallet. Inside was a folded pink slip of paper. He unfolded it and when he saw the woman's name, he remembered Kuali'i saying it as well. *Kelikoa'elakauaikekai Pahanui. Keliko.*

"I have known Tobi for many years…mostly when he was a boy actually…just a *keiki.* I remember how intently he listened to his *kūpuna*…his elders, even as a small boy."

"He told me that you could help. I forgot…I forgot all about it."

Keliko Pahanui patted his hand.

Ben looked at her curiously. "Did you know who it was?"

"Only that he was at the meeting…but I could have told you it was not Nelson Ala'ipaleile. That I could have told you."

Ben sighed. "We got the real man…tonight."

"I know."

Before he could ask how, she told him that 'people have been watching you…the little people…'

Ben let what Keliko said pass without comment. He knew she was referring to the Menehune, a mythical tribe of dwarflike people who completed gigantic feats of construction at night. Irrigation ditches, fish ponds, and stone monuments—all built in one night. Stories of the nocturnal Menehune pervaded Kaua'i like no other legend. He supposed they'd make good spies, as well.

"Ben, what do you think about Sovereignty?" Keliko asked in a soft voice.

She'd come right to the point.

"I think it's something I'll have to learn more about."

"Have to learn…or want to learn?"

Ben looked at her. She asked questions just like Tobi.

Slowly, smiles developed on each of their faces.

"Let me tell you what I think. Then when you are home, you can give it some thought…make up your own mind. It would be a mistake for you to decide about such an important thing without giving all aspects of it complete consideration."

"You sound like Tobi."

"Mahalo…a nice compliment."

Ben thought a bit and realized maybe it was the other way around—maybe Tobi sounded like her.

The girls seated around the perimeter of the platform whispered, some giggled, soon their voices became noticeable.

The teacher of *hula* said to them, "I think you should listen to this as well."

In the flickering torch light, the abrupt silence was eerie.

"Come closer."

The girls scurried across the platform and formed a small semi-circle in front Ben and Keliko.

The wind died down and everything was quiet. Ben looked out over the cliff at the sea. It was hard to tell the ocean was there at all. They were far above the noise, the curls of white surf weren't visible, there were no cries from the seabirds, who probably now nested for the night. No craft on the water, no running lights. No reflection of the moon, which had set behind the cliffs.

Ben felt strange, a little trapped, hesitant, knowing he was about to inherit something he wasn't ready to own.

"First…the concept of Sovereignty should not exist."

The smallest of the young *hula* dancers gasped.

Keliko grinned. "Maybe what I should have said was there should not be *a need* for Sovereignty. That better?"

The little girl smiled and nodded.

"None of this land is ours…it belongs to no one. We believe in *mālama 'aina*, taking care of the land. We are here to take care of it for future generations. Does anyone know what *mahele* is?"

One of the older girls called out, "Sharing."

"Very good, *keiki.* We believe in sharing with our *'ohana* and our neighbors. Our wealth should not come from owning land. Our wealth is our skills…our thinking skills, our healing skills, our farming and fishing skills. That is the way it should be. But unfortunately, we are beyond where we can return to that way of life. It just is not practical, but that does not mean we cannot find a good solution."

The air became completely still and the hoot of an owl, *pueo*, came from a nearby tree.

Ben noticed right away that Keliko didn't use contractions in her speech. Something he'd learned about Tobi. Tobi believed 'contractions are for lazy people.' Knowing Tobi's parents had died when he was young, Ben began to wonder if Keliko Pahanui might have been the one who raised him.

Keliko's hands unfolded and she brought them in front of her lips, as if she was about to pray. Then she lowered them to her lap. "At first, when I was younger and I heard my mother and father talk of Sovereignty, they spoke of it in a different manner, they called it 'returning to the *ahupua'a*.' That means going back to the time when each Hawaiian community was responsible for a strip of land that went from the sea to the top of the mountain in the center of the Island. That way the people had to share, some supplied the fish from the ocean, others taro from the riverlands, vegetables from the rich lowlands, herbs and medicine from the forests…also flowers for *lei*s and royal capes, and a place to honor Pele at the mountain top.

"But now I understand, if we are to accomplish any of this, we have to do it in modern times, mixing city life with the ways of old. The only way to get the people who decide things like this to listen to our cause is to have a common stance, a common goal. Some people for Sovereignty want all the land returned and foreigners to leave. Some want some lands…and are willing to let people with some Hawaiian blood stay. Some people do not care. If we do not find a way to work within what is here now, with all the people who are here now, the Sovereignty

Movement will fail and our culture will disappear. We must have *kōkua*, cooperation, among the different Sovereignty groups. That is all I have to say."

Ben's eyes moved from girl to girl, the younger ones looking around as if they were trying to understand, those in the middle looked straight ahead, staring at a spot at the center of the platform, the heads of the oldest *hula* dancers were bowed, and soon the other girls did the same.

Kelikoa'elakauaikekai Pahanui gestured for Ben to help her stand.

When she was upright, she came closer to him, nodded to him that he should sit. She stood behind him, her hands rested on his shoulders.

She addressed the others. "This man is a detective from the Island of Hawai'i."

Ben expected a murmur from the girls, but there was none. The young *hula* dancers were very serious now.

"Like you, he is mainly Hawaiian. Unlike you, he did not have the opportunity to grow up knowing the ways of his ancestors. But like you, he wants to learn. Tonight, I will give him a gift that is most sacred. Something I think he wants more than he knows."

Keliko placed both of her hands on his head, one hand on top of the other.

"My husband joined his ancestors long ago. His name was Ke'ala Pahanui. Ke'ala means the 'pathway.' Tonight, Ben, I am giving you his name."

Ben's heart pounded. This was something that bothered him for a long time, not having a Hawaiian name. His eyes felt glazed, he tried to wet his lips, but his tongue was dry as sandpaper. Once again, he felt thousands of cold pinpricks over his arms and neck.

"Except I want to change it a little. Your Hawaiian name will be Ke'alahou. The 'new pathway.' Maybe you can help find the right pathway for Sovereignty. This is my gift to you."

With that she removed her *lei* and placed it around Ben's neck, then came around and stood in front of him, bent, and kissed him on each cheek.

And when the young *hula* dancers shouted in unison, 'Ke'alahou,' tears filled his eyes.

"Now…Ke'alahou…would you like to see our *hula*?"

Ke'alahou could only nod.

0-595-27417-X

Printed in the United States
1242600003B/188